The Texans

Previous Books by Georgina Gentry

Cheyenne Captive
Cheyenne Princess
Comanche Cowboy
Nevada Nights
Quicksilver Passion
Cheyenne Caress
Apache Caress
Christmas Rendezvous (anthology)
Sioux Slave
Half-Breed's Bride
Nevada Dawn
Cheyenne Splendor
Song Of The Warrior
Timeless Warrior
Warrior's Prize
Cheyenne Song
Eternal Outlaw
Apache Tears
Warrior's Honor
Warrior's Heart
To Tame A Savage
To Tame A Texan
To Tame A Rebel
To Tempt A Texan
To Tease A Texan
My Heroes Have Always Been Cowboys (anthology)
To Love A Texan
To Wed A Texan
To Seduce A Texan

Published by Kensington Publishing Corporation

Diablo

The Texans

Georgina Gentry

ZEBRA BOOKS

KENSINGTON PUBLISHING CORP.

http://www.kensingtonbooks.com

ZEBRA BOOKS are published by

Kensington Publishing Corp.
119 West 40th Street
New York, NY 10018

All Kensington titles, imprints, and distributed lines are available at special quantity discounts for bulk purchases for sales promotion, premiums, fund-raising, educational, or institutional use.

Special book excerpts or customized printings can also be created to fit specific needs. For details, write or phone the office of the Kensington Special Sales Manager: Attn. Special Sales Department. Kensington Publishing Corp., 119 West 40th Street, New York, NY 10018. Phone: 1-800-221-2647.

Zebra and the Z logo Reg. U.S. Pat. & TM Off.

ISBN-13: 978-1-4201-0850-7
ISBN-10: 1-4201-0850-6

First Printing: February 2010

10 9 8 7 6 5 4 3 2 1

Printed in the United States of America

*This story is dedicated to any woman
who looked with her heart,
not her eyes,
and loved a man
who was scarred in body or soul.*

Prologue

He Not Worthy of a Name crouched with his knife, watching the big herd of longhorns grazing in the coming twilight. On the flat plains, there was nothing— not a hill, not a tree, only hundreds of fat longhorns munching the arid buffalo grass.

He was so weak and sick that he swayed a little, knowing that he would only get one chance to kill a steer. If he missed, the spooky animals would all turn and thunder away, bellowing a warning to the others. If he managed to bring one down, he would have to eat it raw, but he had been eating anything he could catch raw for weeks now, and he felt the Spirit of Death hovering over him. He had one chance to fill his shrunken belly, and if he missed killing a beef, he would fall to the ground and die because he was too far gone and too fevered to walk farther. He had seen only fourteen winters, but he did not expect to see another.

* * *

By the campfire, Trace Durango dismounted with a tired sigh and looked up at the fading sunset. As always, the wide Texas sky was splashed with purple, orange, and scarlet as the sun sank low to the west. "God, I'm wrung out like a dishrag. Cookie, you got any coffee?"

"Boss, don't I always?" The grizzled old man took a tin cup off the backboard of the chuck wagon and hobbled over to the big pot on the fire. "The boys about got all the strays rounded up?"

Trace accepted the cup gratefully and knelt by the fire as he fumbled in his denim shirt for his makin's. "Yep. Another day, we'll have them all headed south for the ranches before the Blue Northers blow in." Damn, that coffee was good. He sipped the strong, hot brew and rolled himself a cigarette.

In the distance, wafted on the cool wind, he heard a steer bellow a warning, and then another picked up the cry. The giant herd moved restlessly, stamping its hooves as other cattle took up the lowing. "Oh hell, don't tell me we've got a lobo or some coyotes sniffin' around the edge of the herd. They'll start a stampede." Irritably, he threw his coffee in the fire and stood up as Maverick, his half-Comanche adopted brother, rode up at a gallop.

"Trace, you hear that?" In the twilight, Maverick's eyes gleamed as gray as a gun barrel.

"*Sí*, let's get out there and see what's upsettin' the steers." Trace swung up on his black stallion.

"I already sent some of the boys up to the north end of the herd, but figure they'll need backup if it's a pack of coyotes."

"Damn, and things had been goin' so well all day." Trace pulled his rifle out of the boot, checked to make sure it was loaded, then spurred his horse. "We don't need a stampede."

Trace, followed by Maverick, took off through the milling herd of lowing longhorns.

"Hey, boss!" One of the McBride cowboys rode toward him. "You ain't gonna believe what we got cornered up on the north edge of the herd."

Trace hardly paused. "If it was coyotes, why didn't you just shoot them? You know how nervous these steers can get."

"We didn't know what to do with him, but none of us wanted to tangle with that big knife."

Trace reined in. "What the hell are you—?"

"You'll see. I told the boys to do nothin' 'til you got there."

Trace cantered past him, leading the trio now as they pushed through the milling cattle. He didn't know what was going on, but he was bone tired and not in the mood for games. They rode through the uneasy steers on this land that was as flat as a peso, heading into the twilight for the big group of riders circled on the far outskirts of the herd.

"What's going on, amigos?"

He swung off his stallion as the men made a path for him. What he faced took him a minute to take in, and even then, he didn't quite believe it.

A scrawny boy, probably not more than thirteen or fourteen, crouched in a defense mode behind a newly slaughtered steer. The boy wore nothing but a breechcloth, and his black hair was long. The fading light reflected off the bloody knife in his hand, and the boy's face was smeared with fresh blood. *Half-breed*, Trace thought, *like me.*

The boy was almost handsome until he turned his right side toward Trace and Trace got a good look at him. "Good God! What's going on here?"

He Without a Name did not give ground, still gripping

his knife. He had not gotten to eat much of the steer, only a few hurried raw bites, and now this white man would hang him. He knew by bitter experience that one did not kill the white man's cows without retribution. Well, he would go down fighting even though he was almost too sick to keep his balance.

"Boss," one of the McBride cowboys took off his hat and wiped his forehead, "we just followed the noise, thinkin' it was a coyote, and here's what we found. What'll we do with him?"

Trace watched the boy, horrified and fascinated at the same time. The kid was so thin his ribs showed. He must not have eaten much in weeks, and the right side of his face . . . Trace shuddered. What was left of it was swollen, disfigured and burned.

Maverick whistled. "Looks like someone took a running iron to him."

"Who would do that to a kid?" Trace demanded and stepped forward.

The kid promptly waved his knife at Trace and took a shaky step backward.

"Some bastard who valued his cattle more than people, I reckon," one of the other cowboys muttered.

"Hey, Trace," Maverick said, "this is about like it was when you found me all those years ago. He's certainly a half-breed; let me see if I can talk to him." He stepped forward and said softly in Comanche, "We will not hurt you."

The boy looked puzzled, swayed on his feet, and brandished his knife.

"He didn't understand you," Trace said. "Let me try some Spanish or Cheyenne." He asked the boy his name in both languages, and the starving kid blinked and shook his head.

"Hell, this isn't doing any good," Trace said. He

stepped toward the boy slowly, holding out his hand. "Give me the knife," he commanded. "We will help you."

"Watch out, brother," Maverick warned. "He looks desperate enough to kill you."

He Not Worthy of a Name looked around at the circle of cowboys. He hadn't a chance against so many, but he would rather die fighting than hanging. He could speak a little English he had learned when the Sioux went to trade, but he did not trust these men. He might be a worthless half-breed slave, but he could die like a warrior and he would fight even though he was having a hard time staying conscious.

Trace watched him warily. The boy was near fainting, and he swayed on his feet. In the shape he seemed to be in, it was a wonder he was still alive. At that moment, Trace charged him suddenly, grabbing for the knife. The boy fought valiantly, but in his starving condition, he was no match for the big half-Spanish, half-Cheyenne cowboy. Even as Trace struggled with him, the boy lapsed into unconsciousness and collapsed.

"Hell," Trace threw the bloody knife away and swung the boy up in his arms. "This kid is all but dead. Maverick, ain't there a town about five or ten miles to the west? Ride in there and see if they've got a doctor."

Maverick wheeled his horse. "A doc ain't gonna like riding out here at night for an almost dead half-breed kid."

"Then persuade him," Trace snapped and lifted the limp boy up on his black horse and swung up behind him.

Then he turned to the crowd of curious cowboys. "You men see if you can quiet this herd, and Mac, you bring in some of that butchered steer. We'll all have steak tonight."

The men scattered, and Maverick galloped away into the coming night. Trace cradled the boy in his arms as he rode back through the milling herd to the campfire.

Cookie came out to meet him. "What you got there?"

Trace handed the boy down, then dismounted and turned his horse over to one of the cowhands. "Some wild boy eating one of our steers raw. He's burning up with fever." He took the boy in his arms again and carried him over by the fire, laid him on a blanket. As the fire crackled, the boy opened his dark eyes, glanced at the fire, and evidently terrified, began to fight Trace.

He was no match for the big cowboy. "Take it easy," Trace whispered, "no one's gonna hurt you."

Whether he understood or not, the boy continued to fight while Trace held him down. "God, he's scared. Cookie, get him some water."

"No wonder," Cookie grumbled, limping toward the chuck wagon. "Looks like someone took a brandin' iron to his face." He brought Trace a tin cup of water and Trace held it out to the boy.

The boy hesitated and stopped fighting. Then slowly, he reached for the water and gulped it, most of it running down his chin from his shaking hand.

"Get him some more, Cookie." Trace handed the cup back to the other man and stared at the right side of the boy's face. "I'd say it was a running iron, not a regular branding iron."

"Rustlers?" Cookie hobbled over to refill the cup, brought it back, and handed it to the boy, who drank it in three gulps.

Trace shrugged. "Well, those are the ones who usually use a makeshift branding iron. Maybe he interrupted a gang of them changin' brands on someone else's cattle, and that's how they punished him."

"Sick bastards," Cookie grumbled.

The fevered boy looked around, leaning on his elbows. He tried to speak. "Texas?"

"What?" Trace asked, taken off guard.

"Texas?" The boy looked up at him with big brown eyes. He would have been handsome if it weren't for the burnt, swollen right side of his face.

Trace nodded, puzzled. "Texas. *Sí*, this is Texas."

The faintest ghost of a smile crossed the boy's mouth, and he sighed. "Texas," he whispered and nodded, then fainted.

Trace put his hand on the boy's forehead. "He's burning up with fever and so near dead, I don't know if we can save him or not."

Mac rode up just then with a haunch of the butchered steer. "Hey, Cookie, looks like we all eat good tonight."

"And here I was plannin' on giving you a special treat: beans," Cookie said wryly.

Trace examined the boy. "Cookie, see if you can get some broth boilin' for the kid, and Mac, go get me a fresh bucket of water from the spring. If we can't get his fever down, he won't make it 'til the doc gets here."

Cookie paused and looked at the boy's feet. "Oh, hell, Trace, look at his feet. They're raw and bloody. He must have walked a hundred miles."

"Or maybe more," Trace said, shaking his head. "I reckon killin' a steer and eating it raw was his last effort to stay alive. Why do you think Texas was so important to him?"

The others shook their heads, and Cookie took the beef from Mac, began to cut it in chunks.

Trace took the boy's chin in his hand and gently turned the head so he could see the right side of his face. It was swollen and, in places, burned black. "Somebody tortured this kid. I wish I could get my hands on that bastard."

Mac had gone for the water and now returned to the fire. "You think he's from around here?"

Trace shook his head and began to wet the blanket the boy was wrapped in. "Don't think so. He didn't understand either Comanche or Cheyenne. Must be from farther north, maybe Colorado."

"Ute?" Mac squatted by the fire and poured himself a cup of coffee.

"Who knows?" Trace shrugged. "From the looks of the soles of his feet, he may have walked several hundred miles. He might even have started with a horse and, when it gave out, began walkin'. Wish I knew why Texas was so important to him."

Cookie got a pot of broth boiling and then began frying steak and making biscuits. The scent brought most of the Triple D and the Maverick-McBride ranch hands in to dismount by the fire.

"Whose turn is it to ride night herd?" Trace asked.

"Ted and Bill," a tanned cowboy said as he dismounted and strode over to stare at the unconscious boy. "God, he looks almost starved to death. What are you gonna do with him, Trace?"

Trace sighed and pushed his Stetson back. "Well, I reckon I'll take him home until I find out where he belongs. Cimarron will bring him through if nobody else can. You know how she is with all the hurt critters the kids bring in."

The others nodded agreement.

Cookie said, "Suppose he don't belong nowheres?"

"Well, then," Trace reached to pour himself a cup of coffee. "I reckon we might keep him. That's what we did with Maverick years ago, and it worked out okay."

The boy barely stirred as Trace tried to clean his burned, swollen cheek. Then old Cookie squatted and spooned broth in between his lips. "He's in pretty bad shape, Trace; he may not make it."

He Who Is Not Worthy of a Name heard the man's voice deep, deep in his soul as he felt the life-giving broth run down his throat. So they weren't going to torture him yet for killing the white man's cow. They would wait until someone named Maverick returned. It didn't matter. He was too weak to fight any more and he had made it to Texas. That had been his goal all these long, hungry moons and now he was here. He could die now.

Trace stared down into the boy's sweating face. "He's running a terrible fever. Didn't I see some willow trees over at the stream?"

A cowboy behind him said, "Yep, I saw 'em."

"Go peel the bark off some of them, and Cookie, you get ready to boil that. It's an old Indian remedy."

It was long past dark when Maverick returned with a cranky old doctor on a thin horse.

"If you'd told me how far it was, I wouldn't have come." He dismounted and reached for his black bag.

Maverick spat to one side. "You would have come if I'd had to throw you across your saddle."

The grizzled doctor rubbed his mustache and squatted by the fireside, staring at the boy. "You dragged me away from my dinner for a boy who's almost dead, and an Injun at that?"

Trace frowned. "Do you know who I am?" His tone had a warning edge to it.

"Uh, well, no, I reckon not."

"Trace Durango of the Triple D ranch."

The older man swallowed hard. Everyone knew the

Triple D empire that covered hundreds of thousands of acres. "Oh, sorry, Señor Durango, I didn't realize—"

"Now see what you can do for this boy. There's gold in it for you if you save him."

The greedy old man's eyes lit up, and he reached for his bag in a hurry. "I'll see what I can do, but I can't promise anything. My God, what happened to his face? He looks like a monster!"

Trace shrugged. "We don't know for sure; maybe someone took a brandin' iron to it."

The doctor opened up his bag, took out some carbonic acid, and wiped the area around the swollen wounds. "Some back east got this new theory about something called germs, say you can kill 'em by disinfecting the area."

"We've been spoonin' willow bark water down his throat to bring his fever down," Cookie offered.

"Old Injun hogwash," the doctor snorted. "Don't think it's worth a damn."

"It works." Trace frowned.

The crew gathered around to watch silently as the old man cleaned the wound. "It's swollen up some, and he'll always be as ugly as hell. Too bad; looks like he was once handsome." He pulled down the blanket and looked the boy over, then turned him on his side. "This kid is almost starved to death, and he's got old scars on his back."

"Oh?" Trace stared at the boy's back, nodded. "He's been treated bad, maybe over a number of years. Take a look at his feet."

The doc squinted and frowned. "Good God, how far has he walked?"

Trace shook his head. "We don't know. We found him trying to eat a steer raw. He don't speak Spanish, Cheyenne, or Comanche, so he has to be from farther north, I reckon, or maybe west."

The doc shuddered as he cleaned and put medicine on the boy's soles, then leaned back and sighed. "Reckon I've done all I can for him. He needs food and rest, and even then he may not make it."

Trace stood up. "If I can get him home to my wife, she'll take care of him; she's the one who doctors all our cowboys and critters. Stay for supper, doc—we're having steak and biscuits."

"Sounds good," the old man grinned for the first time.

Later, Trace sent the man on his way with a very generous fee. Then he watched Cookie spooning broth into the boy's mouth. The Indian kid was barely conscious.

"Well, Maverick," he said with a sigh, "If I head back to the ranch with the kid, can you take over here?"

"You know I will, Trace. We'll move these steers farther south before the weather turns·frosty."

The next morning, Trace fashioned a travois behind his black horse, which shied nervously as the men put the semiconscious boy in the blankets. "It'll take me a few days to get home, but I know where the water holes are along the way, and I can kill enough game to keep us fed."

"You watch out for that kid," Cookie warned, rubbing his chin with a flour-dusted hand, "I think he'd try to kill you if he got a chance."

"He's in no shape to kill anybody," Trace said as he mounted up, "but he's game enough to try. I'll see you boys back at the ranch in a few days. Adios."

Cimarron glanced out the window of the big white hacienda and saw her husband dismounting in front of the courtyard fountain. "Trace!" She flew out the door and into his arms. "Honey, what are you doing home early?"

"Hi, darlin', he kissed the tip of her nose. "Nothing

wrong. I just brought in a half-breed kid we found up in the Panhandle."

She stared at the boy on the travois. "Oh, the poor thing!"

Trace watched her hurry to the half-conscious boy. She might be older than the first time he saw her in 1864, but to him, this yellow-haired wife had only grown more beautiful. "Oh, Trace, double damnation, what happened to him?"

Trace shook his head. "It's a long story, and we may never know all of it. I figure if anyone can help him, you can."

Cimarron turned and ran toward the house, shouting for vaqueros and the house servants. "Come quickly! *Muy pronto!* We have a very sick boy to help!"

Cimarron planned to put the boy in a bedroom of the big hacienda, but Trace wanted him put in the bunkhouse. "Darlin', I know you aren't thinking about this, but this kid could be dangerous. We don't know a thing about him."

"He's hurt—that's all I need to know. All right, we'll put him in the servant's quarters at the back of the house."

"Okay, I give up. See if Maria can cook up something he can eat. He may try to get away, but he won't get far with those feet. He's too weak to stand anyway."

Over the next several weeks, the boy improved. At first, Cimarron knew he was terrified, but he seemed to gradually realize no one would hurt him. The roundup crew was back at the ranchero by the time the boy was hobbling around the floor. His face was healing, but the right side would always be so scarred and twisted that little children backed away when they saw him and ran to their mothers who crossed themselves and muttered prayers. Cimarron had all the mirrors removed from the house so that he would not see his disfigured reflection.

The weather was spitting snow the day that he limped across the room toward a chair and the man who had saved him came in and shut the door. He Not Worthy of a Name backed away. He had no weapon to defend himself now if the white cowboys were going to torture him.

Trace smiled and gestured him into the chair. "Are you feeling well?" he asked in English, feeling foolish because he did not know what tongue the boy spoke.

The boy nodded.

"What is your name?" Trace asked.

The boy had not spoken for a long time and it was hard to mouth the words. "I am called He Not Worthy of a Name. I have not earned one."

"Do you want me to give you a name?" Trace leaned back in a chair and reached into his shirt for a cigarillo. "You can be a Durango."

The boy shook his head, watching Trace's hands. "I must earn my own."

"All right then." Trace searched his pocket for a match, and when he struck it, he saw the fright in the boy's dark eyes as he shied away.

Trace noted the terror and, remembering the boy's burned face, shook out the match. "We will not hurt you," he whispered.

The boy did not look as if he believed him.

"What tribe are you?" Trace leaned back in his chair.

"Santee Dakota."

Trace snorted in disbelief. "That tribe is hundreds of miles north of here."

The boy only looked at him.

"All right then." Trace decided not to pursue that. "The servants say you scream at night in your sleep."

The boy flushed and looked away.

"It is all right," Trace assured him. "We all have nightmares now and then. Are you afraid?"

The boy hesitated. Evidently, he was ashamed to admit his fear.

"If you are afraid, I can teach you to handle a pistol; then no one will hurt you."

The boy smiled for the first time. "You—you would do that?"

"*Sí.*" Trace nodded. "How old are you? Do you know?"

The boy's face furrowed. "I—I think fourteen winter counts."

"Would you like to stay here at my ranch?"

"Is this Texas?" The boy looked out the window.

"Yes, this is Texas," Trace assured him, wondering why it was so important to him.

"Texas." The boy smiled. "Yes. I got here. I did not think I would."

Trace waited, but the boy did not elaborate. "Are you good with horses?"

The boy nodded.

"Fine." Trace leaned back in his chair. "You can move into the bunkhouse and be part of my crew. I will pay you to help with chores and care for horses."

"Pay?" The boy looked puzzled.

"*Sí.*" Trace nodded. "You know, you work and I give you money for it."

"I have never been paid to work. I was a slave to an old Santee woman."

Dios! What all had happened to this boy in his short life?

"Well, now you will be paid. When you feel like it, you can come eat with the other cowboys."

The boy evidently did not believe him. "You—you are not going to torture me for killing your cow?"

Trace shook his head. "Is that what happened to you before?"

Terror crossed the boy's face as he seemed to remember something, but he did not answer. There was something very dark and terrible in his past, Trace thought, something the boy might never tell—maybe something more terrible than the branding.

"All right then," Trace stood up. "When you feel like it, we will begin lessons with the pistol, and I will show you around the ranch. This is a good place. Ask Maverick when he comes to visit. I found him as I found you. You can have a good future here in Texas." Trace went out and closed the door.

He Not Worthy of a Name stared after him. He could not believe everything the man had said, but then this was Texas. Hadn't his friends told him how wonderful it was before they died?

Over the winter, Trace taught the boy to handle a gun and allowed him to take care of the ranch's prize quarter horses.

One day in the early spring, he watched the boy through the window. "Cimarron," he mused, "this kid has an amazing talent for horses and pistols. I think he's better than I am."

"That's saying a lot, honey." She leaned over to kiss him. Trace Durango might be getting a little gray in his hair, but he still had a reputation as the best gun in Texas. "Don't you think we should give him a name?"

"I tried," Trace shrugged and sipped his coffee, "but he says he must earn his own name. Until then, we all just call him 'kid.'"

They watched their young children, Ace and Raven, run across the yard toward the boy. "Hey, kid," Ace yelled, "you want to saddle up and ride today?"

The boy nodded.

Cimarron smiled. "And you warned me he was dangerous. Our children love him."

"We still don't know a damned thing about him," Trace said. "But he does seem to have a special way with children and animals."

"Well, I don't care. If he wants to stay on the Triple D the rest of his life, we can always use a good hand."

Trace nodded. "I told him that. I also told him I have a few thousand acres over in the Big Bend country I'd sell him cheap if he ever wants to go out on his own. There're lots of wild horses there. He could make a good livin' catchin' and breakin' them, and he wouldn't have people staring at him all the time."

Cimarron's eyes misted. "It would be lonely for him without a woman."

"*Sí*, but look at him, darlin'. He looks like a monster. Can you imagine any woman lovin' him?"

"A special woman," Cimarron whispered, "a woman who loves him for his heart, not his looks."

Trace shook his head as they watched the boy saddle up three horses. "It would take a special woman all right, but I'm afraid he won't find her."

"I'm going to teach him to read and write," Cimarron said. "If he's lonely, he can always lose himself in a book."

Trace grinned at her, loving her more than ever. "Darlin', whatever you want to do."

And so she taught the mysterious boy along with her own children and the children of the vaqueros. There was something very sad and angry about him that she was unable to fathom. It had to be worse than just mistreatment, she thought, but he would never let anyone get close to him. He was a loner—an angry loner.

One warm spring day, she happened to be looking out the front windows toward the big fountain with its pool of water. The kid, passing by, stopped to stare at the fountain, then looked into the pool.

Cimarron wanted to run out and stop him, but he was already staring at his reflection, first in disbelief, then in horror as he backed away. Since she had taken down all the mirrors, he must not have realized how he looked, and now the terrible reality had sunk in and there was nothing she or anyone could do to protect him from that. She ran out the French doors onto the veranda.

"It's all right," she reassured him and tried to put her arm around him, but he shook his head and backed away, tears gathering in his eyes. Then he turned and ran into the barn, where he hid.

She told Trace what had happened.

"Leave him alone," he said. "The kid will have to learn to live with it, painful as that might be. I don't think there's anything we can do except be kind to him."

One day she was reading her little class a book of fairy tales when the kid interrupted suddenly, evidently disturbed. "Why is it the beautiful yellow-haired princess always kisses the beast or the frog and he becomes a handsome prince? Couldn't she love him if he were not handsome?"

Cimarron winced. Why had she not remembered the boy's disfigurement? "Of course she could," she answered softly, "if she were the right kind of girl—a kind, caring one."

"I don't want to hear any more of those." He turned over his chair as he ran out, slamming the door behind him. It was weeks before he came quietly into her class again, but she read the class no more fairy tales.

Events at the ranch went along quietly for the next few months as the half-breed boy grew tall and lithe. Then one late summer morning, Trace found a note on the veranda table as he sat down for breakfast.

Cimarron came outside, saw Trace's ashen face. "What's the matter?"

He offered her the note. "The kid has left."

"What?" She took the note from his hand. She had taught the boy to read and write, and here in his simple handwriting, he was thanking them and moving on. "But why? He's still just a boy, and we gave him a good home." She began to cry.

"I think I've always known he wouldn't stay," Trace sighed. "He's as restless as a wild mustang, and we never really knew much about him. I think he has unfinished business somewhere in his past, something terrible, more terrible than brandin', and maybe he can't rest until he takes care of it."

"How could anything be more horrible than that?"

Trace shook his head. "I don't know; I reckon no one does but him."

"But how will he live?" she whispered and crumpled the note. "And what will I tell the children?"

"I've taught him well, maybe too well," Trace sighed. "In a year or so, he'll probably be the best gun in Texas, better than me or even Maverick. There're plenty who would pay a top gunfighter to do their dirty work. I hear they're looking for hired guns in Lincoln County, New Mexico. There's talk of a range war there."

"A gunfighter." Cimarron sank back in her chair. "They never live very long; there's always a better, faster gun."

"I know, and to think I taught him. He was a strange, moody kid, with a terrible life before I found him. He never did tell us much, and now I reckon we never will know his secrets."

"Maybe he'll come back to us someday, and he'll find a girl and be happy," Cimarron said doubtfully.

"Not likely. You think any girl could love a man with a face like a monster?" Trace rolled a cigarette. "Maybe we'll never know what happened to him. I shouldn't have taught him to handle a gun."

"He wanted that badly, and he was so afraid, and full of so much rage," she reminded him.

"And he never got a name," Trace mused. "Maybe he'll finally 'earn' one. It seemed important to him. With that scarred face, if there's news of him, people will remember, and the tales will travel all across Texas."

Cimarron ducked her head and blinked back the tears. Gunfighters didn't live long, everyone knew that. No doubt he'd die in the middle of a dusty street somewhere far away. She closed her eyes and said prayers for the strange, maimed kid and hoped he would find happiness, or whatever it was he was seeking.

Chapter 1

On a northbound train to Wyoming, early April 1892

Diablo paused between the swaying cars, looking through the door to see who was inside before he entered. No gunfighter worth his bullets would enter an area without checking out the lay of the land, especially since this car was full of Texas gunfighters, all hired killers like himself.

He had come a long way since Trace Durango had found him fifteen years ago when he was a Santee slave known as He Not Worthy of a Name. Well, he had earned a name now, and when men heard it, they turned pale and backed down from the big, half-breed gunfighter with the scarred face. He dressed all in black, from his Stetson down to his soft, knee-high moccasins. The superstitious peasants along the Rio Grande had given him the name: Diablo, the devil. It suited him just fine.

Now finally he was headed north to take care of unfinished business. He had waited a long, long time for this, and all these years he had been planning and perfecting his aim. Though the Wyoming Stock Grower's Association was paying exorbitant money to bring this trainload of killers north, the money did not interest Diablo. What interested him was vengeance, and now, finally, he would have it. He was no longer the small and weak half-breed slave. No, now he had a name and was respected and feared throughout the West. Diablo had gained a reputation as a fast, deadly gunman.

Trace Durango had done well in teaching him to use a Colt, and he had used it time and time again in range wars and saloon showdowns. His gun was for hire, and he had fought side by side with men like Billy the Kid. Billy had been dead more than ten years now. Many of the others were dead too, before they reached middle age. In the end, that would probably be his fate, but for now, all that mattered was finishing his business with four men. His biggest fear was that they might now be dead and no longer able to face a showdown.

Diablo swung open the door and stood there watching the others inside. The shades had been ordered drawn, and the light in the swaying car was dim. Most of the men turned to stare at him, unsmiling, cigar smoke swirling above their heads. They did not nod a welcome, and he had expected none. These were hired pistoleros like himself, Texas gunfighters, on a special train to Wyoming where a range war was about to start. An hombre named Frank Canton had come down to hire twenty-five of the best, offering great pay and bonuses for every rustler and nester killed.

The train swayed, and the tracks made a rhythmic click-clack as conversation in the car ceased. All the men were looking at him, but he stared only at the men in the first row of seats. Diablo liked to have his back against the wall. The two men withered under his frown and hurriedly got up and retreated down the car. Diablo took the space they had vacated as if it were his right.

"Who in the hell is that half-breed?" The growling voice drifted toward him.

"Shh! Be quiet, Buck; that's Diablo. You don't want to make him mad."

"The Diablo?" Now he sounded impressed.

"There's only one," said the other.

"He don't look like so much."

"You challenge him, you'll find out."

"Maybe I'll just do that when we hit Wyoming."

Diablo sighed, pulled his black Stetson down over his eyes, and leaned back against the scarlet horsehair cushions, then opened the shade, stared out the window at the passing landscape. Quickly he averted his eyes, not wanting to see the reflection of his scarred face, and closed the shade again.

He probably didn't look like much to the others, who sported noisy, big spurs, fancy silver conchos and pistols, and boots of the best leathers in bright colors. Diablo dressed in the color of the night, and he wore moccasins, the better to move silently against an enemy without them knowing he was coming. Silver conchos and pistols had a way of reflecting light that an enemy could see for a long way. He not only moved silently, but his appearance was as black as a thunderstorm, with no bit of reflected light to give him away.

Now he stuck a slender cigarillo between his lips, but he did not light it. He never lit them. The flash of a match or the slightest scent of tobacco smoke would also give a man away, and he had learned from the Santee Sioux that he must move as silently as a spirit—kill and be gone. No wonder the Mexicans averted their eyes and crossed themselves as he rode past.

Hours later, Diablo decided he would have a drink and moved toward the club car. Balancing lightly in his moccasins as the train rumbled and click-clacked along the rails, he was acutely aware of each man he passed, sensing whether each was a threat or not. One or two eyed him, hands fidgeting nervously, as if thinking of being the one who killed the infamous Diablo, but each seemed to think twice and let him pass unchallenged.

In the club car, five men hunched over a table playing cards. Diablo paused in the doorway, looking them over. Then slowly the conversation ceased as each turned to look at him.

"Good God, look at his face!" the big, unshaven one muttered. He had red hair, and freckles showed through the balding spots.

"Be quiet, Buck," warned a pudgy one with missing teeth, and a greasy ponytail of brown hair. "You want to die before you ever get to Wyoming?"

"But he looks like a monster."

Nobody else said anything, waiting to see if the newcomer would take offense, but Diablo pretended he had not heard the remark. If he killed or challenged everyone who commented on his scarred face, his six gun would never be in its holster. Instead, he walked softly to the small bar and addressed the black waiter. "Beer."

He felt the gaze of the others on his back, but he ignored them.

"Hey," the one called Buck asked, "you got a big rattlesnake hatband and rattles on that Stetson. You kill it yourself?"

Diablo nodded as he took his beer and moved across the scarlet carpet to a comfortable chair with its back against a wall and sat down. Play at the poker table seemed suspended.

"Hell," snorted a short man in a derby hat, "it ain't no big thing to kill a giant rattler. Anyone can shoot them."

Diablo drilled him with his hard stare. "I didn't shoot

it. When it struck at me, I put my foot on its head and killed it with my knife."

The man with the ponytail raised his bushy eyebrows, and the light reflected off the silver conchos on his leather vest. "Man has to be fast as greased lightnin' to kill a snake that way."

Diablo didn't answer, and he knew they all stared at his rattler hatband with the dozen rattles still attached. Now he took out a fresh cigarillo, stuck it in his mouth, and gazed out the window.

"Hey, half-breed, you need a light?" The one called Buck half rose from his chair, his voice challenging. He wore big spurs, and when he moved, they rattled like the tin pans on a peddler's cart.

The others tried to shush him.

Diablo was in no mood to kill someone today. He merely looked at the challenger, dark eyes glowering, and the man sat down suddenly.

"Well, boys," Buck huffed, his dirty, freckled hands as nervous as his unshaven face, "let's get this game goin', shall we?"

Diablo watched the country gliding past the train windows for a long moment. They were only hours from Wyoming, and he was weary of the long trip. He reached for a newspaper on the nearby table. Cimarron Durango had taught him to read, and that made up for his loneliness. The others raised their heads and watched him as if astounded that a gunfighter was reading, then returned to their poker game.

Sunny sat between her father and Hurd Kruger as Hurd drove the buggy along the dusty road toward the train station in the town of Casper. Early spring flowers now bloomed along the way and in the fields where hundreds of cattle grazed.

"Thank you, Mr. Kruger, for inviting me along," she said politely, looking up at him. He was a big, beefy man with yellow teeth that he sucked constantly. His hair and mustache were coal black, and when he sweated, little drops of dye ran down the sides of his ruddy face.

"Now, Sunny, dear, you ought to at least call me Hurd. I'm not really your uncle."

The way he looked at her made her feel uneasy. He'd been looking at her that way ever since she'd gone into her teens, and now that she was eighteen, he looked at her that way more and more often. She brushed a blond wisp back under her pale blue bonnet. "All right," she agreed and looked over at her father. Swen Sorrenson did not look pleased.

"Hurd, I still don't think much of this idea," he said, his Danish accent still strong after all these years.

"Now, Swen, we've been through this before, and anyway, we shouldn't discuss this in front of our Sunny, should we?"

It upset her that her father seemed uneasy. Her mother had died giving birth to her, and Sunny felt obliged and guilty about Dad's loss. If it hadn't been for his obligations in raising a daughter in this rough land, he might have re-married or even returned to Denmark. He had always seemed frail and ill suited to this wild wilderness.

"Uncle Hurd, I mean Hurd, why are we going to town?" she asked.

"Business. The Stock Growers Association business. You know I am the president. But don't you worry your pretty little head about that, Sunny—you can go shop-pin' while your dad and I tend to it."

That didn't account for the unhappy look in Swen's pale

blue eyes, but she decided not to ask any more questions. A trip to a big town was a rare treat for a ranch girl.

They were approaching the town, and her excitement built. In the distance, she heard the distinctive wail of a train whistle. "Oh, a train! Who do you suppose is coming in?"

Her father started to say something, then closed his mouth.

"Some men," Hurd said, sucking his teeth, "part of the cattlemen's business."

They came into town on the main road and headed toward the train station. Others were gathering, too. The arrival of a train in this small, isolated town was big news.

They pulled into the station, and Hurd got down and tied the horse to the hitching rail. Then he came around to help Sunny out of the buggy, but her father got there first.

Hurd frowned. "Now, Sunny, dear, you go along and shop. Your dad and I and some of the other members will meet the train."

"But it's so exciting!" she protested, shaking the dust from her pale blue cotton dress and readjusting her skewered bonnet, "I want to see who's getting off."

"Next year," Swen said to her with a smile, "maybe you will ride the train to Boston and go to college."

Hurd frowned. "Aw, don't put such high-falutin' ideas in her head, Swen. Maybe she'll want to get married instead. There ain't much need for a ranch wife to get an education."

Swen looked like he might disagree, but instead, pulled his Stetson down over his sparse hair as pale as Sunny's and turned toward the station.

The crowd of curious onlookers was growing on the platform as the trio joined them. In the distance, Sunny could see the smoke from the engine and hear the whistle as it chugged toward the town.

"Casper! Coming into Casper!" The conductor walked up and down the aisle and into the next car, "Casper next stop!"

On the sidewalk near the station, Sunny Sorrenson smiled at her father. "Oh, Dad, I never saw a train up close!"

"Yes, dear," Swen smiled back at her with eyes as blue as hers. "Hurd's been expecting it."

"Yep, this is a special train." Hurd walked toward them, smiling. "Now we'll get some action."

"What's going on?" Sunny smiled up at him. She was petite next to the big man.

"Now, sweetheart, never mind," Hurd paused in sucking his yellow teeth and nodded. "It's just cattle business—nothing to worry your pretty little head about."

"All right, Uncle Hurd." She saw a slight look of worry pass over her father's tanned face. He didn't often disagree with Hurd Kruger, their neighbor from the big K Bar ranch, especially since Hurd held the mortgage on their small spread and had been extra nice to them.

The train pulled into the station, puffing and blowing acrid smoke. People started gathering on the platform. The train arrival was always a big event in town. The three of them walked to the station in time to see the conductor step down and begin unloading baggage. After a moment, the passengers began to disembark. They were all men—tough-looking, weathered men, all wearing gun belts. The newcomers looked over the crowd, not smiling, then strode to the stock car, started unloading horses.

Sunny shielded her pale eyes from the sun. "Look at all those cowboys. Do you think they'll be able to find work here? I thought there were plenty in the area."

"Uh," her father cleared his throat, "Hurd brought them in."

"Be quiet, Swen," the other man snapped; then he smiled at her and said, "Now, Sunny, dear, why don't you run along and do some shopping? We men have things to discuss."

There was something wrong here, but she wasn't quite sure what it was. There must be almost twenty-five or thirty of these tough-looking cowboys milling about on the platform, gathering up their carpetbags and unloading their horses.

A tall, straight man with a mustache got off the train and strode over to them, smiling. "Well, Mr. Kruger, I brought them. Handpicked them, too, twenty-five or so of the best from Texas."

"Shut up, Canton," Hurd said, glancing at her. "We'll talk later."

She felt the men were withholding something because of her, but she was always obedient, as was expected of a young lady, so she walked away down the platform as Canton, Dad, and Hurd went to meet some of those men. They gathered and began to talk as she looked up at the train.

Then one final man stepped into the doorway of the railcar, looking about as if checking out the landscape. He caught her attention because he was so different than the others—taller and darker. He was dressed all in black, his Stetson pulled low over his dark face, and he wore moccasins instead of boots. From here, she could see the left side of his face, and he was handsome, with dark eyes and just wisps of very black hair showing beneath his hat. *A half-breed*, she thought. Unlike the others, he wore no silver conchos or spurs, and his pistol and gun belt were very plain and worn low and tied down. This was no ordinary cowboy, she realized with a sudden interest.

At that point, he turned his face toward her, and she took a deep breath and stepped backward in shock. While the left side of his face was handsome, the right side was scarred and twisted. "Oh, dear Lord," she whispered, trying not to stare but unable to take her eyes off the stranger.

He seemed to sense her horror, and he winced and turned quickly away so that his right side was hidden again.

Diablo watched her from the car step. He was almost hypnotized by the girl. She was certainly not yet twenty, and small. Her blue dress accentuated her eyes, which were as pale as a Texas sky, and her hair was lighter than corn silk. The tight waist accentuated her tiny body, and she was fragile and delicate, almost too delicate to be in this cold, harsh country. He had never seen anything like her before. He found himself staring at her full, pink lips, and without thinking, he turned his head to get a better look.

Too late he saw her hand go to her mouth and the way she stepped backward in dismay. Diablo turned his face away, too aware that his scarred face had frightened her, and the old anger arose in him. He would always have this effect on women, always. The fact made him angry with the beautiful, petite girl, although he knew it was not her fault.

Two men walked up to join the girl, not looking at Diablo. The older one had wispy hair, almost snow blond, and eyes as pale as the girl's. The other was middle-aged, perhaps in his forties with a small potbelly, and hair and mustache dyed too black to hide the gray.

Diablo's hand went to his pistol as the old memories flooded back. Then he forced himself to concentrate and not think of that long-ago day. He would pick the day and time, and this was not it. He grabbed his carpetbag and stepped back into the shadows of the car door so the men would not see him. He stared at the girl again, thinking he had never seen anything so fragile and beautiful. He wanted her as a man wants a woman, but was angry because she had recoiled from him. What could he expect? Didn't women always shrink back from his ugly face? And yet, he always hoped there would be one who wouldn't. Sunny, yes, that was what they had called her, and that was a good name for her. This girl was a magnificent princess; she could have any man she wanted, and she would not want him. He sighed and turned his attention again to the men congregating on the platform.

The man called Canton had joined the other two, and everyone's attention was on the crowd of gunfighters as they gathered around.

Diablo heard the big man say something to the girl about going shopping. She nodded, but Diablo saw that she was still staring back at him in a sort of horrid fascination.

"But Uncle Hurd, what about you and Dad?" the girl asked.

"We've got Stock Growers Association business to tend to. Now don't worry your pretty little head—you just run on, and we'll meet up with you later in the day. Here," the big man reached into his pocket, "here's some extra money to spend."

The older man objected. "But Hurd, I give her money all ready."

"So I give her some more. I've got plenty to spoil her."

The girl tried not to accept it. "Oh, Uncle Hurd, it's too much—"

"Nonsense. Now you run along and buy yourself something nice to wear at the party I might give soon."

The girl took the money, hugged both the two men,

and left. Diablo's gaze followed her until she disappeared down the brick sidewalk and past the station. Then he watched the two men she had accompanied, and a terrible rage built in him as he remembered something too horrible to be voiced.

After fifteen years, he had returned as he had always promised himself he would. He cared nothing for the cattlemen's war. Diablo had come to Wyoming for one reason and for one reason only: he had come to torture and kill certain men, and one of them was one of the two men the girl had embraced.

Chapter 2

Before dark, Sunny joined her father again at the train station. "Where's Uncle Hurd?"

Swen helped her and her packages up into the buggy. "He—he and some of the other ranchers rode with the Texans back to the K Bar."

He climbed in, flicked the little whip at the bay horse, and they started up the road.

"Dad, who were all those men? They looked pretty rough."

Swen hesitated and kept his eyes on the road ahead. "The Stock Growers Association has been having a lot of trouble with rustlers."

"I know," she nodded.

"Well, Hurd, as president, got everyone to pitch in, and they've got a pot of about a hundred thousand dollars."

"So much?" she gasped. "Dad, did you—?"

"No," he shook his head, "I don't approve and didn't have any money anyway."

A sense of foreboding came over her as they drove along the road. "I take it there's a connection among these men, the rustling, and the money?"

"Don't ask me, dear. The less you know, the better."

She wanted to ask more, but she had to quell the rebellion she sometimes felt. Then she always felt guilty because she was all her dad had besides a small, mortgaged ranch. "What about that one dressed in black?"

"Uh-huh." He didn't seem to be listening, lost in his own thoughts, so she didn't pursue it. Of course that scarred one was one of the Texas gunmen the ranchers had brought in to deal with the rustlers. That one was the most dangerous, virile man she had ever seen, and it gave her a naughty thrill to picture him staring back at her.

"Dad," she tried again, "about that one—"

"Sunny, the less you know the better," Dad said. "And don't speak of this to Hurd. He wouldn't think it was fitting that a girl knew too much about the cattlemen's actions."

She started to protest, then took a deep breath and hushed. She must not cause her father any more grief than she had already caused him, when her birth resulted in the death of his young wife.

The next night, back at the ranch, Sunny watched her father comb his sparse yellow hair and polish his boots.

"You're going out?"

"Yes, dear," he nodded. "Hurd's decided to throw a barbecue at his place tonight for the uh, new cowboys."

"Oh." She blinked. "Aren't the ladies invited?"

Swen shook his head and frowned. Evidently he did not approve of something, but of course, she never questioned her father about his decisions. "Sunny, these are a rough sort. You saw most of them at the train station."

She remembered the one who had made the biggest impression. "I know what you mean. That half-breed dressed all in black—"

"Half-breed?" Swen shook his head. "Don't remember that one."

Had she imagined the big man with the piercing dark eyes and the scarred face? "Reckon it doesn't matter."

"Anyway," Swen said in his slight accent, "there's business to be discussed. I'll take our hands with me. It'd be dull for the ladies."

"All right. I'll find something to do, maybe some sewing."

"That's my good girl." He smiled and kissed her cheek as he dressed.

She sighed. Everyone remarked on what a dutiful daughter she was.

"And I'll keep a close eye on that dun mare for you."

"Oh, I don't think she'll foal for a few more days, but I want to be here when she does. Yes, there's a lot riding on that fine foal. We can use the money."

"We'll never get Hurd Kruger paid off," she complained. "In fact, we seem to get further behind each year."

"Now he's been a good friend to us," her father chided, "we wouldn't have made it this long without him."

"Oh, I wasn't complaining," she put in quickly. She tried not to do or say anything that would upset her father, even when she had to grit her teeth to be agreeable.

A few minutes later, she walked her dad out to where he saddled a good chestnut, and nodded to his mounted cowhands waiting for him. They all doffed their hats and smiled.

"Evenin', Miss Sunny."

"Good evening, boys," she nodded.

"Now, Sunny," Swen said, "Will you be all right here?"

"Of course, Dad." She leaned over and kissed his weathered cheek. "You know I can handle a rifle if any coyotes come around. You just enjoy your barbecue."

He frowned. "Not likely," he muttered and mounted up.

She looked up at him. "You don't approve of whatever Uncle Hurd is up to, do you?"

"I didn't say that," he sputtered. "Remember, we're owing to Hurd for everything he's done for us. If he hadn't sold me land at a cheap price and lent me money, too, we couldn't have made it in this rough country."

She nodded and waved as Swen turned his horse and all the men rode away. She'd heard her father had a reputation in the county for not being a very good businessman, but they'd managed all right, thanks to Hurd Kruger. She frowned as she returned to the ranch house. She didn't really like Uncle Hurd. Sometimes, the way he looked at her made her skin crawl.

The sun went down, and she ate a cold supper and settled in to sew. As darkness descended, she got an uneasy feeling and went to check on the prize mare. The mare was in the barn and stamping uneasily. Sunny looked her over. Oh, darn, the mare was going into labor and seemed to be having trouble. There wasn't a man in the place, and Sunny knew she couldn't handle this by herself.

She hesitated as she petted the nervous horse. What should she do? Dad had told her ladies were not welcome at the barbecue because of whatever Uncle Hurd was planning. On the other hand, they couldn't afford to lose this foal, much less the mare.

For a minute, she struggled with her dilemma. Dad might be upset with her, but on the other hand, this was an emergency. She dare not ride astride where a bunch of the neighboring ranchers might see her though. The Sorrensons owned a light buggy, and Sunny could harness a horse. In fifteen minutes, she was driving at a fast clip through the darkness, her pale hair blowing in the wind.

At the barbecue, many of the gunfighters stood with a mug of beer, laughing and joking around the big bonfire in the clearing near the barn.

Diablo watched them all from his place in the shadowy trees. He hadn't joined the group, but had hung back, following them to their destination. As far as the locals were concerned, he didn't even exist, and that was the way he wanted it. In his black clothing, he blended into the shadows, not mingling, but watching and sizing up every man there. He knew most of the gunslingers by reputation, but there were a lot of locals, ranchers, maybe.

He watched as the slight Swen rode up with his crew and dismounted. They lined up for barbecue. The wind was blowing toward Diablo, so he could pick up most of the conversation.

Hurd said, "You want a beer, Swen?"

The older man frowned. "Hurd, you know I ain't had a drink in fifteen years. Not after—"

"All right, never mind," the burly rancher snapped. Then he stepped over to the roaring fire and held up his hands for silence. The crowd, sipping their beer and eating their barbecue, grew silent.

Diablo watched the men, gritting his teeth. All four of the ones he came for were in this crowd. He doubled his fists in rage, then reasoned with himself for control. He had waited a long, long time, but he could wait a few days longer. Nothing in his twenty-nine years was as important as this.

Kruger shouted, "Now I hope all you gents have enjoyed the eats. There'll be another celebration once we bring law and order back to Johnson County."

A murmur of agreement and head nodding among the others.

"You tell 'em, Hurd!"

"Anyway," Hurd continued, sucking his teeth, "we'll start tomorrow when we ride toward Buffalo. These rustlers and thievin' homesteaders have cleaned us out and robbed us long enough. It's time we taught them that law-abidin' ranchers can take charge and we ain't gonna take it no more!"

The crowd roared in approval, but Diablo noted that Swen frowned at the other man's words.

One of the gunfighters drawled, "What about the law?"

"What about the law?" Hurd challenged. "Frank Canton, here, used to be the sheriff, and he's with us. Oh, that sheriff in Buffalo is of a different mind maybe, but every rancher in Johnson County is with us. Most ain't gonna interfere with good citizens bringin' law and order to the area. I can guarantee you that."

Another roar of approval, with men clapping Canton and Hurd on the back.

Hurd looked around the big fire. "Anyone got anything else to say?"

Swen cleared his throat and looked as if he might say something, but the big, beefy rancher glared at him, causing the old Dane to lapse into silence, although he didn't look happy.

"Well, since that's settled, I reckon there's nothing else to talk about. We've got about forty men marked that we'd like to be rid of, and there's a bonus for every rustler you men kill. I'll give you the details of how we'll handle this in the morning. You Texans can spread your blankets in my barn or under the stars, but tonight, you're welcome to stick around and eat some more. There's plenty of beer."

Another roar of approval. The crowd now broke up into smaller groups, talking to Hurd or some of the other ranchers. A big crowd of the gunfighters gathered around the beer barrel, while some scattered out through the woods and shadows to visit with each other.

Diablo didn't want to be seen. The other gunfighters seemed to have forgotten he was ever on the train, which suited him just fine. He was always alone but not lonely. His anger kept him company. Instead, he decided to scout

out the terrain around the ranch house and barn. Sooner or later, he might need that information. Somewhere a big dog barked and snarled. *It must be chained or in the house.* He walked around behind the barn and saw a magnificent black stallion in a pen. The moonlight reflected off its shiny coat and long mane and tail. It had whip marks on its hide. That made Diablo frown. He didn't like men who mistreated horses. When the stallion saw Diablo, it reared and stamped its hooves, rolling its eyes and baring its teeth. *A man-killer,* Diablo thought, *but fine bloodlines.* A stallion like this could cost a man a fortune.

He checked out the terrain around the ranch and then returned to the trees in the shadows near the ranch house, making sure no one saw him. Around him, he heard loud, coarse laughter as the gunfighters visited and drank.

Sunny drove her buggy through the cool spring night and up to the Kruger ranch. She jumped down and ran up to the ranch house door, where a bent Indian woman answered her knock. "Where are the men?"

"Down by the barn," the old housekeeper pointed.

Sunny turned and ran down the trail in the darkness. There were a lot of men here at the barbecue tonight. She could see all the horses tied up and men drinking beer and talking in small groups in the distance. She had to walk through a shadowy grove of trees to reach the barn, so she slowed her gait. Dad would not be pleased she had disobeyed him, but with the prize mare in unexpected labor, Sunny felt she had to come.

Near her, a man stepped out of the shadows, and she started. "Well, hello, there, girly, you comin' to the barbecue?"

"No," she shook her head and attempted to step around him, but he blocked her path. She took a deep breath and realized the stranger was drunk and stank of sweat and dirt.

"Let me pass," she said with dignity. "I need to find somebody."

He grabbed her arm. "My name's Tom. Will I do, sweetness?"

"Let go of me, or I'll tell my dad." She attempted to retreat, but the swaying man didn't release her.

"Oh, honey, you're the sweetest thing I've seen since I left Lubbock."

Should she scream? That would bring a lot of people running and would create an embarrassing scene. In that second while she tried to decide, the man pulled her to him and clapped one dirty paw over her mouth.

"Come on, honey, give old Tom a few kisses out here on the grass, and then you can go."

Her heart pounding in her throat, Sunny struggled and twisted, but he was a big man and she was no match for him. She bit his hand, and he only laughed as he stumbled back unsteadily, pulling her deeper into the shadows.

And then a soft, deep voice said. "Let go of her, you bastard, or I'll carve your belly open and feed your guts to the timber wolves."

Her attacker froze, swaying on his feet, and she struggled again but could not break free. She tried to cry out, but all she managed was a weak whimper.

"I warned you," came the deep voice again, and it sounded like a rattlesnake about to strike.

"Go get your own woman," Tom held onto her. "I ain't givin' this one up."

She saw only a large shape looming out of the darkness, and then in the sudden moonlight, a scarred, angry face shone above her and a muscular arm wrapped around the attacker's neck. There was an abrupt, cracking sound as Tom's neck broke. With a dying sigh, his grip loosened. He slid to the ground, and she was free.

"You got no business here!" the deep voice snarled,

and with a strangled sob, Sunny fled down the trail toward the barn. For all she knew, the new man intended to molest her himself. She ran down the trail past groups of curious men and right into the arms of Hurd Kruger.

"Why, Sunny, dear, what are you doing here? This ain't a place for ladies."

She wasn't sure exactly what had happened up there in the shadows, but she wasn't one to start a fuss. Sunny managed to smile and look at her father's frowning face as she stepped away from the burly man. "It—it's an emergency, Uncle Hurd." She turned to her father. "Dad, that mare's gone into labor. I thought I'd better get you."

"Good thinking," Swen nodded. "We're through here anyway, aren't we, Hurd?"

The other man nodded. "Until tomorrow, Swen."

Swen took his daughter's arm, and they walked back up the path. She looked around for her attacker, but saw nothing—no body, no second man lurking in the darkness. Could she have dreamed all that? No, she couldn't imagine that much real terror.

Swen didn't have anything to say as he tied his horse on behind the buggy and helped her up into it. Then he grabbed the reins and took off at a fast clip.

"Dad, what was going on here tonight? Was that half-breed here?"

"Who?" Swen looked puzzled.

"You know, the gunfighter dressed all in black, the one with the scars."

Swen shrugged. "Don't remember that one, but there's a lot of trouble in that bunch. They should have stayed in Texas."

She didn't see how he could forget that one, but maybe he had a lot on his mind. "Dad, what was happening?"

He didn't answer, although in the moonlight, she saw

the frown on his face. "Something Hurd got up. It ain't for young ladies to be involved in."

She was already involved because she'd been attacked on the trail by one of those strangers and rescued by another, but she was a dutiful daughter and let it pass. She didn't like Hurd Kruger, although she tried hard not to show it because they were so beholden to the rich rancher.

"Don't worry, Dad; everything will be fine."

"I don't know that it will," Swen said and glanced over at her. "This ain't been much of a life, Sunny, looking after me. I always intended to send you back east to school."

She knew they didn't have the money for that, and anyway, she liked ranch life. "I don't care anything about some fancy education."

"Your mama would have wanted you an education, I think. You know, your Aunt Mary lives in Boston, and I got a little saved to send you."

She doubted that. Times had been so hard, and anyway, rustlers always seemed to be stealing their steers so they never had a profitable year. "Dad, you know I'd never leave you. Besides, as tough as things have been, I understand how there couldn't be extra money for that."

"I got the money," he insisted. "Aunt Mary would take you in if I could get you there."

"Let's talk about it some other time." She patted his arm. She couldn't imagine why Dad was suddenly so upset. Was it because he expected trouble with all these tough strangers in the county? She liked living on a ranch, but the winter cold of Wyoming bothered her. She wished Dad had settled a lot farther south.

In the meantime as they drove home, she wondered again about the scarred stranger who had stepped out of the darkness to attack her . . . or save her?

Chapter 3

Diablo dragged the dead man off the path as the girl ran away. When he returned, he didn't see her anywhere. No doubt she had gone back into the house where she belonged. He leaned against a tree some distance from the barn and stuck a cigarillo in his mouth. Damn that girl, she had complicated things. He had known it was the petite girl from the train station coming down the dark path from the ranch house the moment he smelled the dainty lilac perfume and saw the flash of moonlight on her long, pale hair.

That gunfighter, Tom, would have raped her and maybe killed her to cover up his crime. Troubled, Diablo leaned against the tree and stared up at the moon. He had acted instinctively in rescuing the girl. Now he couldn't decide if it was because Texans automatically protected women or because she looked like the princess in the fairy tales—the one an ugly man could never have. If that silkey-haired girl was Kruger's daughter, he knew his revenge should include her. There were a lot of ways to retaliate against a man, and that included his family.

* * *

The next morning, Kruger had just finished his coffee and stepped out on the back porch, sucking his teeth. "Good day to start running the nesters out of the county," he noted with a grunt of satisfaction.

His attention was diverted by one of his hired hands running toward him and shouting. What the hell was it now?

"Hey, boss, we got a dead man!"

"What?" Kruger strode to meet him. "Who? Where?"

The wiry cowboy pointed. "In the woods between here and the barn. Think he's one of those Texans."

Kruger started for the little patch of trees and soon came upon the big, burly gunfighter lying at an odd angle, his eyes wide in surprise. He squatted and looked him over. "Neck broke. Guess he fell last night—drunk, more than likely."

"I'd think it'd take more than a little fall to do that."

Kruger shrugged and yawned. "Don't matter. He's one of those Texans, and they ain't nothin' to us. Just get the boys to bury him and don't turn this into a big thing. What's one Texan more or less?"

He strode toward the barn and found Smitty, Joe, and Wilson saddling up. The three had been with him more than fifteen years, and he could always count on them. "Hey, boys, you got my horse saddled?"

Smitty nodded his unshaven chin and grinned. He was as big as a mountain and twice as stupid. He scratched his crooked nose. "You know we have, boss."

"I can always count on you three, no matter what I need."

Wilson rubbed the knife scar on his ugly face, and big muscles rippled under his torn shirt. "We gonna kill us some settlers today?"

Joe, the meanest of the three, spat through gapped teeth. His was the sharp face of a weasel. "We're lookin' forward to it, boss."

Kruger grinned back in anticipation. "You know it, and the Texans will do most of the work."

Joe mounted up, took off his hat, and ran his hand through greasy brown hair. "Them nesters tryin' to move in on our country."

"That's right." Kruger mounted the fine sorrel Wilson led out. "I fought Injuns, wildfires, and bears for this range, and my wife and son was the first people buried in the town cemetery. Now that we made it easy to live here, them farmers want to move in and put up fences and take over."

"We stand behind you, boss," Smitty mounted up. "You know we always have, whatever you wanted us to do."

Kruger nodded, and the four wheeled their horses and took off to the meeting place up the creek. They would overrun these farmers, cut their fences, shoot their damned oxen pulling the plows that tore up the grasslands. Tonight they would set some barns on fire and shoot up some cabins. In a few days of organized terror, they would have the settlers packing up their wagons and moving out. It was only just. Tough men like Hurd Kruger had tamed this land and built empires here after losing wives and children to Injuns, disease, and blizzards. No one was going to take this away from them without a fight, and that's the reason he had called in the professional gunfighters.

They met up with the Texans and some of the other big ranchers at Crazy Woman Creek. Kruger looked around with satisfaction at the Texans. Yes, this was a gang that could spread terror and fast. There were so many of them he couldn't remember one from another, but it didn't matter. None of them had any stake in this fight except the money they'd get for killing farmers and burning their places. Now he scowled as he looked at the other ranchers. "Swen Sorrenson's not here."

A wiry old rancher shifted his weight in his saddle.

"Aw, you know Swen—he don't approve."

"Maybe he's scared." One of the Texans guffawed.

Kruger frowned. "Naw, he's just got what he calls principles, so he'll let us do the dirty work to protect his land from these dirt-scratchin' clodhoppers."

"I'm Buck," a big red-headed one with a ragged beard grinned and spat tobacco juice to one side, "and this is my amigo, Pug."

Pug, a smaller one with a dirty ponytail, nodded with a grin of missing teeth.

Kruger smiled. "You two look like you can do some damage."

"We aim to," Buck said, putting both freckled hands on his saddle horn. "We can use the money. You just tell us what to do, and we'll get her done."

Kruger and some of the other ranchers chuckled. "Now there's the kind of attitude I like."

"I ain't seen many women up in these parts," Buck complained. "Is it all right if we help ourselves to the farmers' pretty ones while we're shootin' and burnin' things down?"

"Be my guest," Kruger nodded with a wink.

"Aw, now, Hurd," one of the other ranchers objected, "hurtin' their womenfolk don't seem right—"

"It'll move them settlers out much faster," Kruger argued, "and what do we care about a bunch of farmers' daughters? Buck, consider that a little extra treat."

Some of the gunfighters raised a cheer.

"Now let's get started," Kruger snapped. "Hemmings, you take part of these men; Rawlings, you take some of the others and go south. Some of you Texans stay with me. Today we spread out, cut fences, and scatter livestock. When it gets dark, we'll fire some barns. In a few days, these settlers will move out of here so fast you'd think their drawers were on fire."

The men roared with laughter and broke into three groups, spreading out across the county.

From a small foothill in the distance along the base of the Bighorn Mountains, Diablo leaned on his saddle horn and watched the dust rise up from the horses' hooves as the crowd broke into three groups and rode out. Dawn was just bathing the prairie with a pale pink glow. Probably no one had missed him, and if anyone did, they'd think he was with one of the other groups. He guessed what the men were up to, but he hadn't come to tear down fences and chase terrorized calves. Such mischief was beneath his dignity.

In a way, he felt a little sorry for the settlers, but they should have known better than to trespass into ranch country and put up barbed wire that would injure cattle and horses. Farmers needed to stay in more civilized places and not subject their women to the dangers of the frontier. He thought of his own mother and frowned. Yes, a damned farmer had brought a fragile white woman into a hostile area, and she'd died by her own hand after that Indian uprising, her rape, and Diablo's birth.

He must not think of his mother. After all, he'd never known her except what the old Santee woman had told him. *Women.* That made Diablo remember the fragile girl with the almost-silver hair. If he hadn't stopped it, she would have been raped last night by that brute. Now he couldn't decide if he had saved her to protect her or was merely saving her for his own revenge. What was her name? Sunny. Well, if she was Kruger's daughter, she would be part of his revenge. There was no room in his heart for pity when anger and revenge were what drove him. The feel of the slight girl in his arms last night came to his mind unbidden, and he frowned. Her skin had been soft and her figure rounded. Her hair had felt like silk, and she had smelled of soap and the faint scent of lilacs. He felt the need arise in him and was angry with himself.

"You ugly monster," he muttered, "you ain't ever gonna get a woman like that unless you take her by force."

Diablo frowned. No, he wanted more than that. He wanted . . . he wasn't sure what the hell he wanted because he'd never had any contact with women except for Cimarron Durango and a couple of very drunken whores. There had to be more to women than that.

"Stop thinking about her," he muttered and reminded himself again that he was here for one thing and one thing only: revenge. He had waited and thought of nothing else for fifteen long years. Certain men were going to die, but not quickly. He would kill them as his Sioux warrior father might have and make it long and painful. These white men were going to reap what they sowed.

Soon the last snow on the mountain peaks would be melted, and the farmers should be planting now. However, within a few brutal days, they would be lying dead in their own cabins as the Texans picked them off. The settlers didn't stand a chance against hired guns. No doubt Buck and some of the others would rape a few of the prettier women. *Rape.* Diablo thought of his own mother and winced. Rape was always the ultimate revenge and so disgraceful that many women, like his own mother, would kill themselves, especially if they found themselves with child after the terrible event. His mind did not want to go into the horror of his own past, but he couldn't control the memories of a terrified boy. Women weren't the only ones who could be raped.

Now Diablo rode along a hilltop, saw movement in the valley below, and reined in his blood bay horse, watching. A man wearing striped overalls ran toward a barn, while another man on a paint horse pursued him. It wasn't his business, Diablo reminded himself; he was in

Wyoming on his own mission. Yet after a moment, he felt forced to help the poor settler, and he turned his mount down into the valley, riding along behind a string of straggly brush. The rider below him laughed, and the wind carried the sound up the hill. Diablo recognized that laugh. It brought back memories of that day fifteen years ago.

Diablo saw a flash of light as the man on horseback pulled a pistol and shot the running man in the back. The farmer stumbled and went down. The big man on the paint horse dismounted and walked over to the prone body, kicked it with his boot, laughed again.

Diablo winced. Shooting a man in the back was loathsome, but he knew the rider was capable of worse than that—far worse. Silently he rode toward the man who was intent on staring down at his victim. *Some poor nester*, Diablo thought as he dismounted and walked toward the killer, his soft moccasins making no sound.

"All right, drop it!" Diablo snarled.

The huge man called Smitty turned slowly, surprise on his unshaven face.

"I said drop it, or I'll kill you right here and it won't be a clean kill."

Smitty's face paled. "Who—who are you? Are you one of them Texas gunfighters? Ain't you on our side?"

Diablo frowned, looking down at the dead man and the little cabin and barn in the distance. "You shot him in the back, you bastard."

"Remember, we're just supposed to clean 'em out; don't matter how we do it."

"I'm not here to kill settlers and farmers," Diablo growled. "Drop your gun belt."

Sweat broke out on Smitty's pale face and ran down his crooked nose and dripped off his fat chin. "Look, I'll let you take credit with Kruger. That's fifty extra dollars in your pocket with none of the work."

Diablo merely smiled without mirth. "Take a good look. You don't even know me, do you?"

The middle-aged cowboy peered at him and shook his head slowly. "God, I'd remember that face—I mean—"

"Yeah, this ugly face," Diablo agreed. "Think back fifteen years. Know me now?"

Smitty's hands began to shake, and his eyes widened as he seemed to recognize Diablo. "Some—some rustlers and an Injun kid, there was an Injun kid—"

"And you laughed when you made them dance on air, and then you all turned to the kid."

"Oh, God!" Smitty moaned, "I—I didn't mean nothin' by it. I was just followin' orders."

"You loved every minute of it," Diablo snapped. "You laughed while you were doing it."

"We was all drunk." Smitty's face was white as milk. "That was a long time ago; we thought you was dead."

"One thing you forgot, you and the others, was that I might survive and come back. Now mount up."

"What—what are you gonna do with me?"

"I'm going to give my friends justice, but first, you're gonna bury this poor devil." Diablo motioned toward the dead farmer.

"Then how will I claim my fifty dollars?" Smitty objected.

"You can't spend fifty dollars in hell."

"What?"

"Shut up and dig," Diablo ordered.

"But I ain't got a shovel."

"Then use your hands," Diablo said.

The other man looked like he might argue, then got down on his knees in the plowed dirt and began to dig. Sweat poured off his pale face and dripped off his crooked nose. His shirt turned dark and wet with his labor.

Diablo glanced up at the sun. He didn't have a lot of time to make this a proper burial. Besides, neither one of them were fit to read a Bible over the dead man. They were both lost souls bound for hell, and Smitty was going tonight. "All right, that will have to do. Turn him face up and put him in the hole."

Smitty was sweating profusely as he obeyed. "I was just followin' orders," he whined.

"Now take off your shirt and cover him up, you rotten bastard. I don't cotton to throwing dirt in a dead man's face."

Smitty blinked and obeyed. His bare skin was fatty and milk white under the shirt.

"Maybe his folks will find him and give him a proper service." Diablo watched until Smitty was finished, trying not to remember how a small, injured half-breed boy had tried to bury his friends with his bare hands because he had nothing to dig with. He didn't want to remember that day, but never an hour passed that he didn't. Maybe when he killed all the men involved, he could forget it. "Now get on your horse."

"I at least ought to get a trial," Smitty whimpered.

"You didn't give those three cowboys a trial."

"Let's talk this over," Smitty begged as he mounted up on his paint horse. "My God, you can't just kill me."

Diablo swung up on his own horse. "Those cowboys begged, too, and you laughed, you and the others. The world needs to be rid of scum like you. Now get riding."

It was near sundown when Kruger led some of his posse toward his ranch, satisfied with his day's work. They had raided three nesters' farms, tearing down their fences and shooting anyone who tried to interfere. By nightfall, the word would have spread across Johnson County, and farmers would begin to pack up and move out. Some might try to organize and fight back, but there was always tomorrow to deal with the braver ones. A few barns burned and people shot would terrify even the most stubborn ones.

It was dusk as they rode toward the big ranch gate with the K Bar sign hanging overhead. There was something hanging from the sign that threw distorted shadows across the road. It was a big white object, dangling and swaying from a rope that creaked and shadowed the riders as they approached the gate and reined in.

"What the—" Kruger spurred his sorrel horse closer. The horse snorted and shied from the dangling object. Kruger stared and blinked. It was a heavy, shirtless man, swaying in the wind, his back toward the riders. Then as he rode closer, the body swung slowly around so that Kruger saw the unshaven face. "Oh, my God!"

A yell of surprise and horror came from the riders behind him as he looked upward. It was Smitty at the end of that rope, his eyes wide and staring, his usually florid face pale as flour. Blood ran out of his crooked nose. Kruger stood up in his stirrups, reached out to touch the body. It was still warm.

The other men rode up beside him, looking in hushed silence for a long moment as the body swayed in the wind and the rope creaked. "Goddamn, what's happened?"

Kruger ground his teeth in rage. "Some of them damned clod-breakers got more balls than we thought. It's an insult, a spit in the face, lynchin' a K Bar hand. The damned farmers are sendin' me a message. Joe, you and Wilson cut him down."

Joe and his other man obeyed. Smitty fell like a bag of potatoes onto the trail. "What'll we do with him, boss?"

Kruger shrugged. "He's no good to me now. Just bury him someplace."

Joe squatted down to look at the body, then up at him, a frown on his weasel face. "We ain't gonna do no service or anything?"

"Naw, we ain't got time for that."

"But, boss," Wilson objected, "he worked for you almost twenty years."

"Yeah, but he ain't no good to me dead." Kruger shrugged. "Now the rest of you, let's get some food and a little rest. Tonight, we'll get even with them nesters. We'll burn every one of their barns in the county. Me, I'm going over to see if I can get Sorrenson to join us. We can use him and his cowboys."

Kruger was still cursing as he turned his horse. *How dare the nesters show any guts?* He had expected them to pack up and run like frightened rabbits. If the farmers killed any of Kruger's men, it might be the Texas gunfighters who backed off.

It was dark as he rode over to Sorrenson's place and dismounted.

Old Swen was out on the porch in the moonlight. Swen frowned. "What brings you here?"

"A little problem," Kruger said.

Sunny came out on the porch just then.

"Dad—" She paused when she saw Kruger.

"Hello, dear," Kruger doffed his hat and gave her his warmest smile. She had never looked so lovely and desirable.

"Hello, Uncle Hurd."

"You know, you could just call me Hurd."

She didn't say anything.

"Umm," Hurd sniffed. "Smells like you're cookin' up something good for your dad. You gonna invite me to stay for supper?"

"Sure," she said, but she didn't look happy about it.

"It'll be ready as soon as I put the biscuits in." She turned and went back into the house.

Kruger watched her go. He wanted her more than he ever had, wanted her more than a bigger ranch and more cattle. "Your girl is turning into a real beauty, Swen. It's about time she was married."

Swen shook his head. "No, I've saved a little money, Hurd, in spite of hard times. I'm gonna send her back east to her aunt. Sunny can live with her and go to college."

Kruger snorted and sat down in the porch swing. "Now why does a girl need to go to college? She'd make a good rancher's wife and give a man some fine sons."

"Why did you come by?" Swen asked, evidently wanting to change the subject.

"We're startin' to give them nesters trouble."

Swen frowned. "I don't want to hear about it. You know I'm a great one for live and let live."

"Aw, I was hoping you'd changed your mind and you and your crew would help us run them out. After all, they're stringin' barbed wire across all these lands we always run cattle on."

"They got rights, too," Swen said.

"You gonna say that when one of them clodhoppers wants to marry Sunny or runs you out of business 'cause they're plowin' up all the grass we graze our cows on?"

"I'm just talking about what's right, Hurd."

"I ain't got the luxury of worrying about right," Kruger sneered, "and you ain't either. If it wasn't for me helping you out, you wouldn't still be in business."

"I've had some hard luck," Swen admitted. "But I'll pay you back someday."

"Not if the nesters crowd you off the land," Kruger argued.

Sunny stuck her head out the door. "Supper's on." She did not smile.

Kruger stood up. "Good. I'm so hungry, my belly thinks my throat's been cut."

He followed her into the house, Swen coming along behind him. Kruger watched the girl walk ahead of him. He wanted her. He had always wanted her, and by God, he would have her. He hadn't cared about his homely first wife; he had married her for the little money she'd inherited and brought her out to the wilds of Wyoming, knowing she was frail and not the sort to be a rancher's wife. It was the son he'd lost that pained him. What good did it do for a man to build a rich empire if he didn't have sons to leave it to? Yes, he would marry Sunny. They would have a dozen sons to take over this state some day. For the last four years, that was all he'd been working toward.

"You keep a fine house, Miss Sunny, real homey." He looked with approval at the homemade curtains, the tidy living area, and the table loaded down with steaming food.

"Remember," Swen said proudly, as he pulled out a chair, "she won the blue ribbon in the pie-baking contest at the county fair last year."

"I remember," Kruger nodded as he sat down. "Not only pretty, but a great cook, too. Miss Sunny, you'll make some man a good wife."

She didn't say anything, only started dishing up the stew and hot biscuits; then she turned toward the cupboard for some homemade jam.

Kruger watched her. The lamplight caught the brightness of her hair and the soft curves of her figure. Yes, he was enlarging his kingdom so he could lay it at the feet of this beauty. There was only about twenty years' difference in their ages—well, maybe a little more than that, but everyone said young girls preferred mature men, especially those with property. He desired her more than anything else in this world, and Hurd Kruger was used to getting what he wanted.

"Hurd, you had a reason for coming?" Swen asked as he took a biscuit.

"Later," Kruger shook his head and dipped into his stew. He didn't want to upset the lovely Sunny by telling Swen about Smitty's lynching yet. If he couldn't persuade Swen and his crew to join him, he still had plenty of help to set fires to a bunch of the farmers' barns tonight.

After supper, he thanked Sunny profusely and took Swen outside to tell him what had happened to Smitty.

Swen filled his pipe. "The nesters fighting back?"

"Yes, damn them. Didn't expect it. I'll get even with them tonight."

Swen shrugged. "Smitty was a varmint with no conscience. I hate to say it, but he deserved it."

"Swen, damn it, whose side are you on? I thought you and your men might reconsider and join us."

Swen shook his head. "I'll have no part of it."

"You used to go along with me."

"Don't remind me." Swen lit his pipe, and the fragrant scent drifted on the cool spring night. "I ain't never forgot what we did that long-ago night."

"Oh, hell, you still thinking about that? Them cowboys was stealing my beef."

"They was maybe just hungry," Swen replied, "and the Injun kid didn't deserve what he got."

"We was all drunk," Kruger shrugged, "but I'd do it again, and I reckon so would Joe and Wilson. To hang on to what's yours, you have to set some limits."

"Over a few cows," Swen sighed, "over a few damn cows."

"Oh, stop your whining." Kruger snapped. "It's over and done with. For the last time, you going with us tonight?"

"I think I'm finally getting the courage to say no to you after all this time."

"Then damn your cowardly hide," Kruger swore and untied his horse. "I been looking out for you all these years, Swen, but I'm not sure I will anymore. You're too weak for this rough country." He mounted up, spurred his sorrel horse savagely, and rode away, already regretting his temper. He would have to try a different tactic, or Swen would never let him marry Sunny. The old Dane was in debt up to his ears, Hurd had seen to that, rustling some of Swen's cattle every year so the old man could never quite make a profit. He'd have to tighten the screws so that Swen couldn't say no to accepting him as a future son-in-law.

Diablo had built himself a small camp in the foothills of the Bighorns, and now he watched the moon against the black velvet of the night. After an hour, a faint orange glow began in the distance and spread along the silhouette of the range line. The smell of smoke drifted to his nose, and he frowned. The gunfighters must be setting fire to the nesters' barns. As one man against more than fifty, there wasn't anything Diablo could do about that, although he was tempted to try. He reminded himself again that he had waited fifteen years and come a long, long distance for only one reason, and saving barns was not part of that reason. Still he felt sorry for the homesteaders. Once a barn was fired, there was no way to put it out, with the prairie wind blowing. The modest cabins would be next.

He mounted up and rode toward the biggest fire on the horizon. He came within sight and saw a mass of riders galloping away. He started to follow them, and then he heard a scream from the house and reined in.

"Come on, men." Kruger gestured as he led them away at a gallop.

The other men guffawed and followed him. "That Wilson, he's got an eye for the women, all right."

"We should stay and help him," Joe laughed.

Kruger cursed. "We got more barns to burn; there ain't no time for women right now."

Joe shouted, "Where's Swen?"

"Where do you think he is? He ain't comin', the coward!" Kruger swore as they rode away.

Diablo watched the riders top the horizon and then disappear into the night. He rode closer to the burning barn. A dead man lay sprawled in the barnyard. Diablo dismounted and checked. The young farmer was dead, riddled by a dozen bullets, probably shot down as he attempted to protect his barn.

From the house, the woman screamed again, and as Diablo turned, she ran out of the house, half naked, holding her torn, faded dress around her. Wilson was right behind her, the flames from the burning barn lighting the old knife scar on his face.

Neither of them seemed to see Diablo. The young woman was a beauty, her dark hair streaming out behind her as she ran barefooted across the grass.

"Hey, honey, let's do it!" Wilson yelled and ran faster, gaining on her. "You never had a man as good as me before!"

She sobbed uncontrollably as she fled, and then she seemed to see the dead man sprawled in the barnyard and ran to him, fell down next to him, trying to take him in her arms.

Her dress fell down exposing beautiful full breasts, now smeared with the dead man's blood.

"Here, honey, don't cry for him," Wilson sneered and

grabbed her, pulling her to him as he groped her breasts. "You got a better man here."

She fought him, but she was no match for the big man.

Diablo winced, thinking of his own mother, and then he rode up behind the pair and threw a loop over Wilson's shoulders and tightened it, dragging him away from the hysterical girl.

"What the hell?" Wilson battled the noose.

"Get on your horse!" Diablo ordered.

The girl had run back to the prone body of her husband, sobbing uncontrollably, not even seeming to see Diablo or realize what was happening.

Wilson stared at him. "Ain't you one of us?"

Diablo shook his head and smiled very slowly. "It's time you got your reward, Wilson."

Wilson seemed uncertain. He mounted up on his skittish palomino horse and tried to loosen the rope around him. "Reward? What reward? What the hell do you think—"

"Just ride," Diablo said. "You got a lot to answer for."

Wilson looked confused. "Now look here, Kruger said I could have her as long as I didn't take long—"

"Kruger ain't in charge now," Diablo snapped. "Now get riding."

"What is it you want?"

"Revenge," Diablo said and turned his scarred face so that Wilson could see it in the glowing light of the fiery barn. "You know me?"

"Hell, no," Wilson shook his head. "You loco?"

"Think back fifteen years," Diablo muttered. "Think about a lynching and torturing a half-breed kid."

Wilson's knife-scarred face turned pale, and sweat broke out under his beady eyes. "Kruger, he told us to do it."

"You enjoyed every minute of it. I remember how you laughed as you flipped me over on my belly."

"We was just havin' a little fun since there was no girls available in town. And anyway, we was all drunk."

"No excuse," Diablo said and pulled the rope tighter.

"Kruger ain't gonna like this," Wilson blustered.

"He doesn't get any say in this. Now ride."

There was nothing Diablo could do to aid the woman, he thought with regret. Maybe she had family who would help her bury her man. At least Diablo had saved her from one horrid experience. Diablo remembered, shuddered, and nudged his horse forward. Some things a man can't forgive or forget, and being drunk was no excuse for the unspeakable things the men had done to him that long-ago night.

It was almost dawn as Kruger and Joe rode into the barnyard at the ranch.

"Good night's work," Kruger grinned.

"Yeah, we set fire to half the barns in the county."

"I don't see Wilson's horse," Kruger dismounted. "Surely he can't still be humpin' that farmer's wife."

Joe snorted as he swung down from his white mare. "You don't know Wilson. He could go all night, and he especially likes the ones that fight and claw."

"Well, that's one of the rewards of this raid. You see a woman you like, Joe, you take her." He dismounted.

Joe grinned. "I got an eye for old man Sorrenson's daughter, and he ain't helpin' us none."

Kruger saw red rage as he grabbed the other by the throat. "You bastard, you pass the word that nobody's to touch Sunny, you hear me?"

Joe managed to free himself from the other's grip and coughed, stumbled backward. "Boss, I didn't mean nothing—"

"I'm going to marry that girl, you hear me? Nobody's to bother the Sorrensons' place."

"Sure, boss, sure." Joe felt his neck and coughed again.

"Now let's put our horses in the barn and get some sleep; it's nearly daybreak. We'll rest up through the day."

"Sounds good to me." Joe led his horse into the barn, followed by Kruger.

The coming daylight silhouetted a bundle hanging from the barn rafters.

Kruger said. "What the hell?"

Joe took one look, and the bile rose up in his throat as the limp form swung around, revealing, in the pink light of dawn, the terrified, knife-scarred face and wide-open eyes of Wilson, staring down at him from the swaying rope. "Oh, my God."

Wilson would never rape another woman or fire another barn. He hung from the rafter, and the rope made a squeaking sound as his weight pulled and strained at it.

"Goddamn!" Kruger said, and for once in his life, he was really frightened. "Goddamn! What's gone wrong that all my men are gettin' lynched?"

Chapter 4

That night and the day after, Sunny had watched the sky light up all pink and red and smelled smoke on the wind. They walked out on the front porch the next morning.

"Dad, what's happening?"

Swen looked troubled, shrugged.

"It's the Stock Growers Association behind this, isn't it?"

Swen didn't answer.

"Dad, don't you think we ought to go into town and tell the sheriff?"

"I'm sure he knows what's going on." He sat down in a porch swing and sighed.

She had never questioned her father's judgment before, and now she hesitated. "What do you mean? Won't he help?"

He didn't look at her. "Would you go up against real gunmen with a handful of inexperienced deputies and a few farmers?"

"But surely burning barns and running off cattle isn't right."

Swen hesitated, fiddled with his pipe. "Honey, you've got to look at this from the cattlemen's point of view. They've fought Indians, blizzards, and rustlers all these years to hang on to what they've got, and now farmers are pouring into Wyoming and plowing up the dirt. This is a hostile land, Sunny, and sometimes you have to fight to hang on to what's yours."

"That doesn't sound like you; that sounds like Hurd Kruger. And anyway you aren't taking part." She sat down across from him, took his hand.

He stuck his pipe between his teeth. "I don't know if I've got ethics or if I'm just a coward."

"Dad, how can you say that? You know this isn't right. Who are all those strangers that came in on that train?"

"They're Texas gunfighters, the cream of the crop. The Stock Growers Association has made up a pot of one hundred thousand dollars to run all the homesteaders out of Johnson County. You know Hurd has a wife and son buried out here on these plains. Some of the other ranchers have buried families too, and they intend to hold on to what's theirs. They figure they've paid for the land in blood. They resent the farmers and the small ranchers moving in and fencing off grazing."

"So you're saying the end justifies the means?"

"I don't know what I believe anymore, Sunny. I've been so alone since your mother died."

"I'm sorry, Dad."

"You got nothing to be sorry about, honey. You're a good daughter."

"I—I try not to cause you any trouble," she said. "I figure I owe you that."

"You don't owe me anything, Sunny. I'm not much of a business man, I guess. We probably should have pulled up stakes and left Wyoming a long time ago." He seemed lost in thought, and Sunny wondered if he were thinking of her mother.

"I'm sorry I even brought this up, Dad. I suppose it's not my business."

"No, you've made me see the light. I think I'll go into town to see if the sheriff can do anything to rein this in before the county has no law at all. Maybe I should go ahead and send you to your aunt."

"Oh, Dad, I can't leave you—not at a time like this. Can I go to town with you?"

She saw him hesitate. "By jingo, with the way things are going, I'm afraid to leave you alone."

She smiled. "I'll get my sunbonnet, and you hitch up the buggy."

When they drove into Krugerville, Sunny saw three wagons piled high with household goods tied to hitching posts.

"Looks like it's started," Swen muttered.

"What, Dad?"

"Never mind, honey." He patted her hand. "You wait here, and I'll go talk to the sheriff."

He swung down from the buggy and walked along the wooden sidewalk to the sheriff's office, went inside.

Sunny waited dutifully for a while; then curiosity got the better of her. She got down from the buggy and walked over to one of the wagons, where a tired, worn woman sat on the seat nursing a baby.

"Hello, I'm Sunny Sorrenson."

"You're one of the cattlemen's clan," the woman said, glaring at her.

Sunny had never felt such shame before. "Are you just coming to town to shop?"

The woman shook her head, adjusted the whimpering baby at her breast. "We're leaving, just like most of the others. But then you'd know that, since you're part of the ranch bunch."

"I'm sorry, I don't know what you're talking—"

"What do you want?" A thin, tired man came up to the wagon. "Here to gloat?" He swung up on the seat.

"I beg your pardon?" Sunny blinked.

"You cattle people have beat us all right, murdering and raping, burning our barns." He turned to the wagon behind him and yelled, "Let's go, Ned."

Sunny stepped back, and the man slapped the reins against his team of thin mules. The two wagons started up, driving slowly out of town as Sunny watched.

With a sigh, she turned back toward her buggy and saw that gunfighter, the one with the scarred face, walk out of the general store as her Dad came out of the sheriff's office and bumped into him. Her father started, and his face went white. She couldn't hear what was being said, but it was a brief encounter.

Diablo had come into town for supplies. He hadn't expected to bump into Swen coming along the sidewalk.

Swen paled and hesitated. "You—you came back after all these years."

"Didn't you know I would?" He stared down at the older man.

"I—I thought you were probably dead."

"I forced myself to live. Dead men can't take revenge."

"I am so sorry," the old Dane said, "So very sorry. If we hadn't all been drunk—"

"You don't need to be sorry," Diablo snapped.

"I have been for fifteen years." He didn't look at Diablo; he looked at the wooden sidewalk. "I'm ashamed I didn't stop it."

"You tried."

"Maybe not hard enough." Swen looked up at him. "I want you to know I ain't had a drink since that night."

"That don't bring my friends back to life or fix this." Diablo gestured toward his scarred face.

"I can't undo it, but I want you to know it's always

haunted me. I've wished a million times I could undo what happened that day."

"So have I." Diablo watched the pretty girl visiting with some of the nesters that were being run out of town. Then he brushed on past the older man and went into the Longhorn Saloon.

Who was that man Dad was talking to? Then she remembered the big frame and the black clothes of the half-breed she had seen at the train station and how she had shuddered at his scarred, horrible face. She wondered what they had to discuss. Then she watched the man in black move silently down the wooden sidewalk and disappear into the saloon while her father strode down the street to the livery stable.

She walked back to her buggy. It was warm sitting here waiting for Dad. She turned her head and watched the homesteaders' wagons disappear slowly up the dusty road.

Maybe she ought to say something to Hurd Kruger about all this. After all, he was president of the Stock Growers Association. She shook her head. Her father wouldn't approve of her sticking her nose into men's business, and anyway, Uncle Hurd would tell her not to "worry her pretty little head about it."

After a few minutes, she grew fidgety and remembered that she needed some thread. Dad had told her to stay with the buggy, but surely he wouldn't mind if she went into the general store a few minutes while she waited. She got out of the buggy and walked into the old store. The dim light after the bright sunshine made her blink, and she took a deep breath of the spices and pickle barrels before she smiled at bald old Mr. Blake. "Good day, sir."

"Why, hello, Miss Sunny. What you doing in town?"

"Dad had some business, and I just remembered I was out of thread."

The old man rubbed his hands together. "What color you need?"

"White."

He went over to a shelf, looking up and down the spools. "Lot of traffic in town today."

She nodded. "I talked to one of them. Settlers pulling out of the county. Reckon that'll hurt your business?"

He frowned as he came back to the counter with the spool of thread. "Not really. Them farmers ain't got a dime between 'em. Don't blame the ranchers for chasing them out.

Johnny-come-latelies wanting to fence off good grazing land after the ranchers made it easy for them by civilizing this country."

"But do you think they should have brought in all those Texas gunfighters?"

The storekeeper shrugged. "That ain't for me to say, miss. You know Hurd Kruger purty near runs things hereabout, him bein' the biggest rancher and the president of the Stock Growers Association."

She didn't know what to say. She'd been taught that a lady never voices an opinion or argues with a man. She took the spool of thread. "Put this on my bill, Mr. Blake."

"Sure thing." He turned back to filling his shelves, and Sunny took the spool of thread and went out the side door, intending to walk down to the livery stable. She ran head on into the scarred gunfighter who had just stepped out the saloon's side door.

Without thinking, she took a deep breath and cringed back against the wall.

The gunfighter seemed startled and turned his face away from her.

She looked up at him, saw the surprise in his dark

eyes, and felt the hard muscle of him before she backed away. She realized abruptly that she was alone with this cold-blooded killer in this deserted side street and she whirled and ran, losing her sunbonnet in the process.

Diablo watched her run, her pale hair glinting in the sunlight. There was something about her that stirred him in a way no woman ever had. Oh, a few times when he was drunk and overcome with need, he had paid some ugly whore to lie down, close her eyes, and take him on, but she had always demanded money in advance and he had been ashamed and humiliated that he'd stooped to such a low. Now he stood watching the girl's soft curves and the glimpse of her trim ankles under the blue calico as she hurried toward the buggy.

He wanted her with all the need any man ever felt for a beautiful woman. He wanted to crush that soft, moist mouth beneath his, run his hands over that ripe body, and take her completely so that she was his in sweet surrender.

"Fat chance of that," he grunted. Then he noticed the forgotten sunbonnet lying in the dirt at his feet. He leaned over, picked it up. It was a blue flowered calico with a trim of eyelet around the face. When he held it close to his nose, he smelled the scent of her soft hair. It smelled of sunshine, soap, and lilacs. He ought to return it to her.

Even as he took a step, he saw her reach the buggy, and then Hurd Kruger came across the street to speak to her and lifted her up onto the seat.

So she was Kruger's woman, or maybe his daughter. Diablo gritted his teeth in rage as he watched. Well, then she would be part of his revenge. But not yet. Diablo had waited fifteen years for this, and he would not let emotion hurry his plans. Diablo folded the sunbonnet and slipped it inside his shirt. Then he went around back of the saloon, mounted his black stallion, and rode out of town, still thinking of the girl.

Sunny had hurried to her buggy. "Oh, hello, Uncle Hurd." Sunny noted the man with a sigh as he came across the road.

"Oh, now Sunny, you can just call me Hurd." He stood sucking his teeth and staring down at her in a hungry way like a coyote might look at a rabbit. "What you doing in town?"

Somehow, she thought any information might lead to trouble for her father. "Just—just picking up a few supplies. I might ask you the same thing." She gave him her warmest smile to distract him.

"I was at the barber's getting a shave and a haircut." Hurd put his hands on her tiny waist and lifted her up onto the buggy seat.

She saw the black dye still wet on his sideburns, too black on his gray hair.

"Where's Swen?" He frowned, looking up and down the street.

"Oh, I don't know. Maybe at the saddle shop." She wished he would go away.

About that time, Swen came out of the livery stable and strode toward them. His weathered face paled as he saw Kruger.

"Well, Swen, what business you got in town?" Kruger smiled, but his cold dark eyes did not.

"Uh, just—just gettin' some supplies, that's all."

"Yes," Sunny blurted, "we had just been discussing how successful the Stock Growers Association has been about running the settlers out of Johnson County." She tried to smile at the heavyset man.

That seemed to divert his attention because he smiled

too, and nodded. "Yep, them Texas gunfighters is doin' the trick."

"She don't need to hear the details," Swen snapped as he climbed up onto the seat.

Sunny wanted to comment on the pitiful, poor families and their ragged wagons, but knew she was expected not to start a controversy.

Hurd smiled at her, looking at her intently in a way that made her feel he was mentally undressing her. "Well, it'll be dark soon and I got things to do. Swen, you ought to come join us. We're meetin' at my place tonight."

Swen swallowed hard and fidgeted with the reins. "You know I won't, Hurd."

"Some people forget when a favor is owed, I reckon. Well, good-bye, Miss Sunny. It was good to see you again. You're the prettiest gal in the county, bar none."

"Thank you," Sunny tried not to pull her hand back as Hurd grabbed it and waited until he had walked away before she wiped her hand on her blue skirt.

"How long he been here?" Swen asked as they watched him mount up and ride away.

"Just a minute or two." She didn't want to even think about the matter.

Swen shrugged. "Just what I thought, sheriff said I ought to be on the side of the ranchers and he ain't gonna get involved or he'd get voted out of office or maybe killed."

"Can't or won't?" Sunny challenged.

"I don't know, and you can't blame him none. There're at least twenty-five of the best Texas gunfighters here right now, and the Stock Growers Association is big and powerful. There's liable to be more trouble, Sunny. I worry about what would happen to you if something happened to me."

"Now Dad," she put her hand on his arm as he snapped

the reins and the buggy moved out down the dusty street, "nothing's going to happen to you."

He glanced over at her. "Where's your sunbonnet?"

She touched her head, feeling a bit foolish. "I—I don't know. Reckon I lost it someplace. I'll make myself another." She must have dropped it in the alley when she was surprised and frightened by that cold, scarred gunfighter. She'd been in a panicked hurry to escape from him. The intensity of his dark eyes and his unsmiling face, his wide-shouldered masculinity had frightened her. He looked like the kind of man who took what he wanted, and the hunger on his scarred face told her he wanted her.

"Honey, what are you thinking about?" Swen said as he took the buggy at a fast clip toward their ranch.

"Nothing," she lied. "I reckon as soon as the cattlemen scare all the settlers out of the county, they'll send all those gunfighters packing?"

"Reckon so," Swen sighed. "There's one . . ."

She waited for him to finish, but her father seemed lost in thought as they drove the rest of the way home.

Tonight, she thought, *there'll be some more barns set afire and settlers shot.* She felt helpless to stop it. Then a thought occurred to her: Uncle Hurd seemed to have a soft spot in his heart for her. She'd ask him as a special favor to stop the killing and bloodshed.

Diablo rode out to his camp, still thinking of the girl. Because he had been raised by the Santee Sioux, he could live outdoors, but living with the Durangos had gotten him used to having coffee and bacon. He'd seen Kruger in town with that beautiful blonde, so this was a good chance to scout out Kruger's ranch. Most of his men would probably be out killing settlers or driving off cattle. He'd decided from what he'd heard that Kruger valued only certain things, so Diablo intended to destroy or steal them. He intended to see that Kruger ended up with nothing.

He tied up his horse at a distance and moved silently toward the ranch house. There didn't seem to be a soul around except an old Indian woman working in the kitchen. Diablo could see her and hear her singing as she walked out on the back porch to empty dishwater. He went around the house and through a window into what looked like the living area. The furniture was rough, but there was a bearskin rug before the fireplace. The sunlight gleamed on the rifle with silver and gold etchings on its barrel. It had to have cost a fortune, and Kruger must be so proud of it. He would be mad as hell when he realized it was gone.

With a smile, Diablo reached up and took it off its mounts and went back through the window. As he walked away, he heard a dog barking and walked over to see a big, thin dog at the end of a chain. It looked like a cross between a wolf and some kind of shepherd. The dog snarled and strained at the end of his chain.

Diablo liked dogs, and this one looked mistreated. "Be quiet boy, or you'll alert the housekeeper. Your life not so good at this place? I'll see what I can do."

He strode to his horse, put the prized rifle in the boot on his saddle, and got the rabbit he'd snared this morning. He could get another one, and the dog was evidently hungry. He returned and tossed the rabbit to the dog, who shied away as if used to being beaten. It blinked and hushed barking at Diablo, then grabbed the dead rabbit.

"I'll bring you another tomorrow," Diablo promised in a soft voice.

The savage dog watched him as if it couldn't believe a man was being kind, then wolfed down the unexpected treat.

Diablo rode back to his camp, still thinking of the girl. He intended to take everything Kruger valued before he killed him; he owed him that much. And if that meant Kruger's beautiful daughter, so be it.

Diablo pulled the sunbonnet out of his shirt and examined it. It was made of some fabric with tiny blue flowers and lace. When he closed his eyes and sniffed it, it seemed he could smell the scent of her pale hair and the lilac scent she wore. In his mind, he remembered every detail of her lovely face and large blue eyes. His manhood rose at the thought of her round curves and soft skin. Oh, there was a lot he could do with Kruger's woman to extract the revenge he craved. He owed it to his dead friends. But for now, he must be patient. He had waited fifteen years, he could wait a little longer.

Kruger rode home from town, still picturing Sunny's face. The more he saw of her, the more he knew he must have her. She was a little young, but she was the most beautiful woman in the whole county and other men would envy him. He could only imagine the pleasure he'd get from her pure, virgin body, and she would give him sons to carry on his empire.

He entered the ranch house, went into the living room, and plopped down before the fire. He stared with satisfaction into the flames. These early spring days were still chilly.

Now he looked around the room, imagining what Sunny would think of his house, then frowned and shook his head. No, this old log cabin was big and roomy enough for him, but for his future wife, he needed to build a fine mansion, maybe one of those expensive Victorian things with all the stained-glass windows he'd seen when he was on a cattle-selling trip back east.

Back east. That was where Swen kept talking of sending Sunny to school. Of course the old man was bluffing about having the money to do so. Hurd would have to put a stop to that nonsense if he was to wed her. He walked to the window, grinned as he thought about the perfect location for the fine new house. When he got finished running all the settlers out of the valley and was in control of the whole county, he would build that mansion and lay his empire at Sunny's feet. With all the power and money he offered, how could she turn him down?

He frowned, thinking of Swen again. He didn't think Swen had any idea Hurd wanted to wed his daughter, but Hurd was almost certain the old man wouldn't approve. Yep, Swen Sorrenson was a problem. Sucking his teeth in thought, Hurd returned to his worn leather rocker and leaned back to feast his eyes on his prized Winchester. He looked again, blinked.

"What the hell?"

He jumped up, ran into the kitchen, and confronted the bent old woman. "Maria, anybody been here today?"

She paused in her cooking and shook her head. "No, sir, just your men working around the barn."

"You stupid squaw," he snarled, "did you take my fancy rifle down to dust it?"

She looked baffled and shook her gray braids. "You mean, the one that hangs over the fireplace?"

"Of course the one that hangs over the fireplace. Anyone been in the house?"

"No, sir."

"Maybe Joe or one of the boys is playing a trick, the bastards! I'll teach them to touch what's mine!" He went storming out the back door toward the barn, pausing to kick at the snarling dog. "You son of a bitch, what kind of watchdog are you?"

None of the men in the bunkhouse admitted to having any knowledge of the fancy gun even though Hurd raged and slammed things around. "By God, if one of you took it, I'll have his hide pinned to the barn!"

"Now, boss," Joe made a soothing gesture, "We'd know better than touch it, knowing how much store you set by it."

"By God, it's one of them settlers! They're getting even with me by comin' right into my house! They're thumbin' their noses at me, and I won't stand for it—"

"Aw, boss," one of the men shook his head, "they wouldn't have the guts to walk right into your house—"

"Well, someone's got the balls! I'm gonna tie that half wolf up at the foot of my bed from now on. If they can get past Maria and all my men, walk right into my house, and take stuff I value, that's getting too close."

Joe tried to soothe him. "There's been plenty of strange stuff already, boss, like hangin' Smitty and Wilson instead of just shootin' them."

"By God, I just won't have it, you hear me? I'm president of the Stock Growers Association, and I'm gonna drive all those farmers out of the county. By God, they better not mock me."

One of the crew shivered and looked uneasy. "Boss, you reckon it's a live person?"

"What do you mean?"

The man shifted his weight uneasily. "I hear the Indians have put a curse on you for all the Indians you killed."

Hurd paused in sucking his teeth. "Are you sayin' a ghost or a spook? That's the damndest thing I ever heard."

Nobody said anything. Blind with rage, but still uneasy at the thought that some unseen spirit might be shadowing him, he shuddered and turned toward the door, then stopped. "Oh, Joe, after we get these settlers run out, I want you and the boys to start clearing off that hill with the good view."

"What?" Joe blinked.

"I'm going to build a big, fancy house. It ain't fitting

for the owner of the biggest cattle empire in Wyoming to be living in a tumbledown old ranch house."

"Whatever you say, boss."

"And there's a thousand dollars in gold for the man who brings back my fancy rifle."

"A thousand dollars?" one of them repeated, and a murmur of excitement ran through the crowd. That was almost a year's wages.

"Yeah, and keep a sharp lookout. You boys must have been half asleep to let whoever it was walk right into my place and take my most prized possession."

Joe said, "Boss, you can't blame us if this thing movin' so quiet around the place ain't human."

"Oh, hell, it's human, all right, and I'm gonna nail his balls to a log and leave him for the coyotes to eat."

Still he wasn't sure himself as he turned and stomped out of the bunkhouse. He didn't really think any of the nesters had the grit to come onto his property and steal from him. As he passed the chained dog, he kicked at it again and it growled at him. "You mongrel sonovabitch, you ain't worth the bullet to kill you. For letting someone take my rifle without raisin' the alarm, you don't get no food today."

He kicked at the dog again, and it snarled at him, straining against the chain. Maybe he ought to rethink chaining the beast in his bedroom. If it ever managed to break that chain, he had no doubt the dog would tear his throat out. He returned to the house and stomped up and down, thinking of all the ways he could torture the man who took his prized rifle. The settlers were getting too bold. Maybe it was time to turn up the heat, really let these nesters know he and the other ranchers meant business. Nate Champion and his friends were some of the main ones suspected of rustling. Tomorrow Hurd and his boys would gather up the others, attack the Champion place. When it was burned down and those rustlers killed, the nesters would get the message and move on.

Finally he went to bed and dreamed of Sunny. She would make him a dutiful, beautiful wife, and in turn he would lay his fortune at her feet as well as that new mansion, which would be the finest in the state. Surely when Swen saw all that Hurd had to offer Sunny, he couldn't object to the marriage. Or could he?

Chapter 5

Diablo watched from a distant rise as the smoke from the burning cabin curled in a thin black snake toward the blue sky. The dozens of men who ringed the burning cabin fired intermittently, evidently waiting for the flames to drive their prey out into the yard. So the Texas gun-fighters and the big ranchers were escalating their war.

Diablo frowned and cradled the prized rifle he had taken from Kruger's den. Such unfair slaughter troubled him. They ought to at least give the poor bastards a fighting chance.

As the flames gradually engulfed the building, a lone man, his clothes on fire, ran out into the yard, shooting as he came. He was greeted by volleys of rifle fire that almost cut him in half. He stumbled, took another step, and went down in a second barrage of gunfire.

Diablo brought the fine rifle up to his shoulder, looked down the sights to center on Hurd Kruger, who had now stepped out to stand over the prone body. He had Kruger in his gun sights. It was a long shot, but Diablo could easily take him out from here. It was a big temptation. Diablo imagined the look of surprise on the man's beefy face as he went down, wondering what had hit him.

No, that wouldn't do. Reluctantly, Diablo slipped the rifle back into the boot on his saddle. He had waited a long time to kill this man, and when he did, he wanted Kruger to know who had killed him and why and then to die slowly and in agony.

He had been paid to take part in this slaughter, but the unfairness of it needled him. Damn, he must be getting soft. What was it to him if the farmers and little ranchers were slaughtered? Yet he wheeled his horse and galloped toward the little town of Buffalo. He reined in as the sheriff came running out of his office.

"Stranger, what's goin' on? I've been trying to get through to find out."

"They've cut the telegraph wire!" Diablo shouted, "and right now, the Stock Growers Association is burning down another ranch!"

"I'll bet that's Nate's place; I heard he was at the top of their list. Thanks! I'll take it from here!"

As Diablo rode out, the sheriff commenced ringing the church bell and people ran up and down the street to find out what all the excitement was about.

Diablo galloped out of town. No doubt the Buffalo townsmen would catch the killers by surprise. He found himself blinking as he rode toward Kruger's place, wondering why he'd done it. He never gave a damn about killing men, and now he was trying to save the underdogs. Maybe that was it: he'd been an underdog all his life.

He rode cautiously to the K Bar, but there didn't seem to be anyone around. All the hands must be out in that killing party. He fed the wolflike dog, which now wagged its tail at him. Diablo walked over, squatted to pet the big beast. "I'll take you next," he promised as he stroked the big head. "And then I'll get the horse. I will take or destroy everything that means anything to that bastard before I kill him."

That brought the girl to his mind. *Sunny.* It was a good name for the beauty, with her pale hair and sweet smile. He remembered the silhouette of her curves in the blue flowered dress, and he imagined lying with her in a nest of hay, her body warm against him as he kissed those full, soft lips.

"Who are you kidding?" He chided himself as he mounted up and rode out. "She's the beauty, you're the ugly beast. You'd be her worst nightmare. The only way you can ever possess her is to take her by force."

The thought repulsed him, but the thought of using her for bait in a trap did not. Still, a girl like the delicate Sunny was meant to be cherished and protected by a man who would fight to the death to be the one she chose to give her love to.

Sunny looked out her kitchen window, watching the smoke curl skyward a long moment before she wiped her hands on her apron and went out on the porch. "Dad, there's something going on over at Nate Champion's place."

Swen frowned. "The damned Stock Growers Association. Hurd is convinced Nate and his friends are rustlers."

"Are they?"

"I don't honestly know." Swen smoked his pipe.

"Can't you do anything to stop him?" She put her small hand on his arm. "I know I never question anything, but I saw some of those farmers in town the other day. It seems to me there's room enough for all of us in Wyoming."

"You know how tough things have been for us, honey," Swen nodded. "Those homesteaders and rustlers must have been stealing my cattle for a couple of years now. I didn't want to worry you by telling you, but if Hurd hadn't been helping with the mortgage, we'd probably have lost the ranch by now."

She frowned at the mention of her dad's friend. There was something about the beefy rancher that made her uneasy. "Dad, you know good people can't just stand by and let Uncle Hurd and those hired gunfighters murder everyone in the valley."

"You're right, honey." Swen stood up. "I'll ride into Krugerville and talk to the sheriff again. This thing has gotten out of hand."

"It always does when people take the law into their own hands."

"I should have said something to Hurd a long time ago, but I hated to, since he's been so good to us." Swen stepped off the porch and strode toward the barn.

Sunny returned to the house and the apple pie she was making.

In about an hour, she was just pulling it from the oven when she heard hoofbeats and grabbed her father's rifle, went to peek out the front window. Hurd Kruger and a couple of his cowboys rode up. She frowned. One of them was that Joe and she had never liked the man with his weasel face and sneaking ways.

"Hello the house!" Kruger called as he dismounted.

Sunny came out on the porch, still carrying the rifle. Kruger grinned at her and fingered his black mustache.

"You're smart to be cautious, Sunny, with all the trouble in the county."

She started to say it was trouble he and the Stock Growers Association had created, but decided it would only cause trouble for her dad.

"Where's your father?" Kruger looked around.

"Uh, out on the south forty checking fences," Sunny leaned the rifle against the wall. She knew the rancher wouldn't like it if he found out where Swen had really gone.

Kruger took a deep breath. "Umm, do I smell fresh apple pie?"

"I just took one out of the oven." She knew she ought to be polite and offer him a slice, but she didn't want him to stay.

Kruger turned to Joe. "Take our horses, and you men go water them. They've had a hard ride. I'll visit with Miss Sunny a while." He dismounted and took off his Stetson, revealing black hair that gleamed like shoe polish, as the others rode off to the barn.

"Where are your usual men, Wilson and Smitty?"

Kruger's beefy face frowned. "Homesteaders got them; lynched them both."

"What? From what I've seen of the farmers, they don't seem like that kind of people."

"Oh, but of course they've got a sweet little thing like you fooled. They've been in my house, too, took that fine rifle I set such store by."

"With all the gunfighters you've brought in, I'd think your place was pretty safe."

"Well, from now on, I'm bringing that guard dog I bought inside so if there is the slightest noise, I'll know about it."

There was a moment of awkward silence.

"Uh, Miss Sunny," he fiddled with the brim of his Stetson, "ain't you gonna invite me in for pie?"

There was no way of getting out of it without being disagreeable. "Uh, of course, Uncle Hurd, come on in." She didn't really want to be alone with the man, but she was too timid to know how to handle it. He followed her through the house to the kitchen, walking too close for comfort. She managed to get a chair between them.

"Sit down, and I'll make some coffee to go with it."

He took a chair, grinning up at her. "You're a great

cook and pretty, too. It's about time you was thinking about gettin' married, Sunny."

She busied herself at the stove dishing up the pie. With him sitting down, she could see the bald spot on the crown on his head, despite the blackness of his hair and mustache. There was gray at the roots of that black hair.

"My dad needs me. I reckon it'll be a long time before I marry, Uncle Hurd."

She set the pie before him, and before she could move away, he took her hand. "You know, I wish you would just call me Hurd. Uncle Hurd makes me feel so old."

He was old enough to be her father, she thought and pulled her hand away. "Let me get you some coffee." She busied herself with the pot, wishing one of the cowboys would come to the door or her dad would come home.

"Umm," he took a big bite. "Yep, you're a good cook, Sunny, and you keep a tidy house. I'll bet you'd be good with kids, too."

She had a feeling about what he was driving at, and the thought horrified her. She poured him a cup of coffee without looking at him. "Maybe I should take some pie out to your men."

"Aw, let them come up to the house for it," he dismissed the thought with a shrug, looking up at her, while sucking his teeth. "You know, Sunny, I'm the richest man in the county, and lots of women been hoping I'd ask them to marry."

"Oh? There's that nice widow, Mrs. Crandall, if you're wanting to marry again." She busied herself at the stove, not wanting to get too close to him.

He snorted. "Much too old."

"Well, there's that new school marm—"

"Not pretty enough." He sipped his coffee. "I can be very choosy because the woman that marries me will have anything she wants. In fact, I'm about to build a new house."

"That's nice." She wished fervently that one of his men or her dad would come in and interrupt this conversation.

He leaned back in his chair and beamed at her. "Got in mind to build myself a real mansion, good as anything from back east. Yep, the boys are gonna start clearing that little hill tomorrow. You know, the one with such a good view of the valley."

"I'm sure it will be lovely."

"It'll have the best of everything: them stained-glass windows and turrets, best furniture shipped in from back east and lots of servants, maybe even one of them fancy butlers. Why, if I decide to marry again, the lady wouldn't have to lift a finger—there'll be maids to do her bidding and lots of trips back east to buy fine dresses."

She tried to think of something to say—anything to change the course of this conversation. In her mind, she imagined being married to Hurd Kruger. She was barely aware of what it was that men and women did to beget children, but even the idea of getting into bed with this potbellied man made her shudder.

"You know," Kruger stood up, still sucking his teeth. "I could use a woman's opinions on what should go into a house. Maybe this week we could take a buggy and drive up there so you could see it."

"I'm very busy looking after Dad," she mumbled.

"You know, when I marry, I'm gonna be generous to the whole family, forget debts and give a life of ease to old relatives."

She thought about how hard her father worked and felt guilty. She knew what Hurd was hinting at, and she pictured the good things his money could do to help her father. Hurd stepped forward like he was going to put his hands on her shoulders, and she sidestepped, not looking at him. "I—I think I'll take some pie out to your men," she gulped and grabbed some forks, saucers, and the pie pan, and fled out the door.

Hurd watched her go, cursing silently. Maybe he was handling things all wrong; after all, she was a shy, innocent little thing. Maybe he was being too bold. He'd have to hold back, although it had been all he could do just now to stop himself from grabbing her and kissing her hard. He ached to throw her down across that kitchen table and take her like he'd taken many of the younger women who had worked in his house.

He shook his head. Everything with this pretty thing had to be correct and above board. He had waited a long time for Sunny Sorrenson to grow up so he could make her his. He'd been in love with her from the first time he saw her, and she had been only a lovely child then.

He would ask Swen's permission to court her, and it would be hard for the old man to say no to him. Yep, it would all be done properly. Then he would put on the biggest wedding Johnson County had ever seen. He would have the new mansion finished by then, and his new wife would get the best of everything his money and power could provide.

He stepped to the back door and watched her dishing up pie for his men. He saw the lust in their eyes, but none would dare approach her because Hurd had made it clear that he had his eye on this beauty for the future Mrs. Kruger.

Swen. Hurd frowned. The old man would probably be glad to have Hurd for a son-in-law, despite all his talk about sending his daughter away to school. Who wouldn't want to have the richest rancher in the county for a son-in-law?

Well, first he had to finish running all the nesters out of

Wyoming. Then he would talk to Swen and start courting Sunny. She'd be swept away by his devotion and all the pretties he was going to buy her. And in turn, she would give him strong sons to help him run his empire. He pictured cold nights with the beautiful Sunny in his bed. Oh, he'd be good to her, and she'd love him as he adored her.

He went out the back door and strode to the barn, smiling at the girl as he did so. "Okay, boys, we got to go; finish up that pie."

The men nodded, gobbling the treat and saying thanks to the lady.

As they all mounted up, Hurd smiled at the girl. "Now, Miss Sunny, I meant it about you coming over to help me make some choices on that fancy new house."

"Sure, Uncle Hurd," she said and looked away.

"Tell your pa we came by. Tell him he can quit worryin' about Nate Champion and his friends rustling cattle."

Her lovely face paled "What happened?"

"Oh, nothing for you to worry your pretty little head about." Hurd grinned and sucked his teeth. "Swen will understand. Well, adios."

He wheeled his horse, and the others followed, trotting out of the barnyard. Sunny stared after them, annoyed with Kruger's attitude. He treated her like some pretty, stupid doll, but then a lot of men treated women that way. They didn't think women had any brains or feelings about anything. Of course she'd been raised that way, too, and sometimes she felt guilty that she wanted to rebel. She felt too deep a debt to her father to embarrass him by not being a dutiful, obedient daughter.

An hour later, her dad rode in and dismounted. Sunny went out to greet him.

"Hurd Kruger was here with some of his men."

"What'd you tell him?"

"I told him you were out mending fences." She started

to tell him about Kruger's attitude toward her, decided against it. Dad had enough worries right now without that, and besides, he might think marrying Kruger was a good idea.

Swen sighed as he tied up his horse. "I don't know if the sheriff can't or won't do anything, although, to give him credit, I don't think he and his deputies would stand much of a chance against all those Texas gunfighters."

"They got Nate Champion," Sunny said as they went inside.

"I got mixed feelings about that," Swen muttered. "I don't know if they've been rustling beef like Hurd says, but I don't think you ought to shoot men like mad dogs."

"So the sheriff in Krugerville isn't going to do anything?" Sunny looked at him anxiously as she poured him a cup of coffee.

He sat down at the kitchen table with a sigh. "He said it was out of hand. He said he might wire the governor."

"Isn't the governor a friend of the Stock Growers Association?" Sunny cut him a piece of pie.

"Well, yes, but if the violence gets too much, people will hold him responsible and vote him out. The sheriff said maybe Governor Barber might get the president to send in troops from Fort McKinney."

"It's going to be too late," Sunny predicted.

"I'm afraid so," Swen said as he ate the pie. "I wish now I hadn't been so weak when Hurd first talked about this. But I'm so beholden to him for helping me keep the ranch, I guess I'd go along with about anything he wanted."

Sunny didn't say anything. Yes, her dad was very beholden to Kruger. No doubt if the rich rancher asked for her hand, Swen would think it was a good idea, or at least, very hard to say no to.

"Dad, don't feel guilty. You've done everything you can

do. Maybe Sheriff Angus from Buffalo will get involved. That area is more farmers and small ranchers."

He frowned and paused with his coffee cup halfway to his lips. "I just hope Hurd doesn't find out who went to the sheriff in Krugerville. It'd be real hard to get back in his good graces if that happened."

Sunny bit her lip and kept quiet. Yes, her father might think marrying Kruger was a good idea. It would certainly solve a lot of their problems. "Uncle Hurd is going to build a fine new house," she said. "He wanted us to come over and have a look at what he's planning."

"Wonder what brought that on in the midst of a range war?" Swen mused and leaned back in his chair.

"Who knows?" Sunny lied as she shrugged. If her dad wanted her to marry Kruger, she wasn't certain she was brave enough to say no. She had always been such a good, obedient daughter that people remarked on it. They didn't know she felt so guilty about being the cause of her mother's death.

Swen finished his pie and went out to the barn to check on his new foal while she tidied up the kitchen. When she took a deep breath, she could still smell the smoke from the Champion ranch. Things had gotten so bad that maybe only government troops could bring order to the chaos now.

It was turning dusk as Kruger rode back to his ranch, still thinking about Sunny Sorrenson. Her lips were so soft and moist, and she smelled of some delicate scent, like maybe lilacs. He'd like his big new house to smell like her. If Sunny would just agree to marry him, he would buy her anything, give her anything she wanted. He already had money, power, the biggest ranch in the county, but nothing mattered if he couldn't have the beautiful blonde as his wife.

He'd never even admitted it to himself, but he'd built this cattle empire bigger in the last four years just so he could lay it at Sunny Sorrenson's feet. After they were wed, they'd take the train back east anytime she wanted to go or maybe down to Cheyenne, and he'd buy her the fanciest surrey in Wyoming with a pair of matched horses in shiny harness to pull it. When she'd drive past with his children at her side, men would take off their hats respectfully, and women would whisper in envy, "There goes Mrs. Hurd Kruger—her husband is the richest, most powerful man in the state. And aren't his sons handsome?"

And having her in bed with him and making love to her as often as he liked. *Ahh.* Kruger was still grinning to himself as he dismissed his men. "Where's Joe?"

The cowboy shrugged. "Don't know, sir—think he was checking on what happened after we left the Champion place."

Hurd nodded. "He'll report in then. It's been a long day. We'll bed down and get an early start in the morning."

Hurd was satisfied with his day's work as the cowboys rode off, and he started into the house.

About that time, Joe rode in at a gallop, his white mare covered with foam. He was out of the saddle even as he reined in at the hitching rail. "Boss, something terrible has happened!"

"What?"

Joe took a deep breath. "After we left the Champion place, that red-haired sheriff, Angus, from Buffalo rode up with a bunch of nesters."

Hurd swore under his breath. "Wonder who alerted them?"

"Anyway, the sheriff's posse chased the ranchers over to the T.A. ranch and had them pinned down there."

"Somebody wire the governor for help?" Hurd frowned.

"Tried to," Joe spat to one side, "but we cut the telegraph wires ourselves, remember?"

Now Hurd really cursed. "They get a rider out to Cheyenne?"

Joe nodded. "Governor Barber contacted Washington, and President Harrison sent in the troops from Fort McKinney. Stopped the nesters from wiping us out."

"I thought we had this thing over and done," Hurd griped and strode up and down the porch. "What's gonna happen?"

"The troops took all the big ranchers in to jail."

"They can't do that. The governor will get them out."

Joe grinned like a big rat. "Can't press no charges if witnesses leave the state or disappear."

Hurd grinned. "That's right. Take a couple of them Texas gunslingers, find out who might press charges, and take care of them. After things cool off, we'll start all over again."

Joe hesitated. "You sure that's wise, boss?"

"You questionin' my judgment?"

"No, sir," the weasel-like wrangler shook his head. "I only thought—"

"Let me do the thinkin'. Have you forgotten them damned farmers lynched Smitty and Wilson? You think them damned cattle-rustling nesters are trying to send me a personal message?"

"I don't know, boss."

"Well, I ain't scared," Hurd blustered. "But you start keeping a sharp lookout around the place. From now on, I'm gonna sleep with that damned dog tied at the foot of my bed."

Joe nodded. "That mean mutt ought to set off an alarm if anyone gets within a half mile of the place."

"You're right about that. Tomorrow, we'll hit the south

end of the county with all them gunfighters. It shouldn't take more than another week before the rest of them farmers are scared shitless and they pack up and move out."

"Sure thing, boss."

"Remember about makin' them witnesses disappear. See you in the morning." Hurd dismissed him and went out to unchain the big wolf mix. The dog snarled at him, and Hurd kicked it. "You hairy bastard, I'll learn you to try to bite me. Maybe tomorrow, I'll take you along and turn you loose on some of them farmers' children. When they hear their kids screaming, they'll forget about taking a stand."

He led the dog into his bedroom, tied it at the foot of his bed. He thought about feeding the dog, decided it would be more alert and dangerous if it were kept hungry.

Then he went to the kitchen and made himself a cold roast beef sandwich, thinking about Sunny. *What a woman.* He sighed, picturing her. Yes, she deserved to be treated like a queen. He could already picture her in his kitchen, but especially in his bed, her pale long hair spread out across the pillows like gold silk. And he'd buy her sheer silk nightgowns so he could see her slim body when he looked at her. He closed his eyes, getting aroused as he thought about her scent and the softness of her skin. Yes, he'd ask Swen for his permission soon, and in the meantime, he'd get started on that fine new house.

The old cook had gone to her cabin, and he was alone. Carefully, he checked all the locks on the doors and kicked at the snarling dog as he pulled off his clothes. He had a pistol under his pillow and twenty or so gunfighters camping out around his ranch. Anyone who tried to get in would either have to be loco or some kind of supernatural being.

The images of Wilson and Smitty came to his mind, their mouths open, their eyes bulging in horror as they swung back and forth in the breeze. They were two of his toughest, most dependable men, and yet someone had gotten the drop on them and lynched them rather than shooting them. Was someone trying to send him a message?

"Won't do any good. If Injuns, wildfires, and blizzards couldn't scare me, nothing can." He blew out the lamp and crawled into bed. His pillow was smeared with the black dye from his hair. He wondered if Sunny suspected that he dyed it. Probably not. He was still a fine figure of a man, even if he was past forty.

Who had lynched Wilson and Smitty? Those dumb nesters were cowards and stupid besides. Could it be Injuns? Naw, if they were going to take revenge for all he had done to the local tribes, they would have done it long ago. There were few of them left in this county anymore.

Hurd reached to touch the loaded pistol under his pillow. He was one of the best shots in the state. Whoever took his prized rifle wouldn't come back with Hurd in the house. If he did, Hurd would nail him because he had an ear for the slightest sound, and he'd like nothing better than blow a couple of dumb farmers to kingdom come. Besides he had the dog lying on the rug at the foot of his bed, and the part-wolf would growl if anyone got close and eat a hapless trespasser alive if one got into his bedroom. Thus satisfied with his precautions, Hurd closed his eyes and settled down for the night, dreaming happily of setting fire to more farmhouses and making love to the beautiful Sunny.

Diablo watched the big ranch house from the little rise. When he saw the lights go out, he dismounted and tied up his horse. Then he sniffed the wind and listened for a moment. All the gunfighters were asleep in their blankets or drinking around their campfires. He waited until the moon went behind a cloud; then silent as a shadow in his moccasins, Diablo sneaked toward the ranch house. He had an object in his hand, an object any rancher would recognize. Without thinking, he reached up to touch his scarred face. He had waited a long, long time, but he would wait a little while longer. His need for vengeance was only overshadowed by his anger, a slow-burning anger that was as hot as a branding iron.

He tiptoed up on the porch and turned the knob. The door was locked. So Kruger was getting cautious now that someone had been in his house and stolen his fancy rifle. Diablo went to a window and slid it open. Then, silent as his warrior father, he climbed inside and moved toward the bedroom. He knew the layout from the time he took the rifle. Diablo paused at the bedroom door and listened to the man inside snoring.

Slowly he opened the door. Diablo had eyes like a wild thing himself, and he could see the silhouette of the dog lying on the rug and hear the rattle of the chain. The dog growled very softly and then seemed to catch Diablo's scent and went silent, its bushy tail thumping the floor gently.

Diablo smiled, a rare thing for him. This was going to be easy, almost as easy as torturing a fourteen-year-old half-breed kid.

Hurd came awake suddenly, listening. Nothing. He must have had a bad dream. He sighed and lay back with a smile. The first faint rays of dawn were coming through his window, and he had a lot of work to do today. He swung his legs over the side of the bed, scratching himself and reaching for his boots. That's when he saw the end of the chain and the collar lying on the rag rug. The dog was gone. "What the hell?"

He looked around the room, blinked, and tried to focus his eyes on a shadowy object lying on the quilt at the foot of his bed. "What?"

And then he recognized it. The object was a crude running iron, the kind rustlers used to change a brand. He was frozen in fear as he stared at it and then again at the chain at the foot of his bed. As impossible as it seemed, someone had come into his room, taken his vicious watchdog, and left a rusty old running iron on his bed. Kruger took a deep breath, grabbed for his pistol, and yelled for help.

Chapter 6

Kruger grabbed for his boots while screaming and cursing.

Joe ran into the room. "What's goin' on, boss? I was in the kitchen havin' a cup of coffee and—"

"Damn it! Everyone asleep in this place?" Kruger swung at Joe with his boot.

Joe stumbled backward, spilling his coffee. "What is it, boss? What is it?"

"There!" Kruger gestured wildly toward the steel rod and the empty collar and chain. "Look, damn it! Someone came right into my bedroom and took my damned guard dog!"

Joe walked over and picked the rusty object up off the bed and stared with big eyes. "A running iron? What's that about?"

"How the hell should I know?" Kruger grumbled as he pulled on his pants and sat back down on the edge of the bed to put on his boots. "It's a damned insult, that's what it is! Stealing my guard dog and leaving a rustler's tool on the foot of my bed."

"It must be meant as a message," Joe mused and laid the running iron on the mantle, dusted the rust from his hands. "If someone got that close, they could have just killed you."

"Of course it's a message, you fool!" Kruger paused, thinking. "Didn't hear a thing, and I'm a light sleeper from all those years fightin' Injuns and rustlers. I didn't figure a grasshopper could get in here and mosey around without waking me up. Yeah, it's a message, all right."

Joe shuddered and looked around the room. "You don't reckon it's some of those evil spirits the Injuns are always talkin' about?"

"Ha! Injun spirits?" Kruger stood up and reached for his denim shirt. "More likely some of them damned nesters tryin' to scare us off. Well, it won't work. They can't spook me; I got the numbers on my side. We'll start in today as soon as I grab a bite. You round up them gunslingers, and we'll go to work on them farmers again. They may think they can scare me off hanging Wilson and Smitty and now, comin' into my bedroom, but it won't work. Today, we burn some more cabins and barns, and when I see that damned dog again, I'll shoot it. Now get movin'!"

"But what about Sheriff Angus and the troops?" Joe blurted.

"To hell with them! This is my county, and I'll run it my way!"

Diablo sat before his campfire up in the hills, cooking bacon and smiling at the dog in the early dawn light. "Hey, Wolf, you're gonna be a good friend. Here, have some bacon." He tossed a slice to the black dog, and it wagged its tail and took the bite. Diablo paused and petted Wolf. "You'll have a better life with me," he promised.

He settled down to eat the fried eggs and bacon, sharing with the dog as he watched the sun come up. Kruger should be up by now, and he'd be mad as hell and maybe a little shaken that someone had been in his bedroom, close enough to kill him.

He poured himself a tin cup of coffee, thinking aloud. "Yeah, you bastard, I could have shot you or cut your throat, but that would have been too easy. I want you to suffer. I want you to be scared loco, and I'll take or destroy everything you ever cared about before I finally kill you."

He sipped his coffee and thought. What else did Kruger value? That fine-blooded black stallion, his ranch, and that beautiful girl, probably his daughter. Yes, Diablo had plans for those, too, before he finally killed Kruger. He had spent fifteen years waiting and planning for this revenge, and he wanted to enjoy every minute of it. His whole life had centered on nothing else. For a moment, he wondered what he would do with his time when he finally finished here. Certainly there was nothing else in his life. Being a gunfighter was an empty, lonely existence, drifting from one town to the next.

"You ugly bastard," he muttered to himself, "you can't have any other kind of life—no wife, no kids. Women scream and shudder at the sight of your scarred, twisted face."

That made him think of Kruger again. Whoever said revenge is sweet certainly knew what he was talking about. He wondered if Kruger had any idea why the running iron had been left on his bed. Did he even remember what he and the others had done that long ago day?

The girl. What was her name? Sunny, yes, it suited her. Diablo pictured the shy beauty in his mind and sighed. He couldn't keep his mind off her, her full mouth, her soft skin. What was the worst thing he could do to the girl to upset Kruger? No, not kill her—Diablo could never kill a woman. Rape and dishonor, that was it. Diablo cringed and patted the dog. No, he didn't think he could do that—

not after what had happened to his white mother, what had happened to him.

Though he didn't want to admit it to himself, the thought of holding the girl in his arms, taking her, making her his completely, made him breathe heavier. But he wanted her to desire him, not to be forced. He laughed without mirth. Fat chance of that happening, with him looking like something out of a nightmare.

As the sun rose, he watched the horizon and soon saw smoke. The raiders must be burning another barn. *Poor bastards.* Diablo wished he could do something to help them, but one man against an army of gunfighters didn't stand a chance. Besides, he had only come to Wyoming for one reason. When Kruger was dead, the range war would collapse, and the farmers and big ranchers would have to find a way to live together in peace. There was no stopping progress, and the days of the giant ranchers were numbered.

He thought of the old man, Swen Sorrenson. He had been there, too, and drunk as the rest of them, but . . . Diablo winced, not wanting to remember that night. He still had nightmares about it just as he did about his days as a Santee Sioux slave.

He wanted to talk to the old man. Kicking dirt over his fire, he saddled up, and the dog trailed alongside him as he took a back trail to the Sorrenson's ranch. He tied up his horse in the brush and approached the cabin cautiously. There didn't seem to be anyone around. They were either all at the barn or out rounding up cattle. Diablo had noted no one from this ranch seemed to be involved in burning and looting the farmers.

He crept up to the cabin as quietly as his Sioux warrior father and peered into the window. It was a homey cabin with calico curtains at the window, a homemade braided rug on the scrubbed floor, and a fresh pie on the table.

Out of curiosity, Diablo pushed up the window and stepped inside. The place smelled of cinnamon and coffee. His eyes watered a little. This was just the kind of warm, homey place he'd always dreamed of for himself with a wife and children. "Don't be a fool," he whispered to himself, "you're a gunfighter, a killer. You'll never be able to live like a regular rancher. Besides with your hideous face, what woman would have you?"

He looked around and saw his reflection in a parlor mirror, winced, and turned away. Then by an old, scarred desk, he paused. On it was a small photo in a gold frame, and the girl in the photo was Sunny. Confused and puzzled, he picked up the photo and stared at the beauty. Now what was a photo of Sunny doing in old Swen's house? Had he been wrong about the relationships?

In the distance, he thought he heard the sound of a horse's hooves approaching. He grabbed the framed photo and went back out the window, leaving it partly open behind him. He looked at the photo one more time before putting the small gold frame in his shirt pocket. He realized now the approaching horse was coming from the other side of the ranch house, and he crouched down to watch. The dog whimpered, and Diablo patted him and shushed him to silence.

When he peeked around the corner, he saw the old man dismounting and tying his horse to the hitching rail before he went inside the house. Diablo gestured for the dog to be quiet, and it wagged its tail and obeyed.

Old Swen went to the stove and poured himself a cup of coffee. Diablo watched him, trying to decide what to do. This was probably not a good time to approach him; his cowhands might return at any time. As Diablo tried to make a decision, he heard another horse approaching.

The dog raised its head and growled.

"Be quiet, Wolf," Diablo commanded. "You'll give us away."

The dog obeyed, and Diablo peered around the corner and saw Kruger dismounting and tying up his sorrel gelding. The old man came to the door. "Oh, hello, Hurd. You not burning barns today?"

"Enough of your sarcasm," Kruger snapped and looked around. "Where's Sunny?"

The old man shrugged. "Over at Mrs. Brown's. She's gone into labor, and you know Sunny's such a help."

"Good. I'd just as soon she wasn't around to hear what I got to say." He lit a cigar and blew out the match. "Someone got into my place last night."

"What you mean? With all them guards you got?"

Kruger's hands shook. "I tell you, someone was in my room, close enough to kill me."

"Well, evidently, he didn't. You're here, ain't you?"

"That's what's so strange about it." Kruger sat down in a chair with his back to the window. "Whoever it was took my dog."

"As mean as that dog was? I can't believe that." Swen poured him a mug of coffee.

"Believe it," Kruger snapped and sipped his coffee. "Worse yet, he left something on my bed, maybe as a warning."

"What was it?" The old man sat down across from him.

"A rusty running iron."

There was a long pause.

"A running iron?" The older man scratched his white head. "That don't make no sense."

"An old, rusty running iron. I figure it's an insult or a dare from those damned nesters."

The old man shook his head. "Still don't make no sense."

"Don't know who else it could be."

A strange look crossed the old man's face. "Oh, my God."

"What?" Kruger asked.

"Never mind. It was just a thought."

"Tell me." Kruger looked annoyed.

"Naw, it was a stupid idea anyway."

Kruger turned his head, and his profile really looked annoyed. "You might be the next one, Swen. Maybe you should move over to my place."

Swen shook his head. "We'll be fine here. I probably ought to tell you who I ran into in town. You aren't going to believe this."

"Yeah, yeah." The other seemed to dismiss him with a wave of his hand. "This probably ain't the time to bring it up, Swen, but the way things are goin', we'll have these nesters cleaned out soon and I'll buy up their ranches and have the biggest cattle empire in the county, maybe even in the state."

Swen frowned. "You know I don't approve."

"It's time we got something straight about Sunny's future," Kruger said and puffed his cigar.

"I got her future planned," Swen said. "Soon, I'll be sending her back east to Boston to live with her aunt and go to college."

"You can't afford to do that," Kruger scoffed. "You're barely makin' it now. If I hadn't been helpin' you along, you'd have already had to sell out."

"Sure, but I got that dun mare and her fine filly I can sell, and a little money put away," Swen said and puffed his pipe.

Outside, Wolf's ear pricked up, and Diablo tensed, listening. In the distance, he heard the thunder of approaching hoofbeats. He peeked around the corner. A bunch of Kruger's men were coming strong, but Diablo couldn't tear himself away from his listening post, even though he knew every second he stayed put him in more danger.

Inside, Swen said, "Yes, she's going to Boston. I hid a little away for it."

"You might ask Sunny how she feels," Kruger sipped his coffee. "She might like being married to the biggest rancher in the county. I'm planning on buildin' a big fine home on that hill overlookin' the ranch, and I'll be able to buy her anything she wants. You'll have a comfortable old age."

"I knew you been wanting her." Swen shook his head and stood up. "No, I can't give my permission. You're old enough to be her father."

"You think I been helpin' you all these years outta the goodness of my heart?" Kruger stood up too, blew a cloud of angry smoke. "I been watchin' her for years, waiting for her to grow up. Why don't we ask Sunny what she thinks?"

"I tell you no, Hurd." Swen's face turned dark red. "I won't stand for it, I tell you, and we don't have to ask Sunny. You know she's an obedient girl, always does as she's told. She's going back to Boston, and that's the end of it."

"Not quite, you stubborn old bastard." Kruger snarled, and before Diablo or the old man could react, Kruger pulled out his Colt and fired, hitting the old man in the chest.

Swen staggered, surprise on his weathered face; then he tumbled and dropped his pipe. It clattered against the floor as he went down.

Outside, Diablo drew his pistol. Fury overcame him. He would kill Kruger now, although this wasn't the way he'd meant to do it.

The thunder of hooves in the distance grew louder. They must have heard the gunshot. Even as Diablo hesitated, trying to decide what to do, Kruger ran out into the front yard waving his arms and shouting. "Hear that shot, men? Some damned nesters shot Swen, and I got here just in time to see them ride away! Go after them, boys! I'll ride and tell poor Miss Sunny what's happened!"

Diablo looked through the window, his vision blurring. Swen was dead; there was no doubt about it. The old man had tried to help him that long-ago day, and Diablo had come to express his gratitude. Now it was too late, forever too late. Diablo was so angry his hands shook, but he would have to wait. He would make Kruger pay even more when the time came.

In the confusion of cowboys coming into the house and others taking off on a wild goose chase after the phantom killers, Diablo and his dog slipped silently away back to his horse. He watched a long moment from the hill, and then he rode back to his camp to think. Kruger had thrown a rock in his plans, and now Diablo wasn't certain what to do.

He took out the small photo of Sunny and stared at it. So the beauty was Swen's daughter, and now Kruger planned to marry her. Would she be tempted by all the wealth and land? Diablo must tell her about the killing. He half rose, then sat back down to brood. She certainly wouldn't believe the gunfighter. How could he even explain to her what he'd been doing at her house? No, he couldn't tell her, and now he could only wait to see if she was selfish and greedy enough to marry her father's killer. That would tell Diablo what he needed to do next.

Kruger was shaking as he mounted up and rode for the Brown's ranch. Behind him, his cowboys were galloping away to look for the killers of Swen Sorrenson. Hell, he hadn't meant to kill the old man, but his anger had made him lose control. He'd always thought that Swen knew he intended to marry Sunny and was okay with the idea.

Well, this would work out just fine. Swen was popular in the county, and a lot of ranchers who hadn't been in favor of running the farmers out would be in favor now. It would all work to Kruger's advantage. And as for the blond beauty, her father was right; she was shy and obedient. She'd marry Kruger without asking any questions. He licked his lips, thinking about the voluptuous girl naked in his bed. He'd be the envy of every man in Wyoming and the richest one, too. He and Sunny would have a dozen sons to continue this empire he'd been building. Losing his dog and gun were minor things right now. Kruger grinned all the way to the Browns' ranch.

He galloped his sorrel to the ranch, swung down. "Hello the house! Anyone home?"

Young, lanky Brown came out the front door as Kruger tied up. "What's going on, Hurd? You come to see the new baby boy?"

Kruger put on a sad face and took off his Stetson. "I—I got bad news. Is Miss Sunny here?"

"Sure, she's helping with the baby. Come on in."

Kruger went inside, keeping a sad face and fumbling with the brim of his Stetson. Sunny came out of the bedroom, carrying a whimpering bundle. *In another year, that will be our baby she's holding,* Kruger thought.

"Why, Uncle Hurd, what's wrong?"

He gestured to one of the plump neighbor women to take the baby. "Sit down, Sunny; it's bad news."

Sunny's pretty face paled as she handed the baby over and sat down, leaning forward. "What—what is it? Has something happened at the ranch? Has something—"

"Oh, my God," Kruger took out his bandanna and wiped his eyes. "I—I just don't know how to tell you, Sunny, the news is so bad. It's Swen." He managed a fake sob.

Now her face turned ashen. "Dad? Something happened to Dad? I must get back to the ranch, I must—"

"He's dead, Sunny." Kruger shook his head. "Them nesters ambushed him."

"Dead?" For a moment she blinked in disbelief, then began to sob uncontrollably. "No, it can't be true!"

"I'm so sorry, my dear."

She collapsed against him and he put his arm around her small shoulders. "Oh, I can't believe it."

The neighboring women whispered in hushed tones among themselves. "And we thought most of them was good people."

"Yep, them rotten farmers," Kruger growled. "There ain't nothin' too low for them to do."

"But why?" Sunny sobbed and sobbed while Kruger hugged her to him. "Dad had always gotten along well with the nesters."

"Just goes to show you how bad they are. Don't worry, dear," Kruger patted her shoulder, "I'll take care of you and the ranch. Everything will be all right."

"How can it be with Dad dead?" she sobbed. "Oh, I just don't know what to do."

"I'll take care of everything," Kruger assured her. "You don't have to worry, Sunny, and the faster we get those clodhoppers out of the county, the better off we'll all be." He held her close and smiled to himself. Yes, things were working out fine for him. The ranchers and gun-fighters were all out of jail and likely wouldn't be charged, so the fight could continue. As soon as this was over, he was going to marry the most beautiful girl in the county and she'd be an obedient wife. Now all he had to do was bury Swen and finish this range war.

It all seemed so unreal to Sunny. She let herself be led to a buggy and driven to Kruger's big house. She was too numb to think or feel anything but crushing grief. Her father had been her whole life. She had never made an independent decision or had any responsibility. Dad had wanted it that way.

Soon they brought Swen's body in a wooden coffin on an old creaky wagon with all his cowboys following along behind.

Zeke, his foreman, wiped his red eyes as she came out to meet the wagon. "Oh, Miss Sunny, it's just terrible. Here we been so good to them nesters, and now they reward old Swen by killin' him in cold blood."

"Are you sure that's who did it?" she asked.

"Of course, my dear." Kruger came out on the porch and put his arm around her shoulders. "Who else could it be?" He turned to Swen's cowhands. "Yes, it is terrible, boys. Now after the funeral, will you ranchers help us chase them damned farmers out of the county?"

The angry cowboys shouted in unison and waved their fists in the air. "We will! We'll get them killers."

"I—I don't think that's what Dad would have wanted," Sunny whispered, but she was drowned out by the big rancher. "Oh, of course it is, Sunny. Now someone ride to let the folks in Krugerville know what's happened. We'll have the funeral in the morning, and then we'll show them nesters they can't get away with killin' a good man like this one."

Sunny suddenly felt faint at the possibility of even more bloodshed, and she swayed a little. "If—if you don't mind, Uncle Hurd, I'd like to see my father and then pick a few flowers for the coffin."

"Of course, my dear." Very gently, he turned loose of her and gestured to the cowboys. "Bring the coffin into the parlor, boys, and we'll set it up for the viewing."

Sunny sobbed as she followed the coffin into the house. They set it up on two chairs and took off the lid.

Biting her lip, she approached the coffin as the cowboys took off their hats and stepped back respectfully. Her eyes brimmed with tears as she took a step. Swen looked so old and pale. Very gently, she brushed his sparse, pale hair from his forehead and then began to sob. "I just can't believe anyone would do this!"

Hurd stepped forward and put his arm around her shoulders. "There, there, Sunny. I'll take care of everything. You just don't worry. Let me and the men make all the decisions now."

She realized she had never made an important decision or taken a stand on anything in her whole life. She really wanted to take Dad back to the ranch and bury him there, not stay in Uncle Hurd's house and bury Dad in the town cemetery. However she didn't argue. "Whatever you say, Uncle Hurd. I'd like to be alone. I think I'll pick a few flowers outside. Dad did love wildflowers."

"Of course, my dear, whatever you wish." He turned to the men. "Everything stops until after the funeral tomorrow; then we'll deal with these damned murderin' nesters."

She went outside to pick wildflowers and sat down on a rock and wept and wept. What would she do now? Where would she go? She was faced with big decisions and had no idea what to do next. They owned a few cattle and a mortgaged ranch, some average horses, and the dun mare and filly—not much to show for all these years of hard, back-breaking work. Uncle Hurd would know what to do, and he had been Dad's best friend. She could trust him to look out for her. Yes, she would let him take the responsibility.

Diablo and his dog watched from a hilltop as the early morning funeral procession wound its long way down the dusty road from the K Bar to the little cemetery at the edge of town. The black hearse, drawn by two black horses, came behind a fancy buggy. A group of people, old and young, walked behind the hearse.

Wolf's ears went up, and he growled. Diablo patted him. "Be quiet, boy. We don't want them to notice us."

For the first time in his life, he felt a great sadness. He had been too caught up in his vengeance to really thank Swen for what he'd tried to do that long-ago day, and now it was too late.

The procession stopped, and six cowboys carried the wooden coffin to the freshly dug hole among the tombstones and set it on the ground. People began to gather around.

As Diablo watched, Kruger, in a fine suit, stepped out of the buggy and helped Sunny down. She wore a black dress and a hat with a long black veil that blew around her pale face. She looked so vulnerable and dazed as Kruger took her arm and led her to the grave side.

The pastor began to speak. Diablo could only catch a word now and then. The breeze picked up and blew Sunny's light hair and black veil about her reddened eyes. It stirred the bright wildflowers on the coffin.

Now a little choir of ladies began to sing. They were a little off-key but trying valiantly as the wind picked up.

"Shall we gather at the river, the beautiful, beautiful river, shall we gather at the river . . ."

Diablo's eyes abruptly grew blurry, and he cleared his throat. But he gritted his teeth as he noted how Sunny leaned on Kruger's arm. *Damn her.* She was greedy and ready to go along with anything her father's killer wanted. She'd never believe Diablo if he told her the truth.

Now they were lowering the coffin and filling the grave. People were tossing in clods of dirt. The big rancher was leading Sunny forward to throw in a handful of dirt. She looked so frail and helpless that Diablo almost felt sorry for her; then he hardened his heart. She was more like

Kruger than her father, and if she married that rancher, Diablo would soon make her a widow.

Kruger led Sunny back to the buggy and patted her hand, helped her in. Then the whole procession drove away, winding like a black ribbon away from the graveyard. After a while, there was nothing but the tombstones and the fresh dirt on the new grave and the wind blowing dust about.

Diablo waited for a time, and then he rode down to the grave site and dismounted. The place was silent except for a meadowlark. The wildflowers were already wilting on the grave.

"Well, old man," he took off his black Stetson and knelt on one knee, "I never got a real chance to thank you, but I'll get revenge for you, too. I don't know what your daughter is made of, but I'm afraid she's not like you. You didn't want her to marry Kruger, and I'll see that she doesn't. Or at least, I'll make her a very rich widow, and she can do what she wants with all the land and money."

Having made that silent vow, Diablo mounted up and rode back to his camp, the dog following along behind.

Back at Kruger's ranch, Sunny sat in a chair in the parlor, a plate of uneaten food in her hand as people hovered over her, offering their condolences. "We are so sorry, Miss Sunny. What will you do now?"

"I—I don't know." And she really didn't. She was a doormat, she thought, always letting men decide for her. Well, it was mostly the way of frontier women.

"My," said the plump pastor, shaking her hand, "Mr. Kruger has been so nice to step in, hasn't he?"

Everyone in the parlor murmured assent.

"Yes, he has," she nodded. "I don't know what I would have done without him."

Uncle Hurd stepped up, his face sorrowful. "Oh, I'm just trying to be a good neighbor. You know, Swen and I were best friends."

"Yes, thank you, Uncle Hurd." She looked up at him and blinked away tears.

In the background, she heard women wondering what would become of her and others commenting that she couldn't possibly run the ranch alone.

She couldn't think past today. All she could do was sit there numbly and let people shake her hand and tell her how sorry they were. After what seemed like an eternity, they all went away, and Uncle Hurd came over and sat down next to her. "Why don't you eat something, my dear?"

"I—I don't think I can." But obediently she took a forkful of roast beef. "Uncle Hurd, do you know anyone who had a grudge against my father?"

"Of course not." He patted her hand, his mind evidently on something else.

"Well, there was a man in town, one of your Texas gunfighters, I think. He had a scarred face—"

"Yes, yes, Sunny, dear." He seemed to brush her words aside, not really listening. "I know this is not the time or place, but you've got decisions to make."

She began to cry. "Not yet. I—I don't know what to do."

He took out his handkerchief and wiped her eyes.

"There, there, dear, everything will be okay."

"I don't think anything will ever be okay again."

"There's something I haven't told you, Sunny, dear." He took her hand in both of his. "You know, I was the one who heard the shot and rode up to your house as some of those killers were escapin'."

"Why didn't you try to stop them?"

He blinked, evidently caught off guard. "Why, I was

more worried about Swen. I rushed in and found him lying in a pool of blood and knew he was dyin'."

"Did he say anything?"

"Matter of fact, he did." Hurd looked sorrowful. "I took him in my arms and said, 'old friend, is there anything I can do? Anything at all?'"

"Yes?"

"He was breathin' his last, but he took my hand and he said, 'Hurd, you are my best friend. Marry Sunny and look after her. Please promise you will.' And I promised solemnly. Then he died in my arms."

"Dad said that?" She was surprised. "Why Uncle Hurd, I hadn't thought about marriage. Dad had something about me going to college—"

"Of course that was a pipe dream." His voice was kindly as he patted her hand. "He always talked about putting money away for you, but I know he hadn't an extra penny. You know the ranch hasn't done well in years. I've been loanin' him money."

"Oh." She didn't say anything else. *Marry Uncle Hurd?* Why he was at least twice her age. She thought about getting in bed with him and almost shuddered. But if that was Dad's dying wish . . .

"And just think, Sunny, you'd be married to the biggest rancher in the county. You could have anything you want. Why, I've already drawn up plans for a new big house up on the bluff and now you'd be able to pick out all the furniture and carpets. Imagine going to New York to buy wallpaper and drapes. Oh, it would be the finest home in Wyoming on the biggest ranch."

The fine home and the giant ranch interested her not at all. "You know, Uncle Hurd, I don't love you in that way."

He got down on one knee. "But you could learn to love me, dear. Oh, you might never love me like I love you." He kissed her hand. "I worship you, I always have. Nothing in my empire matters as much as havin' you for my wife."

"If you're sure that's what Dad wanted—" she began uncertainly.

"Oh, he made me promise!" Kruger took both her hands in his. "Swen would be so happy that I was lookin' after you."

Everything in her wanted to shout no, but she was an obedient, dutiful daughter. She couldn't turn her back on her father's dying wish. "All right, then. I'll marry you."

He grabbed her and tried to kiss her but she turned her head slightly so that he kissed her cheek. It felt wet and sloppy, and she tried not to shudder. "You've made me the happiest man in the world. Oh, you won't be sorry, Sunny."

She was already sorry, but she didn't answer. If this was what Dad wanted, she would marry this potbellied, balding man with the dyed black, black hair. She didn't even want to think about their wedding night, but she began crying anyway and couldn't stop.

Hurd comforted her and told her she mustn't weep over her dead father. As her husband, he would take care of everything.

Chapter 7

Diablo kept a watch on Kruger's ranch, and one night when things were quiet, he tied up his bay horse in the brush and told Wolf to stay. The dog lay down obediently. Then Diablo sneaked down to the corral where the big stallion was kept. The moon came out and silhouetted the black stallion as it moved restlessly about its pen, laying its ears back and rolling its eyes wildly.

"It's okay, big horse," Diablo whispered, "I am your brother, and I have come to save you."

The stallion paused and watched Diablo, its ears going up, its shiny hide trembling.

Diablo nimbly went over the corral bars and into the sandy arena. He stood on a log for a moment, singing a horse song to the stallion. "I am your friend and brother, great one, and I have come to free you from this cage."

The horse stretched out its neck and regarded the man with wonder at his bravery. The stallion had killed more than one handler with his strong teeth and slashing hooves, and yet, here was one standing only feet away, singing and chanting to him in a soft voice.

In a moment, the stud made a soft, whickering sound in his throat and approached Diablo. Diablo held out his hand and did not run for the fence. "Brother horse, your name is Onyx, like the black stone, and we shall be partners forever until that time we both ride across the sky in the spirit world."

The horse stepped up to Diablo and Diablo offered him a bit of apple. The horse paused as if uncertain about whether the man's other hand might hold a whip. Diablo slowly held out both hands to the stallion. The horse had whip marks on him, and Diablo cursed Kruger for his treatment of animals.

Diablo had infinite patience when it came to horses and dogs. He stood still as a sigh, waiting until the stallion decided that it could take the apple and that the man meant him no harm. After it ate the apple, it stood placidly while Diablo ran his hands over the great horse and sang a warrior's horse song in its ears. Then he breathed his breath into the stallion's nostrils. "We will be one with the wind, great Onyx, and I promise you will feel a whip no more."

He had brought a rope with him and it now hung on the corral gate. Diablo fashioned a makeshift halter from it and put it on Onyx. Then he opened the gate and swung up on the great horse bareback. "Now, Onyx," he whispered, "we will leave this place, and you will be my friend and never have to return to this cruel master."

The horse seemed to understand, and they rode out quietly. No one in the ranch or the bunkhouse stirred. The place was silent and sleeping. Diablo rode up to where he had tied his blood bay, untied it, and whistled to Wolf. The four of them returned through the night to the camp up in the foothills. Diablo smiled, and he dismounted and staked both horses out to graze. If Kruger had been angry to lose his fine rifle and dog, he would go into a screaming fit when he discovered his fine-blooded stallion was gone. Diablo was only sorry he wouldn't get to see the anger.

Three days passed, and every morning from his campsite, Diablo watched new fires dot the horizon and heard gunshots echoing through the valley. He was torn as to whether he should or could do anything to stop the violence and then remembered that he had come to Wyoming for only one reason: his own revenge. He presumed Sunny had moved into Kruger's fine ranch house, and he pictured the middle-aged rancher making love to the grieving daughter and hated them both for it. He waited and made his plans.

Kruger mounted up and rode away from the ranch, Joe at his side. He had been in a fury ever since his blooded stallion had disappeared. "Joe, I want you to fire whoever was careless enough to leave that gate open so that stallion could get away and post a reward for him. He couldn't have wandered too far."

"Maybe he didn't stray; maybe somebody stole him," Joe said, rubbing his sharp nose.

"Ha! As wild and dangerous as that horse is? Why, he's killed two handlers—nobody could steal him without gettin' trampled to death. He's gotten out an open gate, I tell you, and I want him back. Damn it! First some sodbuster steals my rifle and dog, and now my pedigreed stallion is gone. Things have got to change around here as soon as we get through runnin' off these farmers."

"Yes, sir." Joe nodded.

"Now, there's three more farmers we'll burn out today," Hurd said. "That ought to start the rest of them on the move. By late spring, there won't be a nester left in the valley."

Joe tipped back his hat as he rode. "They do say word has gotten to the governor."

"The governor's in my pocket," Kruger laughed and sucked his teeth. "He won't do anything."

"But there's so much talk in Cheyenne, they say he'll be forced to take some action."

Kruger shrugged. He did not believe it. Besides, his mind was on Sunny. She was living at his ranch now, but she was in deep grief and hardly came out of her room. He had already begun work on that fine new house on the bluff. That should bring her out of her melancholy. Kruger loved her deeply—no, he worshiped the beauty— and he could already imagine the wedding of the richest rancher in Johnson County and the most beautiful girl in the whole state. With that, his life would be complete. It was what he had planned and schemed for all these years.

They rode to the clearing by the three cottonwoods on the creek to meet the other ranchers and their cowboys. A big crowd of them were waiting there. Kruger reined in.

"Everybody here?"

They shouted the affirmative.

"Joe, you take half these men and hit the two farmers living on the other side of Crazy Woman Creek. The rest of us will wipe out that little church area on the far side of the valley."

"Wait a minute," a rancher protested, "I don't hold with burnin' a church."

"Aw, it's a farmer church. It ain't like it's one of ours," Kruger said. "Then we'll burn down their school."

There was a murmur.

"What?" Kruger snapped.

"We are gonna let the kids get out first, ain't we?" A cowboy asked.

Such weaklings. Who cares about a bunch of nesters' kids?

"Yeah, we'll start shooting as we cross the pasture so

they'll have warning,‚" Kruger conceded. "Remember, we're doing this for old Swen and my two men they hanged like common rustlers."

A cheer went up. "Yes, for old Swen."

"Now let's get riding!" Kruger shouted.

They split up into two groups and took off in a cloud of dust, Kruger in the lead as befitted the president of the Wyoming Stock Growers Association.

Ahead of them lay the little farming community with its simple church and school. The riders began firing shots in the air, and children ran out of the school, screaming and crying.

"Burn the damn thing down!" Kruger shouted. "These farm brats don't need no education!"

He paused to light a torch himself and tossed it upon the church roof. All around was confusion and smoke. Crying children ran everywhere. People came out of houses, standing about, confused and uncertain. Dust rose, and horses reared and whinnied. In a pasture, cows bawled, and chickens flew everywhere, cackling. Here and there a farmer tried to make a defense and was shot down.

Abruptly over the far hill came riders in blue uniforms, galloping and shooting.

"Oh, damn!" Kruger shouted, "the army! Who the hell sent for the army?"

The cavalry was almost upon them, and that only added to the dust and confusion.

"Let's get the hell out of here, boys!" Kruger bellowed, and his raiders needed no encouragement. They scattered and galloped out of town. "Everyone break up!" Kruger ordered and spurred his sorrel horse, heading back to his ranch.

Halfway there, he was joined by Joe riding his lathered white mare. "Soldiers, boss! We ran into soldiers!"

"Hell! I know it! So did we. The whole of Fort McKinney

must have been sent to the county. Damn the governor anyway. I thought I had him in my pocket!"

"Does that mean we're finished?"

"Reckon it does," Kruger snarled. "That bastard governor, just wait until next election time. Let's head for home!"

They rode back to the ranch, and Kruger gave his horse over to Joe. "Take them in the barn and unsaddle them. If anyone asks, we don't know anything about any raidin' parties."

"Someone might have recognized us," Joe said.

"Nobody will talk," Kruger said, "if they know what's good for them. At least, we've run out so many farmers, the rest will probably pack up and go."

He turned and went into the house. Sunny sat in the parlor doing needlework.

"Aw, Sunny, my dear, you weren't up when I went out. How are you feelin' today?"

"Fine, I guess." She sighed. "I'm just having such a time getting over Dad's murder."

He sat down next to her and took one of her dainty hands in his two big paws. "Aw, you know Swen wouldn't want you to be unhappy."

She managed a weak smile as she looked at him and disengaged her hand. The gray of his hair showed at the roots of the black dye. "Yes, I'm so grateful for your help, Uncle Hurd. I don't know how I would have managed without you."

"And you don't ever have to worry again, my dear. After our marriage, I will take care of everything. You will have nothing to worry your pretty little head about. All you have to do is enjoy the comfort and prestige of being married to the richest man in the county. I'm gonna put the biggest diamond on your hand you ever saw."

"Yes, I know." She looked down at her hands instead

of into his eyes. The thought of getting into bed with this man made her gag.

"You could act a little more enthused," he scolded. "Swen knew I would take good care of you. Don't you think we should go ahead and plan the wedding?"

She looked up, startled. "So soon after Dad's death?"

He nodded. "I know it's a bit soon, but I don't want you being gossiped about by livin' here without marriage."

"But we've done nothing wrong."

He put his hands on her slim shoulders. "I know, my dear, but people can be such cruel gossips. It will be a simple affair, just a few close friends, and I can have the dressmaker make a lovely dress, black of course. People will understand."

She pulled away from him, biting her lip. "What— whatever you think, Uncle Hurd."

"My dear," he stood up and faced her, leaned over to kiss her forehead. "You really must stop calling me 'uncle.' From now on, call me Hurd."

"All right . . . Hurd." It sounded too intimate. After all, he must be at least forty years old to her eighteen, but marriages like that weren't unusual on the frontier.

From outside came the distant sound of hammering. She turned her head. "What—"

"Oh, the boys have started the new house," Hurd smiled and sucked his teeth. "Didn't I tell you I was going to build you a mansion befittin' a queen? Let me get the plans, and we'll take the buggy up to the bluff and have a look."

"I'd rather not."

"Oh, it will do you good to get out. In fact, I insist." He took her by the arm, pulled her up out of her chair, and led her to the door. "I'll get the plans, and you get a wrap. Joe will hitch up the buggy for us. Later this afternoon, we'll drive into the dressmaker and talk to the parson."

"All right," she sighed, "whatever you think."

"That's my good girl, always eager to please. You're going to be a wonderful wife, Sunny dear, and such a good mother you'll make."

In a few minutes, they were in the buggy headed up to the bluff. The men had evidently been working for several days because there were foundations and some framework up.

"Oh, Un—Hurd, it's going to be huge."

"We'll need a big house for the children, dear. You do want children, don't you?"

"I—I suppose." She did want children, but not with this man. "You know, Hurd, I need to be honest with you. I don't love you."

"Oh, but of course you do," he shrugged that off and lifted her from the buggy. "And if you don't, I love you enough for both of us." He caught her hand. "You'll learn to love me, Sunny. I'm going to be so good to you and buy you everything your little heart desires. You can't help but love me."

She stood there a moment, and then, thinking he was going to kiss her, pulled away, walked toward the growing skeleton of the house. "My, it is big."

"I'll bring the plans and show you every room," he smiled and returned to the buggy.

From his hilltop, Diablo watched the pair and frowned. What was going on here? For a moment, he'd thought Kruger would kiss the girl, and he'd gritted his teeth. *Damn her, doesn't she know or care this villain had killed her father?* No, how could she know that?

Now Kruger had gotten a handful of papers from the buggy and was walking with Sunny, showing her the pages and pointing out details about the house to her.

He was building this giant mansion for her, Diablo realized suddenly. He was going to move the blond beauty into this elegant home. Well, women were always smitten by riches. Diablo ground his teeth in rage. Kruger would never live in this fine house because Diablo was going to kill him.

Right now, the rancher was out of even rifle range. However, Diablo could wait for his vengeance, and as far as that fine mansion, he would take care of that, too.

Now the rancher kissed the girl on the forehead and lifted her back into the buggy. Then they drove down the hill toward the ranch. Diablo followed them at a distance. They went into the house.

Diablo waited in this shadows. In the afternoon, when he was about to give up and ride back to his campsite, they came out of the ranch house and drove toward town. Diablo followed at a distance.

Outside town, he took the long way and started for the saloon, but he reined in when he saw all the soldiers on the street and many of the Texas gunfighters crowding into the saloon. He edged up to a soldier, keeping his face turned away. "What's going on?"

"President sent us in to bring order to this county," the soldier said. "Reckon all these Texans will be leaving on the next train."

Diablo grunted and moved away. There were a lot of people in town, and after a while, a train chugged in from the north. He watched a dozen weary, dusty gunfighters heading to the train station, leading their horses. They were leaving, all right. Of course, Diablo thought, they probably wouldn't all go, but most of them would be happy to get back to Texas. The army would put an end to the range war.

As he watched, Kruger's buggy came into town. It paused before the little dress shop, and Kruger helped Sunny down and walked her inside. Then he got back in the buggy and drove over to the railroad platform and mingled with the gunfighters. The soldiers had all gone into the saloon. Diablo watched Kruger paying off the gunfighters. Then the train pulled in and the men began loading their horses. Diablo looked for Buck and his pal Pug, but didn't see them in the crowd.

Finally, the train pulled out, chugging and leaving a trail of sooty black smoke on the cool spring air. Kruger got back in his buggy and drove to the little church. He got out, tied up, and went inside. After a while he came out with a big smile on his face. Evidently he was a happy man, and everything was going his way.

Then as Diablo watched, Kruger drove to the little dressmaking shop and went in. Soon he came out with Sunny. He was still grinning, and just before he lifted her up into the buggy, he gave her a quick kiss on the lips. Diablo couldn't see her face, but he was angry.

Well, the two wouldn't be happy for long. There were only Joe and Kruger left to take care of.

The buggy drove out of town. Diablo started to follow them, but decided to stay in town and have a drink instead. He was furious with the girl—*how dare her let her father's killer kiss her?*

He needed a drink. He didn't go into saloons much because someone always wanted to pick a fight when they realized who he was, but right now, he was so enraged it didn't matter. He went into the side door of the saloon, moved silently to the bar, got himself a drink, and retreated to a shadowy corner so that he could think. He did not want to talk to anyone, although the saloon was half full of soldiers and gunfighters. The locals had abandoned it to their overwhelming numbers. Then he spotted Pug and Buck at a far table playing cards. The light reflected off Buck's red hair and the silver conchos on Pug's leather vest. They did not seem to see him.

It started almost immediately. A young tough, wearing sleeve garters and his gun tied low, leaned against the bar and studied him. He might have been handsome except for the pimples on his baby face. "Now who the hell is that over there with the scary face?"

"For God's sake, Brant, that's Diablo. Leave him alone."

"Diablo?" He moved out into the center of the worn floor, sneering as he looked Diablo's way. "He don't look like much. Hey, you, you really the big gunfighter?"

Now two men tried to discourage him. "Brant, you don't want to mess with him. Leave him be."

He shook off the men's hands. "Aw, he can't be much, skulking back there in a dark corner like a rat."

The saloon grew quiet. Even the piano gradually stopped playing. Diablo sighed. He wasn't in the mood to kill a green punk today. The kid reminded him of his old friend, Billy. Sheriff Pat Garrett had seen to it that Billy didn't live to middle age, and that was the same path this kid was on. Well, Diablo didn't want to be the one to kill him. He finished his drink and got up, started for the side door in his silent moccasins.

"Hey, big gunfighter! Hey, you with the rattlesnake hatband!" the kid shouted, "you gonna run out without facing me down?"

Diablo ignored him and kept walking. The saloon was silent as a grave.

"Hey, big man, you hear me? I'm challengin' you!"

"For God's sake, Brant," another man pleaded, "don't—"

Diablo heard just the slightest sound as the kid's hand hit leather, and he whirled, his hand a flash as he reached for his Colt. His gun was out and firing even as the kid attempted to clear his holster. He saw the surprise and shock on the boy's sneering face as Diablo pulled the trigger. The force of the Colt sounded like thunder in the silence, and the power of the slug struck the kid between the eyes. The kid slammed backward against the bar and went down, blood running between his blue eyes even as his pistol dropped from his dead hand.

For a long moment, no one made a sound. The acrid smell of the gun smoke drifted across the saloon and overpowered the scent of stale beer and cigars. There was a collective sigh from the crowd of men as Diablo holstered his gun, turned again, and went silently as a shadow out the side door.

He heard the murmur of voices behind him. "You see that? God, he was fast! Brant had it coming, though."

Diablo mounted up and rode down the back alley, angrier than before. The killing had left a sour taste in his mouth; it had been so useless. More and more he was now challenged by young punks who wanted to be the Man Who Killed Diablo. Trace Durango had been right: once you started killing, there was no end to it.

He passed the back door of a bordello. From inside came the sound of laughter and piano music. A whore with too much face paint and a skimpy red dress came out on the back porch and tried to light a cigarillo. She was so drunk she couldn't manage it. He glanced at her and kept his face so that she could not see the scarred side.

"Hey, fellow, you want a little fun?" She was more than drunk; she was hanging onto the porch post and swaying. Her hair war a strange blond color not her own, and her lip rouge was smeared across her face.

He reined in, still angry and now aroused, thinking of the pale blond hair of Sunny and the intimate way his most bitter enemy had kissed the girl. Now his rage and passion combined. "Sure, why not?"

He dismounted and tied his horse to the hitching rail, and now the woman gasped as she saw his ruined face. "Goddamn! You're a monster!"

He wanted to strike her, slam her hard against the peeling painted wall for all the hurts and insults he had endured in his life, but Diablo would never strike a woman. "I'll pay double, you bitch."

"That'll be a twenty-dollar gold piece then." Her eyes were wide with distaste, and she smelled of liquor, dirt, and cheap perfume.

It was highway robbery, but he didn't care. He'd only had a couple of whores in his life and they'd all been drunk old broads that would ignore his ugly face.

She took his hand, and he had to catch her elbow to keep her from falling. She led him through the door and up some rickety stairs that led up to her room. Diablo looked around. It was dim and dirty. He scowled with distaste.

"Gimme the money first."

He tossed the gold piece on her nightstand.

"God, you're ugly!" She tittered and lay down on her back, yanking up her skimpy red skirt. She wore no drawers. "Get it over with." She seemed to be gritting her teeth as she closed her eyes.

Diablo started to unbutton his pants, staring down at her, and abruptly, his need left him. She was old and dirty, and she smelled bad. In his mind, he pictured Sunny, all clean and fresh and wanting him, really wanting him. And he would kiss her, and she would throw her arms around his neck and say, "I love you. I don't care about your scarred face; I love you."

The whore opened one bloodshot eye. "Well? I ain't got all day. Get it over with."

"I—I changed my mind." He turned to go.

"I ain't givin' your money back." She sat up on the bed.

Abruptly, he realized how pathetic they both were: a man desperate enough for a woman's embrace that he would pay for it and a woman needing money bad enough to take on an ugly monster like himself. It made him very sad. "Never mind. You can keep the money." He started to leave her room.

"You loco, mister?" She got up off the dirty bed, swaying on her feet. "Or ain't you a man?" she challenged. "Can't you do it?"

He wanted to strike her, but he only shrugged. "I changed my mind, that's all." And with that, he went out and down the stairs, the tinny piano playing in the background as he strode outside and mounted up, taking deep breaths of the fresh, clean air and feeling ashamed and sad for them both.

As he rode out of town, he saw the latest edition of the newspaper being put out front of the little office and stopped to pick up one; then the shock of the headlines almost caused his vision to waver, although he was not drunk.

LOVE OVERCOMES TRAGEDY, read the headline.

> *Despite her father being recently murdered in the range war, Sunny Sorrenson has accepted the proposal of prominent local rancher, Hurd Kruger.*
> *Mr. Kruger said to this editor, "I know this is unusual, but I feel that Miss Sorrenson needs my protection and can't run her ranch alone. Of course I will continue to hunt down her father's killer and bring justice to this county. In the meantime, the wedding will be a tasteful affair, and all the town is invited."*

Diablo couldn't read any further without crumpling the paper in his fist. So she was going to end up in the bed of his worst enemy. And now he hated the blond beauty as he hated her fiancé and he would wreck havoc on her as well. As he rode out of town, Diablo vowed this wedding would never take place—because he was going to murder the groom.

Chapter 8

The next afternoon, Diablo rode to a cliff overlooking Kruger's ranch, Wolf at his side. On the bluff behind it, he could see carpenters hard at work. The framework of the fine home was expanding on the hill.

Even as he watched, Sunny and Kruger drove up to the site in a buggy, and Kruger helped her down. Then he got out a set of plans and spread them on a rock, showing them to the girl as he pointed out the features of the fine new home.

Seeing Kruger smile made Diablo grind his teeth as he patted the dog. Of course the rich bastard was happy. Soon he would be bedding the most beautiful girl Diablo had ever seen. The thought that she would make love to her father's killer made him shake his head in disbelief. Of course she might not know that Kruger was the killer, and there was no way to let her know. She certainly wouldn't believe Diablo if he told her.

He remembered the whore and the way she had withdrawn from him in horror and distaste. His eyes watered, and he blinked rapidly. Even if Sunny knew the truth, would she pass up a chance to marry the biggest, most powerful rancher in the county? Like most women, she was probably greedy for fine dresses and trinkets. Well, Diablo would make her a widow before she was ever a wife.

The sun set all gold and red in the west as Diablo watched the pair get in their buggy and drive back down the road to Kruger's ranch. Now the workmen began putting away their tools and leaving. The wooden skeleton of the fine new house was silhouetted against the pink evening sky as they all left. It looked like the bare bones of a giant carcass as the light faded behind it.

Sunny would never be bedded in this fine new house, Diablo promised himself. This mansion was one more thing that Diablo would take from Kruger. He would take everything the man held dear, and then he would take the girl. Diablo smiled to himself at the thought. When he took her, he could make love to her as he had dreamed of doing, and she would be helpless to protest because she would be in his power.

Late that night, Diablo rode up the hill to the frame of the new house, dismounted, and splashed kerosene around on the lumber as his horse and dog watched. He mounted up and tossed a match into the piles of wood. Then he rode back to another bluff where he could watch the red fingers of flames reaching higher and higher. He grinned, but it was not because he saw anything funny. He was imagining Kruger's shocked face when he saw the burned skeleton of his fine, new house still smoldering and in ruins in the morning.

The smell woke Sunny up, and she blinked, puzzled and wondering what had awakened her. Then she took a deep breath and realized it was smoke. The ranch house must be on fire. She ran out into the hall, forgetting her slippers and robe as she looked around. Then she saw the scarlet reflection on a nearby window glass and peered out. In the distance, she saw the flames devouring the skeleton of the new house on the hill. She hurried for the outside door shouting, "Fire! The new house is on fire!"

She ran out into the moonlight, the slight wind whipping her sheer nightdress around her slender legs. "Fire! Fire!"

From his high spot, Diablo watched her, the moonlight highlighting her pale hair, the breeze pinning her sheer blue nightgown against her full soft curves. She had never looked so vulnerable and desirable as she did right now. He wanted to ride down there and sweep her up, carry her off to his blanket to kiss her, and tangle his fingers in that soft, long hair.

Even as he thought that, Kruger came stumbling out of the ranch house, looking confused and sleepy. He stared and blinked as if he could not believe what he was seeing. Then fury contorted his heavy jowls, and he began to run about shouting orders and cursing. Diablo smiled and watched sleepy cowboys tumbling out of the bunkhouse, confused and trying to organize a fire brigade.

"Goddamn it!" Kruger roared. "Put that fire out! Who in the hell . . . ?"

Joe ran up to him, and Kruger growled something. The cowboys were grabbing buckets and pumping water like crazy, trying to get a wagonload of buckets and start up the road. They must have known they had no chance of putting it out, but Kruger's shouts and curses spurred them on. They got one wagon hitched up and loaded with buckets of water, then took it up the road. The moon showed that the jolting wagon was spilling much of it as they tried to get to the fire. The little bit they got up the hill with them didn't seem to make any dent in the roaring blaze, Diablo noted. People were running and shouting, but everyone seemed powerless to do anything to really quench the flames. After a while, even Kruger seemed to realize that. He stood with shoulders slumped, watching his new mansion burn; then he limped back down to where Sunny still stood in her nightdress, staring up at the fire. They both stood there a long time, watching the fire burn. Then Kruger took her hand and led her back inside. He walked like a frustrated, defeated man.

Diablo, on the other hand, kept his post until the big house was only a pile of glowing embers. He was almost satisfied. He had taken almost everything that Kruger valued: his horse, his dog, his fine rifle, his new house. There were only two things left to take: the woman Kruger loved and, finally, Kruger's life.

Diablo was looking forward to taking the girl. He would make Kruger suffer the misery of the damned before he finally killed him. Now he need only wait for his chance to kidnap Sunny.

Kruger sulked and thought for several days, barely speaking to anyone, including Sunny. At first he thought the workmen had been careless; then he found the empty kerosene can. It seemed as though the last remaining nesters had spit in his face by burning down his new mansion.

"I'll build it bigger and better," he promised Sunny as his mood lightened. "I'll send back east for stained-glass windows and some of those fancy Tiffany lights."

"It doesn't matter," Sunny shrugged as they sat at breakfast. She was still grieving the loss of her father and not at all looking forward to her upcoming marriage.

Kruger smiled as he looked across the table at her and beckoned for Maria to pour more coffee. He couldn't believe his own good luck. He was going to marry the most beautiful, desirable woman in the whole state, and with the demise of the nesters, he would soon own most of the county. He and Sunny would have sons to inherit his empire, so his life would be complete. True, he had killed his best friend to own her, but he loved her more than life itself and nothing meant as much to him as possessing her. The thought that she would soon be in his bed, his to make love to every night, made his heart race.

"Are you all right, Uncle—I mean Hurd?" she asked, picking at her omelet.

"Yes, my love." He reached across and took her hand. "Remind me to buy you the finest weddin' ring money can buy."

She looked at him, a potbellied, middle-aged man with dyed-black hair and a habit of sucking his teeth that drove her crazy. Then reminded herself that he had been her father's best friend and Swen's dying wish had been that she marry this man. He would take good care of her, of course, but what she yearned for was a handsome prince on a big stallion who would carry her away. "It doesn't matter," she sighed, sipping her coffee. "A plain gold band will do."

"Honestly, Sunny, I do wish you would be more enthused. Half the county is comin' to the ceremony."

"I'm sorry. I'm still thinking about my father."

"Oh, yes. I'm so sorry I didn't understand." He patted her hand and gave her an adoring smile. Nothing else mattered to him if he could marry this beauty. "I've called a meeting of the Stock Growers Association," he said. "We're meeting at the Browns' ranch. It won't interest the ladies. Maybe you'd like to go into town shopping instead. Shouldn't your dress be ready by now?"

"Oh, yes." She started as though she had not given their marriage a thought. "I suppose it is ready to be picked up."

"That would be a fun trip to town for you," he said, pushing back from the table. "I'll get Joe to drive you into town, and while you're there, look around in the shops. Anything you want, you just have them put it on my bill. Nothing is too good for the future Mrs. Kruger."

She smiled. "Thank you, Hurd. You are too good to me."

"Then how about a kiss for the groom?" He leaned over and gave her a wet kiss on the lips before she could turn her head away. "I'll be back late, but I'll tell Joe to hitch up the buggy."

"All right." She didn't look all that happy about a trip to town.

When Hurd left the ranch, however, he didn't go right to the Brown ranch. Something had been bothering him, something Swen had said about having money hidden to send Sunny away to school. He thought Swen might have been bluffing, but he needed to make sure. He rode to the Sorrenson ranch and made sure no one was around; then he began to dig through trunks and drawers. He took the place apart one room at a time but found nothing.

Diablo had watched from his hilltop as Kruger left the ranch and, out of curiosity, had followed him. Now he sat up on a ridge and viewed the small ranch house as Kruger entered, wondering what the man was looking for. Surely it wasn't the small picture of Sunny that Diablo had taken?

After a while, Kruger came out, looking satisfied, mounted up, and rode away north.

Diablo watched until the rancher was out of sight; then he and his dog crept down the hill and entered the old cabin. Things were strewn everywhere, drawers pulled out, books tumbled off shelves. Whatever Kruger had been looking for, had he found it?

Still mystified, Diablo went back for his horse and

rode to Kruger's ranch. Kruger had ridden north, so that meant he wasn't headed home. This might be a good time to kidnap the girl.

As he watched, Joe drove the buggy out of the barn and around to the front door. Then Sunny came out. She wore a black dress of mourning and a shawl pulled around her blond hair so that her face was difficult to see. Joe helped her up into the buggy and got in himself. Then the buggy started at a leisurely pace toward town. Diablo followed along at a safe distance, his dog trailing after him. He would never get a better chance to take the girl. He was not sure what he would do with her. He only knew that kidnapping Sunny would throw his enemy into a frenzy and that was what mattered to Diablo.

He followed along behind them on the long dusty road into Krugerville. Then from a rise, he watched Joe tie up at the hitching rail before the general store. He helped the lady down and escorted her into the dress shop next door. When she disappeared inside, Joe headed for the saloon.

Sunny tried to paste a smile on her face as she entered the dress shop. Young Ellen West was at the counter, and her mother came out of the back room at the tinkling of the bell on the door.

Ellen, who was too thin and not quite pretty, walked around the counter. "Well, you're looking good, Miss Sunny."

Sunny tried to smile. "As well as can be expected, I suppose."

She tensed as the buxom older woman rushed forward to hug her.

"There, there now. That's all in the past, and it's a small cloud that don't bring someone some blessings.

After all, you are about to marry the richest man in the county." There was a bit of envy in Mrs. West's voice.

"Now, Mother," Ellen rushed to say, "I only went to a barn dance with Mr. Kruger once. He was never really interested in me. Why, everyone knows he's always had an eye for Sunny."

Sunny didn't even want to discuss that. "I know it must seem unusual to rush into marriage like this, right after my father's death, but Hurd—"

"Well, he's right!" Mrs. West put her hands on her generous hips. "You can't live on your own ranch alone, and it don't look right, an unmarried girl living under Kruger's roof. People might talk."

Sunny bit her lip. "Actually, Ellen, I came by to ask if you would be my maid of honor."

"I'd be delighted." Ellen's plain face lit up, and even Mrs. West's dour countenance smiled.

"Well, now," the older lady said, "this is an honor, and I reckon there'll be a lot of eligible young men there. Maybe Ellen will find a husband."

"Mother!"

Sunny took out a hankie and coughed slightly. "Excuse me, I may be coming down with a cold."

"Ah now," Mrs. West took her by the arm and led her to a chair. "What you need is a little nip of sherry. It is a mite chilly out there today."

She didn't want any sherry, but she was never one to assert herself. "About the wedding, it will be an informal affair," she said as Mrs. West hurried to get the decanter and three glasses.

Mrs. West poured two small ones and a large one for herself. "Considering the circumstances, we all know that's proper, even though he is a very rich man."

Sunny tasted her drink. "He says next year, when things

have settled down, he'll throw the biggest first anniversary party the county has ever seen."

"That will be nice," Ellen said, sipping her sherry.

"Ah," nodded her mother, taking a big gulp, "after all the unrest and these nesters causing so much trouble, it should be peaceful by then. Now if we can just get the army to clear out of town and leave us alone."

Sunny fiddled with the drink in her hand. She was feeling too warm and not well at all.

"Oh, yes, forgive me," declared Mrs. West, as she put her drink down, "you came to pick up your dress."

"Yes," Sunny said and put her sherry on a nearby table.

"It's glorious, even if it is black," the buxom lady declared. "Too bad it couldn't be white like Queen Victoria's, but after all, you are still in mourning."

"Mother, must you be so blunt?" Ellen made a face.

"I didn't mean anything by it." Her mother disappeared into the back room and came out with the dress carried across both plump arms. "Ellen stayed up half the night sewing the lace on. Why, there are twenty yards of the best black silk money can buy. No one else has been able to afford such goods. Be sure to tell everyone where you got it."

Ellen scowled at her mother again, and Sunny rushed to stop the confrontation by standing up. "Why, it's lovely!" She ran her hand over the dress. It *was* magnificent.

"You should try it on," Mrs. West suggested, "in case it needs alteration."

She didn't feel like trying it on, but she nodded. "Of course."

Ellen said, "I'll help you." She took the dress from her mother, led Sunny to the back room.

"Oh," called her mother, "and we took the liberty of making white lace drawers and a bust improver with little pink ribbons. That should make Mr. Kruger very happy."

She giggled, and inside the dressing room, Ellen rolled her eyes.

"You'll have to forgive her, Sunny. This is the biggest news in this county's history. The newspaper's out, and the ladies can talk of nothing else."

"That's all right," Sunny said listlessly as she took off her plain black cotton and put on the elegant black silk. "My, this is beautiful."

"I'm glad you like it," Ellen said wistfully, adjusting the bodice. She put a long, black sheer veil on Sunny's pale hair. "Now go out and look in the big mirror out front."

Sunny sneezed.

"Bless you," Ellen said.

"I'm sorry; I'm afraid I'm coming down with something."

"Well, let's hope you're well for the wedding. It's next Saturday night, isn't it?"

Sunny nodded as she went out into the front room and looked at herself in the full-length mirror. It was a gorgeous dress that fit her beautifully with a small waist and a tiny bustle. The black lace of the top fitted around her shoulders, leaving a wide expanse of bosom. The veil was made of some filmy, sheer ebony lace.

"Of course you know Mr. Kruger ordered some very fine jet jewelry from back east. It had to be rushed to get here." Mrs. West went behind the counter and got out the earrings and necklace. "They say Queen Victoria herself has a set like this. It's become all the rage back east, I hear."

She put the necklace around Sunny's neck. "My goodness, my dear, you feel like you might have a fever."

"I'll be fine," Sunny brushed her off and went to survey herself in the mirror again. A couple passing by on the street paused to look and smiled at her, nodding their approval. "I suppose I can take it off and you can box

it up now. Joe will be wanting to drive me home before it
gets dark."

"Yes," Ellen said, "it's clouding up like it might rain."

From his hilltop, Diablo could see the girl standing
before the mirror in the fine black dress and sheer veil.
She wore a necklace of black beads around her slender
pale neck. Sunny had never looked so desirable, and for
that Diablo hated her. He did not want to get emotionally
involved with this girl; she was only part of his revenge.

Diablo watched and waited as she disappeared from
view, absently patting Wolf and sucking on an unlit cigarillo. After a while, she came out of the shop with a big
box and the woman who worked there, carrying her purchases. They put everything in the back of the buggy, and
they exchanged a few words. Then Sunny went next door
to the general store.

No doubt she was shopping for her wedding, Diablo
thought in anger. She must be like most women—money
meant everything to them.

Diablo noted the sun low in the sky. If the pair didn't
head back to the ranch soon, they might get caught out
on the road at dusk, and it was clouding up.

Finally Joe walked out of the saloon and went to stand
in front of a shop. Sunny came out then with packages,
and Joe tipped his Stetson, took the things, and put
them in the back of the buggy. Then he helped Sunny
up into the buggy, and they started at a nice trot back
down the road toward the ranch in the coming darkness.

Diablo followed along the ridge line, keeping the
buggy barely in sight. There was a shadowy curve in the
road up ahead that he remembered. There, he thought,
was the perfect place for an ambush. He would take the

girl and hold her for ransom or use her to lure Kruger in his death.

Now he came down the ridge line, following closer to the buggy, Wolf trotting silently behind his horse. He wasn't certain he would kill Joe right now. He needed someone to carry a message to Kruger.

Sunny sighed as they drove along. She didn't feel very well, and the wind picked up abruptly and smelled of rain. She tried to make conversation with Joe, but he'd had a few drinks and wasn't in a talkative mood. A drop of rain spattered on the buggy and thunder rumbled in the distance.

"Reckon we'd better hurry," Joe mumbled. "Boss won't like it if you get wet."

"Well, I do feel bad," she admitted and wiped her nose. She paused now, listening. "Did you hear that?"

"Did I hear what?" Joe sounded peevish and hungover.

"Oh, nothing I guess. I thought I heard a horse."

"Of course you heard a horse." He gestured toward the bay pulling the buggy.

"No, I meant, maybe following us. Oh, never mind." She felt like a fool. In truth, she wasn't eager to get back to the ranch to face more of Hurd's adoring stares and wet kisses. She was also annoyed with herself that she had taken him at his word and bought a bunch of things in town. Not that she cared about any of it—she'd only been prolonging the shopping trip and avoiding returning to the ranch.

"I reckon we're gonna be late gettin' home," Joe grumbled, "or we're gonna get caught out on the road after dark and in a spring storm. Hurd will have my head. He can get really mad."

"I'll tell him it was my fault. I shopped too long."

"Yeah, but he'll hold me responsible. You can't do anything wrong. He adores you, you know." Maybe that should have made her feel good, but it didn't. She was already beginning to feel like a small animal in the trap of Hurd's obsession.

"You know," she turned in her seat and looked behind them in the growing dusk. "I swear I hear a horse coming. Maybe you should speed up a little, Joe."

He whipped up the horse, grumbling under his breath about nervous women.

It was dark as ink with the coming storm. Diablo cantering along behind, saw the girl turn in her seat and look back and then Joe picked up the pace a little. The buggy was barely visible, and the few raindrops began a sprinkle.

Diablo smiled without mirth as he spurred his horse. He had taken or destroyed almost everything that meant anything to Hurd Kruger, and now he would take the thing the man valued most: his beautiful bride.

He spurred his horse, easily overtaking the buggy. Joe looked back, alarm on his weasel face, as Diablo rode up next to them. The girl stared up at him, her pale blue eyes bright in her pale face. Fear and surprise were etched there.

"Stop this buggy! This is a holdup!"

The girl screamed, and Diablo's black stallion reared, neighing. Joe grabbed for his Colt, but he was drunk and clumsy and Diablo shot it from his hand. The buggy horse came to an abrupt stop, and packages and boxes from the back flew everywhere, dumping the contents on the road.

Diablo reached for the girl, who seemed paralyzed with fear as she stared up at his disfigured face. Cursing and crying, Joe clambered down as Diablo grabbed for Sunny.

Joe cut the buggy traces and jumped on the bay, whipping it with a cut rein as he took off down the road, abandoning her to her fate. Diablo reached for her and swung her up to his saddle even as she screamed and struggled. Her skin felt warm and very soft, and it excited him.

The big box had fallen into the road and spilled its contents, a sumptuous tumble of black lace and silk. Diablo held onto the struggling girl easily, grinning as he deliberately whirled his stallion so that it trampled the fine dress into the dirt of the road. This was one dress she would never wear. He turned his stallion, and with Wolf running along beside, he vanished into the trees lining the road while the girl cried and trembled in his arms.

"I—I have money!" she cried, "I'll give you money!"

"I don't want money." He almost whispered it, as he took off at a gallop with his captive in his arms. "I got what I want. I want you!" he shouted triumphantly, then spurred his horse and took off through the darkness of the night.

Sunny had never felt such terror as she did now, cradled in some robber's strong arms and held tightly as they galloped through the night. Joe had abandoned her. No, maybe he was going for help. "My—my fiancé will be looking for me," she cried.

The shadowy face grinned down at her as they rode, white teeth gleaming. "He won't find you."

"What—what is it you want?" Maybe she could bargain with him.

"I want revenge," he said in a voice so soft she had to strain to hear him. "Now shut up."

"But—"

His free hand reached up to clap across her mouth, and he pulled her tighter against him. "I told you to shut up."

His stern voice brooked no argument. Sunny had always been a very obedient girl. Maybe if she cooperated with whatever this robber wanted, he would let her go. If not, Kruger would soon have every cowboy in the county out scouring the plains for her. He was a proud man. No one could take his future bride without his power and anger coming down hard on them.

Diablo felt her body warm and full against him. It aroused feelings in him, mixed feelings. Because she trembled, he wanted to hold her close and protect her. But more than that, he wanted her in the way a man desires a woman, and she was his captive. When he got her back to his camp, he could do anything he wanted with her, and no one could stop him. Yes, she was Kruger's bride, but Diablo could take her virginity. That would be the best of his revenge, to dishonor Kruger's woman and make her his own. When Kruger came looking for her, Diablo would taunt him with that knowledge, and then he would kill him. In his mind, he told himself that he had taken the girl as part of his vengeance on Kruger, but his heart knew that he had stolen her because he could not bear the thought of this beauty surrendering her lush body in Kruger's bed.

Tonight, he could not think of Kruger or revenge; all he could think of was stripping off the selfish beauty's black mourning dress and making love to her on his blankets by the campfire.

Chapter 9

The downpour began in earnest as Diablo galloped back to his camp, the girl frozen in fear against him. He had expected her to fight and scream, but she seemed too terrified to move. They were both soon soaking wet, although he tried to shield her from the cold rain with his big body. At least the rain would wash out Onyx's tracks, so they couldn't be trailed.

He drew up in front of the cave and dismounted, Wolf barking in excitement. Easily, he lifted the slight girl from his saddle and carried her inside. "Stay here," he ordered, "while I put away my horse."

Sunny was too terrified to do anything but nod and stare, as he poked up the dying embers of a fire inside the cave entrance. She tried to remember where she had seen him before. Then he turned as he left so that she saw the scarred side of his face, and she drew back in horror.

"That's right," he snarled. "I'm an ugly bastard, and I know it." Then he led his horse away.

Could she make a run for it? She wasn't even sure where she was, and it was pitch black except for the tiny fire and an occasional jagged streak of lightning. She retreated toward the back of the cave.

In moments, he was back, and in a flash of lightning, she watched him building up the fire.

"What—what are you going to do with me?"

He had the fire going now, building into a roaring blaze. "Now what do you think?"

All the stories she had heard of women being ravaged by outlaws and Indians came back to her, and she tried to draw herself up and make herself very small. "I—I don't know."

He grinned without mirth. "Let's just say your bride-groom will have to delay the wedding, courtesy of Diablo."

Diablo. The devil. Yes, he looked like a devil in those black clothes and with that black Stetson. This was the Texas gunfighter she'd seen getting off the train a few days ago, the one who had rescued her that night at the barbecue, and the one she had run into in the alley by the saloon—the one who had startled Dad that day.

She was shivering, so she moved closer to the fire in spite of her fear. "Mr.—Mr. Kruger will pay a lot of money to get me back unharmed." She tried not to let her voice tremble as her body was doing. Yet she felt as if her skin were on fire.

"I don't want Mr. Kruger's money." He finished tending the fire and sat back, cross-legged, in satisfaction as they both watched the rain fall outside the cave.

She was mystified. "Everyone wants money. He's got a lot."

"Princess," he glared at her with eyes as black as his twisted soul, "there's not enough money in the world to buy you back."

Her heart sank as her terror grew. "He'll—he'll be searching for me. He'll have the whole county looking."

"Of course he will." His scarred face grinned without

humor. "I plan on that, but he won't find you. This is a secret cave I found as a boy."

"You've been in Wyoming before?"

He nodded, his dark eyes cold. "I was a slave of the Santee Sioux when I was a child. When I ran away, I hid in this cave."

She shivered again.

He suddenly really seemed to look at her. "Are you cold?"

"What—what do you care?" She coughed.

"I can't have you dying on me—that would ruin my plans."

"I wouldn't want to do that." She was trying to be sarcastic, but she felt too ill to care much right now.

He reached out and put his hand on her face, and she drew back.

"You're burning up," he growled. "Why didn't you tell me you were sick?"

"You didn't give me a chance when you kidnapped me."

He grabbed a blanket and began to dry her off. "You are soaked to the skin," he said and wrapped the blanket around her. "I'd better get you warm."

Now that she was convinced she was in no immediate danger, she was less afraid. "If you were really concerned about my health, you'd take me back to Kruger's ranch."

"No, the plan is that he comes to me. You're the bait in my trap." He reached for a big metal coffeepot. "If I can get some food in you, you'll be all right."

He bustled about, making coffee, while the rain poured down outside. She watched his hands. They were fine hands with long fingers. He could have been a surgeon. Maybe that was why he was skilled as a gunfighter. She stared at the Colt tied low on his hip.

"You can quit staring at my gun, Princess. You can't move fast enough to get it."

"I wouldn't try," she lied.

"You got more grit than I expected." He sounded admiring as he handed her a tin cup of coffee. "I figured you as a typically soft, helpless female."

She took the cup in both hands, warming them around it. Most of the time she was just what he said, but maybe her fear had brought something out in her she didn't know was there.

"You won't get away with this."

"I already have." He sat back and sipped from his own cup, turning to watch the rain pouring outside.

"Hurd will have his cowboys out hunting as soon as Joe gets back to the ranch."

"If he doesn't kill the cowardly bastard for deserting you to your fate. I wouldn't have left you to fend for yourself if I'd had to fight off a gang of outlaws or a whole Sioux war party. What a bunch of warriors liquored up on white man's rotgut would do to a beauty like you is unspeakable."

She tried not to imagine the images his words brought to her, but she shuddered and sipped her coffee. It was hot and strong, and she felt its warmth all the way down. "You're Injun, aren't you?"

"A half-breed. My father was a Santee warrior."

"Looks like you're following in your father's footsteps." He shrugged. "Don't know. I never knew him."

She wanted to ask a million questions, but she guessed she would not get any answers. There was silence except for the big black dog yawning and the rain pouring down outside. She wondered what made this man tick.

She pulled her blanket around her closer and watched Diablo stare out at the rain, wondering what he was thinking and how he had been connected to her father. *Could this man be Dad's killer?* Her anger grew, but she dared not ask. "Are we just going to sit here? Aren't you going to write a ransom note or something?"

He frowned. "It's raining. Besides, I told you this wasn't about ransom."

"Then what is it?"

He looked at her a long moment, and she drew back from his scarred face. "Princess, this is about settling an old score. Now shut up. You're noisy as a chattering squirrel."

She was feeling worse by the minute, but she didn't say anything. There was nothing she could do to help herself right now, and she knew that even if Hurd started a posse tonight, they'd get nowhere in the dark and rain. It was black as the back of this cave beyond the little fire except for an occasional flash of lightning. The icy drops still poured down in sheets. She watched him open the can of stew with his big hunting knife and put it in the glowing coals. With his wet black shirt clinging to him, she could see every muscle and sinew of his broad shoulders. His waist was almost as narrow as hers, and his hair was black as a raven's wing. She realized then that he wore knee-high moccasins. He might only be a half-breed, but inside, he was as savage as his warrior father.

Now he dished up the stew in two tin plates and handed her one. "Nothing fancy like Kruger's been feeding you, but this is all a poor cowboy can offer."

She took it. "You're not a cowboy—you're a killer."

He shrugged and began to eat his stew. "A lot of cowboys are killers; they just sneak around to do it."

"What do you mean by that?"

"Nothing. You wouldn't believe me anyway."

She began to eat the stew. "I'll live to see you hang."

"Maybe. That's what happened to my father at Fort Lincoln back in '62."

She didn't know what he was talking about. She ate her stew and felt a little better, then began to shiver again.

He looked concerned and put down his plate for the dog. "You really are cold. You need some dry clothes."

"I'll be all right."

But he was already digging in his saddlebags. "I've got an extra shirt. As tiny as you are, it will reach down past your hips."

"I'm not going to change in front of you."

"You can go to the back of the cave." He gestured.

She turned and looked. It looked shadowy and scary. "Suppose there's a bear hibernating back there?"

"No, there isn't. Wolf would have found him by now."

At the sound of his name, the dog raised his head and wagged his tail. Diablo petted his ears.

"That's Hurd's guard dog," she suddenly realized.

"Used to be, but he was mean to him, so I took him."

"And that horse you're riding, that's his prize stallion."

"He was beating the horse, so I took him."

"You're lying. Hurd isn't mean."

His face turned stern. "Princess, if you were a man, I'd kill you for calling me a liar."

"A killer with honor?" She sneered.

"Princess, you are trying my patience. Now change out of those wet clothes, or I'll take them off for you."

"You wouldn't dare!"

"Would you like to try me?"

This was a real man, a stallion of a man. She realized suddenly that one did not argue with a man like this, and besides, she was feeling worse by the minute. "I'll— I'll put on the shirt."

She grabbed up the shirt and retreated back into the cave. It was cooler there, but she felt like her skin was on fire. She began to take off her wet dress.

"If you'll bring your blanket and come up here, I'll rub you dry," he called.

"Not likely."

"Suit yourself." he shrugged and poured himself another cup of coffee.

She was shivering violently as she pulled off the wet dress and reached for the black wool shirt. It swallowed her small form, hanging halfway to her thighs. The shirt smelled of him—male, smoky, and salty. The sleeves hung down past her fingertips.

"Bring me your wet things, and I'll hang them up near the fire to dry," he called.

"All right." She tiptoed barefooted back to the fire and handed him her wet dress.

He looked her up and down admiringly. "Looks better on you than it did on me."

She looked down, saw that she hadn't buttoned it completely and the curve of her breasts showed. She buttoned it up, sat down on her blanket, and wrapped her arms around herself protectively.

"You're sick," he said.

"No, no, I'm not," she said, but she coughed and shivered again. If he thought she was sick, would he think she was too much of a burden and kill her? She had to stall for time until Hurd could come to her rescue. Looking out at the driving rain she figured that might be sometime tomorrow, and who knew what this killer would do before then?

"Here, take down your hair, and I'll dry it for you."

"I can dry my own hair, thank you," she said, but she began to take out the hair pins. He was right: if she got her hair dry, she wouldn't be so cold. It fell in wet waves down her shoulders and back.

Diablo stared at her. "It's the palest, finest hair I've ever seen."

"I'm Danish and Swedish," she said and began drying her hair with the edge of her blanket.

"Here, let me—you'll never get it dry the way you're dabbing at it." He took the edge of the blanket away from her, despite her protests, and began to dry her hair.

In the firelight, it looked almost like cream-colored silk. Her skin was as pale as milk in contrast to his dark hands, and her eyes were as blue as a Texas sky. She was delicate and fragile, but her full breasts made the black wool shirt stand out from her slender body. She had missed the top button, and he could see the rise of her breasts in the vee of the neck.

He wanted her then as he had never wanted a woman before, and she was his captive, his plaything for the taking. If he died tomorrow, he could certainly count this night worth it if he made love to her. She was so very young and innocent. Her mouth looked full and moist, and it trembled slightly, as if she knew what he was thinking. He reached out and put one big hand on her forehead. "You're burning up with fever."

She pulled back against the cave wall. "Don't touch me, or Hurd will kill you."

"It might be worth it."

"What have you got against Hurd? What has he done?"

"That's not your business. It's between men."

"And I'm just a pawn in this war?"

He nodded, then smiled. "Or maybe a prize."

She caught his meaning and gasped. "Don't you even think about it, you—you paid killer."

He ran his hand through her long hair. "If I want you, you can't stop me."

He was right. She was his captive, his toy for the night if he so chose. She was too sick to be terrified anymore. "What—what are you going to do with me?"

He shrugged. "You're my hostage to draw Kruger out. Don't worry; I don't intend to hurt you."

She didn't know whether to be grateful or terrified. She shrank back from him. He was a big, powerful man. If he decided to take her virginity, there was no way she could stop him. She would go to her marriage bed disgraced, and Hurd might not—no, he would adore her anyway. He had always seemed almost obsessed with her.

In her mind, she imagined it, Diablo so powerful and big as a stallion, she spread with his virile body between her slender thighs.

"Go to sleep," he ordered. "You're sick, and I'm very tired. The princess is safe."

He was so cocksure of himself that she wanted to slap him, beat on his chest, but he could easily overpower her and he was half savage. She was too sick to do anything except lie down on her blanket. The dog curled up next to her.

Diablo watched her a long moment. She was the most beautiful, fragile thing he'd ever seen. If she was his woman, he'd protect her, cherish her, and never let her go. Then he chided himself. *You poor, ugly bastard, she'd shrink from you and your scarred face. You'll always be alone; no woman will ever love you.*

After a while as she slept, he pulled a blanket over her bare, slender legs. He could imagine them wrapped around him, returning thrust for thrust as he buried his disfigured face in her full breasts. His manhood rose at the images, but he knew that could never be. If he took her, she would be screaming and fighting him, not returning his love like he wanted. In the fairy tale, the princess had kissed the frog or the beast, and they had turned into handsome princes. Diablo would always be scarred and frightening, and so of course, he would always be alone, drifting from town to town until some younger, faster gun took him out and he died in the dust of a frontier street or the sawdust floor of a dirty saloon.

That didn't matter, he told himself stubbornly as he spread out at the mouth of the cave. What mattered now was getting Kruger after all these years of waiting. The girl was only the bait in his trap. That was what he told himself. Deep inside, he realized now that he had taken her because he couldn't stand the thought of this fragile beauty ending up in Kruger's bed.

Joe galloped the old buggy horse home, but in the rain, the road was sloppy and slow. It was late before he reined up before the K Bar house and jumped off, shaking because he was going to have to face a man in a fury and he had seen Kruger when he was in a blind rage.

He ran into the entry hall, leaving a muddy track behind, and he heard Maria coming out of the kitchen, clucking in annoyance over the mess he was making. He didn't care. He ran into Kruger's bedroom where the rancher paused in pacing up and down before the fire.

"Thank God you're home!" Kruger whirled. "Where in the name of heaven—"

"He—he took her," Joe tried to shake the water from his soggy hat as he stood dripping on the carpet. "He took her. I tried to stop him, but—"

Kruger grabbed him by the arm. "What the hell do you mean? Where's Sunny?"

"A—a monster came out of the darkness riding a horse straight from hell! It was rearing and neighing, and there was a wolf with red eyes and gleaming teeth—"

"Damn it, are you telling me she's not with you? You let someone take her?"

"He—he was not human, I tell you! He was like one of those Injun spirits out of hell we been talkin' about for years."

Kruger took a whiff of the cowboy's breath. "I knew it! You been drinking!"

"I only had a little, Boss, while I was waitin' for Miss Sunny, and—"

Kruger had never known such fury. He slammed the man back against the fireplace and hit him in the face. "Then how'd you get away? You let a man take her and you get home safe?"

"I—I couldn't help it, boss," he threw up his hands to defend himself while rain and blood ran down his face, "He reached out and grabbed her with her screamin', and I cut loose the buggy horse and took off to get help."

"You cowardly bastard!" Kruger raged and hit him again, knocking him against the wall. "You yellow dog! You let some outlaw take my fiancé, and you ran away?"

"I was comin' for help," Joe babbled. "I swear, there was nothin' I could do, I had to come for help."

"Better you should have stayed and died to protect her," Kruger snarled and hit him again, "I would have."

"I'm sorry, boss," Joe gasped, "I—I couldn't do nothing, I tell you."

"You didn't try, you yellow bastard!" Kruger was in a red rage. He hit the cowhand again and again until Joe was a babbling wreck, smearing blood all over walls and furniture. He knew Maria had come out in the hall to clean up the mud and the maid would hear, but he was past caring. "Get up, Joe!" He dragged the man to his feet. "Go get the boys out of bed. We'll start a search."

Joe stumbled backward toward the door. "But the rain will wipe out the tracks—we won't have no luck in this darkness."

"We got to look for her anyway," Kruger said. "I can't

bear to think of my darling in the hands of some rapin' bastard."

"Maybe in the morning there'll be a ransom note," Joe gasped and wiped his bloody mouth.

"We can't wait for tomorrow, we've got to find her before . ..." In his mind, some vile farmer was tearing off Sunny's dress and ravaging her while she screamed for Hurd to rescue her. Tears came to his eyes. He adored the girl almost to the point of worship. Nothing must happen to her. He had waited all these years, made all these sacrifices, even killed her father, to possess her and he would not be denied.

If some lout dared deflower his pure bride, he would kill the brute himself, slow and sure. He ground his teeth together. "You heard me, Joe: Get the boys out of bed, and let's look for her. Then spread the word. By tomorrow morning, we'll have every rancher in the county on the alert. No nester is going to insult Hurd Kruger by stealin' his bride right out from under his nose. That's an insult I will not take, and I'll make a final example out of the man who dared do this."

"I told you—it ain't a regular man, it's some kind of Injun spirit, an ugly one, coming to get you for all the Injuns you've killed over the years."

"I ain't done nothing I didn't have to do to hang on to this land," Hurd yelled, "and I did it all for her, so I could lay it all at her feet. We'll get her back unharmed, or I'll turn this whole county into a big prairie fire! Tell me again what he looked like."

Joe backed away, his weasel face turning black and purple with bruises. "He—he was big, and dressed in all black. He was dark, too, maybe Injun."

Hurd paced up and down. "A hired gunman of the farmers, maybe. Well, don't just stand there—get movin'!"

In less than thirty minutes, they were riding through the

pouring rain back down the trail to Krugerville. Several of the men carried lanterns, but it was difficult to see through the driving spring rain. Hurd was in such a rage, he spurred his horse needlessly, thinking of how he'd do the same to the man who took his darling. No, he promised himself, he'd do more than that—he'd geld the bastard with all the cowboys looking on. Word would spread across the whole state that Hurd Kruger was not a man to put up with insult and no man should even give an admiring glance to the future Mrs. Kruger. Sunny was his to love and protect.

They rode through the mud until they reached the disabled buggy. The glow of the lanterns showed packages scattered everywhere and the box containing the fine wedding dress lay on the trail. The dress itself had been trampled into the mud as if by deliberate insult, but there was no trace of the girl. "Spread out and see if you can find a track!" Hurd bellowed, "a hundred dollars in gold to the man who finds a clue!"

A murmur ran through the wet, tired cowboys. A hundred dollars in gold? He worshipped that girl more than anyone had realized. They all spread out and dismounted, holding up lanterns to see the muddy ground, but the tracks were gone.

"Boss," Joe said through swollen, bloody lips, "It ain't no use—the tracks have been washed out."

"Damn it, keep lookin!" Hurd ordered. "Two hundred dollars to the man who finds the trail!"

They searched for another hour, and the lanterns began to burn out for lack of oil. Hurd himself was soaked through, and rain dripped off his Stetson and ran down his beefy neck. He tried not to think of what might be happening to his darling at this very moment. "All right, I reckon we'll have to quit until daylight; then we'll start again. I'll give five hundred dollars to the man who captures this bastard and I mean alive! I want to kill him myself an inch at a time."

"Boss, I still think it's one of them Injun haunts," Joe insisted. "No man alive would dare to take something that belonged to you!"

Hurd cut him across his face with his quirt. "They've taken my horse and my guard dog and my fancy rifle, and burned down my new house. Takin' my woman is the last straw. Just wait 'til I get my hands on him! Dale, you ride into town and alert the sheriff so he can get a posse together at dawn. Joe, you ride to the fort and see if the captain can turn out a patrol. Bob, you ride down to Cheyenne and let the Stock Growers Association know what's happened. They need to know these damned farmers are fighting back."

"It's a long way to Cheyenne," Bob protested.

Hurd slashed at him with his quirt. "What the hell! You think I don't know that? I want every lawman, soldier, cowboy and rancher out scouring the county. Get the newspaper to do some notices and hang them from every tree from here to the border. I'll give a thousand dollars in gold for Sunny's return . . . and the man who took her. If you men never seen a public torture and execution, you'll see one now!"

The rain continued to pour down, and Hurd was so weary and angry that tears came to his eyes. "All right, you've got your orders. We'll lock Johnson County up so tight a flea can't get through our lines. Now everyone move!"

The men scattered, and Hurd spurred his horse as he galloped back up the trail to his ranch.

Chapter 10

It seemed as if the rain would never end. Diablo watched it from the mouth of the cave, then looked toward his captive. She lay bundled up in her blanket, but from here, he could see that she shivered. Noiseless in his moccasins, he crept back and put his hand on her forehead. Her pale skin felt burning hot. She was sick, really sick, and now he felt guilty, knowing taking her through the deluge into no more shelter than a cave had added to her misery. The dog raised its massive head and thumped its tail, but he motioned it to silence.

He knew an old Indian medicine for fever; Trace Durango had used it to save Diablo's life. Hunching himself against the cold rain, he went out into the night near a small stream where he knew a stand of willows grew. He cut several branches and carried them back to the cave where he got a pot of water boiling and dropped the peeled bark into it. The steeped tea would lower her fever. In the meantime, he was cold himself. He stripped off his wet shirt and hung it over a rock to dry. She was wearing his only dry shirt.

He started to wrap himself in his sleeping blanket, but after seeing her shiver he instead spread the blanket over her. Her face in repose was so soft and gentle, her lips full. He resisted the urge to kiss those lips, reminding himself that she was part of his revenge and he must not let down his guard. Still, he could not resist stroking her pale hair. He had never felt anything so soft, and he wanted to tangle his fingers in it. Of course if she woke up, she would scream, so he backed away. While she slept, he could pretend that she might smile at him if she awakened, instead of screaming at his misshapen, burned face.

Now he returned to stoking up the fire and tending to his willow bark tea. The heat had dried much of the moisture on his muscular body, and he was not so cold.

Behind him, he heard a movement, and he turned toward her. She had arisen on one elbow and was staring at him with those pale blue eyes, blinking as if not sure where she was. Then she seemed to realize and shrank back against her blankets. "What—what are you doing?"

"Making you some tea." He pulled the pot off the fire. "It will be good for your fever."

"What happened to your shirt?" The look of fear in her eyes made him cringe.

"I had to go out in the rain to get the willow bark so I hung it up to dry. You've got my only other clean one."

She looked down at herself as if to see if he spoke the truth. "You—you've got scars on your back."

She had seen the old whip marks from his days with the Indians. He turned so she could not see them. "I'm scarred all over. When I was little, the old woman who owned me used to beat me."

She looked like she might ask something more, but he had already revealed more to her than he ever had to anyone.

"Here, I've made you some willow bark tea." He poured a steaming tin cup and brought it to her.

Perspiration beaded on her ivory skin, and she shrank back against the cave wall. "No."

"It isn't poison. Look, I'll taste it to show you." He tasted the brew and tried to hand her the cup, but her fingers shook. "You're gonna spill it. Let me help you."

Though she tried to edge away and protested, she was small and sick. He put one strong hand under her neck and held the cup to her lips with the other. She tried to avoid it, but finally opened trembling lips and took a swallow.

"More!" he commanded gently, and she drank. Then he put the cup down and wrapped the blankets around her. "I can't have you dyin' on me. Kruger wouldn't like that."

She lay curled up in the blankets. "Who—who are you?"

"I think we've already had this conversation."

"No, I mean, who are you, really?"

He sighed and squatted down next to her. "I'm a gunfighter. I kill people for money."

An expression of distaste crossed her pretty face. "Oh, now I remember; you came in with that trainload from Texas."

He nodded. "Kruger and the Stock Growers Association got up a hundred thousand dollar pot to pay to wipe out the nesters."

"That's just a rumor. I don't think Hurd would do that."

"You don't know him as well as I do."

"But if you're working for Hurd, why—"

"I'm not." He sat down and leaned against the cave wall. "I didn't come to kill settlers; I came for Kruger."

"But why?"

"Princess, you ask too many questions." He stared at her. Her eyes were as blue as the Gulf of Mexico—blue and deep enough to swim in. Her lips were moist and slightly parted. He wanted to kiss them and kiss them again, but of course, she wouldn't allow that and he wouldn't, couldn't force her.

"Are you really from Texas?"

"Don't you recognize my Texas drawl?"

"I see your hat has a rattlesnake hatband. Is that to tell everyone how dangerous you are?"

He glanced at his Stetson lying on a nearby rock. "I'm more dangerous. A rattlesnake will give you warning before it strikes; I won't."

The tea must have been working. She was feeling better and sleepy. She tried to ask more, but he shook his head.

"Shut up and go to sleep. You can hardly keep your eyes open now."

She blinked, obviously trying to stay awake. "What— what are you going to do?"

"Nothin' right now. Go to sleep." He reached out and, with surprisingly gentle fingers, pulled the blankets up around her shoulders.

She tried to stay awake, but she couldn't.

Diablo watched her sleep. She was still shivering, and he had no more blankets. He was cold himself. He crawled over and felt his shirt by the fire, but it was not dry. If he built the fire up much higher, someone might smell the smoke and find his hideout.

After a while, he lay down next to her and pulled the two blankets over both of them, holding his breath because he knew if she woke up, she would scream. In her sleep, she moved toward his warmth, and he opened his arms to her, pulled her close. He hardly dared breathe for fear of waking her, but she only moved closer, snuggling against his big chest with her head on his shoulder. She seemed so dainty and frail in his powerful embrace. Her warm breath felt good against his bare skin. He pulled her close and held her, wanting to warm and protect her while telling himself she was only part of his revenge and that he must not let his emotions get in the way of his plans. After a while, he slept, too.

Sunny woke with a start, trying to decide where she was and then realized in horror that she had slept in the half-breed's strong embrace. *Had he—? Oh, my God.*

"Let go of me!" She came up fighting and clawing, pushing him away.

He rose up on one elbow and smiled ever so slightly. "Well, I see you're feeling better."

"You monster!" She sat up, shrinking against the cave wall. "Have you dared—?"

"No, I haven't, but if I want to, you aren't big enough to stop me."

That was true. She was at least feeling stronger, though she was still shaky. She looked toward the mouth of the cave. It had stopped raining, and a pale dawn washed the inside of the cave with gray light. "Hurd will have half the county out looking for me."

"But he won't find you." Diablo yawned and crawled out of the blankets to the smoldering fire. He began to poke it up. "I hid in these foothills when I was a small boy. I know this county better than any man alive." He reached for the coffeepot.

"Is my dress dry?"

He grinned at her. "I like you in my shirt, although it's way too big for you. What do you suppose Kruger would think if he showed up and found out we'd been sleepin' together and you're wearing my shirt?"

"You cad! He's a proud man who wouldn't under-stand." She crawled up to reach for her black dress, hating her kidnapper with every ounce of her being. "We're sup-posed to be married next Saturday."

"I got news for you: you won't make it."

She felt an odd sense of relief that she couldn't understand.

"You don't look too sad about that." He put the coffeepot on to boil.

"That's none of your business. How much ransom do you want to free me? Hurd is a very rich man."

"I told you before—this isn't about money."

"You gunfighters kill people for money, don't you?"

"Sometimes." He didn't smile. "Sometimes we do it for free."

"You rotten rascal."

He shrugged. "You can go to the back of the cave and put on your dress."

She took the black dress and crawled back into the shadows, looking to make sure he was tending the fire before she unbuttoned the big shirt and took it off.

Diablo sneaked a quick look. She was even more petite than he had thought, with a trim waist and long legs. Her yellow hair spilled down her shoulders and half hid her generous breasts. For a moment, he fought the urge to take her, hold her, claim her in the way men have made women theirs for millions of years. Then he squelched the urge. No, he didn't want her that way, screaming and clawing at him, tears running down those ivory cheeks. Last night, he had held her against him, warm and safe, and he couldn't change that feeling. He returned to slicing bacon and throwing it in the skillet.

He heard her putting on the dress. Then she crawled forward and tossed him his shirt. He took it and held it a moment. It was still warm from her slender body, and it held the faint scent of her skin and perfume. Then he put it on, thinking how it had clung to her curves. "There's coffee."

She held out a small hand and he put a tin cup into it.
"Be careful," he warned, "it's hot."

She sipped it, and he sneaked a look at her as she stared
out at the dawn. Her eyelashes were long, and there were
half a dozen freckles on her nose.

"So what happens now?" she asked.

"You afraid?" He handed her a tin plate of bacon and
fried bread.

"Of course I am." She seemed to stifle a sob. "I've been
kidnapped by a gunfighter—a—a—"

"Ugly monster," he said, and then he sighed and sipped
his coffee.

"I didn't say that."

"But you were thinkin' it. All women do."

She didn't deny it, and they ate in silence.

Finally she said, "You know, they'll be scouring the
county for me. Your life won't be worth a plugged nickel."

"I knew that when I took you."

"Then why—"

"Shut up and drink your coffee," he snapped.

"I—I need to . . . *you know.*" She looked embarrassed.

"Okay, you go off in that brush over there, and I'll see
about my horse. Wolf will go with you."

At the sound of his name, the dog wagged his tail.

She got up and started out of the cave, the dog trailing along behind. "No funny business," her captor yelled
after her. "You can't get away."

But of course that was just what she intended to do.

After she relieved herself in the brush, she looked
back toward the cave. She didn't see the half-breed. He
must be around the bend, taking care of his horse. She
didn't have to get very far; she only had to find a road or
a rancher's cabin or a place where she could scream

long and loud, bringing someone out to see what the noise was about.

Taking a deep breath, she zigzagged through the brush, the dog following along behind. There was no sound behind her. The ground was muddy and pulled at her little shoes. He'd be able to track her, but maybe it would take him awhile.

Behind her, she heard the half-breed yell, "Wolf?"

The dog with her began barking.

"Hush!" She tried to grab the dog's muzzle to shut him up. "Hush, Wolf!"

But the dog pulled away from her and continued barking.

"Damn, damn, damn!" She muttered to herself and began to run, crashing into trees and falling in the mud, getting up and running on. She never swore, but now she was furious and scared. There was no telling what the gunfighter would do to her for running away. He seemed like the kind of man that others obeyed. Was he behind her?

She couldn't hear anything but her own little feet splashing through the mud, but he was part Indian and he wore moccasins so he might move as noiselessly as a deer.

Her breath was coming in gasps, and she tripped and fell again, clambered to her feet, and kept running. Her dress was dripping wet with mud, but all she cared about was escaping. He might be able to hear her gasping for air, or at least the dog barking as it followed behind her. She was still weak from her fever, and she was slowing down. She tripped and fell again.

Even as she tried to get to her feet, the gunfighter came out of the brush and was on her, grabbing at her as she fought him, both of them covered with mud. He ended up on top, one hand over her mouth and his face etched with anger.

"I told you you couldn't get away from me. I know these woods."

He could feel every inch of her warm body from her slender thighs to her soft breasts, beneath him, and he wanted her. He wanted her bad.

She clawed at his face, and in answer, he grabbed both her hands in his free one and held onto her.

"Stop it, Princess!" he commanded. "Stop it now. How dare you pull a stunt like that?" He put his hand over her mouth.

In answer, she bit his fingers.

"You little bitch!" He pulled back like he might strike her, then seemed to think better of it. "I might forget you're a woman!"

He stood up and pulled her to her feet, the dog dancing around the two of them. "Now all you've done is get your dress wet and muddy."

She stood breathing hard. "I don't care."

"Well, I do, Princess. You might get sick on me again." He looked puzzled, as if unsure what to do. "You still got any clothes at your old place?"

She nodded. Maybe some of her dad's cowboys might be still on the ranch, although Hurd had ordered them to move all the Sorrenson livestock to the Kruger barns.

He took her by the hand and started back toward the cave.

She was breathing hard, and she stumbled. "I—I can't go any farther."

"Well, I ain't leaving you behind, if that's what you think." He swung her up in his strong arms and set off at a rapid pace toward the cave. He hadn't buttoned his shirt, and she laid her face against his bare chest and gasped. He was strong all right; she didn't stand a chance of outrunning him.

Diablo walked more slowly. He wouldn't admit even to himself that he liked the feel of the petite body in his arms, the softness of her face and the warmth of her breath against his skin.

"You're more trouble than I thought."

"Then why don't you just drop me off somewhere near a town and ride back to Texas? I won't tell anyone what happened."

"Liar. Besides, this isn't about you; it's something between me and Kruger." He stood her on her feet and wiped the mud from his chest, buttoned his shirt. "If you aren't a mess. Stand here 'til I get my horse saddled, and we'll ride to your place."

"All right. I'm too tired to run anymore."

He went around the boulder and saddled his horse, paused for a split second to gaze at the small picture of her in his saddlebags. He'd been stupid to take it. If she ever saw it, she'd know he'd been in her ranch house, yet he couldn't bring himself to throw the picture in its ornate frame away.

"Are you coming?" she shouted.

"Yes." He put the small photo back in his saddlebags and swung up on the ebony stallion. He rode around to where she stood. He swung down and took out his bandana. "Come here, Princess."

"No."

She tried to step away, but he grabbed her arm. "You think I want you to see the trail back to this cave?"

He tied the bandana across her eyes, then swung up on the black stallion while Wolf sat down on his haunches next to the girl. Then he reached out one hand and lifted her lightly up before him. He held her against him as he rode down the twisting trail to the prairie.

"Don't touch me," she snapped.

"Shut up," he said, enjoying the feel of her warm body against him. She was his, he thought. He could possess her anytime, anyplace he wanted, as many times as he wanted, and there was nothing she could do about it.

It was almost as though she read his thoughts or maybe felt his manhood rigid against her body. "Hurd won't pay to get me back if—if anything happens." She said in a trembling voice.

He merely grunted and rode toward her ranch, every nerve alert to possible riders or ambush.

Finally, he reined in before the old house, dismounted, and reached up for her. "Come on."

"I—I can't see."

"You don't have to see; I'll catch you."

But instead, she yanked off the bandana before she jumped. He caught her, set her on the ground, but he didn't let go of her. She was hardly chest high on him, but when she looked up, he saw fear in the big blue eyes and it disturbed him.

"I—I'm getting you muddy."

"I know it," he snapped and stepped away, tying up the horse to the hitching post. He tried the door and it was unlocked. "Come on."

There were tears in her eyes. "I haven't been back here since Dad was murdered."

"I know." His voice was gentle. "But you need some clothes." He wished he could tell her what he knew, but she would never believe him.

They went inside, and, as Diablo remembered, the place was ransacked already by Kruger.

"Oh, my," she sighed. "To some people, nothing is sacred. We didn't have much."

"Then what were they looking for?"

She shrugged and wiped her eyes. "I'm not sure. Dad always said he had money hidden away to send me back east to school, but I always thought it was just wishful thinking. In fact, if it hadn't been for Hurd helping with the mortgage, we would have lost the ranch years ago. He was my dad's best friend, and I'm beholden to him."

Diablo started to say something, decided it was no use. She didn't know as much about Kruger as he did, and she wouldn't believe it anyway.

"Well," she took a deep breath, "if there was any money, hidden, I reckon it's gone now. The place is a wreck."

"We can't stay too long," Diablo cautioned her.

"I know." She paused by her father's favorite rocking chair and ran her hand over the back. "I can almost see Dad sitting here."

"He was a good hombre." Diablo said.

"How would you know?" she flared at him, then marched into her room and began going through the drawers.

"Just grab a few things, and let's get out of here. Someone might happen by."

That was what she was hoping. She stalled as much as she could, gathering up some white cotton drawers and a blue gingham dress. She had never really owned much, but Hurd was promising her the finest of everything. All she had to do in return was sleep with him and let him father her children. She shuddered at the thought.

She changed into the blue gingham dress and dropped the black one on the floor. If anyone came along and found the muddy dress, it might give them a clue.

"Come on," Diablo said again, "we've got to get out of here. We can't take a trunk full of stuff."

"I'm just getting a few things." She finished and came back into the parlor where the gunfighter stood.

He looked her over. "You're pretty in blue."

"I feel guilty. You know, I'm supposed to wear black mourning for a year."

"That can't be helped," he said, looking around. "It looks like they've pulled out every can in the kitchen and every book on the shelves. If there was any money, do you reckon they found it?"

She shrugged. "Don't reckon it matters now, but I don't think there is any. I don't have much alternative except to marry Hurd."

The disfigured man scowled. "I told you, he isn't going to live long enough to bed you."

"We'll see. You have no idea how much power and wealth Hurd Kruger has in this county, and he'll bring it all to bear against you for daring to kidnap me."

"Then I might as well enjoy you to the fullest," the gunfighter said, and he didn't smile. "What is the old saying, 'in for a penny, in for a pound'? In Texas we say, 'might as well get hung for stealin' a sheep as a goat'."

"You're no gentleman," she scolded.

"Neither is your intended."

"That's not true. Hurd is a wonderful, caring man. He'll make a fine husband."

"You didn't say that with much enthusiasm." He led her out to the horse.

"That's not true. I—I'm looking forward to being Mrs. Hurd Kruger."

He took her handful of clothes and stuffed them in his saddlebags, then pulled out his bandana.

"Let me take one last look," she pleaded.

"Sure." His voice softened.

She took a long, long look around at the home of her

childhood. She had never lived anyplace else. "My dad came here when mother died in childbirth."

"He never remarried?"

She shook her head. "I always felt so guilty and tried hard to make it up to him."

"You love this country?"

"Not really. It's too cold for me, but I loved ranching. I always hoped Dad would move farther south, but he wasn't a very good businessman, I'm afraid. Only Hurd's help kept us afloat."

There was so much he wanted to tell her, but he knew she would never believe him. "Let's go."

He tied the bandana over her eyes and mounted up. Then he lifted her up before him. "Come on, Wolf."

The dog came running at his whistle, and Diablo headed back along the twisting trail that led to his hideout up in the foothills. What he would do next was uncertain, but he meant for it to lead to Joe and Kruger's deaths.

Chapter 11

Kruger was in a frenzy over Sunny's disappearance over the next several days. "How dare anyone kidnap her? It's spittin' in my face, that's what it is!"

He wired the governor and rode over to the fort to talk to the commander there. The sheriff at Krugerville deputized extra deputies, and every member of the Stock Growers Association and all their cowboys soon knew of the kidnapping. As the days passed, Kruger had reward posters on every tree and fence post in the county, offering a big reward in gold for information leading to her safe return.

He called Joe into the ranch house again and made him go over every detail about what had happened. "Tell me again: was there more than one kidnapper?"

Joe backed away, as if fearing he might be beaten again. "I—I'm not sure, boss. If there was, some of them were hiding because I only remember one. I'd swear he was riding your black horse, and that part-wolf dog of yours was with him."

"What?" That sent Kruger into a rage of gritting his teeth and slamming his fist against the wall. "The gall of him! I'll take his hide off slowly, an inch at a time. Takes my woman, my horse, and my dog? it's a deliberate insult, that's what! Can you remember anything about what he looked like?"

Joe tried to remember, his weasel face screwing up in thought.

Kruger wanted to hit him, beat him. "If you hadn't been drunk, you might have saved her."

Joe threw his hands up before his face. "Now, boss, he came out of nowhere, all dressed in black. I still ain't sure it wasn't some kind of devil."

"What'd he look like?" Kruger sucked his teeth and tried to imagine the scene.

"I'm not sure. His face was in shadow, but I think he was dark."

"Injun? Mexican?"

Joe tried to remember, shook his head. "Not sure. Wait, I do remember he was ugly, ugly as a monster." That puzzled Kruger. He chewed his lip. "Ugly? That could be a thousand men."

Joe struggled, his face furrowed. "No, I—I mean like one side of his face had been caught in a meat grinder or a forest fire."

Hurd lit a cigar but didn't offer Joe one. "If he's that ugly, seems like we'd remember if we ever saw him in the county before."

"He looked like something out of my worst nightmare," Joe said. "There's something familiar about him, but I'm not sure what it was."

"Looks like if he was that bad, you'd remember," Kruger snapped.

Joe seemed to be struggling as he played with the brim of his Stetson. "It's—it's almost there, but I can't quite get a hold of it."

"Oh, hell," Kruger shoved him, "you're an idiot! Go out and help the boys. I want a reward poster on every tree in every surrounding county and town within fifty miles."

Joe sighed. "Boss, we already got them in Krugerville and over in Wildfire. That's all the towns there are for quite a few miles, unless we put them up in Buffalo and that's a farmers' town."

"You heard me!" Kruger roared. "It has to be a ransom thing, knowin' I've got money to save her."

"But he ain't tried to get a message to us," Joe answered as he started for the door. "What else could it be?"

"Revenge?" Kruger muttered to himself and motioned Joe to leave before he lost his temper and beat the cowboy senseless. "No, that don't make no sense. Swen didn't have an enemy in the county—even those damned nesters liked him."

He leaned against the fireplace and smoked his cigar. Maybe it wasn't revenge against Swen; maybe someone was trying to get even with Hurd because Sunny was only a few days away from being his bride. Because of his power and money, he had a lot of enemies. *Well, important men always do.*

Would any of the farmers have the sheer gall to snatch the girl to get even with Hurd? He didn't think any of them had the courage for that, yet on the other hand . . . his gaze went to the mantel, where he had placed the old running iron that an intruder had left on his bed. Yes, there was a message there, but what was it? His mind went to Smitty and Wilson left hanging where he could find them. If it was a farmer or small rancher, why hadn't they just shot his cowboys instead of going to so much trouble?

A memory tried to come to his mind, but he couldn't quite grasp it. He'd done so much violence to different people over the years, defending his empire against all this poor riffraff, that there were a lot of people who wanted him dead. Yet though the intruder had entered his bedroom and could have killed him, he had instead left a running iron, a trademark of the rustler, on the foot of Hurd's bed. It didn't make any sense.

He poured himself a whiskey and sat down in his rocker. Whiskey. He had done some of his most foolish deeds with a few drinks under his belt, so he didn't drink much anymore, not in a long time. Swen didn't drink at all, not since that night. . . .

He tried to remember why Swen had stopped drinking, but he couldn't reach that far back for the memory. He remembered the whiskey haze and some violent horseplay that had happened on a night long ago, but his mind had glossed it over and he wasn't sure what it was. He thought they had hung a couple of rustlers, but then he'd done that a number of times. Oh, hell, what did it matter?

He gulped the drink and went outside into the warm spring morning. The woman he loved more than life itself, for whom he would sacrifice anything, even his beloved ranching empire, was missing, and who knew what was happening to her? She might already be dead or worse yet . . . he tried to block the thought of the shy beauty being used for some owl-hoot's pleasure from his mind. She'd probably kill herself before she'd submit to that shame.

He slapped his quirt against his leg as he walked to the barn, imagining slamming it against the kidnapper's bare back until it was a raw, bloody mess. No, he'd come up with a slower, more painful torture for the bastard. If a reward was asked for, he'd pay it all right, but then he'd set a trap for the upstart. No man could take something that belonged to Hurd Kruger and not suffer the consequences.

His whole remuda of cowboys now squatted before the barn or leaned against the hitching post.

"Mount up, boys. We're gonna do a sweep of every bit of land for miles around where Miss Sorrenson was taken."

"We already done that once, boss," Kit objected.

Kruger hit him full force with the quirt in his hand,

knocking him against the barn. "Goddamn it! We'll do it again and again until we find some clue!"

As he led out his sorrel horse and mounted up, he saw the men scowl and exchange glances as Kit wiped the blood off his face. There was a muttering behind him.

He turned in his saddle. "Any man don't like it can draw his pay and quit."

Joe cleared his threat. "Boss, I know it's important to you to get her back, but there ain't no work being done around the ranch. We got calves that need brandin', fences that need fixin'. Things will go downhill fast if we don't keep workin'."

"You think I give a damn about that?" Kruger roared. "I built this spread up for her, and if she ain't my wife, I don't give a damn about the ranch. It can fall down for all I care."

"Boss," Joe said gently, "I been riding for your brand for more than fifteen years, and this ain't like you. You're tired; we're all tired."

Another cowboy chimed in, "Joe is right, boss. You're riding us into the ground. We spent days chasing down all those nesters, and burning barns and cabins; now we're spending hours in the saddle looking for Miss Sunny. A man can only take so much before he wears out."

"You!" Kruger pointed at him. "You're fired. Joe, see he gets paid off. Now if the rest of you want to ride for the K Bar ranch, let's get off our rumps and see if we can pick up a clue. There's money to be made by any man with a keen eye and some guts."

With a collective sigh, the many cowboys of the K Bar outfit fell into line and rode out to search the prairie again.

Back at the cave, Diablo sat before the fire, gazing out across the valley.

"Are we just going to sit up here forever?" Sunny asked.

Diablo shook his head. "Depends on your lover."

"He isn't my lover; he's my fiancé."

Diablo didn't answer. In the distance, he could see a faint cloud of dust showing that a large group of horsemen were riding away from the Kruger ranch.

"No doubt Hurd is already offering a huge reward for me," she said.

"No doubt."

She was exasperated. "So why don't you work out a trade? You can be a rich man and hightail it back to Texas."

"I know that."

"Then what are we waiting for?" She looked at the side of his face turned to her. He was a handsome man until he turned his head, and then she tried not to shudder.

"If you were Indian or at least, a half-breed," he said softly, "you would understand the value of patience when you're after game. When the Sioux kill a man, they know how to torture him for days before he begs for the release of death."

"And that's what you intend for Hurd?"

He nodded and watched the distant cloud of dust.

"You'll have to get him away from all his cowboys first. He's always got twenty or thirty men with him."

"Maybe as time goes on, some of them will quit, realizing they're working for a madman."

She shook her blond hair back. "I think you're the madman."

"No, everything I'm doing is carefully planned. I've had many years to think about this."

"I think that's the reason you're mad," she argued. "No sane person goes through all this over an old grudge. A sane man would finally forget it."

He turned his damaged face toward her. "Every time I look at my reflection in a stream or a barroom mirror, every time a woman backs away from me in horror or a little kid sees me and runs screaming, I remember."

"Are you saying Hurd did that to you? He wouldn't do that."

He didn't answer. She got up and walked over into a spot of shade under some trees, and he watched her with mixed feelings. It was getting more difficult to sleep near her at night and listen to her soft breathing without wanting to reach for her, take her, make her submit to him.

Even now as he watched her profile with the delicate ivory of her fair skin and the soft rise of her breasts in the lace bodice of the blue calico dress, he felt his desire rise. He wanted to take her in his arms and kiss her eyes, her cheeks, her full, moist mouth. Then he wanted to rip off her dress, caress those fine breasts, and plunge into her, conquer her.

She would scream and struggle if he did, and that made him wince. For a moment, he imagined her coming willingly into his embrace, returning his kisses, touching his lips with the tip of her tongue, pulling his dark head down to kiss her throat with his warm breath against her soft skin, and finally, helping him undo the pearl buttons of her bodice.

He must not get emotionally involved with his captive because she belonged to his most bitter enemy, and Diablo hated her for that—hated that she couldn't see what a cruel, evil bastard the rancher was. Once he figured out how to lure Kruger to his doom without an army of cowboys accompanying him, he could take the girl and make her his in the most primitive sense of the word. He shook his head. No, rape was a loathsome crime; he knew that because . . . he didn't want to remember. Instead, he imagined a willing Sunny, her dress half torn away, begging him to take her again and again and again. Then he would torture Kruger and finally lynch him, leaving his body to swing in the wind and rot as Kruger had done to Diablo's friends.

He came back to the present and scowled at the girl, "You might as well take a nap or find something to do. Today isn't the day he'll come for you."

"And what are you going to do?" she flared. "Just sit upon this hill and stare into the sky?"

"I am going to read a book," he said, and reached for the small tattered volume under his blanket.

"You can read?" she snorted. "That's unusual for a cowboy."

He got a faraway look in his eyes. "Someone in Texas taught me."

"A woman?"

"A woman." He nodded and smiled faintly.

"Was she your lover?"

"Why would you want to know that?" He thought of Cimarron Durango, Trace's wife who had helped saved his life and shown him the only kindness he had ever known. "She was more like a mother. In fact, her husband, Trace Durango, offered to give me their last name."

"Don't you have one of your own?"

"Not that I know of." He thought of his white mother raped by a Santee warrior during the uprising and then killing herself because of the disgrace. The white family had dumped him on the Sioux. Neither white nor brown had wanted him.

So Diablo read, and Sunny fidgeted and made her plans. She didn't exactly know what the gunfighter's intentions were, but she was uneasy about the intensity of his dark gaze when she caught him staring at her. Yet the killer intrigued her with his dark skin and scarred back. He was as lithe as a panther, and she had seen the broad shoulders and the rippling muscles under his shirt. Maybe she could seduce him into letting her go, although she wasn't sure what it took to interest a man and she knew Hurd would be in a rage if she gave herself to this cold-blooded killer to buy her freedom. Or perhaps Hurd need never know what it had cost her.

Hurd hadn't been able to rescue her so far, and maybe he couldn't. She might either have to seduce Diablo with her innocent body or find a way to escape and make her way back to the K Bar ranch. She clenched her small fists and smiled, thinking of the punishment Hurd would mete out to this half-breed. Then she could sit on the front row at a public hanging while the state of Wyoming meted out justice. She wanted Diablo to see her grinning up at him before the hangman opened the trap and left him kicking and gasping at the end of a rope.

It was almost dusk that warm spring night as Diablo finally put down his book. "I shot a rabbit this morning. We can roast that for supper."

"All right. You know this is Saturday."

He shrugged. "So what?"

"If you hadn't kidnapped me, I'd be walking down the aisle to marry Hurd right now."

"So I saved you." He actually chuckled as he got up and went to pick up sticks for the fire.

Saved you. In a couple of hours, had Diablo not stolen her, she would be giving her virginity to a man old enough to be her father. She made a small face at the thought of his dyed gray hair and potbelly, then felt guilty. If Dad had asked with his dying breath that she marry his friend, who was she to question it? Hadn't she always been an obedient and dutiful daughter? So therefore, she would make an obedient and dutiful wife, just like Hurd wanted.

Diablo came back with the firewood and began skinning the fat rabbit. "Princess, you want to start some coffee?"

"Sure." As she got a bucket of water from the stream, she thought about scalding him with the kettle once she got it boiling, then decided he was too smart for that. As she made coffee, Diablo put the skillet on the fire and put some cut-up potatoes in it to fry. He put the rabbit on a sharp stick and hung it over the flames. The sizzling scent made her mouth water, and even Wolf licked his chops and whined.

Diablo laughed and petted the dog. "You'll get a bite, too."

They ate in silence, and then she cleaned up the tin plates without being asked.

"You'd make a good ranch wife," he said in an admiring tone.

"That's what I intend," she answered.

"But not Kruger's wife," he said and stuck a cigarillo in his mouth.

"Don't you ever light those?" She sat down on a log next to him.

He shook his head. "The smell of tobacco can carry a long way."

"So can a campfire."

He shrugged. "Yes. I'm half Sioux, but I'm not savage enough to eat my food raw."

She took a deep breath. "Look, I've seen the way you look at me sometimes. I know you want me."

He didn't smile, and the way he looked at her with those burning eyes almost made her feel naked. "Wouldn't any man?"

She looked away first. "I—I wouldn't know about that."

"Don't be so modest. Kruger is willing to lay everything he owns at your feet to bed you."

She felt her face flush. "Don't be crude."

He shrugged. "Princess, you started this conversation."

Her throat felt dry. She licked her lips. "What—what I

meant to say was, suppose I offer you first chance to bed me as the price for letting me go?"

"Sunny," he said, and there was a trace of a smile on his grim mouth as he threw the unlit smoke into the fire, "why should I bargain for something that I can take anytime I choose to?"

She felt the blood rush to her face at the truth of his words. "I—I reckon so, but wouldn't you rather I be willing?"

He shook his head, and there was a cold, hard expression in his dark eyes. "The only women who've been willing were whores so drunk they'd let me bribe them while they closed their eyes until I was finished." He looked embarrassed and ashamed at the confession.

"But you've had willing women kiss you?"

"With this face?" He snorted.

"Oh." She didn't know what to say.

He looked at her. "Sunny, have you ever been kissed?"

She drew back. "Only a couple of times, mostly on the cheek."

"Then you've had more experience than I've had. Now shut up, and let's bank the fire and go to sleep. Tomorrow's another day."

She wasn't certain why or what, but impulsively, she leaned forward to kiss him.

He jerked away. "What the hell you think you're doing?"

Then she felt foolish. "Never mind." What had she been thinking? "I—I just wondered what it would be like."

"You think I haven't asked myself the same question?" Before she realized what he was doing, he leaned over and kissed her.

For a moment, she froze in surprise, and then his arms went around her and he returned her kiss, taking it over, forcing her lips open to touch the tip of his tongue to hers. She could only gasp at his strength as he dominated her, put his tongue deep into her mouth while one of his big hands covered her breast through the thin blue print of her dress. He was breathing hard, almost as hard as she was, and, abruptly, she was unnerved by the strength and virility of the man. He tasted of salt and wood smoke and sheer maleness as he tangled one strong hand in her pale hair and kissed her deeply, thoroughly. Then he pulled back, drawing ragged breaths.

"You little bitch," he growled as he pulled away from her. "There. Now how far are you willing to go to seduce me?"

She breathed hard, her breasts rising and falling as she remembered the savagery of that kiss. This was a man, a stallion of a man, and she might have awakened something in him that she would fear to unleash. But this might be her way to escape. "I'll let you make love to me," she whispered, "if when it's over, you'll let me go."

He swore. "Get back in that cave, you little tart, before I take you up on your offer."

"Aren't you tempted?" She asked as she turned away.

"Princess, I told you, you can't use as a poker chip what I can take any time I want."

She hadn't realized a woman could have such power over a man; at least, she sensed that she had that kind of power over this man and he was riled by it. "All right." She crept to the back of the cave.

Diablo stared into the fire, still breathing hard. She had affected him deeply like no woman ever had, and the little bitch knew it. She was the most beautiful woman Diablo had ever met, and now he could see why Kruger would give everything he owned to have her in his bed, to put his seed in her so she would give him strong sons. That was one more pleasure he would deny the rancher, Diablo thought with satisfaction. Maybe as he lynched

Kruger, he ought to take the girl right beneath the rancher's feet. Worse than dying would be the thought that your executioner was lying between the creamy thighs of your woman, riding her hard in ecstasy even as you watched and fell to your death at the end of a rope.

No. He winced. He could never be guilty of rape. That would make him no better than the men of the K Bar or his own warrior father.

Sunny watched his back as he hunched in front of the campfire. What was he thinking about? Had he been as deeply moved by the kiss as she had? She might have sealed her fate, and the aroused gunfighter might insist on taking her virginity tonight when he crawled to the back of the cave. The thought excited her, and that shocked her. What kind of trollop was she becoming? He might look like a monster, but she sensed he was all man and could make a woman glad to be a woman and submit to him over and over again.

Her own thoughts shocked her. She was scared and desperate, that was all. It was dark now, and Diablo still sat staring into the fire. The dog, Wolf, lay asleep near him. She looked beyond the cave mouth to where two horses grazed. Could she take one of them? She was an excellent rider, but still a little afraid of the big black stallion. She knew that Hurd had never managed to ride the fiery brute, but Diablo seemed to manage the horse easily. She looked around, trying to make plans. Diablo was wearing his pistol, and the fine rifle lay across his lap, so there was no way to get that.

Worse yet, she had no idea exactly where she was or even if she was still in Johnson County. No matter. If she could find her way to a ranch or stagecoach station, they would know who Hurd Kruger was and help her get back to the safety and the luxury of the life the rancher intended to give her. All she had to do to live this carefree lifestyle was to submit to Hurd's lust and let him bed her whenever his need arose.

That thought made her shudder. So did the idea of kissing him while he ran those big rough hands under her nightgown. Somehow, she was sure his kiss wouldn't excite her or make her come alive as the gunfighter's had.

Very quietly, she crawled toward the fire. Picking up a chunk of rock, she hesitated. If she missed knocking him out, there was no telling what he would do. He might kill her or beat her or even rape her on the spot. She'd always been docile and obedient, but now she had to change and take the initiative for her own safety.

She raised the rock, watching him.

He must have heard her breathing because he whirled away from the fire, throwing his hands up to protect himself just as she brought the rock down on his forehead. He gasped and made a slight sound as he slid to the ground and lay still.

She felt a twinge of shame and regret. She hadn't wanted to hurt him, but there was no other way to escape. At least he was still breathing, though a small wound bled on his dark forehead. Maybe he would be unconscious for a few hours, long enough for her to make it to safety.

Wolf raised his head and whined.

"No, Wolf, you stay here. He's not dead. I've got to leave." Quickly she saddled up Diablo's blood bay horse and mounted up, wending her way down the twisting trail in the darkness. Once at the bottom of the hill, she reined in, listening. No sound from the campsite. Diablo would be in a fury when he awakened and discovered his bargaining chip was gone. She hadn't the slightest idea where she was with clouds now scudding across the sky so that she could not see the stars. She wasn't even sure which way to go, but she needed to put some distance between her and her unconscious kidnapper.

Sunny picked a direction at random and started off at a canter. She was afraid to ride any faster; her horse might step in a gopher hole and break a leg and then she'd be afoot in hostile country with rattlesnakes beginning to come out of their dens in the warm spring. Some said there were panthers and a few bears in this part of Wyoming. She'd never seen any, but that didn't mean there weren't some.

Worse than that, there might still be a few nesters left who wouldn't feel any kinder toward her than Diablo had. She kept riding. Somewhere she'd find a friendly cabin or cowboys out on a roundup—they'd help her, especially for the big reward she was sure Hurd was offering.

She rode for several hours into a wild thicket of brush near a creek. Was that a campfire up ahead?

She smelled smoke and then heard men talking. A horse raised its head and whinnied, and her horse answered.

Now she could see the outlines of two cowboys sitting by a campfire and one of them picked up a rifle and stood up. "Who's there? Show yourself."

Relief flooded over her. Hopefully it was one of Hurd's cowhands.

"Don't shoot! I'm a woman!" She rode into the light of the fire and reined in. Then her blood seemed to freeze in her veins. Both men were dirty and unshaven, but they didn't look like cowboys. "Any chance you two work for the K Bar?"

"We did as gunfighters runnin' the farmers out." The tallest grinned and stood up, his red hair shining in the firelight as he walked toward her. His big spurs jangled loudly. "Almost everyone's gone back to Texas except us."

She had a feeling of unease as she tried to decide what

to do. Her instinct told her she should clear out of here. "I—I've been kidnapped. If you'll take me to Hurd Kruger, I—"

The big man grabbed her bridle with freckled hands, and her horse neighed and stamped uneasily. "Come on down, honey, and join us."

She saw the lust in his eyes too late and tried to slash him across the face with her reins, but he cursed and hung onto her bridle. "You little bitch! I'll make you pay for that."

She tried to gallop away, slashing at him, but he hung onto her bridle. "Hell, Pug, ain't you gonna help me?"

"I'm comin', Buck." The smaller one ran toward her as she fought to get away, her horse dancing in circles as the bigger man hung onto her bridle. And then he reached to yank her from her horse. "Look here, Pug, we got a purty lady, just what we been wantin'."

She bit and clawed as Buck pulled her from her horse.

"Gawd, Buck, that's the girl the big reward is up for." Pug's greasy brown hair was pulled back in a ponytail, and some of his front teeth were missing. The fire reflected off the silver studs on his leather vest.

"Hell, I know that, Pug." He twisted her arms behind her so that she screamed in pain, "But we can sample her a little and then turn her over to that rich bastard. He won't know the difference, and she won't tell, will you, sweetie?"

"Let me go! Hurd Kruger will kill you for this!" She clawed and screamed and bit.

Buck held her close as she fought him. He smelled of dirt and whiskey. "Yes sir, Pug, the lady will be too ashamed to tell him she's used goods, won't you, sweetie? Now stop fightin', and let's get this over with if you want to get home to your rich rancher!"

Chapter 12

Diablo slowly opened his eyes, his head beating like a war drum. His vision blurred, but finally the image of the dog registered on his consciousness. He felt the warm, wet tongue licking his face and heard Wolf's whining. He reached up and touched his head, brought his fingers down to stare at the sticky liquid on the tips. Even in the darkness, he realized it was blood.

Damn that girl. He sat up slowly, his head aching. He remembered then what had happened. He had been careless, thinking her too docile and afraid to attack him. Maybe she had more grit to her than he had thought.

How long had she been gone, and how long had he been unconscious? He wasn't certain, because it was still dark. He staggered to his feet and looked toward the horses. The bay was gone. Maybe she could find her way back to Kruger or at least to someone who would take her to the ranch for the reward. Of course she might run into trouble, a beauty like that out alone on the prairie at night.

Hell, she deserved it. He told himself he wasn't really worried that she might be in danger. Then he swore at himself for being a damned fool because he knew he lied.

The sky now turned cloudy and troubled, the way it

often looked back in Texas when a bad storm was brewing. He ignored the headache and saddled Onyx, then made sure he had his rifle and whistled to Wolf. He started out to track her. If she escaped, he had no way to lure Kruger out to a place where he could be easily ambushed.

With the sky so troubled with building thunderclouds, he wasn't certain he could find directions, but then, she couldn't either. And it was too dark to track her. Then he had an idea. "Wolf, find her for me. You can follow the scent."

The dog whined and put his nose to the ground, sniffing and running in a circle. Then he took off at a run, Diablo and his great horse following him through the darkness.

In the meantime, Sunny fought Buck as he dragged her to a blanket by the fire. What had she gotten herself into? Out of the frying pan and into the fire. "Look," she tried to pull away, "Kruger will pay a big reward to get me back. With that much, you can buy half the girls in Wyoming and plenty of whiskey besides."

The dirty one with the missing teeth and the ponytail laughed. "No deal. Now sweetie, we're gonna have some fun, and then we'll return you. You ain't gonna tell that rich rancher we done took a little sample. Kruger wouldn't like the idea of takin' two saddle tramps' leavin's. He's too proud."

She had to outwit them; they didn't look too smart. She stopped fighting and forced herself to smile with lips frozen in fear. "Well, maybe it will be fun. Why don't we all have a drink first?"

"Now you're talkin,'" the shorter man said and reached for a half-empty bottle.

"You're bein' smart, sweetie." Red-haired Buck relaxed his grip. "You can't escape, so you might as well relax. Who knows? You might even like it."

The two men cackled like crazed hyenas, and she forced herself to keep smiling while she tried to think what to do next. Could she get them both drunk and grab their guns? If nothing else, she could delay this. The sky looked like it might be about to break open in a downpour soon. All she could do was hope she'd get a bit of luck.

They all took a drink, passing the bottle around. She pretended to sip it. Finally Buck seemed to notice. "Hey, Pug, I think the bitch is just stallin' us."

"Oh no," she said, "let's just have another drink, okay?"

"Naw, you've stalled us long enough." Buck wiped his mouth with the back of his hand and lurched toward her, his big spurs jingling.

She tried to elude him, but he grabbed her. She kicked and bit, but he caught hold of the bodice of the blue calico and yanked. The fabric tore, exposing her breasts as she fought to cover her modesty.

But now Pug, the shorter one, was on her, pulling at her skirt. She kicked him hard in the face, and he stumbled backward, cursing. Buck reached up to grab her shoulder, and she turned her head and sank her teeth into his freckled arm.

"God! You little whore! You ain't gonna get away with that!"

However, she was already on her feet and running into the darkness, holding her torn dress to her slender body. Her horse grazed past the two thugs on the other side of the fire, and there was no way she could get to it. Faint thunder echoed through the night. Maybe she could hide, and they'd lose her in the darkness.

Sunny crouched down behind a bush, her breath coming in raw gasps. If they couldn't see her, they could surely hear her. Now she regretted her rash escape from the half-breed. At least he had treated her like a lady, more interested in his revenge than her body.

Silence. She held her breath, listening to the sounds of the two men cursing and walking through the brush. With the spurs and pistols, they jangled like tin cans tied together.

"You see anything of her?"

"I think she went off down that ravine there."

Huddling behind the bush, she prayed. Even if she managed to elude them all night, come morning, they would find her. If she could only reach her horse . . . but it was on the other side of her assailants.

Minutes seemed to turn into hours. Her breath slowed, and she finally quit gasping for air. Maybe she still had a chance to escape. Maybe—

"Gotcha!"

She screamed even as Pug leapt out from behind her and pounced on her like a ragged tomcat on a trembling mouse. "You little bitch, you'll pay for all this trouble!"

She tried to kick and bite, but he was so much bigger than she was. He grabbed her up and slung her over his shoulder, carried her to the fire. "Come on, Buck, I got her!"

Buck sounded like a pile of tin cans striding over to grab her.

Pug snarled as he wiped the blood from his lip and slouched toward the fire. "After she kicked me in the face, she's gonna pay for that. She knocked some more of my teeth out. Lady, you ain't ever been rode like I'm gonna ride you!"

Even as she struggled, Buck threw her down on the blanket by the fire. "God, look at them tits!"

She cowered against the blanket, trying to cover her body with her arms. Her hair hung loose and fell down around her slim shoulders. "Please," she begged. "Please! Kruger will only pay you if I'm returned unharmed!"

Buck guffawed and spat to one side. "We ain't gonna harm you, sweetie—we're just gonna love on you a couple of hours before we take you back. We just want a little sample of what that rich sonovabitch is gonna get."

He reached down and caught the front of her dress she was holding against her breasts and pulled it out of her small hands. "Gawd, you ever see such pale skin, Pug? She's purty in the firelight, ain't she?"

"You know it!" Pug's face was dark with lust as he advanced on her, wiping blood from his mouth where she'd kicked some teeth out.

Buck grabbed the skirt of calico and ripped it away. She wore nothing now but her little shoes and her lacy drawers. The two threw long shadows across her in the firelight as they stood over her. "Now, sweetie," Buck growled, "take off them lace drawers so I won't have to rip them. They probably cost a purty penny."

She trembled but she was also furious. "You'll have to take them off me, you rotten rats! You'll rape me only after I'm dead!"

Both men threw back their heads and laughed.

Pug wiped his eyes. "That's plumb funny. You ain't no good to us dead. Get her, Buck!"

Buck moved in and grabbed her up, tearing at her lace drawers. She bit and fought, but now she was naked and he was running rough, freckled hands over her bare body. "Sweetie," he breathed heavily, "you're worth more than gold or water to a thirsty man. I ain't ever had anything as good as you before!" He twisted her hands behind her back and bent his head to nuzzle her bare breasts.

She moved fast as a rattlesnake to sink her teeth in his ear.

"Goddamn!" He roared. "Come on, Pug, help me hold her down before she eats me alive!"

The two of them had her now, fighting to get her flat on her back. Finally they had her pinned down, and Pug ran his hand down one of her thighs. "She feels like silk."

"What you think she'll feel like on the inside?" Buck laughed and tried to kiss her, and she smelled the sour whiskey on his breath. She managed to turn her head and avoid his wet mouth. They might rape her, but she would do the best she could to bite or scratch, no matter if they killed her in anger later.

"Who gets her first?" Pug asked.

"Why, me of course," Buck snorted. "You hold her for me, and then I'll hold her for you."

There was the sudden whinny of a horse, and the three of them turned to look even as a snarling, furry devil launched itself onto the two men, biting and snarling. They fell back, shouting and screaming in shock.

"Down, Wolf!" yelled a voice, and it was soft and deadly and full of unspoken fury.

In the split second of silence, Sunny staggered to her feet with a sob, not even aware that she was naked. Diablo sat his black horse just inside the circle of firelight, the half wolf lying obediently near the fire where the two drunken men gaped at the sudden surprise.

Slowly, Diablo dismounted, and his hands dropped to his side where his Colt was tied low on his muscled thigh. "Step away from her, you bastards—I don't want your blood to splatter her."

"Diablo!" She saw him only as her rescuer, forgetting that only a few hours ago, she had struck him down and escaped. Now she got to her feet and ran into his embrace. His warm, muscular arms went around her only a brief moment before he thrust her protectively behind him. She clung to his side, sobbing.

He pushed her to the ground behind him, and she clung to his leg, sobbing while he glared at the two men. "All right, which one of you wants to die first?"

"Now, Diablo," Buck forced a grin and gestured. "We're willing to share her."

"I'm not," Diablo snapped. "You're gonna die for putting your hands on her, so draw."

Buck went for his pistol, but he seemed to know he didn't have a chance against the lightning speed of the half-breed. His pistol hadn't even cleared its holster when Diablo's bullet caught him between the eyes, knocking him backward and into the campfire. He was dead before he hit the ground, big spurs rattling.

"Goddamn you, you miserable Injun!" Pug grabbed for his Colt, but Diablo's shot caught him in the heart. The force of the slug knocked him backward. He stumbled several steps and went down, the silver studs on his leather vest reflecting the campfire.

Diablo stepped forward and dragged Buck's body out of the campfire. "I wouldn't let any man burn, because I know what it feels like," he muttered and then strode over to the prone, naked girl. "Are you all right? Did they hurt you?"

In answer, she burst into tears, and he knelt down and scooped her naked body into his arms. "Hush, Princess," he whispered against her hair, "you're all right now. They can't hurt you."

While only hours ago he had seemed like a vicious brute, now he was her protector, and she clung to him, sobbing as she pressed her naked body up against his lithe hard one. "They—they were trying to—"

"I know what they were tryin' to do." His voice was almost a kind whisper, his dark face close to hers as he brushed her pale hair from her eyes. "It's okay now."

She looked up at him and saw the purple bruise and dried blood on his forehead. "I'm sorry; I'm really sorry."

He didn't smile. "You should be—you almost brained me. If I had any sense left, I'd ride away and leave you."

"No!" She clung even harder to him, and he seemed to relent.

"Okay, I know you wouldn't be in this fix if it wasn't for me." Diablo held her close a long moment. Her naked skin felt like pale silk under his hands, and her bare breasts pressed against his wide chest. When he looked down, he saw the roundness of her bare bottom and was aroused in a way no woman had ever aroused him before. Then he remembered that she had nearly killed him, and for a moment, he was angry with her. She deserved to be dragged over to that blanket and used to slake his lust as the two dead gunfighters had been about to do.

Yet the way she trembled in his arms made him want to hold her closer, protect her, cherish her. "What happened to your clothes?"

"They ripped them to shreds." She looked up at him with those big, tear-filled eyes.

"Okay, well, I reckon I can give you my shirt again until we find something better." He let go of her, peeled off his shirt, and stood there a moment, all wide shoulders and massive chest. "Let me help you put it on."

She stood up, realizing to do so would give him a full view of her naked body, but there was nothing else to do. She took the shirt, and he helped her put it on, his arm brushing across her bare nipples as he did so. The touch electrified her, and she froze.

"Damn it, Sunny, move away before I do something you'll regret."

His harsh tone frightened her, and she obeyed him, too aware he was staring at her nakedness as she slipped into his black shirt. It was still warm from his body and smelled of tobacco, wood smoke, and the male scent of him. It was way too big for her, and it fell below her bare hips.

He stepped up to her and began to button it slowly, very slowly, all the time looking down into her face. She didn't flinch away from his ravaged face; she saw only his dark intense eyes and the need there. She noticed his lips trembled.

Now Diablo seemed to take a deep breath for control and stepped away. "God, if only things were different . . ."

She didn't say anything, but she wasn't afraid of him, somehow. She felt a sense of power. "Now what?"

Standing there bare-chested, he turned and looked at the roiling sky. The wind picked up suddenly, and lightning flashed. "There's a storm brewing, maybe even a twister."

He turned toward the horses. She stared at his scarred back and wondered what kind of difficult life he had had that made him so hard and self-reliant.

She looked up at the sky. "Shouldn't we find some shelter then?"

He nodded. "I think your dad's ranch isn't too far from here. Maybe we can still find you some clothes there. Get on your horse."

"Aren't you going to bury these men?" Obediently, she mounted up.

Diablo shook his head. "We don't have time. There's a bad storm comin'. I'll roll them off in the ravine. In the meantime, grab anything we can use like blankets or grub."

She tried not to watch as Diablo took Buck and dragged him away from the fire and over to the ravine. Her torn drawers had lain under Buck, and they were smeared with his blood. She winced, thinking how close she had come to being raped by those two brutes. She gathered up bacon and supplies, extra blankets. The campfire had dwindled to glowing coals.

"You ready?" Diablo ran from pushing Pug into the ravine. "I'm gonna turn their horses loose; we don't need them. Come on, Wolf."

The big animal barked and ran to stand by Sunny, his tail wagging.

"I'm ready." She tried to mount up, but she was too shaky. Diablo strode over, put his hands on her bare hips, and pushed her up into the bay's saddle. She was too weary to be embarrassed.

The wind picked up, and thunder rolled in this distance.

"We'd better get out of here," Diablo ordered. "Don't want to be caught by a twister."

They turned and rode away at a gallop, the dog following along behind. Diablo knew the landscape now, and he turned toward her father's ranch. Would she be able to figure out where they were so that she might escape later? However, when he glanced back, she rode with her eyes closed, as if she were trying to erase all the horrible things that had happened tonight.

Diablo sniffed the wind, his old life as a Sioux coming back to him. There was trouble in the wind, and a light hail began to fall. "We've got to get to shelter!" he shouted over the gale.

Up ahead was the pale outline of a barn and cabin.

"Let's get into the barn!" he shouted and grabbed her horse's bridle, taking off at a dead run for the barn. The horses and the dog made it inside as the hail became as big as white stones, pelting down on the tin roof with a roar. Diablo tried to say something to her, but the crash of the hailstones made hearing impossible. He could see the cabin from here, but the hailstones were piling up like snow outside and it was death to venture out. He reached to help her down from her horse, and his hands slipped and went up under the shirt. Her bare skin was so soft under his dark hands, and he had to take a deep breath.

He signaled to her that they should feed the horses, and they found some baled hay and some grain in a barrel.

The horses were nervous and snorting, but they settled down once Diablo threw them the hay. Wolf whined and lay down on the hay himself.

The hail still pounded, but it had lightened enough to hear each other. "We'll be here a while!" he shouted at her.

"What about my clothes?"

He shook his head. "We aren't going out in that," he nodded toward the open door and the pounding hail. "It would be sure death."

She noticed he was trembling. "Are you cold?" she asked innocently, pulling away from him.

"Goddamn it, no, I'm not cold."

She couldn't understand why he was so angry. "I'm sorry I hit you in the head with that rock."

"That's not it," he snapped and sat down on a hay bale, ignoring her.

She had liked the feel of his strong, warm hands on her bare skin, but of course, she dare not admit that, even to herself. She sat down next to him.

"Damn it, can't you find a seat clear across the barn?"

The lightning crackled and seemed to split the sky outside.

"I'm afraid." Her voice was tiny and she pressed against him.

"You'll think afraid if you don't move away from me," he muttered, but she didn't move, her gaze concentrated on the thunderstorm outside.

"What do you mean?" She turned questioningly toward him, her lips half open.

"Princess, you are the most innocent, damndest—"

"What?" She looked up at him, her lips slightly parted.

His hands went to her waist, and she knew she should pull away, but somehow, electricity seemed to pass between them and she felt rooted to the spot.

His fingers felt like fire burning through the shirt, and his voice came in a hoarse whisper. "You need to stay as far away from me as you can get, otherwise . . ."

She ran the tip of her pink tongue along her lips. "Otherwise what?"

He cursed and pulled away. "Don't you know I could take you right here in this barn?"

"But you won't," she blinked.

"Now what the hell makes you think that?" He got up and strode up and down.

"Because then Hurd wouldn't pay full price to get me back." Her voice was matter-of-fact.

"I told you this was never about money!" He sat down next to her suddenly, sweeping her into his arms, and kissing her, his tongue slipping inside her mouth, dominating it as he held her to him.

She knew she ought to pull away, but she didn't. She felt hypnotized by his closeness and his mouth devouring hers. Instead, she leaned into him, putting her arms around his neck. His mouth forced hers open even more so that his tongue could caress the velvet of her mouth. Then one of his hands went up under the shirt to cover her breast possessively.

She was both surprised and shocked at the sensation that raced through her like the jagged lightning outside cutting through the black velvet of the night. She moaned and did not pull away as he gently caressed her nipple and it swelled into turgid fullness.

Now his other hand slipped from her waist to her thigh even as he kissed her face, her throat. "You little bitch, I can't do this—you're part of my revenge—" But his hands gripped her thighs, forcing them apart, and she wanted him to reach even higher as she clung to him.

The wind and the hail ceased abruptly, and the silence was so deep it seemed to echo. Wolf's ears came up, and he looked toward the outside, whining.

Diablo's head came up, listening.

"What?" She asked.

"Get down!" he shouted and grabbed her, pulled her to the straw-covered floor.

Was he going to rape her? She struggled to get away, but then she heard a sound like a rumbling freight train and the horses reared and neighed and the dog ran over to curl against them.

Diablo threw himself across her, covering her with his own body.

"What?" She tried to get out from under him, and then the roar outside built.

"Twister! Stay down!" he shouted in her ear as the roar increased, and the roof seemed to lift halfway so that she could see the blackness of the sky past his broad, bare shoulder. For a split second, they were showered with timber and straw, and then the roof came back down with a bang, half collapsing as it whirled by.

Diablo looked down into her face. For the first time ever, he looked frightened. "Are you all right?"

She only managed to nod, then turned to look out into the night. "The ranch! My house!"

Even as she watched, a whirlwind of debris wrapped in rain seemed to come out of nowhere, and the house shuddered and began collapsing. Bits and pieces of it and various debris took to the air in a whirl and blew out over the prairie. "My house!" she sobbed, clinging to Diablo, "My house is gone!"

"But we're okay," Diablo said and sat up, shaking splinters

and bits of trash away as he brushed himself off. He stood up and reached down to her. "Are you all right?"

"I—I think so." How could she have been such a fool? If they hadn't been interrupted by a tornado, even now, the gunfighter would be lying on her, pumping hard and kissing her breasts. The thought both terrified and excited her. What kind of slut was she? This was her captor, a paid killer, and her virginity belonged to Hurd, who would take it in their marriage bed. She thought of Hurd bare-chested as Diablo was now and sighed. There was no denying the virility and the power of the half-breed compared to the potbellied, balding rancher.

She took his hand and let him pull her to her feet. Then she ran to the door of the barn. Through the slackening rain, she could see only a foundation. "Our house is gone."

"You're lucky we weren't in it." Diablo said. "Well, I reckon we won't find much left of value."

"I want to look." Before he could stop her, she ran to the house and stood there, looking around.

"Watch out, Sunny, there's broken glass and all sorts of sharp lumber."

It gradually ceased raining, and now she stood here with tear-filled eyes. "There's nothing left to speak of."

"I'm sorry," he said gently and walked up to put his arm around her.

"Daddy always said he had hidden some money so I could go back east to school."

"Maybe he lied to make you happy," Diablo suggested.

She shook her head. "Dad wasn't the lying type. Well, if there was any money, I reckon it's been blown away. It looks like every bit of everything is damaged or ruined."

Diablo thought of the small photo of her in the ornate frame that he carried in his saddlebag. He wanted to tell her there was one thing that hadn't been destroyed, but then she would think he had killed her father. "Let's get out of here, Princess. It's stopped rainin', and they'll be able to track us soon."

"That's all you think of," she turned, flaying out at him, tears in her eyes. "That's all you care about—using me to lure Hurd to his death!"

She beat on his bare chest with both her small fists, and he caught and held them. "Any other man would spank your little bottom and throw you across his saddle," he snarled.

"Why don't you then? Why don't you?"

"Princess, you do try my patience." He picked her up, with her still beating him about the face and bare chest, and carried her out of the ruins of the cabin. He carried her into the barn and sat her down on a hay bale, where she sobbed uncontrollably. "I'll see if I can find you a dress and maybe a shirt for me."

"I don't want you wearing my dad's things!" she screamed at him.

"Okay," he nodded, "I understand. His shirts wouldn't be big enough for me anyway. Just sit here." He turned and strode back to the ruins of the house while she watched; he picked through the rubble and found a pink gingham dress, but not much else.

It occurred to her she could take a horse and try to make a run for it. After all, she knew where she was now. It wasn't that many miles to the K Bar. Then she decided she hadn't a chance of out riding the half-breed. She had never seen anyone ride as well as Diablo did.

In a few minutes, he abandoned his search, got the two horses, and whistled to the dog. Then he walked over and stood looking down at her as she stared at her destroyed house and wept. "It's just a house, Sunny. Hurd will build you a better one."

"You say that, but you burnt the new house down," she snapped. "Wherever you go, you leave a trail of death and destruction behind."

He looked stung, but he frowned and growled. "Yep, that's me. I'm a gunfighter, and I'll die someday in the wreckage I leave in my wake. Now let's get ridin'."

"I won't go."

"But of course you will. I can do anything I want with you, including spanking that round little bottom."

"No." She could feel his breath warm against her face, and she wondered if he would kiss her again, or more.

"It's not as if you have a choice." He swung her up easily in his strong arms and carried her. "It's been a long night, and I'm tired. Try not to try my patience any more."

"And suppose I do?"

He chuckled. "And to think I once pictured you as a shy mouse of a girl. Get on your horse."

She tried to mount, but she was still shaking and she couldn't do it.

"Do you want to ride behind me?" he asked.

"I can ride," she snapped and tried again, "I don't need your help."

"Of course you don't." His voice was gentle. He walked around and tied a bandana around her eyes, lifted her easily up on his big stallion onto the skirt of the saddle. His powerful arms felt comforting.

"I don't need your help," she said again.

"Maybe not, but you're gonna get it, so hush." She heard him whistle to the dog. "I'll lead the bay."

He swung up into the saddle, and she put her arms around his waist so she wouldn't fall off. He clucked to his horse, and they started off. He said, "I put the pink dress I found in my saddlebag. When we get back to the cave, you can clean up in the stream and put it on."

"You don't like me in your shirt?"

"Princess, I only have two shirts, and I'd like that one returned."

She leaned against his bare back as they rode. She could feel every hard muscle and sinew of his lithe body. "I hate you for using me as bait so you can kill people."

He laughed as they rode. "Kill him? Naw, that would be too easy. I'm going to make him beg for me to kill him."

"You don't have a heart."

"More than he does, Princess."

"Why do you keep calling me that?"

"It's a fairy tale. You ever read fairy tales when you were young?"

"Did you?" She was incredulous.

"Mrs. Durango read me some. There's one about a snooty princess who goes about lookin' for a handsome prince."

"All the princesses in the stories were looking for handsome princes," she snapped.

"Then I won't tell you how it ends because you must already know." He sighed, and she wondered what made him so sad.

"Let's see," she mused, "there was the princess who slept on all the mattresses with the pea under them. There was the one whose father, King Midas, turned everything he touched into gold. There was Sleeping Beauty, who fell asleep and didn't awaken for years until a handsome prince kissed her." She shrugged, annoyed that she couldn't make the connection.

He seemed to chuckle and said nothing.

"Think of all the money you could get for me," she said as she leaned against his bare back in spite of attempts to sit upright. She was very tired, and it felt so comfortable to lay her face against his brown skin.

"I'm not after money, I've told you that," he snarled as they rode "I'm after revenge. Sooner or later, Kruger will come lookin' for you."

"Maybe he won't," she said, too aware of the warmth of his body against hers.

"If you were my woman, I would." He reached down and put his big hand over her small ones. "And I wouldn't rest until I found you."

Her breasts rested against his back, and she was conscious of that, remembering that she had let him kiss her when she'd been so afraid of the tornado. "So you're going to use me to lure him out?"

"I said that, didn't I?"

She waited for more, but they rode in silence. "He must have done something terrible to you."

"So terrible, I can't even tell you about it—something no man should do to another."

"Besides killing or torturing?"

"Yes."

She tried to imagine what he might be hinting at, but she wasn't sure she believed him anyway. Hurd had always been so good to her and her father. "How long ago?"

"Fifteen years."

"That's a long time to hold a grudge."

"Not for what he did. I've waited all these years to settle with him and three of his men."

A chill went up her back, and she remembered that two of Hurd's longtime cowhands had been found hanged. Maybe this killer was willing to go to any lengths to get Hurd. If only she could warn him.

She waited for Diablo to say more, but he kept his silence. Evidently this was a taciturn man who was used to a lonely life where he seldom mixed with people.

After a long ride, she felt him rein in, and she heard Wolf barking and dancing about.

"Be quiet, boy," her captor said and dismounted. Then he said, "You can dismount now."

"That's hard to do with a blindfold on," she complained.

"I'll catch you."

She hesitated, but she knew his strength so she slid off the horse. He caught her easily and carried her over and sat her down on a rock. Then he leaned against her to reach behind her and untie the bandana. His body was hard and warm against her breasts, and she felt his breath hot on her cheek. His mouth must be only inches away. Would he kiss her again? Did she want him to? *Sunny, are you loco?* she asked herself.

"There," Diablo said and moved away.

Sunny looked around. They were back at the cave. It was almost dawn.

"I'll fix us something to eat," Diablo said, and she was conscious that he kept his scarred face turned away from her.

If she was ever going to get away from him, it needed to be soon, before he decided she was too much trouble and killed her. Just dumping her dead body on Kruger's doorstep might be revenge enough for this outlaw. "I can help."

He looked at her, distrust in those dark eyes. "All right, but don't get any ideas." He went over and sat on a rock.

Wolf trotted over to join him, wagging his tail. Diablo patted the dog and played with its ears. She saw a rare smile on his chiseled face.

"I bake a better biscuit than you do," she said. "And if you'd shoot me a rabbit, I'd fry it up."

He looked at her a long moment as she reached for the frying pan. "Sure."

He and the dog got up and strode off through the

brush while she made biscuits. In a few moments, she heard a pistol shot, and then the pair came back to the fire, Diablo carrying a fat bunny.

"Well, that was fast," she commented. "I only heard one shot."

He shrugged. "It only takes one."

"Where'd you learn to shoot like that?"

"Trace Durango. He's one of the best shots in the Texas hill country."

"Is he a killer too?"

He didn't answer, only began to skin the rabbit and toss the scraps to the dog. Then he handed her the meat. Their hands touched, and he looked at her. "Is that how you think of me, a killer?"

"How else am I to think?"

"Just cook the damned rabbit." He strode over and washed his hands in the stream, then came back to sit on a rock and watch her cook.

She felt him staring at her as she got the food ready, and it made her nervous and self-conscious. This man had kissed her intimately, and as much as she hated to admit it, she had liked it. Suppose he had liked it too and decided he wanted more? She must get away from him. Maybe tonight she'd have a chance.

Diablo watched her as they ate. "You can cook," he nodded in approval.

"Thanks." She was having a difficult time keeping her eyes open. It was early morning, but she had had such a long, weary night. She tried to keep her eyes open, nodded, blinked, and finally let her empty tin plate slide off her lap as she dozed.

Diablo thought she looked worn-out. Very gently, he picked her up, carried her back into the cave, laid her down, and covered her up. Then he tiptoed out of the cave and sat down by the fire. She might sleep all day if no one disturbed her, and she needed the rest. He thought of the two gunfighters and clenched his fists. If they'd hurt her, there was no telling what Diablo might have done to them. Killing them wouldn't have been enough.

Careful, he chided himself, *you must not begin to care about her. She's Kruger's woman, and don't you forget that.*

Even though he kept reminding himself of that, when he looked at her lying in his big shirt, sleeping peacefully, he wished she belonged to him, body and soul.

Chapter 13

It was late morning at the K Bar as Kruger shouted at a handful of his men in the den. Maria had quit three days ago, and the whole place was already disheveled.

When Joe showed up, Hurd sent the men to the barn, and he raged at Joe. "You weasel! Where is everyone? Looks like half the crew is missin'."

Joe winced away from his anger. "Boss, they're tired of your rages. Some of them have quit. This keeps up, there won't be enough men left to keep the place goin'. You can't keep a ranch this big runnin' without a big crew."

"The ingrates! The miserable bastards! Once I get Sunny back, I'll right everything that's gone wrong around here. It don't matter unless I get her back." He paced up and down, the smoke from his cigar clouding the room and smelling it up like an old saloon.

"But boss, you've put your whole life into this ranch. That tornado last night took out some fences and destroyed three feed sheds. Besides that, some of the shingles are blown off the barn and house, and they'll leak if we don't fix 'em."

"I don't give a damn." He stopped and eyed the running

iron still lying on his mantel. "All I really care about is Sunny."

"There're other girls," Joe said, "and lots of them would be happy to marry you—"

"Goddamn it! I only want her! I've always wanted her. I've built all this for her."

He paused, hearing a horse approaching the ranch, and ran to the window to see a rider galloping up on a gray horse. "Who is that?"

Joe walked up and looked out at the wiry rider. "I think that's Harry Bicker from the Lazy C."

"Maybe he's heard something." Kruger was almost pathetic as he ran out the door to meet Harry. "You got news?"

The wiry man nodded and slipped from his saddle. "Found a campsite about twenty miles from here. Looks like there's been big trouble. You'd better come, Mr. Kruger." Kruger felt his heart lurch. He wasn't in that good of health, and if anything happened to Sunny, if he didn't get her back, he wasn't sure he could survive the shock. The doctor in Cheyenne had warned him his heart wasn't top notch.

"Joe," he yelled, "get the horses quick!"

"But the men were gonna mend those broken fences today, boss, and there's brandin' and—"

Kruger threw a coffee cup at him, and Joe ducked. It crashed against the fireplace and joined the broken whiskey bottles littering the floor. "I don't give a damn about the ranch, not unless I have Sunny here as my wife. Now get some riders mounted!"

In minutes, they were on the trail.

Kruger turned to the Lazy C cowhand as they rode. "What did you find?"

"Just a campsite, Mr. Kruger, but there was a woman's

dress, so I thought she might have been there, and some other signs."

He didn't want to hear any more. In his feverish mind, he imagined Sunny fending off some brute of a nester as he took her down on the ground and raped her. He'd raped a woman or two in his life and even . . . hell, he didn't want to think about that. He was a rich, important rancher, and the victims were nobodies, so that didn't count.

He chewed his lip and spurred his sorrel into a gallop. His beloved bride would have been screaming for help, and he wasn't there to save her. Oh, he'd kill the man who hurt her. She belonged to him, and there was nothing, nothing he wouldn't do to get her back.

It was mid-afternoon with the horses blowing and lathered as Kruger and his cowboys rode with the Lazy C cowboy and arrived at the campsite. At first, he saw only ashes of a cold fire and buffalo grass trampled, as if a fight had occurred.

His heart beat unsteadily as he saw the ragged blue print dress caught in a thicket. He strode over and pulled it free. It was still damp from the deluge of rain, but he recognized it. "Yes, it's hers, all right," he admitted, although his heart wanted to deny it was true. "See what else you can find."

Joe sniffed the breeze. "I smell something dead."

Hurd sniffed the air and had to swallow hard to keep from retching. It must not be Sunny. It couldn't be Sunny. "You men spread out and look."

In a minute, Joe called, "Hey, boss, over here in the ravine, there's two bodies."

Oh, God. Hurd ran toward the ravine though he wanted to run the other way. "Who—who is it?"

"Two men." Joe scrambled down the ravine as Hurd peered over the edge. Joe struggled to turn the bloated bodies over and when he did, he whistled. "Someone's a good shot."

"Who are they?" Hurd peered down and was joined by the other men, who took a breath and backed away.

Joe said, "Looks like two of those Texas gunfighters, maybe the one called Buck and his friend, can't remember his name."

One of the other cowboys scratched his head. "Wasn't his name Pug?"

"Yeah, that's right," Joe nodded. "One's hit squarely between the eyes; the other's shot in the heart. Mighty fancy shootin.'"

Hurd climbed down to have a look. The red-haired one looked surprised, his eyes wide open in his freckled face with flies crawling about his mouth. The other one's ponytail was stiff with dried blood, and he was missing a number of teeth. Hurd coughed at the smell and frowned. "You're right. Nobody but one of them Texas gunfighters can shoot like that."

"I saw one of them in the saloon kill a man," volunteered another, "the one with the scarred face."

"Scarred face?" Joe asked.

"Yeah," the other nodded. "He was dressed all in black—a half-breed, I think. One side of his face looked like a monster, all burned and twisted."

Everyone turned and looked at Hurd. "You hire that one, Mr. Kruger?"

Hurd shook his head. "Don't remember him. No, I don't think so."

He saw a look of growing horror on Joe's face. "Boss, that sounds like the man who took Miss Sunny."

"What?" Now Hurd was very interested.

"Another thing, boss," Joe climbed back up the side of the ravine, "you remember about fifteen years ago—"

"Oh, hell," Hurd snapped as he climbed out of the ravine, "you're lettin' your imagination run wild." Hurd sucked his teeth, trying to remember, but the memory was fuzzy because they had all been drunk. There had been a half-breed kid and three cowboys. . . .

"Well," said the Lazy C rider, "shall we bury them right here?"

Hurd shrugged. He didn't give a damn about the dead bodies. "Is there no other sign of Miss Sorrenson?" he asked, not knowing whether to be disappointed or relieved. Before anyone could answer, he caught sight of a bit of white cotton fabric that had blown into the brush. "What is that?"

The other men turned, but Hurd was already running to retrieve it. As he did, horror mixed with pure rage. "Goddamn it to hell!"

"What is it, boss?" Joe strode over to join him.

Tears came to Hurd's eyes, blinding him. The object was a dainty pair of women's white lace drawers, and they were torn and soaked in blood. He didn't even want to think about what might have happened, but the torn lingerie told a mute story of its own.

The other men saw what he held and sighed, but no one said anything.

Hurd clutched the torn undergarment and closed his eyes. His Sunny, his future bride. At the least, she had been violated. At the worst, she had been murdered too. He managed to get control of his voice. "Men, she's still out here somewhere. I'm raising the reward to ten thousand dollars."

"Is that dead or alive, Mr. Kruger?" The Lazy C cowhand asked, and Hurd wheeled and put all his fury into

his fist as he knocked Harry down. "You sonovabitch!
She's alive, I tell you, and I want her back!"

Harry stumbled to his feet, rubbing his swollen jaw. "I
didn't mean nothin' by it, Mr. Kruger."

Hurd was aware the men around him exchanged
looks and someone mumbled "gone loco," but he didn't
bother to look to see who it was. Maybe he was going
crazy, but he was obsessed with the girl. He had loved
her all these years and now some rascal had taken her
virginity and maybe killed her.

"I want Sunny back alive or her attacker dead, I'll pay
either way. You hear me?"

The men mumbled agreement and turned away.

"Boss," Joe asked, "shall we bury those two now?" He
nodded toward the ravine.

"Hell, no, they had Sunny. Let the buzzards eat them."

"But, boss," one of his other cowboys said, "that don't
seem right, just to leave 'em to rot like that—"

"Leave 'em to rot!" Hurd said and swung up on his
sorrel gelding. "They don't deserve any better!"

He heard grumbling from the men, but he didn't give
a damn. He didn't care if they thought he was loco or un-
christian. He didn't need them; he didn't need anyone
but Sunny. And God protect the man who might be still
holding her captive.

As they mounted up at the campsite, Hurd looked
toward the hills and the mountains beyond. "Has anyone
looked up there in the foothills?"

Joe shrugged. "I reckon they have, boss; I'm not sure.
It's rough country, too rough for white men."

Hurd swore under his breath. "Idiots likely to skip the
obvious. Let's take a ride up there and look around."

One of his men mumbled, "Mr. Kruger, those hills are
pretty steep, and there's snow and ice farther up. It's
nearin' late afternoon now. It'll be at least dusk by the

time we get into the foothills. We might get caught up there in the dark."

"So what?" Hurd snapped. "We can't miss a single hiding place."

He heard more complaining behind him about being hungry and the horses needing water.

The Lazy C cowhand said, "I need to get back to my own ranch."

"Then go and be damned," Hurd slapped his quirt against his saddle. "The rest of us will look around through the hills."

They started off, his men grousing under their breaths, the horses snorting and lathered. Everyone needed rest and food and water, but Hurd decided they'd just have to manage without. He didn't give a damn if they got caught up on treacherous steep trails after the sun set. Any danger was worth it if he could save his beloved.

"Boss," Joe cleared his throat, "you know there're some steep turns and loose gravel trails up there. We oughta wait and start tomorrow."

"No!" Hurd snapped and stared stonily ahead as they rode.

Joe tried again. "We get caught up in those hills, some of these tired horses might lose their footing and it can be a steep drop—a killer. Besides, everyone says those hills are haunted by Injuns white men murdered."

"That's nonsense," Hurd kept riding. "Any man who doesn't want to go with me can draw his pay and get off my ranch before sundown."

More muttering. Jobs were hard to find right now.

"All right," Hurd turned in his saddle and looked behind him. "So we're agreed?"

The men nodded in hostile silence and followed him.

* * *

Diablo, keeping his watch from a big boulder, noticed the snakelike line of riders heading toward the hills. He jumped down and strode over to the girl, who had just crawled out of the cave, yawning. "Change of plans: I've got to hide you."

"Why?" She yawned again.

"Never mind." He was already leading the horses deep into the cave and scattering his campfire.

"But—"

"No time to explain," he said and grabbed her, whirled her around, tied her hands behind her with a rawhide thong. Then he took off his bandana and said, "Open your mouth."

"Why—" She didn't get to finish because he stuffed the handkerchief into her open mouth. She struggled to spit it out, but she couldn't.

Now he picked her up and carried her into the cave. She was only too aware of his hand on her, and she remembered she wore no drawers. She was naked under his oversized shirt.

He lay her down on a blanket in the cave, and she struggled.

"Be quiet!" he ordered. "Wolf will keep you company."

He ordered the dog to stay with her, turned and left.

How dare he? She struggled to untie her hands or spit out the bandana, but it was no use. *There must be someone coming.*

Outside, Diablo quickly brushed out all the tracks and piled brush against the cave opening so it was invisible. Then he took Hurd's prize rifle and climbed back up on his boulder. It would be dark soon, and in his black clothing, they might not see him. He hunkered down and waited for the riders.

They came single file up the trail like ants. Diablo made sure the Winchester was fully loaded; then he sat and waited.

They were close enough now that he could see the leaders. He gritted his teeth in anger as he recognized Kruger in the lead on his sorrel horse, followed by the weasel-like Joe on a white one and a bunch of cowhands. Kruger hadn't changed much in fifteen years except he was heavier and had more lines in his beefy face.

Diablo could easily pick the front-runners off with his rifle. It was tempting, but he had waited too long for his vengeance and he didn't intend to let his torturers off so easily as a quick, clean death.

The men were almost to the campsite now, riding slowly, and by the expressions on some of the faces, they were none too happy to be here. It would be dark soon, and these hills were steep and dangerous to ride at night if you were unfamiliar with the terrain.

He held his breath and watched them ride closer. There were too many of them. He couldn't get them all if they spotted him, but he'd get the first two and that was all that mattered to him. Now they were riding almost below his boulder. If anyone had glanced up, they might have seen him, but no one looked up—every eye was staring around at the trees or the trail ahead. As he watched, the line of riders rode slowly past him and snaked through the hills going away. He watched them go until they had disappeared into the dusk of the night, and then he sighed and climbed down. They would not get out of these hills before dark, and then some of them might not make it down at all.

He pulled the brush away from the mouth of the cave and went inside. Wolf wagged his tail. The girl twisted and seemed to be cursing at him, but of course, her words were muffled. He picked her up and took her outside, sat her down by the fire. Then he led the horses out and staked them under some trees to graze.

She seemed to be screaming at him behind the gag. He stopped and took it out. "Be quiet, can't you?"

"How dare you?" she seethed. "What was that all about?"

"Your bridegroom just led a search party through here, but he's gone now."

"What?" She tried to get to her feet and run up the path, but Diablo reached out and grabbed her. She started to scream, but he clapped his hand over her mouth and they struggled until she bit his fingers.

"Damn," he muttered, "you're worse than a coyote bitch."

"They were here, and you didn't shoot at them? Why not?"

He shrugged as he untied her. "He isn't going to die that easily."

"You're a cruel, hard killer." She glared at him.

"I am that." He nodded. "Now let's cook some beef and eat."

"Where'd you get beef?"

He grinned at her. "Courtesy of your bridegroom."

"They string up rustlers in these parts," she said.

He frowned. "I know that better than you."

Darkness fell over the foothills like a shroud while she went about cooking the steaks and frying some potatoes.

In the distance, she thought she heard a long, terrified shriek. "What was that?"

"Sounds like someone missed a turn in the trail," he said and reached for the coffee. "This is a deadly place to be in the darkness if you don't know the trail."

"White people seldom come up into the foothills," she

said. "There's an old superstition that it's haunted by Indian ghosts."

He nodded as he poured himself a cup of coffee. "I can believe that. Kruger's riders who do manage the trails won't be home until morning, and they'll be so weary and scared, it may take a while to get over it."

She started to say something, then decided against it.

They ate in the dim glow of the fire, and then he leaned back against the rocks, staring into the flames while the dog gobbled the leftovers.

"I'm not used to having anyone to share my fire with," he said, patting the dog. "You cook good." He almost seemed to smile at her, and she took a long look at him. He would have been a handsome man if it were not for the scars on his face.

"Who did that to you?" she asked impulsively.

Now he scowled, and the spell was broken. "I told you, Kruger and his boys. That wasn't the worse thing."

"I don't believe you. Hurd wouldn't do that."

"He's been slaughterin' farmers and nesters for the last few days; what's one half-breed kid to a mean bastard like that?"

She didn't answer, and he stuck an unlit cigarillo in his mouth, petted the dog, and stared at her.

He was a strange man, she thought, almost warm and vulnerable at times, at others, a taciturn and deadly killer.

She was abruptly aware that she wore only his black shirt and nothing underneath. "I—I think I'll put on that dress you got out of my house."

"Let me get it out of my saddlebags."

"I can get it."

"No," he stood up. "I'll get it."

She watched him walk over to where his saddle lay inside the cave. Was there something in those saddlebags he didn't want her to see?

He tossed the pink dress to her.

"I feel dirty," she said as she caught it, "I'd like to take a bath."

"It's turning pretty cold, but there's soap and a towel over by the stream if you want it."

She walked over to the stream and hesitated, pulled off his black shirt, dipped a toe into the water. He was right; it was cold.

Behind her, Diablo moved so that he could see the bare outline of her naked body as she waded out into the creek and splashed water on herself. There was just enough starlight to silhouette her, and he marveled again at how beautiful and ivory her skin was. He had an urge to pick her up, naked and wet from the water, bring her back to the fire, lay her on a blanket, and make passionate love to her. If she belonged to him, he'd fight an army to keep her, do anything to gain her love.

Of course she did not belong to him and never would. He sighed at the thought, then yelled, "Aren't you gettin' cold? You'd better come back to the fire."

She came back in a few minutes wearing the pink gingham dress and carrying her little shoes. "You're right. The water's cold." She sat down by the fire.

She still smelled faintly of lilacs. He looked at her. Her damp yellow hair hung in ringlets, and drops of water clung to the rise of her fine breasts in the low, pink bodice. She put her arms around herself and wiggled her toes. She had tiny feet.

"Are you still cold?" he asked.

Sunny studied him. He was wearing his pistol, and the rifle was leaned up against a log on the other side of the fire. If she could get close enough to him, she could grab that pistol. "I'm a bit cold." She put on her shoes.

"I can get you a blanket out of the cave." He started to get up.

"That's okay." She smiled again as she gestured him to keep his seat. She got up, moved closer to the fire, and then scooted over close to him. "I think this boulder breaks the wind."

She leaned against him, and he put his arm around her, pulled her closer. He sighed as if content, and she leaned back, liking the feel of his big arm around her shoulders. The dog settled down near them, and for a moment, all three enjoyed the crackle and warmth of the fire. "You're not used to having anyone at all, are you?" she whispered.

"No." He looked down at her. "I reckon I could get used to it, though." He snorted and looked away. "Who are we kidding? I'm a loner and always will be."

"That's sad," she said.

He shrugged. "I'm used to it."

Neither of them said anything for a moment, and then she felt him kiss the top of her head very gently. "If things were different . . ." he whispered, but didn't finish.

His pistol was in the holster on his right side, and she was on his right side. She turned ever so slightly and looked up at him. If she could get his pistol, she could hold him at bay until she could mount up and escape. She was an old hand at riding bareback with nothing but a halter to guide the horse.

He looked down into her eyes, and she let her lips part and her eyes close, knowing he would kiss her.

He did, so gently and so slowly that she was surprised, and she leaned into him so he could kiss her deeper still. He held her so tightly she could feel the pistol pressing into her side. Now he kissed her face, her eyes, his lips caressing her. His mouth moved down her neck ever so gently until his lips were brushing the rise of her breasts.

"Sunny," he whispered, "Oh, Sunny . . . ."

At that moment, she grabbed for the pistol. He seemed caught by surprise, and he cursed as they struggled for the Colt. "Why, you conniving little bitch!"

They fought for the weapon, but he was stronger and she knew that any second, he would twist it from her grasp. She was determined that she was not going to let him take it. At that moment, the pistol went off, the sound like thunder in her ears. She smelled burning powder and felt him jerk as he fell backward, a wet, scarlet stain spreading across his side. His brown hand released the weapon very slowly, and he lay there on his back, looking up at her and gasping. "You bitch!" he breathed, "I should have known better than let my guard down."

She stood up, still holding the pistol, but shaking as she stumbled backward. "Oh, my God!"

He lay there, trying to hold in his scarlet blood with his hands while it ran down his fingers. "Go ahead, finish me off—don't leave me to die slow."

She tossed the gun away and knelt by him. "Honest, I didn't mean to shoot you; I was only trying to escape."

"So now you can," he coughed.

Quickly, she assessed the damage. It looked like the bullet had gone clear through, but she couldn't be sure it hadn't hit a vital organ. He might die.

She stood up, trying to decide what to do. He looked up at her, gasping and evidently in pain, but he didn't beg for help or for mercy. He was proud, and his expression was one of disappointment at her betrayal. "I never trusted anyone before," he gasped, "and you're just like the others. . . ."

Oh, God, what had she done? She hadn't meant to hurt him. She stumbled backward, still staring in horror at the wounded man. She needed money. "Do you have any cash?"

"You're—you're gonna rob me, too?"

"Money!" she demanded; then she thought he might have some in his pockets. She knelt and felt through his shirt pockets, found a few coins.

He grabbed her hand, but he was too weak to hang on to her. "I—I trusted you," he gasped.

She stumbled backward, horrified at his blood on her hand. "I'll be back!" she promised and ran for Onyx.

"Sure you will!" he muttered behind her.

She didn't have time to argue. She was a little afraid of the black stallion, but she knew he was the fastest horse and time mattered. She swung up on the big horse bareback and rode away into the night. The dog ran along beside her. She wasn't sure where she was or which way to go. Then she noted that it was a clear night, and her father had taught her how to find directions by the stars.

Should she try to find the riders who were even now on the backside of the hills? She shook her head. Even if she could find them, Hurd would show no mercy to her kidnapper, she was sure of it. Not that she blamed him for his righteous anger, but it seemed wrong to hang or shoot a wounded man.

Out on the prairie, she reined in once to look around and get her bearings. She knew where she was now. Diablo lay helpless up by the cave and couldn't chase her. All she had to do was ride to Hurd's ranch, and she would be safe and Diablo would slowly bleed to death. She wouldn't have to feel guilty about Hurd riding up to kill him. Well, that was all Diablo deserved. She hesitated a long moment, trying to make a decision. Diablo expected her to desert him, leave him to die because he trusted no one, but in a moment of weakness toward her, he had let her get close enough to grab his pistol.

She had to get him some help. She didn't dare ride into the town of Krugerville. Everyone there would recognize her. But the town of Wildfire was just a few miles to the east. She'd only been there once or twice so no one would know her, and she remembered the tiny town had a pharmacy.

She turned east, the dog trailing along with her. It seemed like she rode for hours before the shadows of the dark buildings lay ahead of her, and she rode across the railroad tracks and down the main street. It must be late, but she had no way of knowing the time. She knew a train came through at midnight, but the railroad station and the whole town seemed to be asleep. The pharmacy was dark, but there was a light on in the living quarters above. She tied up her horse and threw gravel against the upstairs window. No response. Again she threw gravel. A man with tousled gray hair pushed up the window and leaned out. "What do you want?"

"I need some medicine."

"I'm closed. Can't you come back in the morning?"

"No, I need it now."

"All right. I'll be down." Still fussing, he closed the window.

In a moment, through the front window, she could see him coming down the stairs in his nightshirt, pulling up his pants as he came. He carried a lamp as he walked to the door and unlocked it. "Awful dark for a young lady to be out."

"Never mind that, I need some stuff." She pushed past him and into the pharmacy. It smelled faintly of dust and strong medicines.

He sighed and set the lamp on the counter. "What do you need?"

"Some kind of medicine for wounds and some bandages."

"Oh?" He looked curious as he busied himself getting things off the shelves, but she didn't explain.

"You live around here?" he asked as he totaled up the purchases and ran his hand through his unkempt hair.

"Um, yes," she said. "How much do I owe you?"

He handed her the sack and the bill.

She ignored his curious stare as she paid him and took the sack. "Thank you very much." She turned and left the store, mounted up, and rode out. In the distance, she heard the lonesome wail of a train whistle as the locomotive chugged toward Wildfire. It must be near midnight then, but she'd be lost in the depths of the night before the train came through town. She headed toward the foothills.

The storekeeper had followed the mysterious girl in the pink dress to the door and locked it behind her, grumbling to himself. "Could have come in during business hours, but no, got to get me when I'm headed for bed. Homer Bledsoe, you're an old softie." He yawned and returned to get his lamp, stumbled up the stairs. "Wonder if she was from around here? Seemed familiar, somehow."

In the distance, the incoming train whistled, but he knew it wouldn't stop unless a passenger was getting on or off, which wasn't too likely. Homer pulled off his pants and blew out the lamp, got into bed. The train chugged on through town, whistle blowing a warning. Then the sound faded slowly as the train kept moving. Homer listened to it fade, and after a long moment, he drifted off to sleep.

Sometime near dawn, a howling wind woke Homer Bledsoe up. There was something else that came to him. He sat up abruptly in bed, wide awake. "There was a poster. . . ."

Quickly, he got up, lit his lamp, and went down the

stairs in his nightshirt. He stumbled through the darkness to his bulletin board, stubbed his toe, and hopped, cursing. When he reached the board, he held the lamp up high, peering at all the posters and announcements posted there.

"Ah, there it is." He put on his spectacles and leaned closer.

MISSING AND FEARED KIDNAPPED. BEAUTIFUL BLOND GIRL WITH BLUE EYES. BIG REWARD. REPORT TO K BAR RANCH.

"Big reward. Wonder how much?" He sighed and took off his spectacles. Five hundred dollars would be a fortune to him. But suppose he was mistaken? He'd heard about the owner of the K Bar, a stern and formidable man. Suppose he got that man all upset and it turned out it was the wrong girl? Besides that, he'd have to close his store for the day and lose that profit. Well, the big reward was worth the risk. He grabbed his lamp and headed for the stairs. He'd get dressed and drive over to the K Bar. If he kept a steady pace, he might get there a little after noon.

Sunny had left the pharmacy and followed the stars back toward the foothills. The wind picked up and blew dust against her face so that it stung her delicate skin. Had the man at the pharmacy recognized her or heard about the kidnapping? There was no way to tell and nothing she could do about it anyway.

She paused, confused, and looked down at the dog. "Wolf, can you take me back to the cave?"

The dog looked up at her, whining and wagging its tail.

"Come on, Wolf, we've got to get back to Diablo."

The dog barked and took off at a trot. Did he know

where he was going? There was nothing she could do but trust Wolf to find their way through the windy, dusty night.

"I must be the world's biggest fool," she muttered as she rode. "I've spent days planning on how to escape, and once I have, I'm going back to help the gunfighter. I ought to leave him to die."

She should, but it wasn't in her heart to desert a hurt man. What if he had already died by the time she got there? Sunny shrugged off that possibility and kept riding, closing her eyes against the blowing grit. She hadn't meant to shoot him, only get control of his pistol, and she'd sure rather not have his death on her conscience.

It seemed like forever that she followed the dog through the howling darkness, and then Onyx was climbing the hill to the cave.

The campfire was down to glowing embers. She tied up the horse and grabbed her sack of medicine. "Diablo, can you hear me? Diablo, are you all right?"

He moaned softly, and she knelt by his side. His eyes were closed, and his pulse was thready. His bare skin had so much blood on it she gasped.

He felt cold and shivered when she touched him. The first thing she'd better do was build up the fire and get him warm. Even then, she might not be able to save him.

He moaned and thrashed about, said something in a whisper so low she could not understand. *He must be delirious.* What on earth was he dreaming about? From the way he was fighting and muttering, it must have been a horrible nightmare.

Chapter 14

In Diablo's fevered mind, he was once again a Santee Sioux slave, only fourteen winter counts old, and he was running away on this early spring morning. Everyone around the camp was busy, including the grumpy old woman who owned him. He was called He Not Worthy of a Name, and if he were caught, he would be beaten severely as he had been in the past. His back was already crisscrossed with whip scars, and he had decided he had had all the punishment he could take and the risk was worth it.

He went out the back of the teepee and crawled into the brush. At any moment, he expected a cry to go up that he had been missed. His heart seemed to be in his throat as he crawled through the dirt and tall grass, putting more distance between him and the camp. He was hungry, but then he often was. As a half-breed slave, he was always the last one fed. His owner was the mother of one of the warriors hanged because of the uprising, the warrior who had been He Not Worthy of a Name's father. She beat the boy often and blamed him for her warrior son's death.

Now the boy was at least a hundred feet from the encampment. At any moment, he expected to be discovered and whipped, but so far, no one had set off any shouts of alarm. Finally, he got the nerve to stand up and look behind him. The camp was quiet, the horses grazing, small children laughing and playing. He had never been allowed to play. Even when he could barely toddle, he had been made to work, carrying firewood and water, skinning game that the others ate before throwing him the scraps.

As he watched, he wondered where to go and what to do with his new freedom. No other tribe would take him in; they might return him to his owner. He had been to the trading post a few times and spoke a few words of English, but he did not think the whites would welcome him either. Hadn't his white mother's family given him to the Indians after she killed herself?

He did not know where to go, but he knew he must put as much distance between him and the Santee as possible or his life would be even more miserable than before. For the next dozen days, he traveled west, not knowing where he was going and not caring. He was starving and weak when he crossed a stream and drank and drank. Along his journey, he found a few acorns and roots to eat and even dug out a mole and caught a gopher. He knew how to make fire, but he was afraid the scent of the smoke would draw the attention of a Sioux hunting party, so he ate the small animals raw.

Finally, one afternoon, he was so weak he decided he could go no farther. The night had been cold, and he had found a cave up in the foothills. There he had crawled under some fallen leaves, attempting to stay warm. He knew if he did not get food soon, he would be too weak to keep walking. It was tempting just to sit down in the woods and give up, but his will to live was stronger. He had not survived all these years as a slave to surrender and die now.

In another day, he was imagining things. The Great Spirit came to him and told him he would live. The spirit of his father, the Sioux warrior whom the white soldiers had hanged along with all those others, came to him and said he did not blame him. It had been the crooked Indian agent back in Minnesota who had been responsible for the great uprising that Taoya-Teduta, Little Crow, had led.

His eyes blinked open. It was morning again. He had no idea how far he had traveled over the last dozen suns, but his shoddy moccasins were worn through and his bare feet were raw. Every step was painful and left a bloody imprint. His rib bones stuck out like the skeletons of the disappearing buffalo that lay on the prairie from the white hunters' slaughter. All the Indians were beginning to go hungry the last few years.

He took a deep breath to make sure he was still alive and thought he smelled meat cooking. He must be imagining things again in his delirium. He took another sniff and thought it was the best smell he had ever smelled. He was tempted just to lie here and die, smelling the imaginary meat and pretending he had all of it he could eat, but his will to survive was strong and he struggled to his feet and limped down the twisting, crooked path from the cave. Somewhere ahead lay life-giving food. His feet bled as he walked, but he knew he could not stop. To stop was to die.

He did not know how long he walked through the brush, the stones and broken twigs cutting into his sore feet, but he knew it was a long, long time. He sniffed the wind like an animal and followed the scent that floated on the air. Yes, someone was cooking meat. His dry mouth salivated as he followed the smell. Probably at the end of the wind he would find a hunting party, which would return him to the old woman whose son had fathered him, but he was so hungry he did not care.

In the shadows of late afternoon, in a clearing under three cottonwood trees, he peeked around a boulder and saw three white men sitting by a campfire. Their three horses grazed beyond the clearing. A butchered steer lay nearby, and they were cooking strips of beef on sticks over the fire. They laughed and talked with each other as they drank strong coffee from their tin pot and cooked fried bread in the coals.

He watched them gorge on the food while he licked his lips. He was so weak he swayed a little, but he was careful not to let them see him. No white man at the trading posts had ever been kind to him, and so he did not expect these to be.

They were in a good humor and laughed and poked at one another.

"Hey, Tex, you think the owner of the K Bar minds us helpin' ourselves to a few of his steers?" the very skinny one asked and grinned.

"Hell," said the weathered one called Tex, "he's got thousands of them, Slim. He probably won't even miss us stealin' a few."

The third one, an older fellow, looked around nervously. "I don't like it, hombres—rustling cattle is a hangin' offense."

"Aw, Dusty, don't be so scary," Slim said and took another bite. "Likely he wouldn't begrudge hungry men one steer and sellin' a few more so we'll have money enough to get back to Texas."

"Ah, Texas," sighed Tex, "Wyoming is too damned cold. If we can just get train tickets back to Texas."

"Heaven on earth," Dusty nodded, "but I reckon the owner of the K Bar won't feel like buyin' us tickets. He catches us with a running iron, he might hang us on the spot."

"Oh, shut up and eat, partner," Slim snorted, "then we'll finish changin' them brands."

He Not Worthy of a Name watched them eat, licking his dry lips. He had hoped they would be leaving soon and he could eat their scraps or chew the bare bones they threw away, but it appeared they were going to stay a while. One of them took a long iron rod and put it in the fire and nodded toward the cattle grazing on the prairie just past them. "Yep, boys, we'll rustle just a few and go back to Texas."

The boy was so weak he swayed, and when he did, the grass around him rustled.

"Who's there?" Slim was on his feet, pistol drawn. The other two jumped up, reaching for rifles.

Should he run or let them kill him where he stood? He was too weak to run, although he took a couple of tottering steps.

"Come out of there, or I'll kill you!" Slim ordered.

There was no use to run. He put his hands in the air and stumbled out of the brush. They would kill him now. He only wished he had managed to get a bite of their food before he died.

"Why, it's just a half-breed kid!" Dusty said and stood up.

"Looks like he's about done in," Tex said. "Kid, who are you?"

He swayed on his feet, weak and dizzy. He was proud; as he had not begged when the old woman beat him, he would not beg now as they killed him. "I—I am Not Worthy of a Name."

"Are you hungry?" Tex asked.

He only managed to nod as he collapsed by their fire.

Immediately, all three gathered around him. "Good God, look at his feet and those scars on his back," said Slim.

Another held a tin cup of water to his parched lips. "Where are you from, kid?"

He gulped the water gratefully. Maybe they would feed him before they killed him. He tried to remember a little

English. "I—I am running away from the Santee Sioux camp. I was a slave there."

"Get him some meat, Dusty," Tex ordered as he poured a tin cup of coffee and put a lot of sugar in it. He held it to the boy's lips.

He knew about sugar, but he had never been allowed any. The coffee was strong and sweet, and he almost gulped it, even though it burned his mouth and felt warm all the way down.

"Easy, kid," Tex said, "would you like some food?"

He could only nod, not believing his good luck. These men were being kind to him. No one had ever been kind to him before, not in his whole life.

He struggled to sit up, and Dusty handed him a tin plate of beans and roasted beef and fried bread. He ate so fast he choked on some of it.

"Take it easy, kid," Slim said, "there's plenty more where that came from."

He did not know if they would kill him later; he only knew that right now they were feeding him. He gulped more coffee and ate three more plates full before he sighed and wiped his mouth with the back of his hand.

"What are we gonna do with him?" Slim asked the others. The men lay back against logs, enjoying the fire, smoking hand-rolled cigarettes and sipping coffee.

"We could take him with us to Texas," Tex suggested.

He struggled to find a few words of their language. "What is—what is Texas?" he asked.

"What is Texas?" all three asked, wonder in their eyes.

"Why, boy," drawled Slim, "Texas is heaven, the Happy Hunting Ground. It's a big, big land, and the weather is warm there, not like Wyoming, where it's colder than a mother-in-law's heart."

"That's right," old Dusty agreed. "All cowboys want to go to Texas—it's God's country. We came up here on a cattle drive, and now we're tryin' to get enough dough together to take the train back south."

"Dough?" the boy asked and sipped his coffee.

"Money, wampum. We figure we'll use this here runnin' iron," Slim indicated the rod in the fire, "to change a few brands on some steers and sell them."

He knew stealing meant trouble. It had happened to a couple of braves of the tribe. "You steal the cattle?"

"Just a few," Tex drawled. "We hear the K Bar is the biggest outfit in Wyoming, so he won't miss a few since he's got thousands. We got to change the brands. That's what a running iron is." He pointed to the metal bar heating in the campfire.

"Can—can I go with you to Texas?" he asked, hardly daring to hope. It sounded warm and wonderful, with plenty of food. All they had to do was head south.

The three looked at each other.

"If we take him, we'll need more money," Dusty complained.

"What'll happen to him if we leave him behind and the Sioux catch him?"

"They'll kill me," the boy said. "Take me to Texas. I will be your slave if you will."

Tex laughed. "We don't need no slave, boy. You help us with the brandin', and we'll take you. You can be our compadre."

He blinked, puzzled.

"Friend," Tex explained. "Ain't you ever had a friend?"

The boy shook his head.

"Well, now you got three. We look out for each other and share whatever we got."

The three cowboys grinned at him, and he felt warm inside. It was good to have friends, and they would all go to this Happy Hunting Ground called Texas. He already loved the place without ever having seen it.

Tex said, "Slim, rope us a couple of steers, and Dusty, you build up that fire so we can use this runnin' iron."

He Not Worthy of a Name smiled for the first time he could remember. He had never been so happy. He had friends, men who liked him and would help him. They would all go to this wonderful place called Texas, and it would be warm there and there would be enough to eat. Better yet, he would have freedom.

They never got the first steer branded.

About the time they dragged a bawling steer to the fire, a voice thundered, "All right, stick 'em up! You damned rustlers are gonna learn your lesson."

He did not understand what was happening, but the three cowboys put their hands slowly in the air and there was a look of fear on their faces.

"You too, half-breed," the voice ordered.

He put his hands in the air as five men on horseback rode out of the shadows and into the light of their fire. The late afternoon dusk threw weird shadows on the surrounding brush.

The big one with the black hair and mustache held a shotgun, and as he dismounted, he swayed a little.

The boy smelled the liquor on the man and looked at the others. They all seemed to be under the influence of firewater.

"Honest, mister," Tex said. "We was only gettin' one scrawny steer, we was hungry."

The big man swore an oath and knocked Tex down with the butt of his rifle. "I ain't loco, I see that runnin' iron. Now Joe, you and Wilson and Smitty tie 'em up."

The fifth man was an older man with light hair and pale blue eyes. "Now, Hurd, let's not do anything we're gonna regret."

"I ain't gonna regret a thing," the man called Hurd said, and there was anger in his dark eyes. "You rustlers been helping yourself to K Bar cattle too long. Now I'm Hurd Kruger, and I own the K Bar. You know what happens to rustlers."

The older man got off his horse. He'd been drinking, too, the boy thought, but maybe not as much as the other four. "Hurd, why don't you have your men take them into Buffalo and turn 'em over to the sheriff?"

The mean one called Hurd swayed on his feet. He was more than a little drunk, as were his cowhands. "No, Swen," Hurd snapped as he watched his men tie up the three men and the boy, "I need to send a message to every rustler in the county. I ain't sweated and slaved to build the K Bar so every worthless Texas saddle tramp can come in here and steal from me. You men put these damned thieves on their horses."

"Mister," said Slim, "we was just hungry and tryin' to get back to Texas, honest. We're real sorry."

"Not sorry enough," Kruger said, sucking his yellow teeth.

"Hey," said Slim, "the kid didn't do nothin'. He just showed up an hour ago, and we fed him."

Hurd threw back his head and laughed. "So he was eatin' my beef, too? He lies down with dogs, he gets fleas. He's a rustler as far as I'm concerned."

"Now, Hurd," Swen argued, "you ain't really gonna lynch these four? Why, that boy can't be more than twelve or fourteen."

Joe snorted. "He'll grow up to be a rustler like the rest of 'em."

Wilson nodded. "We don't need no more half-breeds in this county, do we, boss?"

"Hell, no!" Hurd spat to one side. "Put 'em on their horses, boys."

Tex protested, "Okay, we got it comin', but the kid just happened along. Let him go."

"Yeah," added Dusty, "he's just a boy, and it ain't right to lynch a kid."

"If his belly is full of K Bar beef," Hurd growled, "that's good enough for me. Tie 'em up and put 'em on their horses, boys."

"You can't do this," the older man, Swen, protested. "Let's turn them over to the sheriff."

The men were forcing the Texans up on their horses. Joe threw three ropes over sturdy cottonwood limbs.

Kruger growled, "The law of the range is that you hang horse and cattle rustlers, and we got them dead to rights."

"You can't do this," Swen protested again.

"Just watch me," Kruger smirked and nodded to his men to adjust the ropes around the three Texans' necks.

Smitty grinned. "The boy don't seem to have a horse. How we gonna hang him?"

Wilson guffawed. "I reckon we could just haul him up an inch at a time so he'd strangle instead of breaking his neck quick."

"No, don't hang my friends!" The boy struck out at the K Bar cowhands, and Joe grabbed him and slapped him. The boy bit Joe's hand, and the man struck him until his mouth bled. "You little red bastard! We'll deal with you later."

He could only lie on the ground in a daze as he watched the scene. Swen was protesting again. His Texas friends had their heads bowed, muttering prayers.

Tex opened his eyes and straightened his shoulders. "Kid, I'm mighty sorry we got you into this."

"If we're gonna die," Slim said, "we'll go out like Texans, like men, not beggin' or cryin'."

The boy felt tears come to his eyes. He finally had friends but this ranch owner was going to hang them. Hanging was a shameful way to die. Real men should be killed with a bullet or an arrow. Every warrior knew that if a man was hanged like the white men had done the Santee warriors at Fort Lincoln, his spirit could not escape up his throat and out of his mouth as he died and would be trapped in his dead body forever. That was how his warrior father had died for raping his white mother.

He turned and looked again at the older man with pleading eyes, but said nothing.

Swen begged, "Hurd, let's not do this. We've all been drinking in town. If we was sober—"

"If we was sober," Hurd muttered, "I'd still hang 'em."

"But at least don't hang the boy," Swen argued. "He's just a kid."

"All right," Hurd agreed and swayed on his feet. "We'll hang the men, but that boy ain't gettin' off scot-free. We'll teach him a lesson he won't forget. Joe, make sure that runnin' iron is hot."

Swen's face paled. "Aw no, Hurd, you can't—"

Hurd hit him then with the butt of his rifle and knocked him to the ground. The man lay there unconscious. Kruger looked down at him. "You may be my best friend, Swen, but you don't know how to maintain order in this wild country. You're too soft to be a rancher."

Now he turned back to his cowboys. They were as drunk as he was, grinning and unsteady on their feet. "All right, boys, show these three Texas sonovabitches what we do with rustlers in Wyoming."

"No!" the boy shouted, but Hurd knocked him down and gestured to his men.

"Okay, boys, let 'em dance on air!"

"The kid didn't do nothin'," Tex protested. "For God's sake—" Then his words were cut off as each of Hurd's men slapped a cowboy's horse on the rump and the startled horses ran out from under the Texans.

He couldn't do anything to help his friends. He could

only watch as the three Texans hit the end of their ropes, like sacks of sand under their full weights. They swung there, the ropes creaking, their boots jerking as they died. The four men on the ground grinned and nodded.

The boy looked toward the older man with the sandy hair. Swen was unconscious, so there was nothing he could do to help.

Now the big man with the black hair and mustache turned toward him. "And now you little half-breed bastard, we'll teach you a lesson."

"Let's all have another drink," the one called Wilson staggered over and got a bottle out of his saddlebags. Behind him, the three Texans swung, throwing strange shadows across the landscape as dusk came on.

"Good idea," Kruger grinned, and they handed the bottle around.

Smitty looked at the swinging Texans. "Shall we cut 'em down and bury them?"

"Naw," Kruger said, "leave them to hang there 'til they rot as a message to any other rustlers that might take a likin' to K Bar beef."

The boy watched them pass the bottle around again. What were they going to do to him? He was not going to beg. If they were going to kill him, he could die with dignity as his three friends had.

The man called Kruger grabbed him and shoved him to the ground. "You know, this kid is almost purty enough to be a girl."

Joe laughed and swayed. "Hey, boss, we didn't get any gals in town."

"Maybe he'll do," Kruger laughed, and his eyes were hot with angry lust. "Flip him over on his belly, Wilson, and you other two hold him down."

"Gawd," Smitty licked his lips over and over, "I ain't never done nothin' like this before."

Wilson laughed as he grabbed the boy. "Who's to know? Just us, and Swen's not gonna object."

Kruger began to unbuckle his belt. "We'll all get a turn, and then we'll mark him so other ranchers will know he's a rustler."

What they did to him over the next few minutes was too shameful to remember. He only knew that finally Kruger sighed with satisfaction and said, "He was almost as good as a girl. Now flip him over on his back, Wilson."

The man jerked him by his arms. It hurt, but he did not cry out as they turned him. He looked up at the four white men.

The one called Smitty grinned. "What you got in mind, boss?"

"Well, Swen was havin' such a fit about hangin' him, so we'll do something else to make sure he remembers not to steal K Bar cattle again."

The men all stared down at him. What they had already done was so shameful he did not care if they killed him now. No matter what they did, he would not cry out or beg. Maybe they were going to kill him slowly the way the Sioux sometimes did their captives.

"Yes, sir," the big man with the black hair and mustache said, "we'll teach him a lesson he won't forget, and any other rustler who sees him will know better than steal cattle. Joe, hand me that runnin' iron."

He saw the cowboy reach for the glowing rod. The others held him down so he couldn't struggle.

"Boss," asked Joe, "you gonna brand his rump or his back?"

"Neither." Kruger grinned, "Let's mark his face so everyone who sees him will know what happens to rustlers in Wyoming."

"Kind of a shame to mark his face," Wilson said. "He's handsome, even if he is a half-breed."

Hurd laughed. "He ain't handsome for long."

The boy watched as Hurd took the running iron. It glowed scarlet from the flames. He could smell it and feel the heat as Kruger brought it closer.

"Hold him, boys."

The others laughed, and now as he realized what the rancher intended to do, he struggled and tried to get away. However, all four men were big and strong, and they held him as the iron came closer. Then Hurd pressed it to his right cheek. He heard it sizzle and burn flesh. He tried not to cry out, but he couldn't stop himself.

Kruger and the others laughed.

Then Joe stumbled away, retching.

"What's the matter with you?" Kruger complained. "You soft?"

"I never seen a man branded before," Joe gulped. "It smells like burnin' meat."

"Well, I ain't through." Kruger said, and turned back to his victim. "That'll teach you to take up with Texas rustlers, boy. Hold him, men, I'm ain't through yet."

The boy struggled while the men laughed. He could not escape as the rancher put the burning iron on his face again and again. He felt as if the whole right side of his face were on fire. He had never known such pain. He bit his lip to keep from screaming, but he bit his lip through and it bled all down his chin and neck.

He felt Hurd put the hot iron on his cheek again, but he was past pain even though he smelled the burning flesh, heard the sizzle of the iron. Then he passed out.

When he woke up, they had wearied of the torture and were drinking again. The boy had never known such agony, but the pain told him he was still alive. He kept his eyes closed and pretended to be unconscious.

"What'll we do with him, boss?" he heard Joe say. "Want me to put a bullet in his brain?"

"Naw. He probably won't live anyway, but if he does, I want him to be a walkin' ad for what happens to rustlers."

"We ought to be gettin' back to the ranch." Wilson hiccoughed. "It's dark now."

"You're right, Kruger swayed on his feet. "Swen's beginnin' to come around. Help me put him on his horse."

"He ain't gonna be happy when he wakes up," Joe said.

"So what can he do about it?" Kruger snorted. "Swen's too soft. He couldn't even be a rancher if I didn't lend him money and give him advice. Let's go home; I'm gettin' a headache."

The boy watched out of the corner of his eye as the four threw the unconscious Swen across his horse. Then the group rode away, laughing and singing a drunken song.

After that he must have passed out. When he awoke, he lay there a long time, fearing the men would come back. He wanted to die from the shame the men had inflicted on him. His face felt as if it were on fire. Finally in the darkness, he managed to get to his knees and crawl through the brush to a nearby creek. He drank deeply and plunged his face into the cold water, which gave him temporary relief.

At least he was alive. The Sioux couldn't kill him, and the white rancher couldn't either. Through his pain he felt the bitter anger and need for revenge. If he lived, he would kill these men someday.

Right now, his main goal was to stay alive. He dipped his aching face in the stream again and again. Then he crawled back to the fire and searched out any scraps of leftover meat and ate them. The fire had died down to glowing coals. He was cold, but he was afraid to build up the fire, afraid the white men might see it and return. The moon came out and threw grotesque swaying shadows from the three cowboys hanging from the tree limbs. When the wind blew, the bodies swayed in the breeze, and the ropes creaked. Somewhere in the distance, a wolf howled.

He wasn't certain what to do. He was too weak to walk, and the cowboys had taken his three friends' horses. He wanted to take them down and give them warriors' burials as befitted brave men, but he didn't even have a knife to cut the ropes.

He crawled back into the brush and raised his hands to the Great Father, praying for help. He was weak and in pain, and he knew he had reached the end of his journey. He did not want to give up, but he did not know where to go and had not the strength to travel anyway. Maybe he should just lie down and die and end his shame and suffering.

"Give me guidance, Great Spirit, and I promise I will seek vengeance against these men who treat other men like the lowest dogs instead of brave warriors."

He would dig graves with his bare hands, thinking somehow, he would get the bodies down. He tried to dig, but the ground was hard and after a few minutes, he stopped, exhausted. He would have to rest a while and then try again.

Now he heard a noise and fell silent, crawling back into the grass and crouching as close to the ground as he could get. If they were coming back to kill him, there was nothing he could do but hide—he was too weak and injured to run.

Soon the noise grew louder, and he recognized the sound of horses walking. One of them snorted, and another one neighed.

He held his breath and peered through the grass as Swen rode in near the old fire. He led a pack mule and another horse. As he reined in, he looked at the hanging men and cursed, long and loud, and maybe he sobbed a little.

Then he dismounted, and as the boy watched, Swen cut the three Texans down and got a shovel from the pack mule. "What kind of bastards won't even give men a decent burial?"

The boy watched from his hideout as Swen buried the three Texans and then leaned on his shovel. "Liquor," he muttered. "It might not have happened if we hadn't been drunk. Oh, God, forgive me."

The boy wasn't sure whether to show himself. He wasn't sure what Swen intended to do now. The older man fashioned three crosses from crude branches and then put them in place, took off his hat, and bowed his head. He murmured a few words and then turned to look around. "Boy, are you out here? Boy, can you hear me?"

The boy watched him from his hiding place and said nothing. He was afraid to trust any white man now.

Swede called again, then sighed. "All right, if you're here, I'm leaving you a horse and a pack mule of supplies. Better get out of this area before sunup—no telling what Hurd and his men will do next. If only I wasn't so indebted to him . . ."

He sighed and mounted up, leaving the horse and pack mule tied to a tree.

Could the boy trust the man? He waited a long time to see if there was an ambush before he crawled out of the brush. His face burned so badly he wanted to scream, but that would only bring predators, human and animal.

He stumbled over to the three graves and couldn't control the tears that came, only adding to the pain of his burned face. He had had three friends for only a couple of hours, and now he prayed for the Great Spirit to bless them and take them on their Sky Journey to where brave men are never cold and hungry and they ride spirit ponies through the clouds forever and ever.

It would be dawn in an hour or so, and he must leave

here. He untied the horse and mounted up, tied the pack mule to his stirrup, and started away. He did not know where to go, but he had to escape both the Sioux and the whites, who might return to torture or kill him.

He looked up at the stars, undecided. Which way to go? Then he remembered his friends and what they had said about Texas. It was a long way south of here, but it was a big land of much happiness and lots of pasture. There would be horses and cattle, and the weather would be warm. He would go to Texas for his three dead friends. He headed south.

For several days, he was half-conscious as he rode, but the horse kept plodding south. His face was agony, but he stopped and splashed cold water on it and kept riding. Sometimes he would go to sleep in the saddle and fall off, but the well-trained horse would wait patiently for him to rouse himself and remount.

Days passed and then weeks. The pain in his face lessened, but then it was replaced by fever. He had used up all the supplies Swen had given him, and so finally, when the pack mule stumbled and fell, and could go no farther, he ate it. Then he rode on, always making sure he was headed south as the days warmed into summer.

Finally his horse gave out and died, and he took his knife and ate the horse raw. The next few weeks, he lived on the few rabbits he could snare or the gophers he managed to catch. He ate snakes and frogs and anything he could find to fuel his ravaged body. Then he began to walk south again on his scarred feet. He did not know if and when he would reach Texas or how he would know it if he did, but he had no will or thought to do anything else now except haul himself to his feet and stumble on south as the days grew hotter.

Autumn was turning the leaves to red and gold as he passed mountains in the distance to the west and kept walking. Then the landscape became endless plains. He was nearly dead from thirst and starvation when he stumbled on the Triple D herd. He knew the punishment for killing the white man's cattle, but he was too hungry and tired to care. He killed one with his knife and was eating it raw when the cowboys rode up and the one called Trace Durango found him. He thought they would kill him or torture him for stealing their beef, but the boss instead had rescued him and told him he was finally in Texas. He could die now, he thought. He had made it all the way to Texas.

Yet his face still felt on fire and his side throbbed with pain. Why was his side hurting? He must be still on the trail and Trace had not rescued him at all; he had only dreamed that.

He opened his eyes slowly and looked around, trying to decide where he was.

A beautiful girl with long, pale hair hovered over him. He could see her in the glow of the fire. Where was he, and what had happened? Was she what the white men called an angel? He tried to move, and the pain in his side made him cry out.

The girl held a tin cup of water to his lips and said, "Don't move, you're hurt."

He blinked and swallowed the water. She looked familiar somehow, and then he remembered. He was in Wyoming again. Sunshine. *Sunny.*

"What—what happened?" he gasped.

"Don't you remember? I shot you!"

Chapter 15

Her words didn't register with Diablo. He struggled to come back into consciousness and failed. When the angel put a soothing, cool hand on his forehead, he relaxed and drifted back into delirium.

Now as Sunny put her hand on his forehead, she wasn't sure what to do next. The gunfighter was burning hot with fever, and the wound didn't look too good. *What to do?* Then she remembered that Diablo had boiled some kind of bark to lower her fever. What was it? Oh yes, willow. It must be an old Indian remedy. She went out into the darkness and searched out a willow tree in the light of the moon. She took the gunfighter's knife and peeled some of the bark, and set it to boiling in a small pot of water on the campfire. After it seeped and cooled a little, she spooned some between his lips.

He was still too warm but shivering. She peeled back the bandage and looked at the wound. It looked swollen and red in spite of the medicine she had bought. It ought to be cleansed, but she wasn't certain what to use. Then she remembered the small bottle of whiskey. She wiped the wound as clean as she could with boiled water, then washed it with the whiskey. Maybe the alcohol would kill the infection.

He moaned in his sleep and thrashed about.

"Stop it," she whispered, "or you might tear it loose and it'll start bleeding again."

The only thing that seemed to quiet him was her putting her hand on his forehead. He muttered and talked in his delirium, and some of the things he revealed horrified her. She had picked up enough clues from his words to know a little about what had happened to his face, but she found it hard to believe Hurd and his men could have done something so cruel. Then she remembered that Smitty and Wilson had been found hanging from trees, and a chill ran through her as she realized that instead of nesters, Diablo must have been the one to do that, determined to take his revenge.

Could he have killed her father, too? She shook her head. Her father had tried to protect the boy from the branding.

Diablo muttered again, and tears came to her eyes. He had had a hard life. Almost no one, from the day of his birth, had been kind to him. No wonder he was such a hard case, such a merciless killer. And she was part of his revenge.

He was helpless now and maybe dying. It would serve him right if she mounted up and rode off and left him. If he died, that would be his tough luck, and it would do away with the threat against her fiancé. *Hurd.* No, she couldn't quite believe he would deliberately torture a half-breed boy.

Would the chilly night never end? Diablo shivered again even though she piled both blankets over him and built up the fire. She could go for help and get him to a ranch, but he might die while she was gone. Anyway, she wasn't certain anyone was willing to help one of the

Texas gunfighters. If she managed to find her way back to the K Bar, Hurd would probably say it was a good thing the cold-blooded killer was dying and the world would be better off without him.

Should she go for help or forget him and find her own way back to civilization?

She mounted up and reined in, looking down at him. To desert him was all he deserved after what he had put her through. At that moment, he opened his dark eyes and looked up at her.

"You—you leaving?" The torment in his eyes told her he expected nothing from her, from anyone. No one had ever done anything much to help him, except maybe that Texas family.

He was ravaged both in body and soul, she thought, and he deserved not the slightest shred of compassion and expected none. "Good-bye, angel," he whispered and closed his eyes again, shivering violently.

Oh, my. No, she couldn't leave him. He might be a hard-hearted killer who deserved to be shot, but the look in those tortured eyes, as though he expected nothing more from her, tore at her heart.

She dismounted and unsaddled the horse, turned it out to graze, and then she built up the fire again.

"Cold," he murmured, "so cold."

She hesitated. If he didn't get warm, he'd probably die before morning. She took a deep breath and took off her dress, crawled under the cover with him, warming his shivering big frame with her own. She placed his ravaged face against her bare breasts and stroked his hair. "It's all right," she whispered. "Everything is going to be all right. I'm not leaving."

She was a fool, she knew, for not taking advantage of his helpless state to ride out and desert him, escape her captivity, but she couldn't bring herself to do it. Instead, she held his shivering body close to her warm naked one and stroked his hair. In the glow of the fire, she could see the ravaged side of his face, all burned and covered with red welts. Once she had thought he looked like a monster, but now she looked with her heart and saw only a sad, angry man who had never seen much kindness. He was no longer a heartless beast; he was only a mistreated, lonely boy who had grown into a hard, bitter killer.

She held him against her bare breasts, and gradually he stopped shivering and slept. She had done everything she knew to help him, and now it was up to the Great Spirit of his Sioux people.

It was almost dawn when she awakened and was startled to realize where she was. His ravaged face still nestled against her breasts, but he was no longer burning with fever. Hurd would never understand if he should come riding up suddenly. In fact, he would probably kill the gunfighter right there in his blankets.

Then she realized Diablo was awake. She felt his warm breath on her breasts, and she stroked his hair a moment, before she got up and stood by the fire, buttoning the pink gingham dress she wore. She knew he was watching, but she didn't care.

He managed to say, "You—you saved my life." He said it with a sense of wonder, as if he could not quite believe it.

"Well, I shot you, so I figured I owed you that." She turned away and busied herself at the fire.

"After what I've done, anyone else would have ridden out and left me, or put a bullet in my brain."

"I reckon I'm a fool," she snapped, feeling a bit silly because what he said was true. "Here, drink the rest of this willow bark brew, and I'll see if I can make some broth from some of that dried jerky."

He just kept looking up at her in wonderment as she

held his head and helped him sip the willow bark brew. "I—I never met anyone quite like you."

"Any decent human being would have done the same." She cradled him close for a long moment before she returned to the fire.

"I reckon I haven't met many decent human beings."

"Now I can believe that." She started making broth.

He rose up on one elbow and winced. "I reckon I'm hurt worse than I thought."

"Lay back down," she ordered. "You're hurt. By the way, I saw all the scars on your body. I'm surprised you haven't died before."

He managed a weak smile. "I reckon I'm tough as a boot heel. Mostly, I just did the best I could for myself when I got shot up."

She had the broth cooking now and came back to sit beside him. "Honestly I didn't think you'd make it through the night."

"That would have been the perfect time for you to escape."

"I know it. I've still got your guns. When I'm convinced you're okay, I'll leave."

"And bring the boys from the K Bar back to finish me off?"

"Don't be silly," she snapped. "I didn't save you to let Hurd kill you. I figure we're even now." She reached for a wet cloth and bathed his face.

"What do you mean?"

"I mean you should wipe the slate clean and ride out."

"In other words, you're trying to save Kruger's life?"

"I'm trying to end this endless cycle of violence." She gently washed the right side of his face.

"Don't it scare you to look at me?"

She shook her head. "No. It's just scars, that's all."

"Most women back away from me in horror."

"I reckon I saw past the scars." She got up and went over to pour him a cup of broth, brought it back, and knelt down beside him. She was aware, that she slipped her arm under his head, her bodice pulled open so that he could see her breasts, but she was too weary to care. He sipped the broth and lay back down on the blanket, looking up at her like a hurt dog.

"I never expected anyone like you," he murmured again.

"So will you go back to Texas and leave us in peace here?"

He managed to pull himself up into a sitting position, although he winced. "I told you I came for revenge, and I'm not finished with it."

"Lay back down before you start bleeding again." she scolded.

"I'm feeling better," he said, but his face was etched with deep lines of pain.

"I'll stay until you can ride," she said, "and then we'll each go our own ways."

"I meant it about not leaving until I finish what I came for."

The dog came over to him and licked his face. It lay down next to him, and he stroked its ears.

"You're a hard case, Diablo."

"No more than you are, trying to save your fiancé."

"Is that what you think?" She sighed at his stubbornness.

His face hardened. "You didn't save me out of the kindness of your heart; you're trying to protect Kruger and Joe."

"I don't want anyone else killed, not even you."

"Are you still going to marry that mean bastard?" he almost snarled.

"I—I don't know." She looked away. "It was my father's dying wish."

"Who told you that?"

"Hurd. He said he found Dad when he'd been shot and that was the last promise Dad insisted on."

Feeling overwhelmingly angry and annoyed, Diablo chewed his lip. He could tell the girl what he knew, but she would never believe him and for some reason, the thought of the burly rancher marrying and bedding this girl set him in a fury.

"What are you thinking?" the girl asked.

"Nothing. Nothing at all." No, she would never believe him. He looked at her and remembered the sweet smell of her, the softness of her skin, and the warmth of her full breasts, and he wanted her as a man wants a woman. If Kruger was going to own this girl, Diablo wanted her first, wanted to take her virginity and rob the rich rancher of that pleasure.

"Lie down," she said gently, "you don't look like you feel too good."

He sank down with a sigh. "This is no good, me lying here helpless. Kruger and his men are searching high and low for you all over the county, and the more time passes, the better chance they have of coming back here. I reckon he's got a reward out."

"A big one," she said, pulling his blanket up over his chest.

"How do you know that?"

"While you were unconscious last night, I rode into Wildfire to get some medicine and bandages. I saw a poster in the pharmacy."

Now he looked really alarmed. "You were in a store? You saw someone?"

"Only the clerk," she shrugged. "Don't worry, I didn't say anything that would lead him to you."

"You're so naive," Diablo sighed and closed his eyes. "Don't you think for any reward, that clerk will ride to the K Bar?"

"I thought about that, but I didn't know what else to do. You needed help." She brushed her hair back from her face.

His hand, lying on the blanket, clenched and unclenched. "It won't go well with you if Kruger finds out you helped me and stayed when you could have escaped."

She reached out and took his hand. It was a brown hand with long fingers, a strong hand that had killed many a man. "Hurd adores me; he always has. He'd forgive anything if I marry him."

He looked at her small pale hand in his. Everything about this girl was delicate and beautiful. He wanted to protect her against the whole world, hold her close, and make her his in the most primitive way. But she was going to marry Kruger, and Diablo had nothing to offer her. Without thinking, he raised her hand to his lips and kissed her fingertips tenderly. He saw tears in her eyes as he did so.

"Don't you have any other name but Diablo? You don't seem like a devil to me."

"That's because you haven't been on the business end of my Colt."

"I think I will call you Jim."

"Jim?" He laughed. "Why?"

"Because it sounds like a good, honest rancher, not a killer. What's your last name?"

He shook his head. "I don't have one. I was fathered by a Santee Sioux brave who raped my mother. That white family didn't want me, so they gave me to that warrior's mother after he was hung." He frowned and turned away, let go of her hand. "The Durangos offered me their last name, but I didn't feel worthy of it since I'm a gunfighter."

"I'm sorry, I didn't mean to cause you hurt." She leaned over and kissed his cheek. "I christen you Jim Durango."

He laughed without mirth. "That might be a good name for a law-abiding rancher, but I'm a hired gun, Sunny. I'll be Diablo until the day a faster man shoots me down in some dirty saloon or a dusty main street."

"But you don't have to be. You can choose to be Jim and go back to Texas, lead a peaceful life. Couldn't you make a fresh start?"

He frowned. "My need for revenge is the only thing that's kept me alive these past fifteen years. Oh, Trace Durango offered to sell me a few thousand acres in the Big Bend country, where I could catch wild horses and break them, but I can't see myself doing that. I can't change—I'll always be a hired gun."

She fought back the tears. "You're so damned stubborn. That dusty street might be right here in Wyoming when you come up against Hurd."

He glared at her. "And now that we get down to it, he's the one you're really worried about, not me. You want to be Mrs. Hurd Kruger, wife of the richest, most powerful cowman in the county if not the state. You're trying to keep me from killin' him."

"Oh, you're impossible!" She got up and stalked away, went out into the woods, and sat down under a tree. She wasn't sure how she felt about the gunfighter. Once she had feared him, but not anymore. Behind her, she heard him up and moving around.

She got up and ran back to the camp. "You'll tear something loose and start bleeding again."

"I told you I was tough." He seemed to be gritting his teeth, but he had found the weapons where she had hidden them under some branches near the cave. "Now, Princess, you're my prisoner again."

"You rotten—" She couldn't find words enough to express her anger, or maybe it was her disappointment in him. "If you're in good enough shape to make it on your own, why don't you let me go now?"

His face looked ghastly white, and she noticed the bandage was slowly spreading fresh scarlet.

"You'd better sit down, Jim," she said softly. "You're bleeding again."

He slid into a sitting position against a big rock, but he held onto the pistol and rifle. "I—I'm okay."

"No, you're not."

"Well, I've got the guns."

"You didn't need the guns. I wasn't going to shoot you or bring someone who would."

He took a deep breath, and she could tell he was in pain. "I can't trust anyone, never have."

"I haven't sold you out, and I've had the chance."

He shook his head and closed his eyes. "I can't figure that."

"Jim," she whispered, "I won't double-cross you. I just want to save you from dying on that dusty street somewhere."

"I can't change, Sunny."

"Of course you can." She put her hand on his knee. "Everyone can change. There's no path in life that's so set it can't be changed."

"Stop talking to me," he snapped. "You're just trying to save Kruger's neck. You know when I get on my feet I'm going to kill him."

"I know." She moved over by the fire. "I guess I was wrong about you, Jim. I think I'll leave now and get on with my life." She got up and walked over to the grazing horses.

He cocked the pistol. "I won't let you leave."

"Are you going to shoot me?" She gave him a very direct look with those big sky-colored eyes and went on saddling her horse.

"Damn you, sit down!" He ordered. "You won't bring Kruger back here when I'm not ready to face him down."

"You know I wouldn't do that." She said it calmly as she saddled the bay.

"I can't take that chance." His voice was cold and hard as his face when she turned to look at him.

"I swear to you I won't bring anyone back here."

"Sunny, don't you understand? I can't trust you— I can't trust anyone."

"You poor, poor thing. You've got to trust someone in this world. Good-bye, Diablo. I reckon that's who you really are."

"I'll kill you, I tell you." He waved the Colt at her, but she ignored him and grabbed the bay's bridle, started to lead the horse past the gunfighter.

"Goddamn you!" He swore and dropped the pistol, grabbed for her. They went down in a tangle of arms and legs, the horse neighing and rearing away from them.

"Let go of me!" She looked up into his face as they struggled, and she did the only thing she could to escape his superior strength. She took her fist and hit the band-aged wound hard.

He collapsed with a shudder and a moan.

"Oh my God, I didn't mean to hurt you!" She knelt by him and rolled him over on his back. Blood slowly spread over the white bandage. She grabbed his hands and pulled him back over by the fire, covered him up. His face was chalky white. "I didn't mean it," she whispered, "I didn't mean it."

She didn't even bother to pick up the pistol or the rifle. He would never use them against her, she knew that now.

Now what? She ought to go ahead and ride out. He surely couldn't stop her now, but he looked so vulnerable lying there, white faced and unconscious. "If only you could be Jim Durango instead of Diablo, the deadliest gun for hire in the whole West."

She kissed his forehead without thinking and brushed his black hair from his eyes. She should hate him and desert him, but she couldn't bring herself to do that.

Druggist Homer Bledsoe could hardly see through the stinging dust that burned against his face. Once or twice, he lost track of the road and had to rein in and check. The sun came out, but with the wind blowing, it was only a pale disk in the sky. He was late finding his way to the K Bar ranch.

A weasel-faced man let him into the big house. It looked dirty and neglected, which surprised Homer. He figured a rich man could afford some household help. "I'm here to see Mr. Kruger."

The cowboy looked him up and down. "I don't know what you're sellin', but Mr. Kruger ain't of a mind to see nobody today."

From inside came a bellow. "Joe, who is it?"

"Some drummer, boss."

Homer Bledsoe drew himself up proudly. "I am not a drummer. I came because of the poster."

The cowboy's bored expression now turned curious. "Maybe you'd better see the boss."

He disappeared and in a minute was back. "Mr. Kruger is in the den. He wants to see you."

Homer followed Joe deep into the big house.

The wind continued to shake the house, and grit peppered against the windows. A big man with a very black mustache and hair sat slumped in a leather chair with a glass of whiskey in one beefy hand. He appeared very sad and defeated.

"Mr. Kruger?" Homer took off his hat and approached timidly.

"Yeah?" the other growled. "What do you want?"

"I saw your poster. I'm from Wildfire." He played with the brim of his derby hat.

"So?"

Joe said "Shall I throw him out, boss?"

Homer held up one hand, as if to stop Joe from grabbing his collar. "I think I might have some information that would interest you."

Now the big man's face lit up a bit. "About the girl?"

Homer nodded. "Yes, sir."

Now the big man smiled. "Joe, bring the man a drink. Pull up a chair, Mr.—what'd you say your name was?"

"Bledsoe. Homer Bledsoe." Homer took a chair near the fire. The wind continued to beat against the house. He noted the important man looked as neglected as the interior of the house. Hurd Kruger needed a shave and looked like he hadn't changed clothes in several days. He was rumpled and dirty.

Joe brought Homer a glass of whiskey, and Homer noted the glass was smudged as he sipped it. "Ahh! Now sir, the information I have might be of some value to you. I understand there's a significant reward?"

The big man moved as fast as a rattler, grabbed Homer by the shirt collar. "Don't play with me. You know something about the missing girl?"

"Yes, yes. Don't get so upset." Homer managed to pull himself free of the man's hands and looked away from his glaring dark eyes. Truly this was no man to tamper with. He might even be a little mad. "Last night, a young lady came into my pharmacy to buy medicine and bandages. She was a pretty blonde."

The other man asked, "What was she wearing?"

Homer had to think a minute. "I—I'm not sure. A pink gingham dress, I think."

"That could be anyone." Kruger scowled and sank back into his chair. "There're lots of pink dresses."

"Oh, but this gal was special." Homer insisted. "There can't be too many like her, hair so pale it was almost white and very big blue eyes. Prettiest gal I ever seen. She bought medicine and bandages."

The other man's face lit up. It was evident he cared very much for the girl. "Was she hurt?"

"I don't think so." Homer shrugged. "At least, she didn't appear to be. No, wait." He screwed up his face in thought. "She did have dried blood on her hand."

"Oh, my God, she's hurt!" The rancher half rose from his chair. "Was she alone?"

"She came in alone," Homer said. "I don't know if there was someone waiting for her outside."

Kruger looked over his shoulder. "You hear that, Joe? It must have been her, all right. But if she got loose, she'd hightail it for here."

"That's right, boss," Joe nodded. "There must have been some bastard out there in the dark holdin' a gun on her."

Kruger's beefy face contorted with worry. "So she's either hurt or whoever took her is, and there might be more of them than one." Kruger's face brightened. "All we got to do is track them from the town—"

Homer cleared his throat. "I'm afraid that might be impossible, sir. The wind was blowing hard in Wildfire last night, worse than here. I doubt there are any tracks left."

Kruger sighed and slumped in his chair again. "We've got to find her, we've just got to, before some of her kidnappers—"

He left the sentence hanging in the air, but Homer knew full well what he meant.

"Aw, boss," Joe said, "they may have already—"

"Goddamn you!" Kruger came up out of his chair, upsetting it with a clatter on the bare floor. "No, they haven't. Sunny would die first before she let a man do that to her. She's so pure and beautiful, and she's mine! You hear? She's mine, and I'm going to marry her when I get her back and woe to the sonovabitches who took her!"

Homer put his glass on the side table. This might be the most powerful rancher in the state, but it seemed he was rapidly becoming unbalanced. "Uh, well, I'll be going now." He stood up.

"Joe, show the man to the door." Kruger gestured, and his eyes were wild. "Mr. Bledlow—"

"Bledsoe," Homer corrected gently.

"Whoever the hell you are, when we find her, I'll make sure you get your reward."

Homer wanted to know how much it was and if he could have it immediately, but he was afraid to ask. Hurd Kruger looked like he might be on the edge of madness or maybe have had too much alcohol, and Homer didn't think it smart to argue with him.

He left, got in his buggy and started back to Wildfire.

Hurd watched him go, then turned to his foreman. "Joe, get the boys out. We'll look in a radius of fifty miles from Wildfire."

"But boss," Joe held up his hands helplessly. "It's blowing a sandstorm out there, and there won't be any tracks to follow. We ain't got too many cowboys left after last night. The Sorrenson hands have all quit, and the men we do have are exhausted after bein' in the foothills all night. Bill has a broken arm, and we got one horse killed and several more are lame—"

"Damn you! Don't nobody follow orders anymore?"

Hurd roared and charged at his foreman, slamming him up against the wall. "Get the boys out lookin'. They ain't that tired. Now that's an order!"

"Yes, sir," Joe sighed and went out the door into the sandstorm. He was beginning to think Kruger was losing his mind, he was so obsessed with this girl. Joe didn't have any doubt that the kidnappers were using her for their pleasure if she was even still alive, but Kruger wouldn't face that. There hadn't even been a ransom note, which puzzled everyone.

Joe shook his head and went to the bunkhouse to rouse out the reluctant cowboys. The ranch had been sliding into ruin and neglect ever since Sunny had disappeared several weeks ago. Kruger cared about nothing but her. Joe had been with the boss more than fifteen years, but he was beginning to think it was time to ride on. He had a bad feeling about this whole bloody mess.

Chapter 16

Days passed, and the weather improved. Diablo drifted in and out of consciousness, and Sunny looked after him. Her common sense told her she should take everything that belonged to Hurd Kruger and ride out. It might take her a few hours, but she would soon find her way back to the K Bar. Then she could marry Hurd as her father had wished and get on with her life.

Yet she couldn't bring herself to desert the injured gunfighter. She wasn't even sure why. She told herself maybe it was guilt because she was the cause of his wound. She kept him wrapped warmly, even as the weather turned warmer, and fed him broth and willow bark brew.

Now he was awake and staring up at her in wonderment. "How long have I been out?"

"Oh, maybe a week," she shrugged.

"You could have ridden away and left me." He rose up on one elbow.

"I know that," she snapped. "Just call me a fool."

"There's probably even a reward out for my head. You could have led Kruger to me."

"I know that, too." She busied herself around the campfire, not looking at him. "Would you like some coffee?"

"Sure." He managed to pull himself up against a big boulder. When their fingers touched, she felt almost a spark between them and shrugged it off.

"You look tired," he said.

"I'm okay. I've been looking after you around the clock."

"I haven't done anything to deserve such good treatment." He sipped his coffee.

"Don't I know it!" she snorted and dipped him a tin bowl of stew out of the pot on the fire.

"I'm afraid my hands are still too shaky to hold a spoon."

"I can feed you," she said and moved to sit next to him with a bowl and spoon.

His gaze seemed to fasten on hers with puzzlement as she fed him. "You know, the only other woman who was ever this good to me was Trace Durango's wife."

"That's pitiful. No wonder you're such a hard case."

"Did I—did I say much while I was out?"

She looked at him a long moment, decided to lie. It would upset him if he knew how much he had said. Besides, she wasn't sure how much of it to believe. "You mumbled a lot, is all. Couldn't make much sense of it."

He sighed, looked relieved. "If I told you the whole thing, you might not believe me."

"Doesn't matter." She fed him another spoonful of broth.

He swallowed and leaned back against the rock. "I reckon you're right, Princess."

"On the other hand, it must matter to you, or you wouldn't be so hell bent on revenge. Was it Hurd? Surely it wasn't my father?"

He shook his head, staring into her eyes. "Not your father. He was a good hombre. If I told you it was Kruger and some of his cowboys, would you believe me?"

She backed away from him, eyes blazing. "Of course not. Hurd is a respected man in this county. If he would do something that terrible, Dad wouldn't have wanted me to marry him."

Diablo hesitated. There was no way he could tell her about the scene he'd witnessed. She'd never believe him. "Then let's just drop it, okay?"

"Okay." She watched him set the cup on the ground. He looked troubled.

"You've tired yourself," she said softly. "Why don't you lie back down?"

"I need to get up." He struggled to stand. "If anyone finds this hiding spot, I don't want to be shot down like a helpless dog."

She rushed to drape his arm over her shoulders as he fought to get to his feet. "You're so stubborn. Why don't you let me help you?"

"I'm not used to dependin' on anyone," he protested as he took a shaky step, but his knees were buckling.

"If there's anyone coming, I'll alert you," she promised.

He slid to the ground, and she pulled a blanket up over him. "There's no reason for you to be good to me."

"Except I shot you and I feel guilty about it. Now lie still and I'll read you a book." She reached for one of the books in his saddlebags and got a book of fairy tales and opened it. "How about *Beauty and the Beast?*"

He shook his head, his eyes closed. "Isn't that the one where the beautiful princess gets carried off by the beast and she kisses him and he turns into a handsome prince?"

"I think so." She wished she had picked something else.

"I hate that one," he mumbled. "In real life, you can't kiss the beast and turn him into a handsome prince. He's always going to be just that, an ugly monster."

"Some women look with their hearts, not their eyes," she whispered, then felt foolish.

However, he had dropped off to sleep, and she figured he hadn't heard her. She stared at him. One side of his face was handsome, the other twisted and burned. Once she had been horrified by his looks, but now she had a lot of sympathy for a lonely half-breed boy who had had to fight his way through the world the best he could.

She reached over and brushed a shock of black hair from his eyes, and impulsively, she kissed his ravaged cheek. She wasn't sure how this all would end, but she wasn't going to let Hurd kill the injured gunfighter if she had to stay with Diablo another month. However, she was concerned that someone would stumble on this hideout and kill Diablo while he was too weak to fight.

That night, he moaned and thrashed about, and she thought he must be having a nightmare again about being tortured and branded. Wolf whined and curled up next to him, looking up at her with mute appeal, as if to ask if there was something she could do to help.

She lay down next to Diablo and put her head on his broad shoulder. He stirred just enough to cuddle her close and dropped back off to sleep.

"It will be all right," she whispered, close to his ear. "Everything will be all right." She knew she lied because he was headed down a one-way road with only death awaiting him in a gunfight somewhere.

She kissed the side of his face, thinking how vulnerable he was now and how he had come in with guns blazing to save her from Buck and Pug. This was a real man who could protect a woman and look after her, but right now, he needed looking after himself.

The next day, she climbed on a rocky outcrop and saw riders a long, long distance away—probably Hurd's men searching for her. She might get their attention with a signal fire or a rifle shot, but she wasn't going to lead them to Diablo. She knew she ought to ride to the sheriff or Hurd and turn Diablo in, but he would fight capture and she didn't want to see him shot down in cold blood.

* * *

Within another day, he was getting around the camp by leaning on her shoulder. He looked down at her, his face close enough to hers for her to feel his warm breath on her cheek. "You aren't terrified of me anymore?" It was a statement more than a question.

"No." She looked up at his weary face. "Now that I've gotten to know you, I realize you mean me no harm."

"You can't be sure of that." He frowned.

"I am sure," she said matter-of-factly.

"Damn, you've certainly changed from the shy, mousy little thing that couldn't make any decisions on her own."

She smiled ever so slightly. "Maybe I've grown up."

"There's something I've been wantin' to do ever since that moment before you shot me," he said.

She looked up at him, waiting, although she was certain she knew what it was.

His big arms went around her, and he pulled her against his wide chest. Then one of his big hands tipped her chin up, and he kissed her, thoroughly and deeply.

For a long moment, she lost herself in the kiss, her heart hammering wildly, wanting more. One of his hands went to caress her breasts, and the sensation shocked her because she wanted him to touch her even more intimately. Then she remembered and pulled back. "I'm an engaged woman." Was she reminding him or herself?

"I know. Maybe you'll be sorry you helped me when I tell you I still intend to kill Kruger."

"Still?" She drew back, appalled. "I hoped you'd forget about that and when you got on your feet, you'd ride back to Texas and leave us in peace to get on with our lives."

He snorted and backed away from her. "So the truth comes out. You thought by helping me, you'd save Kruger?"

There was no point in telling him that she would have looked after him, no matter what. He would never believe her since he trusted no one. "Sure," she lied, "and you're an ingrate not to let him live and ride on."

"I should have known it wasn't because you cared anything about me."

He wouldn't believe her if she told him differently, so she said nothing. He made a disgusted sigh and sat down by the fire pit and poured himself some coffee. "Women! You can't trust any of them."

"You're pretty much on your feet now," she said, angry and disgusted with his stubbornness. "Why don't you let me ride out and go back to the K Bar? I promise I won't lead them to you, and in a few days, you'll be in good enough shape to head back to Texas."

He picked up his pistol, hefted it, and buckled his holster back around his waist. "No. I want to keep you with me . . . as insurance."

"Well, that's gratitude for you." She shook back her hair and glared at him.

He thought she had never looked so beautiful as she did at this moment. He knew not to trust anyone, but she looked so soft and vulnerable in her pink gingham dress and he remembered how she had looked naked and defenseless when he rescued her from the two gunslingers and covered her soft, beautiful body with his shirt. He remembered how she had felt in his arms when he lifted her and carried her to his horse with her arms around his neck and her lovely face weeping against his bare chest. And he wanted her again in the way a man wants a woman. No, he wanted her body and soul. He felt his manhood rise with his need. "I tell you what, let me have you and maybe I'll let you go."

She whirled on him, her face angry and horrified. "You mean, like—like some whore?"

He shrugged. "If that's what you want to call it. I've always intended that Kruger shouldn't take you to his bed untouched."

"Why you bastard!" She crossed the circle and slapped him, and he grabbed her arm, pulled her up against him.

"If you were a man, I'd have killed you for that, and you know it. I've taken a lot off you, Sunny, more than I've ever taken off anyone."

"And why is that?" she snarled as he pulled her hard up against him and she struggled.

He didn't know the answer. He had never felt like this toward any other woman. He wanted to take her, make her his completely in a frenzy of hot passion, yet he wanted to hold her and protect her against anything and anyone who might hurt her. Abruptly, he was ashamed of himself for the brutal way he was acting. He loosened his grip, and she stepped away. Then he leaned back against the rock and sighed.

He didn't want her this way, fighting and clawing and afraid. He wanted her to come into his arms, offering her body to him, offering the passion that the rich rancher was expecting on his wedding night. Well, Diablo still intended to kill Kruger, and now he wasn't certain whether it was because of what had happened that long-ago day fifteen years ago or the image of Kruger panting and groaning as he took Sunny's virginity. Diablo wanted to be that man, but he had no money and no prestige and he knew he was ugly—uglier than ugly, he was a monster. Sunny would never let him make love to her willingly, and he didn't want her any other way.

"Well?" She straightened her pink dress.

"What do you want from me?" he snapped, shrugging his shoulders. "I may be a killer, but I'm not a rapist. I just—" He didn't want her to know how badly he had wanted her, how much he still wanted her. For her own sake, he ought to set her free, and yet he still needed her as bait to draw Kruger and Joe into his trap so he could kill the two of them. He owed them that.

"You know, I could have left any time the past few days. You were too hurt to stop me." She walked toward the cave.

"I know, and I'm much obliged," he whispered.

She sighed, suddenly bone tired.

"Why don't you get some rest?" he said. "You've probably been up for days without any sleep taking care of me."

"And look at the thanks I get."

"Did you expect any?" he snapped.

"From you, I expect nothing." She marched into the cave and lay down on a blanket.

He sat patting the dog and watching her. It was almost dusk. In another couple of days, he should be on his feet and fit enough to ride and shoot. Surely Kruger and his men were out searching for Sunny. Now Diablo just had to figure out how to lure them to a place where he could kill that Kruger and Joe.

After a long moment, he stood up and hobbled over to the cave, where he stood looking down at her. She looked so vulnerable lying there in her pink delicate dress. Her long hair spread over her shoulders, and he wanted to stroke it because he remembered the soft, silky feel of it.

Abruptly he remembered her photo. Had she discovered it when she was digging in his saddlebags for a book? He'd never be able to explain how he came by it. Diablo hobbled over to his saddlebags and checked them. Thank God she hadn't stuck her hand in the far pocket. He reached in and pulled out the small, ornate gold frame and smiled. He liked looking at her picture. Even after they each went their own way, he would always keep the photo to remember her by. She was an unforgettable woman, and he had never felt so lonely as he did at this moment. He would feel lonelier when they finally parted forever.

Diablo ran his fingers over the photo's face, wishing he could touch the real woman that way, but of course that was only a wistful dream. He wrapped the photo frame in an old rag and put it back in the saddlebag. All he could think of at this moment was Sunny. She had bewitched him, and if her kindness had been meant to distract his attention from killing Kruger, she had almost succeeded.

Then he touched his scarred cheek and ground his teeth. No, Kruger and Joe must die for what they had done to him and his three cowboy friends, and for the cold-blooded murder of Swen. He ought to tell Sunny everything he knew, but he didn't think there was a ghost of a chance she would believe him. What was he supposed to do now?

Back at the K Bar, Joe brought the cowboys in. It was dusk, and the men were tired and dirty, the horses lathered, their heads hanging. He dismounted and went into the big ranch house. The place was in complete disarray since Maria had quit. Clothes and newspapers were strewn everywhere. Cobwebs hung from the wood ceiling beams, and the floor was coated in dust. Dirty dishes and pans were piled on tables, and empty whiskey bottles lay everywhere.

Hurd sat before the fireplace, sipping a drink and staring into the flames. He didn't look up. He needed a shave badly, and he hadn't changed shirts in days.

"Boss, this place looks like a dump."

"I don't give a damn about that." Hurd turned and snarled. "You find anything?"

Joe shook his head. "Not a clue, and more hands quit today. They're sayin' you must be loco."

Hurd stood up, turning over his chair as he grabbed Joe by the collar. "I'm not crazy, I just want to get her back and kill that half-breed bastard who's got her. He might be using her for his pleasure every night. When I think of her helpless and in his arms—"

"Don't think about it, boss," Joe soothed and managed to pull out of Hurd's grasp. The man was drunk, and his eyes were a little crazed. Maybe those cowboys were right. "We ought to be branding and rounding up all those cattle we've got spread out over the county. You're a rich man now that so many of those nesters have fled."

"I don't give a damn about that now; I don't give a damn about the ranch." Hurd staggered over and poured himself another drink. "All I care about is getting Sunny back and marrying her. As for that half-breed, I'll geld him if he's touched her and shove his manhood down his throat, and then I'll kill him by inches."

"Boss, that's the reason we're in the mess we're in now because of what you did to him all those years ago."

"And I'll do it again," Hurd promised, drained his glass, and slammed it into the fireplace, where it shattered into a crash of glass. "Damn him, I'll brand him all over and laugh while he screams, you hear me?"

"I hear you, boss." Joe wondered if he ought to be looking for a new job himself. This man was going mad. He had everything a man could want: money, a big ranch, respect. There were a lot of pretty girls who would be glad to marry Hurd Kruger, although, Joe had to admit, none as beautiful as Sunny Sorrenson.

Hurd stared out the window. "Tomorrow, we go out again, and I'll lead the search. They're somewhere in this state, and I'm going to find them, I swear it."

Joe managed to stifle a groan. The whole thing had

become a fool's errand. Sunny might be dead or not even in Wyoming. The gunfighter may have taken her with him and left for Texas. A couple more of these wild goose chases, and they would lose the rest of the crew when there was work around the ranch that needed doing. "What about the branding and taking cattle to market, boss?"

Hurd whirled on him, swaying on his feet. "I told you I don't give a damn about that. Nothing matters but finding my bride before that bastard . . ." He didn't finish. He walked over and sat down in front of the fire, staring into the flames.

Joe lit a smoke and went outside. He'd been with this man over fifteen years, and Hurd had always been business smart and cunning. Now he seemed to be going loco. He dreaded going back to the bunkhouse and telling the men. A lot of them would quit, but he was under orders. If that half-breed meant to destroy Hurd and the K Bar, he was doing a pretty good job of it.

Diablo sat by the fire a long time, watching Sunny sleep. God, how he wanted her. He patted the dog and imagined what it would be like. No, she would never give herself willingly to an ugly monster like him. Besides, he had nothing to offer her. He had a few dollars, a fine horse, a guard dog, and a fancy rifle, all of them stolen, and the woman was stolen, too. Everything belonged to that rich rancher.

He couldn't let himself care about the girl; he had never cared about anyone but himself. Yet he found himself wondering what would happen to the girl after he killed Kruger? He didn't think she could run the K Bar alone. Swen had talked about sending her away to her aunt in Boston so she could go to college, but Diablo didn't have that much cash and he wasn't sure if Swen had been lying when he'd told Hurd he had enough money to send her.

Certainly Diablo hadn't found a penny in that ranch house. Kruger had plenty of wealth, but the rancher wanted to marry her, so he wouldn't give her the money to go back east.

Well, none of this was Diablo's concern. After he ambushed Kruger and Joe, made them pay for what they had done to him and Swen and the cowboys they had lynched, Sunny would be on her own, and what happened to her wasn't really Diablo's concern.

The fire had dwindled down to coals, and the spring night was chilly. He got up and went in to lie down next to her, pulling a blanket over them both. He wanted to cuddle her up against him and bury his face in that mane of soft yellow hair, but that might awaken and alarm her, so he did not touch her. He could hear her soft breathing, and he wished she cared about him instead of being terrified, but of course, the princess wasn't going to fall in love with him, kiss him, and turn him into a handsome prince. After a while, he dropped off to sleep, dreaming of riding back to Texas with Sunny riding with him, her long yellow hair blowing out behind her like a filly's mane as she looked over at him, and smiling, her face saying everything. Diablo knew how a man could throw away riches or a kingdom for a woman's love, and he had neither.

Chapter 17

Sunny awakened with him asleep beside her in the darkness, his arm thrown protectively across her body. She watched him in the shadows of the fire. His face was relaxed, and he looked gentle as he slept. She should have gotten away when he was helpless; now he might never let her go.

Or if she let him make love to her, maybe he would release her and ride out of Wyoming without killing anyone else. Aside from that, he looked so vulnerable and lonely. She leaned over and kissed his ravaged cheek, and he stirred and smiled slightly. She surprised herself by wanting to kiss him. He had such full, sensual lips. She leaned over and brushed her lips across his, a mere whisper of a touch, and his lips opened slightly. Emboldened, she kissed him full on the mouth, and he stirred and his arm went around her, pulling her down to him without ever opening his eyes.

She kissed him again. His mouth opened, and she touched the tip of her tongue to his. His arms went around her, holding her close as he kissed her deeply, thoroughly. His hand went to her breasts, and she let him caress her there, feeling her own pulse quicken. His fingers circled her nipple, and she felt it swell at the touch. She leaned into him, wanting him to stroke her there more and more. She jerked open her dress and pressed her breast to his mouth. She gasped at what his tongue did to her nipples and the greedy way his lips sucked at her breast.

Her breath came in gasps, and she reached to uncover her other breast, offering it to him. He never opened his eyes as he kissed there and fondled her until she was trembling with excitement. She wasn't sure what she was supposed to do next, nor was she even sure whether he was really awake, but she didn't want this to end. Reaching down, she touched between his thighs. His manhood was turgid and throbbing. Her fingers trembled as she undid the buttons on his pants and freed his big maleness. It was rigid as hot stone, and the tip was soft and wet. She took a deep breath and encircled it with her hand. "Dearest," she whispered, "oh, dearest . . ."

In answer, he rolled her over on her side and faced her, rising up on one elbow to kiss her face, her eyelids. His big hand slipped down to touch her mound, and she quivered with excitement. She wanted him in the most primitive way a female can want a male. She had never felt real passion before, and now she was breathing hard, but not as hard as he was as he touched and stroked between her thighs until she was wet and hot. "Please," she moaned, "Oh, please . . ."

He looked deep into her eyes, breathing hard. "Damn you. I never knew a man could want a woman like I want you! I'd give my front seat in hell for ten minutes in your arms."

"If I—if I let you," she gasped as he stroked her breast, "if I let you, will you ride out of Wyoming and never look back?"

He swore a terrible oath and sat up. The glare in his

dark eyes told her the spell was broken. "You're no whore! Why are you acting like one?"

She was afraid of his anger and shrank back. "I—I just thought I could tempt you into making a deal—"

"Does it even occur to you I could take you by force right here and now?" He sat up and began to button his pants.

"But you wouldn't." She knew him well, she thought.

"Princess, don't tempt me. You were within a few seconds of losing your virginity, and Kruger wouldn't want you then."

"He wouldn't care. He loves me."

"He loves his pride more." Diablo swore and leaned back against a rock. "I think I know him well enough to know he wouldn't want my leavings."

"Is that what you call it, 'leavings?'" she snorted and got up from the blanket, flounced over to the fire, and poked it from coals into flames. She reached for the coffeepot.

Diablo watched her making coffee. He had never wanted to possess a woman as much as he wanted Sunny. He studied her pale hair reflecting the dawn glow and the fairness of her skin. She was light to his darkness, innocence to his world-weary cynicism. He realized he was succumbing to her dainty charm, his need to protect her, to take her as his woman. Or was it only that she was Kruger's woman and he wanted to take her as he had the man's horse and dog and rifle? He was not sure, and that unnerved him.

She looked up as she fried bacon, and her eyes were the palest blue like a Texas sky on a summer day. There couldn't be many women as beautiful as this one, and she could command a high price: the riches of a cattle baron and a bed with silk sheets. She was beyond his reach, and Diablo knew it.

She turned the bacon over and looked at him. "What are you thinking?"

He could not tell her—he was still furious with her for leading him on and then attaching a price to it like a common whore. He must use her to draw Kruger close enough to kill him before she caused him to weaken and drop his resolve.

They ate in silence as the sun rose.

She watched him, noting every ripple of muscle and sinew under his dark skin. His maleness had seemed huge, and she had wanted him with every ounce of passion within her, which surprised and scared her. He was not going to be deterred from more killing by a promise of her ripe body. And she had wanted him to take her, possess her completely, and at that time, she hadn't cared about anything else.

She thought about Hurd's flabby, middle-aged body and sighed. The marriage, of course, would mean that she would have to let him use her body for his pleasure and get her big with his child. That didn't seem a fair exchange. At the moment, she wanted the half-breed to take her virginity in wild spasms of passion, so that she would know at least once what it felt like to be loved by a real, virile man.

Diablo stood up. He still felt weak, but he had things to do and the longer he stayed up here hidden in this cave, the better chance Kruger had of finding him before Diablo found him first. "I've got someplace to go."

"You shouldn't ride. That wound might tear open."

She looked up at him, and he wished her concern for him was genuine.

"I've got to get a message to Kruger."

"About me?"

He nodded. "You can quit thinkin' about escaping while I'm gone."

"I could have escaped a dozen times when you were first wounded."

"Then why didn't you?" He had been wondering this.

She didn't look at him. "We've been through this before. Maybe I thought I should get you on your feet before Hurd found you."

"He'd have shot me helpless in my blankets."

She shook her head. "No, he's not that kind of man."

Diablo snorted in disgust. "You don't know anything about men. Here, I'm going to tie you up."

"No." She shook her head and backed away.

"Don't make me chase you down," he snapped. "I'm not up to it."

In answer, she turned to run, but his reflexes were faster. He grabbed her, and they went down, struggling and kicking. He ended up on top. "You keep temptin' me, I may just take you, and you can make excuses to Kruger."

Her face flushed red as he twisted her arms behind her and forced her into a sitting position against a tree. Then he tied her there. In the struggle, her dress had slipped off one shoulder, and one breast was almost completely exposed.

He tore a scrap from her skirt. "I don't want you yelling for help, either."

Before she realized what he was about, he leaned over and kissed her deeply, thoroughly. She bit his lip and tongue, and he jerked back, wiping blood from his mouth. "It was worth it," he smiled.

Then he forced the scrap of cloth between her teeth.

She tried to swear at him, but her sounds were muffled. Then he leaned over and kissed her breast, sucking her nipple while she writhed against her bounds, yet she couldn't help but arch her back, offering more of her breast still.

"Damn you," he whispered, breathing hard. "You keep upping the ante, I may just have to take you up on your offer."

She tried to tell him through her gag that she wasn't making any offer and she'd die before she let him touch her again, but she knew he couldn't understand what she said.

He grinned and reached down to raise her chin. "I'll be back in a couple of hours, and maybe we'll continue this."

She watched him saddle Onyx and order Wolf to stay with her. Then he mounted up and rode out. She looked after him as long as she could see him. She tried her bonds and realized she couldn't slip free, nor could she push the gag from her mouth. She was like a trussed goose, helpless and vulnerable, waiting for him to return and do with her what he willed. If he never came back, she could die here before anyone ever found this secret place.

No, she decided, that was what the old Sunny would have done: wait obediently for the gunfighter to return and untie her and if he never did, die here like a docile prairie lady. Hell, no, she wasn't going to do that. She realized then that her days with Diablo had changed her. She had a mind of her own now. She began to work on loosening the ropes. He had tied her well, and it was a daunting task. She might not get loose before he returned, but she had to try.

* * *

Diablo could think of nothing but the girl as he rode away. She was Kruger's future bride, and he should possess her as he had taken everything else the cattle baron valued. It would serve Kruger right. And yet, Diablo didn't want her that way. He didn't want her screaming and afraid as he forced himself within her, he wanted her to welcome him with open arms and spread thighs, her lips and her mound hot and wet, desiring him and only him.

He had to finish this business with Kruger before he succumbed to his need for the girl. Where could he post a note that might be found and taken to Kruger? It had to lure the rancher out into the open where Diablo could capture him and Joe and repay them for what they had done to him.

He passed a reward poster nailed to a tree, stopped, and ripped it down. He dismounted and took a stub of pencil from his shirt pocket. He turned the poster over and wrote:

> *Kruger, I will meet and return the girl. Meet me tomorrow night just before sundown at the clearing by the three cottonwood trees. You know the place. You and Joe come alone and unarmed.*

He thought about signing it, but decided Kruger would know who sent it. Diablo didn't know if the pair would ride into his trap, but he was certain they wouldn't come unarmed. The clearing by the three cottonwoods was an ironic place to meet, but the horror began there and so it should end there. It was only just.

How to get it to Kruger? He thought about this a long time. Finally he rode into the town of Krugerville, rode down an alley, wrapped the note around a rock, and tossed it through the Longhorn Saloon window. Then he galloped out of town. Someone in the saloon would get it to Kruger, he was certain of that. Tomorrow night at sundown, he would finally get his revenge: torturing Joe and Kruger and then killing them both. After that, he would turn the girl loose and let her do as she would, having served as the irresistible bait in his trap.

In the meantime, Sunny had managed to untie herself and stood wondering what to do. Should she ride for town and the sheriff, or should she ride to the K Bar? She thought she could find her way out of the foothills now.

You little idiot, she thought, *what difference does it make as long as you clear out of here before the gunfighter returns?* There was something about him that drew her to him, but she knew he was dangerous. Was she just some silly moth hovering around a flame? She shook her head. Of course she had to leave this minute. She began to saddle the bay.

Diablo rode back to his hideout. It was near dark now, and the fire was down to a few glowing coals. Wolf came out to meet him, and he dismounted and patted the dog, unsaddled his black horse, and hobbled it so it could graze.

At that moment, out of the corner of his eye, he saw the girl mount up, and he ran for her as she whipped up the horse. "You little bitch!" He grabbed her ankle and pulled her off. They went down in a whirl of skirts and rolled over and over.

The blood bay ran a few yards and stopped, while Wolf barked and ran around the pair as they tussled in the grass. Diablo came up on top, very aware of the soft curves of her body under him. "Princess, you surprise me. I thought you'd sit there like a good little girl until I came back."

"You bastard, get off me!" She tried to get out from under him, feeling the sudden hardness of his maleness through the thin pink dress. She felt her nipples go turgid, and her secret place felt suddenly warm and wet. That both scared her and made her angry. "This is no way to treat a lady."

"You're right." He sighed and very slowly, got up. She had aroused him in a way no woman ever had, and what his body wanted to do was take her, conquer her, make her his in every sense of the word. He reached out and pulled her to her feet.

She dusted herself off, and he got a good look at her breasts as she bent. He fought an urge to grab her, run his hand into her bodice, stroke, caress, and kiss those mounds of delight.

She straightened. "Where did you go?"

"To get a note to Kruger. I told him we'd meet tomorrow night just before sundown if he wanted to get you back."

"What did you ask for?"

He got up and went to the fire, poked it into flames. "Nothing."

"Do you really think he'll come?" she asked.

He nodded. "For a woman like you, any man would walk across live coals."

She flushed at the way he stared at her, his hunger evident in his dark eyes.

"Maybe not. Anyway, you know he won't come alone."

"No, but I want Joe too. Kruger will probably try to trick me and bring a big posse," Diablo said. "But when he sees you tied and staked down naked in the trees, he'll forget his caution and come rushin' in to save you."

"And then you'll kill him." She looked up at him.

"And then I'll kill him," Diablo promised.

"So after that, what happens to me?"

He shrugged. "After I use you as bait, you can go and do as you please."

"You don't have any desire to take me with you?"

He started to say something, then chewed his lip. "A gunfighter leads a tough, lonely life, Sunny. You couldn't take it."

"Hurd is a good shot; so is Joe. They might just kill you."

"Maybe, but I don't think so." He stared into the fire.

She got up. "I reckon I could throw some supper together."

"I shot a rabbit on the way back," he said. "That would be good roasted on a spit."

"You can really live off the land, can't you?"

He nodded. "Texans are pretty self-reliant and independent."

Too independent, she thought. *He doesn't need anyone.* She watched him skin the rabbit and put it on a spit. "So I'll be the bait so you can kill Kruger."

"And Joe," he said as he hung the meat over the fire.

There was no reasoning with this cold-blooded killer, she decided. Maybe later tonight, she could lure him with her body, although there was no guarantee he'd keep his word if she traded her body for Kruger's life. She had to try.

After they ate and shared the scraps with the dog, they both sat by the fire drinking coffee.

She looked over at him. "How are you feeling?"

"A little weak, but I'll make it. I'm tough."

"You're in no shape to get into a gunfight."

"Let me be the judge of that," he snapped.

"Look," she whispered, "I don't want to see you get killed. I don't want to see anyone get killed. Why don't you just ride on back to Texas?"

He shook his head. "Can't. This will never be finished until Kruger is dead."

"You might be the one dead."

He shrugged. "Then you can say I got what I deserved."

"You're a stubborn fool."

"Yep. But there's not much I want out of life except Kruger's death."

"And what about your life after that?"

He shook his head. "I've never given a thought to past Kruger's death. My whole life has been centered on that. I reckon I'll just go back to Texas until someone needs a hired gun."

"Don't you want a home, a family, a woman who loves you?"

His face was sad, and he waited a long time before answering. "Trace Durango offered me some land out in the Big Bend country where I could catch wild horses and break them. I could build a cabin, but no woman would want to live that poor and out in that desolate, lonely country."

"She would if she loved you."

He laughed. "With a face like mine? Besides, I have no money. It would take at least a thousand dollars to make a start, buy supplies."

"Well, maybe you could get it."

He shook his head. "I don't think so. I haven't seen that much money in one hunk in my whole life."

"Maybe Kruger will bring ransom money—"

"He won't bring money—he'll bring cowboys with rifles and plenty of ammunition."

"If you're sure it will be a trap—"

"It'll be a trap; I know the man. But I've got tricks, too."

"So everybody gets killed." She sighed in exasperation.

"Not you," he said. "I'll make sure nothing happens to you. Maybe you can find a way to go back east to your aunt."

"With no money?" She snorted, then got up. "I'm going to bed." She went into the cave, lay down on the blanket. From here, she watched Diablo staring into the fire. She had mixed feelings about the man. She didn't really want to see him get killed, but that seemed inevitable. Well, it served him right.

After a while, he came in and lay down beside her. She heard the dog whine as it settled down near them.

"Diablo, I hate to see any more killing. There's been enough bloodshed already."

"That's not up to me; it's up to Kruger."

"If—if I make love to you, would you stop all this and ride out?"

He snorted in disgust. "Do you care that much about Kruger?"

She didn't answer. She realized suddenly that she cared that much about Diablo, not Kruger. There was something vulnerable and tender about this scarred, tough gunfighter. She reached over and took his hand, squeezed it.

He raised it to his lips and kissed her hand. "If things were different . . ." he began, and then stopped.

"Yes?"

"Nothing." His tone was brusque. "I'm a damned fool, I reckon."

Sunny thought maybe she would be returned to Kruger and marry him and spend many years in his silk-sheeted bed while he huffed and pawed over her. But just once, she'd like to know what it was to be possessed by a real man, a wild stallion of a man. Even if tonight was the only time. Kruger would never have to know.

She rose up on one elbow and looked down at him.

"What the hell do you want?" he snapped. "Go to sleep."

"Not yet," she whispered.

"You're a funny girl," he said. "Don't you realize that if you keep messin' with me, I might not be able to control myself?"

"I know, but I've wondered what it would be like."

"You'd be wastin' your virginity on an ugly killer who has nothing to offer. Save it for some rich, future husband."

"But then I would always wonder if I missed something."

"Look, Princess," his voice was gentle, "I don't know nothin' about making love to a real lady. All I've ever had were a few drunken whores I had to bribe. Each time it was over in a couple of minutes, and then I paid her for it, got up, buckled my belt, and left. You deserve better than that."

She had never felt so sorry and so tender toward anyone as she did at this moment. "Make love to me, Jim Durango."

"I'm not Jim!" he raged. "Jim is some law-abiding rancher with a decent life who'll grow old among grandkids. I'll die before I'm forty on the floor of a dirty saloon or the dust of some Western street, and—"

She leaned over and cut off his words with her kiss. She didn't know what would happen tomorrow, but tonight, she wanted to find out what passion was all about and she wanted this scarred, bitter gunfighter to teach her.

And maybe, just maybe, there was something she could teach him about trust and tenderness. It was worth a try.

He hesitated, then put his arms around her, pulling her close. "Sunny," he whispered, "Oh, Sunny . . ."

She snuggled into the safety of his powerful embrace,

laying her head on his broad shoulder. The kiss deepened, and his grip tightened as if he never wanted to let her go.

She pulled back and looked up into his smoldering dark eyes. He looked confused and troubled. "You could be Jim," she whispered, "just a regular rancher with an ordinary life."

He shook his head. "I've gone too far to return. Everyone knows who I am. There's always some young buck waiting to draw down on me, wanting to be the man who beat Diablo to the draw."

She ran her hand across his scarred face. He started to pull away, but she stopped him.

"Don't. I don't care about your looks, what's on the outside. I've had a glimpse of the inside, and I think there's something there worth saving—something protective and loving."

"Nobody else has ever seen anything like that," he murmured.

"It's there. Believe me, it's there." And she reached up and pulled his face down to hers, kissed his face over and over again. "I think I could love you."

"Don't," he warned her. "You know it will only lead to heartbreak for us both. You're eighteen, Princess, and I'm twenty-nine, and it's been a long, hard road. There's been too much killing, drinking, gambling—too much everything for me to make a go of it with a naive innocent like you. You'd end up leavin' me and I couldn't bear it, to have you a little while and then lose you."

She felt tears gathering in her eyes. "Don't say that."

"For God's sake, don't cry!" he snapped and wiped the tears off her cheeks with a finger. "I—I can't stand to see you cry."

"Then tell me you don't care about me," she wept,

"convince me that you're only holding me as revenge against Hurd."

"All right. I don't care about you. I'm only playing with you. As soon as I kill Kruger, I'll go back to Texas and never give you another thought."

"Liar!" She reached up and pulled his face down to hers, and he couldn't stop himself. He kissed her with all the pent-up love and devotion that a lonely, half-breed had never given to anyone.

Sunny knew he might be making a fool of her, but at the moment, she didn't care. Tonight she was going to learn about love, and she wanted this scarred, vulnerable gunfighter to teach her.

Chapter 18

She was ecstatic with the touch of his lips across hers, and she held on to him and whispered, "Please make love to me."

"You're a little fool," his voice rasped with passion as he kissed her cheeks, her eyes, and then again, her mouth.

She opened her lips in complete surrender. His tongue caressed the velvet of her tongue, and she sucked gently on it, willing him to go deeper still.

His strong hand went to cover her breast, and she reached to unbutton her bodice, wanting the warmth of his hand to possess and stroke her nipple. Then his lips crept to her neck and the hollow of her throat. She felt the warmth of his breath and his tongue as he moved down to caress her nipple with his mouth. She had never known it could feel like this. She held his dark head against her breast and arched her back, offering her breasts to him.

"Sunny," he gasped, "Sunny, I can't get enough of you!" His hand pulled up her calico dress. She felt him stroking her thigh until goose bumps rose at his touch. Then she let her thighs fall apart.

"Touch me there," she demanded. "Touch me there!"

He obliged, his fingers going to her inner thigh and

then to her mound. She knew she was wet with desire, and he stroked her there, sending a thrill shuddering through her. She knew she was on the precipice of something she did not understand and had never known: that moment that a girl becomes a woman, when she becomes one with a special man. She wanted that—no, she demanded that.

As he kissed her lips and stroked her belly, she reached to unbutton his pants. His freed manhood was big and hot and throbbing. He moaned at her touch and tried to pull away. "Sunny, for God's sake, you don't know what you're doing to me. You don't want to waste this on a penniless gunfighter. It's the most valuable thing a woman has to give, and I can't let you—"

"Do it to me," she commanded. "I want it as much as you do."

At her words, he became frenzied and rolled between her thighs, supporting his weight on his elbows as he looked down at her, breathing hard. His dark eyes were intense with passion.

"I—I think I love you," she whispered, pulling him to her.

"Don't make more of this than it is," he ordered as he positioned himself above her. "We have this moment and nothing more."

"Then that will have to be enough," she answered and put her hands on his narrow hips. "Take me!" she begged. "Please take me."

He hesitated just a moment, his rough-hewn face contorted with his need, and then he came into her very slowly.

He was big. She could feel him hot and throbbing as he came down on her. She wanted more. Sunny reached to pull him, locking her thighs around him so that he could not escape until he had given her what it was she needed.

He gasped and plunged into her to the hilt. "Sunny, I—I'm afraid I'll hurt you."

"Hurt me," she begged, "deeper and deeper still. Ride me like a wild filly."

He needed no further urging. He began to ride her, deep and hard. She could feel every hot inch of him invading her velvet depths, and she wanted more and more as she began the rhythm of love, bare flesh slamming hard against bare flesh.

For only a moment, they were locked together, each writhing and pounding, gasping as each time he went deep and hard. She felt emotion beginning deep in her belly. It was like silent music, and he was providing the rhythm. The music reached a deafening crescendo as he rode her harder and faster. Just as she thought she couldn't take any more without crying out, he stiffened and plunged into her once more, sighing as if it were his last breath, and then her own body locked on to his. The silent music became the crashing of drums in her ears, and she took a deep breath and knew no more.

When she finally opened her eyes, he was still lying on her, gasping for air, and she wanted to hold him close and caress his tousled black hair. "Oh, sweet, I think I love you."

He rose up on his elbows and looked down at her, his face pained. "It was only for pleasure, understand? I don't give a damn about you; I can't."

"I know." She didn't believe him, and she reached up and traced his sensual mouth with one finger.

"I've ruined you." He rolled off her and looked regretful. "I shouldn't have taken your virginity. You shouldn't have sold it so cheap."

"I didn't sell it. I gave it away, and I'm glad you were the one." She reached up to kiss him.

He seemed to struggle with self control, and then he

kissed her deeply and passionately, and held her very close. She felt tears from his eyes on her face. "Princess, I don't like this feelin' I get about you. It makes me feel weak and vulnerable."

"I like you that way." She kissed the side of his lips. "Can you do that again?"

"Sunny," he smiled. "You're too innocent to understand a man has to have a little rest before he can do it again." He held her very close and kissed her hair. "This can't work out. You're hardly more than a girl, and I feel old and world-weary next to you."

"You said you were twenty-nine." She looked up at him, feeling loved and protected in his embrace.

"But it's an old twenty-nine. I've got a lot of miles on me," he answered, "and you're so innocent. I've got nothing to offer you."

"I don't think I care," she said and buried her face against his wide chest, "as long as you keep me with you always."

"I can't promise that, Sunny, and I'm bein' honest. I came up here to kill some men, and then I'm gone, alone as always."

"You can't mean that," she whispered against his chest.

He stroked her hair and held her close. "I never realized how lonely I was until I met you. It'll be like tearin' my heart out to leave you."

"Then take me with you," she looked up at him earnestly, tears running down her cheeks.

He reached out with one strong brown hand and very gently wiped the tears away. "And offer you what? A cheap room in a crummy hotel as I drift around the country? You deserve better than that."

"Can't you let me make that decision?"

He shook his head and held her close, kissed her cheek. "No, I can't. I care enough about you that I can't let you make that sacrifice. Besides, I've already set the last chapter of this in motion, and there's no stoppin' this showdown now."

"I hate you for that." She glared up at him.

"And I adore you, Princess," he whispered, and then he kissed her again, deeper and deeper still until she clung to him, weeping. He made slow, gentle love to her by the fire as Wolf stood guard.

After that, he took her one more time that night, caressing her breasts and kissing her belly before he mounted her again. But this time, he rode her slowly and teasingly until she was begging him to speed up his ride, and she clawed his muscular back as he did. Again she heard the music, and it became louder and faster until it disappeared in a wild roar as he gave her his seed.

Afterward, they lay locked in each other's arms by the fire, both content to do nothing else. Finally, they both slept curled up together, and Wolf lay guarding the mouth of the cave.

When she awakened, he lay with one strong arm thrown protectively across her naked body. The pink dress lay crumpled under her. She sighed, and he came awake, grabbing for his pistol, then saw her and relaxed.

She reached up and stroked his face. "Do you always sleep so lightly?"

He lay back down. "I've stayed alive this long by always sleeping with one eye open."

"Well, you can relax," she murmured. "I'm not going to harm you."

He looked as though he thought she would regret last night, but she smiled and pulled him to her, kissing his scarred face. "Make love to me again."

He actually grinned. "Wouldn't you rather have coffee and bacon?"

"Nope."

He laughed. "You little wild thing. Let's have break-fast, and then we'll make love again."

"Cowboy, you've got a deal." She got up and put on the rumpled dress, showing no modesty as he feasted his eyes on her body. Then she took the bucket, walked down to the creek for water.

Diablo watched her walk away, her round little bottom moving seductively as she walked. He felt deeply trou-bled. He had never allowed himself to care about a woman or anyone else. In a few days, she would realize what a bad bargain she had made, wasting her innocence on an ugly, penniless Texas drifter. She would regret it bitterly and wish she had given her virginity to the rich Hurd Kruger. When he thought of her in Kruger's arms, it made Diablo grind his teeth. He couldn't stand the thought of any other man touching her or making love to her. He had made her his in the way no man could ever possess her again, by taking her virginity, and he wanted to keep her—God, how he wanted to keep her!

Sunny came back with the water and began to make coffee. While she did, she watched him out of the corner of her eye. She wished she knew what he was thinking. Had she only been a night's pleasure for him? Certainly it had been more than that for her. Surely it couldn't end with him riding away forever . . . if Hurd didn't kill him.

She fixed breakfast, and they ate the biscuits and bacon in silence, the dog cleaning up the scraps.

"Now what?" she finally said.

"Now nothing," he shrugged and avoided her eyes. "I tried to tell you there was no future with me. I'll be riding out as soon as I get Kruger and Joe."

She felt her face fall with her spirits. "So after what's happened between us, you haven't changed your mind?"

He laughed without mirth. "Is that what last night was about? You thought if you let me take you, you'd save those bastards' lives?"

She shook her head. "I'm not worried about them; I'm worried about you."

He didn't look like he believed her. "You know I've left a note for Kruger. Someone has probably taken it to him by now."

She looked up. "So there's no stopping the show-down?"

"No, so your actions last night were in vain."

So he didn't believe she could really care about him. "I reckon you really are Diablo after all. So you ambush them both and kill them, or they kill you?"

He nodded. "That's about the size of it. I don't have much money, or I'd buy you a train ticket and send you to your aunt."

"You didn't even ask me if I wanted to go to Boston or with you."

"This isn't some fairy tale, baby, where the princess kisses the ugly beast and he turns into a rich, handsome prince. If I took you with me, there'd come a day when you would wonder what you saw in me, regret it, and walk out."

"I don't think so."

He winced. "It would kill me if you did. I can't take the chance."

"Then you don't have any confidence in me—you think I'm a spoiled child, not a woman."

He stared into her eyes and finally said "I don't have any confidence in myself. Nobody ever wanted me—why should you?"

"Because I love you." Tears made crooked trails down her face. She reached up and brushed them away. "There's nothing to keep us from riding out right now. Let's go to Texas."

He shook his head and glanced at the midday sun. "Too late for that. This whole thing should be over before sundown."

"You promised you would make love to me," she whispered.

He raised one eyebrow. "After what's been said, you still want that?"

"One last time," she whispered and swallowed hard to keep from sobbing.

"Baby, I didn't mean to make you cry." He put a gentle arm around her and kissed her tears away.

"Let's not talk." She hid her face against his shoulder. "Just love me for the very last time."

"Oh, God," he muttered and pulled her close, "Oh, God, I didn't mean for this to happen."

She kissed the scarred side of his face; then her lips brushed across his cheek and down to his mouth. His eyes were as moist as hers as he pulled her to him and kissed her as if he would never let her go.

Then they made slow, gentle love and slept again, curled up in each other's arms.

It was late afternoon when they awoke.

He got up and began to check and load his weapons, ignoring her eyes as she stared at him.

Finally he walked over and threw the saddle up on his black horse.

"One thing I can say, baby—I'll never forget you."

She watched him yanking the girth to tighten the saddle. There was no way she could convince him. He was going to kill those two and then ride back to Texas without her.

She saw him reach in his saddlebag and pull out something. She couldn't see what it was.

* * *

Diablo looked at the small photo in the gilt frame. He would be leaving a part of his heart behind when he left Wyoming, but at least he had her photo. In the lonely years ahead, he could pull it out sometimes and look at it, remembering the precious few hours they had had in each others' arms.

"What have you got there?"

He heard her walk up behind him and tried to put the photo back in the saddlebag, but she had already seen it.

"Why, that's the little photo my dad always kept on his desk. What are you doing with it?" She didn't know whether to be shocked or just puzzled. She tried to grab it out of his hand, but he held on to it and they struggled for the photo.

"Not what you think," he said as she tried to take it away from him.

"Where did you get this?" she demanded as they fought.

He knew what she would think if he told her the truth, so all he could do was try to hide it, but it was too late. He was bigger than she was and as they battled for it, he yanked it from her hand and it flew across the clearing. It struck hard against a stone, and the frame came apart with a tinkle of glass.

She ran over to it. "That was my dad's. Where'd you get it?"

He looked guilty as he raised his gaze from the shattered frame. "I—I took it. I looked through the window and saw it, and I wanted it. I fell in love with the pretty girl in the photo."

"Why, you thief!" Abruptly her face paled. "You—you're the one who killed Dad. He caught you robbing the house, and you killed him!"

"Sunny," he gestured, pleading, "I swear to you, I never did anything to hurt your dad."

She slapped him hard. "You bastard! You liar! Making love to me, knowing you shot down my dad in cold blood."

"More than once now, you've done things I'd kill a man for." He rubbed the stinging red place on his cheek.

"Go ahead!" she challenged, "Shoot me down in cold blood like you did my father!"

"Sunny, I swear to you, I didn't—"

"I don't believe you! And to think I gave myself to you, wanted to go to Texas with you!" She seethed and ran over to pick up the damaged gold frame. As she did, folded one hundred dollar bills fell out of the back of the frame. "What the—"

"Well, I'll be damned." Diablo reached to pick up the money and hand it to her. "He said he had money hidden to send you to your aunt's in Boston. I reckon no one ever believed him."

She was past emotion, staring dumbly at the bills in her palm, then slowly at Diablo. "There must be at least a thousand dollars here. Was that what you were after when you killed him?" She began to cry.

"Sunny, I swear to you, I didn't kill him."

"Liar! Then who did?"

He knew if he told her Kruger had done it, she wouldn't believe him. "Not me. I just took the photo. You were so beautiful, and when I saw it, I had to have it."

She walked over and sat down on a rock, clutching the photo and the money. "Dad, my poor dad, scrimping and saving to send me to school. If he saved to send me to school, why did he tell Hurd Kruger he wanted me to marry him?"

Diablo hesitated. She wasn't going to believe him, so he didn't answer.

"Well?" she sobbed and clutched the money.

He shrugged and looked away. "That solves your problem. After I kill those two, you'll have enough money to go to Boston."

"Can't you think about anything but killing?" Her beautiful blue eyes were wide and red with tears.

"That's what I came for—you've always known that. But know this, Princess, I did not kill your dad. I may be a low-down, cold-blooded killer, but Swen was good to me. I wouldn't murder him and then deflower his daughter."

She was in inner pain. "I—I don't know what to believe, even with the evidence in my hand. I'm such a fool to care about you."

"I told you that," he agreed quietly.

"It's hard to believe you would seduce me all the while knowing you had killed my dad and stolen the little money he had," she lashed out.

"I swear to God, baby, I didn't know the money was in the frame." He strode over to her. "Look, I don't need you to finish what I've come to do. Let me take you to the railroad station over in Wildfire. I'll put you on the train to Boston, and you can forget you ever knew me and get on with your life."

She raised her tear-stained face. "Don't you understand? I can never forget about you. I love you."

"Then how can you not believe me?" he snapped, "I know what the right thing to do is. I'm letting you go. I'll put you on that train myself."

She wanted to believe him, believe that he wouldn't lie to her, that he was the kind of man she thought in her heart he was. She looked up at him. "Have you nothing more to say?"

He struggled for the words that must have been hard coming. He was an independent loner who lived by his wits and his gun. He was proud, not a man who wanted to be beholden to anyone. "I—I want you, Sunny. I didn't realize how empty and barren my life was before I met you. Oh, to hell with it! Believe anything you want. Then tell me if I should put you on that train or send you back to Kruger's ranch."

She didn't know what to do. She had always let other people make decisions for her, tried to be the ideal pioneer woman—always obedient, never questioning. She hugged the photo and the money to her breast as she ran into the cave and fell down on the blankets and wept and wept.

Diablo sat outside, watching the sun move across the sky and tossing pebbles against a rock, unable to deal with his feelings. He hated that he'd made her cry and that she thought he was the kind of hombre who would kill an old man in cold blood and rob his house. Well, to hell with everything. If Kruger had gotten his note, the rancher would come to the clearing by the three cottonwood trees, and Diablo would finally get his revenge. Somehow, that didn't seem so important as it once had. *Damn that girl.* She had changed his priorities.

The bartender at the Longhorn Saloon had read the note that was tossed through his window last night. So the kidnapper was ready to make a deal. Hurd Kruger would pay a nice little reward to get this news. He chased the last two drinkers out of the place, hung a CLOSED sign on the front door, and got out his wagon. It was a long drive to the K Bar ranch, but he could be there a little after midnight. Kruger would certainly pay him well for bringing the note.

Kruger sat before the fire, drinking straight from the

bottle, when he heard the knock at the door. He staggered as he got up, answered it, and glared at the man standing in the darkness. "What the hell do you want? It must be one o'clock in the morning."

"I got information, Mr. Kruger." He handed over the note as he came in and looked around the disheveled house. "Uh, sir, what's happened to your housekeeper?"

"None of your damned business," Kruger snarled as he led the way into the den. He hadn't shaved or changed clothes in almost a week. He didn't give a damn anymore about how he looked; he only cared about Sunny. The ranch was in disrepair and most of his cowboys had quit, but he didn't care about that either. He flopped down in his big leather chair and stared at the crumpled paper. Then he got up and hobbled over to the door and shouted, "Joe, get in here!"

"Uh, sir," the barkeep played with the brim of his hat, "I thought you might be grateful for the note."

"So?" Hurd wavered a little as he stared at the man. He hadn't had much to eat these last couple of days, but all he wanted now was another drink. "Get the hell out of my house. You're probably in on this. Everyone's after my money."

"Why, no, sir, I just thought bringin' you that note might be worth a little—"

"Get the hell out of my house!" Hurd shouted.

The burly barkeeper turned and scurried out the door.

Hurd slammed it behind him. "Joe! Where the hell are you? Joe!"

"Yes sir, boss," Joe had been asleep in a chair in another room. Now he came into the den, his eyes bleary and his mouth yawning.

"We finally got a note from the kidnapper. He says he's gonna return Sunny. He wants me and you to come

unarmed and meet him alone in the clearing near the
three cottonwoods."

"Boss, ain't that where we lynched them three cowboys
and—"

"Yes, it is." Hurd grinned and poured himself another
drink. "So our little half-breed has come back for revenge."

Joe licked his dry lips. "Can't blame him after what we
did to him. I ain't never told anyone about flipping him
on his belly and—"

"Shut up." Hurd waved a hand for silence. "We
wouldn't have done that if we hadn't been drunk. He deserved the branding, though, because he was a rustler."

Joe poured himself a drink. "When, boss?"

"Today, about sundown. I reckon he's usin' my Sunny
to lure me up there. I'll geld him like a steer before I kill
him if he's touched her."

"Boss, we ain't goin' up there alone, are we?" Joe's
hands trembled.

"Of course not, you idiot. We'll take the crew, and
we'll ambush him."

"Boss," he hesitated, not wanting to anger the man,
"we only got two men left, and they're both new."

"Two?" Kruger swore long and loud as he poured himself another drink. "Where the hell is everyone?"

"They all pulled out."

"Why?" He glared at Joe.

He didn't want to tell him the cowboys all thought
Hurd Kruger had gone loco and was letting the ranch go
to rack and ruin while he drank and worried over his
sweetheart. "They—they just left, that's all."

"I can't run a ranch without a crew. It'll be worthless,
all the cows scattered, all the fences down before winter."

"I know, boss. Now if we can get this thing settled
about Miss Sunny, maybe you could go to Cheyenne and
hire a new crew—"

"Later. Right now, I don't give a damn about any of that, you hear me? I only care about Sunny!" He threw his tumbler at Joe, and it missed him, hit the wall behind him, leaving a dark stain on the wallpaper. "That Injun bastard. We should have finished him off the first time instead of being so merciful."

Joe scratched his head. "I—I ain't eager to go up against him. They say he's the best of the Texas gunfighters."

"We ain't gonna go against him—we're gonna trick him."

Joe's sharp face paled. "I don't like this. When an Injun wants revenge, he don't quit until he gets it. That's why Wilson and Smitty were lynched."

Hurd cursed again. "Well, the scarred-up bastard is in for a surprise. We'll ambush that devil at the three cottonwoods when he returns Sunny." He strode over to the fireplace and reached up on the mantel for the rusty running iron. "He thought he was leavin' me a message with this, but I'll take it with me and this time, after we geld him, we'll brand him to death."

Joe gulped his drink with a shaky hand. "God, boss, ain't we done enough? Don't you figure some of them Injun spirits is wantin' to take revenge on us? If we don't kill him, we'll be lookin' over our shoulders the rest of our days."

"I don't intend we should be lookin' over our shoulders." Hurd smiled wickedly and drank right out of the bottle. "Once we get Sunny back and safely out of the way, then we'll make him wish he'd never been born. Tell your cowhands what's up. I'll take my rifle—"

"I thought you said we was to come unarmed for the exchange," Joe said.

"We'll hide our guns," Hurd snapped, "and the running iron. He'll think 'raped' once I put that hot running iron up his—"

"Oh, God, boss. Can't we just kill him?"

"You weakling!" Hurd pushed him against the fire-place. "He's humiliated me in front of all Wyoming. Everyone's talkin' about this, him lynching my men, stealing my woman. I want to make sure everyone gets the message that nobody messes with Hurd Kruger or the K Bar ranch, or he'll make them pray for death!"

Joe moved to go out the door. "Boss, you don't think he'd well, you know, take Miss Sunny and ride out?"

"Are you loco?" Hurd snarled. "He wouldn't dare, not with Hurd Kruger's woman. Besides, she's a very obedi-ent, innocent girl. She wouldn't go with him without him tying her up and abducting her. Anyone knows a decent woman would kill herself rather than be defiled by some no-count half-breed Injun."

The man was definitely losing his sanity, Joe thought. "Okay, boss, I'll get some sleep and have the boys ready to ride before sundown. You ought to get some sleep, too."

"Don't tell me what to do!" Hurd threw the bottle at him. "You think I can sleep, knowing my darling is in that Injun bastard's possession? When I think what he might be doing to her in revenge for what I did to him—"

"Don't think about it, boss. We'll hang him up to one of them cottonwoods tonight like we should have done fifteen years ago."

"Damn Swen for that anyway." Hurd mumbled and re-turned to his chair before the fire. "I can hardly wait for sundown. Now get out of here!"

Joe fled, and Hurd only got up to get another drink and stared moodily into the fire for hours. It would be dawn soon, but he didn't feel like sleeping.

Diablo and Sunny did not speak; instead, they both watched the sun move relentlessly across the sky. Finally he began to break camp. "Sunny, it's time. You'd better gather up your stuff."

She came out of the cave, her eyes swollen and red. "I can't convince myself you killed my dad; maybe because of how I feel about you."

Diablo sighed. "I told you I didn't. Now don't make this any tougher than it has to be, Princess."

She swallowed back her tears. "You're so stubborn, and I don't want to see you killed. You've insulted Hurd, and he's a proud man. I doubt if he'll abide by the agreement."

Diablo laughed. "I'd be shocked if he did. Have you decided to let me take you and put you on the train?"

"No. I'll make my own decision about that, but I have decided I'm not going to marry him." She shook her head. "I know Hurd. If I don't go to meet him and let him see I'm all right, he'll never believe I didn't want to marry him, and he'll keep hunting you forever."

He reached for his bridle and paused, staring at her. "Are you sure you've got the guts to stand up to him, or will you let him force you to stay here and marry him?"

"I've changed, Diablo. I'm not a pliant, obedient, ideal woman anymore." Her voice was resolute as she squared her small shoulders. "I'll tell him I've got the money to go to Boston, and he can go to hell if he doesn't like it."

"And after that, I'll kill him," Diablo said as he put the bridle on Onyx.

"You know he'll have tricks up his sleeve. He won't take a chance." She walked over and put her hand on his arm.

"What's that to you?" he shrugged.

She looked at him, torn by conflict, yet she loved him with no reservations. "I don't suppose you'd reconsider letting me go with you?"

He shook her hand off. "You still think I killed your father?"

"I—I don't know what to think. My head says you did,

but my heart says I have to trust you, believe you. I love you, Diablo."

His eyes moistened, and he blinked rapidly. "You're one in a million, baby, but we both know this can't work. We'd be drifting from town to town. I lead a lonely life, Princess, one saloon, one dirty town after another. It's no life for a girl like you. Sooner or later, some young dude will be faster, and I'll die in a puddle of my own blood."

"I thought my love could change you," she sighed heavily and turned away. "I thought you might want to become a rancher with a little spread and a family, but you'll always be a killer, a gunfighter, I reckon."

"I'm playin' the cards I'm dealt." He walked over and began to saddle her horse. "We've talked enough. Gather up your things."

He looked at her, and there were tears running down her face. "I—I'll never forget you," she whispered.

And he would never, ever forget her. He wanted to run to her, take her in his arms, and kiss her and never let her go, but of course, he was headed to a showdown and, knowing Kruger's dirty tricks, he might not walk away from it. *Revenge is a cold, hard master.* "Are you ready to go?"

She looked around the campsite, her eyes blinded with tears. "You'll take the dog with you?"

He nodded. "I need a friend. The trail back to Texas is long and lonely."

"All right then, I'm ready." She swallowed hard. It wouldn't do to break down and cry in front of this proud, cold killer.

"Here," he gestured, "let me help you mount up."

She blinked away her tears and walked over to her horse. He put his big hands on her small waist, and she had to struggle not to throw herself against him and kiss him and kiss him, not caring who he was or what he was.

She loved him just the same. "Hurd and his boys will probably ambush you."

He nodded, his face an impassive mask. "If they do, can you still insist he put you on the train?"

"Yes. I won't marry him, no matter what."

He wavered, looking down into those eyes blue as a Texas sky. For a moment, he allowed himself the luxury of thinking how it could be, sharing a lifetime with this woman. He could build a small spread out in the wild country of the Big Bend, and every night he could hold her and make love to her. And there would be children, pretty little girls like her and big strong boys like him. At night, they would sit before the fireplace, and it would be warm and he wouldn't be alone ever again.

"Diablo," she whispered, "that thousand dollars would give us a start, build us a cabin."

"No! Damn it, no! I can't change now, not after all these years!" He spun away from her, angry with himself that he cared so much about her that he would do almost anything for her.

"Well, then, kiss me one more time, and it's settled." She hungered for one more kiss to remember him by all those lonely years ahead of her. For some women, there is only one man—and this was hers, and she was going to lose him.

"No," he snapped, "let's not prolong this. Mount up."

"Aren't you going to help me up?"

He knew if he put his arms around her, he wouldn't be able to turn her loose. He would pull her so tightly into his protective embrace that he would never, never let her go. "You can mount up by yourself, can't you?"

"Yes." Maybe she had been mistaken. Maybe she had only been a plaything, a pawn in his game. She mounted the blood bay.

He swung up on the big black stallion, not looking

at her. "Gunfighters never change, Princess. They die violent deaths, some sooner, some later."

She didn't answer and choked back a sob. If she tried to speak, she would cry hysterically, and it wouldn't change things. She'd go to Boston, all right, but she yearned for freedom and his love. Together they could live in the wide open spaces of the Lone Star state.

He tried not to look at her because it couldn't work, the princess and the ugly beast, not in a million years. He glanced up at the sun. The day was warm, and the sun was a big orange ball hovering near the far horizon. "Let's ride out," he ordered and whistled to Wolf. The dog ran ahead of the pair as they rode toward the three cottonwoods.

Chapter 19

With a heavy heart, she followed Diablo's lead as they rode out. There didn't seem to be anything she could do to stop this showdown. Either the gunfighter would kill Hurd, or Hurd would kill him. All she could do was watch and then get on the train and leave, no matter which man died. If Hurd won, he would try to talk her into staying, but Dad's last wishes or not, she had made her decision not to marry Hurd Kruger.

Back at the ranch, Hurd took one last drink and stared at the grandfather clock and then looked to Joe. "All right, it's almost time. Get the boys, and let's go kill us a half-breed." He reached to get the running iron off the mantel.

"Maybe he won't bring Miss Sunny to the showdown," Joe said as they went out the door to the barn.

"He'd better." Hurd held up the running iron. "My mistake was not killin' him fifteen years ago instead of just hurtin' him a little. This time, we'll put a hot iron on every inch of him until he looks like a hunk of charred beef. If he ain't dead by then, we'll lynch him."

"You ain't gonna do that in front of the lady?" Joe asked.

"No, I'll have one of the boys take her back to the ranch first. She need never know, but she'd probably be happy to watch, after him holding her captive all these days."

Joe yelled at the bunkhouse, and a couple of men came out.

Hurd said, "Is that all the crew we got left?"

Joe nodded. "I told you that. I haven't been able to hire anyone. Nobody wants to work for a man they think is . . ." He didn't finish.

"Loco?" Hurd laughed and rubbed his unshaven chin. "I'll show you who's loco." He turned to the other two. "You men get your rifles. We're going to meet that damned half-breed."

The two nodded, and the four of them saddled up.

"Oh," Hurd ordered, "bring along that dun mare for Sunny to ride home. She'll be glad to see it."

"The foal, too?" Joe asked.

"Of course the foal, too," Hurd snapped. "That mare ain't gonna want to come without it."

They saddled up the fine dun mare and brought her out, the long-legged chestnut filly gamboling along beside her.

Hurd grinned. "Start of our fine herd of horses . . . when I get that black stud back. Now let's go."

He mounted his sorrel, and the four of them rode out, Joe leading the fine mare, the filly trotting at her mother's side.

Joe looked over at Hurd and took an uneasy breath. The man looked a little crazy. He wondered if it was the whiskey or his obsession with the girl. "Boss, it spooks me that he wants to meet us at the three cottonwoods. You know what happened there."

Hurd laughed. "Hell, three cottonwoods is the right

place to finish this. That's where we should have finished it fifteen years ago, but Swen was too soft-hearted."

They rode along in silence, the sun hanging low, looking like a fried egg in the sky over the far rim of the horizon.

"Boss," Joe licked his dry lips, "you think this hombre murdered Swen?"

Hurd hesitated. "Of course he did. Nobody else had any reason to."

"It don't make no sense," Joe argued. "It was Swen who saved him from bein' lynched."

Hurd snorted. "You think a cold-blooded killer would show any gratitude? Quit thinkin' so much and concentrate on what we got to do."

Joe looked up at the sun. "We're gettin' there early."

Hurd nodded. "I planned it that way. When he arrives, if he does, we'll be ready for him."

They rode into the clearing and dismounted.

Hurd looked around. "Joe, build a fire and hide the horses over there behind them rocks. I don't want him to know how many of us there are. You men," he gestured to the two cowhands, "you get behind those rocks with your rifles. Once we're sure the young lady is out of the line of fire, take that bastard out of the saddle, but don't kill him. I got other plans for him. Also, don't hit that black stud. That horse is valuable."

Both cowboys frowned. "That don't seem right, Mister Kruger. We ought to at least give him a chance."

"Hell, no, we ain't givin' him a chance," Hurd swore, "not any more than you'd give a coyote."

Both weathered cowboys looked at each other, then shook their heads.

Clint said, "This ain't fair play, Mr. Kruger. We didn't sign on to be part of a deliberate ambush. That's murder, and we don't want to be hung."

"Hell, I am the law in this county," Hurd snarled. "I can do what I want. Now you men do as I said."

However, the two cowboys were mounting up. The taller Clint said, "Sorry, Mr. Kruger, me and Mart think we'll ride on and find another spread to work for."

"Damn you!" Hurd reached for his rifle, but Joe grabbed his arm.

"Let them go, boss. We can handle this alone."

Hurd took a deep breath. "You're right, Joe. We don't need no yellow bellies on this here spread. You two get the hell outta the county. Joe and I can handle this."

The two cowboys wheeled their horses and rode out.

Grumbling, Hurd handed over his sorrel horse to Joe, taking his rifle and the running iron with him to the center of the clearing. Joe took the horses over behind a distant boulder to graze where they'd be out of the line of fire. The filly was in high spirits, running and kicking up her heels as Hurd built a small fire in the center of the clearing.

"Boss, what are you doin'? He'll be able to smell that smoke for miles; any Injun could."

The other looked up at him and grinned. "I mean for him to. I want him to know what's waitin' for him when we get him." He thrust the iron into the fire, and after a minute, it began to glow.

Kruger was either drunk or really a little loco, Joe decided. Maybe this whole thing was a rotten idea. He rolled a cigarette with shaky hands.

"Boss, why don't we just shoot him on sight and get the girl back? I've had bad luck and nightmares ever since that day. What we did wasn't natural, and torture is something Injuns do. Let's just make a clean kill and be done with it."

"Not you, too?" Kruger roared. "I'm surrounded by yellow bellies, even my top hand." He picked up the hot iron and grinned, "Oh, this is gonna be fun, Joe, listenin' to him scream!"

Joe winced and backed away. "Boss, the last time, we was all drunk, but I was ashamed after I sobered up. That Injun's got good reason to come after us, and he won't give up 'til he gets us. I want to clear out of this state; I don't wanta be hangin' from the gate like Smitty and Wilson."

Kruger looked up from his fire where he had spread a blanket and lain his rifle under the edge. He stood up and strode over to face the other man. "Why, you lily-livered coyote." He slapped him across the face with his quirt. "And after you been with me all these years."

Joe backed away, rubbing his face. "And you been knockin' me around for more'n fifteen years. I've had a bellyful of your abuse."

"Oh, shut up, damn you," Hurd dismissed him. "Now get over behind that rock with your rifle."

Joe took a deep breath and wiped a trickle of blood from his mouth. "I ain't takin' orders from you no more. I can find another ranch to work on." He shook his head, turned, and started toward his white mare, grazing behind the rocks.

"Hell! You can't quit now—not when I need you to help me take down this half-breed. Come back here!"

Joe kept walking toward his horse.

"Goddamn it! I order you to come back here!" Hurd swore and grabbed for his rifle. Joe kept walking without looking back.

"You low-down—" In a rage, Hurd shot him in the back. Joe took two more steps and then stumbled and went down.

Hurd dropped the rifle, staring at the crumpled figure.

"Joe? Joe, answer me!" He ran to his side, struggled to turn him over. "I—I didn't mean it, Joe. You're the last friend I got! Get up, Joe, I didn't mean it. I was mad—that's all." He turned the body over. Joe's brown eyes stared sightlessly at the sky, and blood soaked his denim jacket. Hurd shook him. "Stop jokin' around. I need you, Joe. I can't take on this gunfighter alone. I can't run the ranch without you."

Joe didn't answer, and Hurd gradually stopped shaking him. What to do now? The sun was almost on the rim of the far hills, and in a few minutes, Hurd would be all alone against the best gunfighter in Texas. *Think, Hurd, think,* he cautioned himself.

After a deep breath, he murmured, "Hurd, you're the biggest, most feared rancher in Johnson County. You can handle one lousy half-breed. You don't need Joe; you can hire more cowhands. You got thousands of cows and the makin's of a fine herd of horses. All you need is Sunny beside you as your wife; that's what matters." He took off his Stetson and wiped the black dye from his sweaty forehead. "Yep, I don't need Joe. I'll get my woman back, my fancy rifle, everything that Injun bastard stole from me."

He dragged Joe's body behind a nearby log in the brush. Then he returned to the blanket by the fire, where the running iron glowed red-hot. He slid the rifle under the blanket and sat down cross-legged in the open to wait for the gunfighter to appear.

Diablo and Sunny rode toward the clearing in silence. The sounds of meadowlarks and the horses' snorting seemed loud in the bright silence. There was so much she wanted to say to him, and yet, nothing to say. Whatever his past crimes, she didn't care, God help her. She loved him, and nothing else mattered. Except he didn't love her as much as he loved his life as a gunfighter.

A shot echoed and re-echoed faintly through the hills.

Diablo reined in, ever alert. "Sounds like we've got a reception waitin' for us."

She shook her head. "I can't believe Hurd would do something that underhanded and dirty. Didn't you tell him to come unarmed?"

He grinned without mirth. "You don't know what Kruger is capable of. He nudged his horse forward, riding toward the rendezvous. He wanted so much to tell her everything, but he did not think she would believe him. Anyway, what did it matter? He intended to try to stick by the agreement: turn Sunny over to Kruger and let the rancher put her on the train to Boston. After she was safely away, they could continue their feud.

He looked back at her as they rode, and he thought he saw tears glistening on her fair cheeks. Maybe her show of emotion was only because she was about to be rescued and was relieved.

On the crest of a hill before they reached the clearing, he reined in and took off his gun belt, hung it over his saddle horn. When she looked questioningly at him, he said, "Remember I told him I'd come unarmed."

She looked surprised. "You trust Hurd?"

He shook his head. "But I didn't want you caught in a cross fire. One more thing." He paused and looked away. He didn't know how to tell her he would miss her and he didn't want to let her go.

"Yes?" she said, with moist, full lips that he remembered so well, looking at him with those eyes the color of a Texas sky. What good would it do to prolong this?

"I—I just wanted to tell you I'm sorry for whatever trouble I caused you. I wish you success in Boston."

She seemed to be having a difficult time speaking. "Good luck to you, too. Take good care of Wolf and Onyx."

"I will."

There was a long, awkward pause.

Then Diablo sighed and nudged his horse forward. "It's almost time. Kruger will be waitin'."

Behind him, she said, "Suppose Hurd doesn't follow the rules? Suppose he's waiting with a bunch of cowboys and an ambush?"

He shook his head without looking back. "I think Kruger will be afraid of hitting you. I'll hand you over, and you ride out of range."

"Diablo—no, Jim," she implored, "why don't you just drop me off and ride on out without getting within rifle range?"

He turned in his saddle and smiled at her. "If that's what you want. I'd hate to kill Kruger in front of you."

"For me, can't you just forget about your revenge? Go on back to Texas and that ranch in the Big Bend you want. While I'm in Boston, I'd like to think you were alive and well out there."

He looked over at her and scowled. "Do you realize what you're asking? This showdown has been all I've thought of for fifteen years, and you're asking me to turn tail and run?"

"Not run," she shook her head. "Maybe Hurd will bring other men with him. I wouldn't want to be responsible for you riding into a trap and getting killed." Tears overflowed her eyes.

"For God's sake baby, don't cry!" For a long moment, he fought an inner battle. "This vengeance means everything to me. I don't have any other purpose in life."

"And if word gets out you killed the biggest rancher in Johnson County, others will be challenging you. You'll always be a gunfighter until the day a faster man gets you. For me, wouldn't you rather be just a rancher named Jim Durango?"

"You ask too much," he murmured.

"Diablo—Jim, if you ever cared even a little about me, just stay out of range, drop me off and ride out. Do it for me."

There was a long silence, and when she saw his throat working and his eyes moistened, he took a deep breath and said, "All right, I'll do it, for whatever I meant to you."

She smiled then. "Good. Have a great life in Texas."

They rode on in the twilight silence, and finally, they spotted the little campfire in the clearing.

She said, "Why don't you stop right here? You're out of rifle range on this ridge. I'll go down and talk to Hurd and tell him I'm not going to marry him."

"He's not gonna like that."

She shrugged. "I don't care. I'll tell him I'm going to Boston, and he can take me to the train. I think he'll lose interest in you once I'm no longer your captive."

"I don't think so." Diablo shook his head. "He knows he has to kill me or he'll always be lookin' over his shoulder. I reckon after fifteen years, he's weary of that."

"Diablo—Jim, in spite of everything, well—" She didn't finish. She rode up close to him and leaned over and kissed him.

He started in surprise, and then his arms encircled her as if he'd like to hold and protect her forever. He kissed her back with a heat and a passion that made her head spin, and she didn't want him to ever let her go. "Goodbye, Jim Durango," she whispered, "I'll never forget you."

He tried to say something; then he swallowed hard, and his dark eyes grew moist. He only managed to nod and gestured toward the trail. "Go on down, Princess."

Her eyes were blinded by tears as she started down the trail and rode toward the small fire, where Hurd sat on a blanket. He was unshaven and red-eyed. She had never seen him look so bad.

"Sunny, is that you?" Hurd stood up and held up his hands to show he was unarmed.

She took a deep breath of relief. So he was going to abide by the rules of the bargain.

He rushed to meet her and help her from her bay horse. "Oh, God, Sunny, my darling, are you all right?" She could only nod and choke back sobs.

He looked anxiously into her face. "Has he hurt you? You're crying. If he's hurt you, I'll—"

"No." She shook her head. "I—I'm all right, Hurd, but I've got something to tell you."

"It can wait, my dear," he embraced her stiff body while she stared at the campfire. There was a running iron in the flames, glowing orange hot. Surely he hadn't intended to . . .

"Now you just get out of the clearing, Sunny," he steered her away from the fire, "and let me deal with this half-breed."

"Where's Joe?" She looked around. "I figured he'd be with you."

"Never mind." He turned toward the trail. "Where's that damned gunfighter?

"He's not coming, Hurd; he's riding on back to Texas. That's good, isn't it? There won't be a showdown, and no bloodshed."

"No showdown?" Hurd began to curse, and when she looked at him, she wondered if he was deranged. "I should have finished that damned half-breed fifteen years ago, and I would have if it hadn't been for Swen."

She blinked. "So you really were the one who branded him?"

He nodded and grinned, and she saw madness in his eyes. "He was riding with rustlers, and I thought we should finish him off when we lynched the other three, but your lily-livered father stopped me. Swen was always too soft to survive in this tough country."

She felt horror and backed away from him. "Hurd, let's ride out right now."

"No, I'll go after that red-skinned bastard," Hurd babbled, "and then I'll take you back to the K Bar—"

"Hurd, listen to me. I'm not going to marry you." She said it resolutely. She was no longer a timid, pliant girl. She was a strong-willed woman, and she would not be silenced. "Hurd, I've found Dad's money, and I want you to put me on the evening train to Boston."

"No," he shook his head and grabbed her by the shoulders. His breath was sour with whiskey. "No, you don't mean that. I love you, Sunny; I've been waitin' for you to grow up so you could be my wife and queen of the K Bar and all of the state."

She tried to pull out of his grasp. "I'm sorry, Hurd. I don't mean to hurt you, but I don't love you. I will not marry you."

He glared down at her, shook her. "You've changed. What is it? It's that gunfighter, isn't it? Have you—have you given yourself to him?"

She knew there was no use to lie—it must be shining from her eyes. "I love him, Hurd, but he wants me to go to Boston, so there's no point in a showdown. He's riding out."

He didn't seem to hear her. "You've given yourself to him?" he screamed at her. "That half-breed saddle tramp, and after everything I've done, everything I've built just for you?"

He was almost rabid, and she suddenly realized she didn't know this man like she'd thought she did. This one might be capable of anything. "I'm sorry, Hurd." She tried to calm him down. "Why don't we go into Wildfire and discuss this sensibly while we wait for the train?"

No!" He roared and hung on to her. "You will marry

me! I didn't kill your father so you could get on a train and leave me!"

She jerked away from him, stunned with disbelief. "But I thought Dad wanted me to marry you—"

"No, but that doesn't matter," he babbled. "Swen's dead and now you're mine, and I'll kill that damned gunfighter and lay his head at your feet as a wedding present, darling."

She screamed and fought to get away from him, and he grabbed her and slapped her hard.

"There'll be no train trip to Boston, my sweet. You'll take me on as you took that damned Injun and give me sons."

She cried and fought him, scratching his face. "I won't marry you. I'd rather be dead!"

Hurd turned abruptly, and she whirled to look the direction Hurd was staring. She heard the sound of hoofbeats coming at a gallop in the twilight. It was Diablo, and he was coming at a dead run, fury etched into his face. "Get your hands off her!"

"Look out!" She screamed, realizing her love was now within rifle range as Hurd dived into the blanket and came up with a Winchester. He laughed madly as he aimed at the coming rider.

She would not stand by and let Hurd kill the man she loved. Without thinking, she grabbed the running iron, glowing red-hot in the coals.

"No!" she shouted, and she swung the sizzling iron even as Hurd aimed the rifle. She caught him across the face with the hot iron. He screamed as the shot went wild, and he dropped the gun.

Hurd fell to the ground, writhing and clawing at his burned face. She grabbed the rifle and backed away, even as the gunfighter came off his running horse. "You dirty sonovabitch!" Diablo shouted as he grabbed Hurd, hit him hard in the face. The rancher stumbled backward, and Diablo followed him, struck him again and again. "How dare you hit a woman!"

She saw Hurd dive behind a log, come up with a pistol. Diablo was unarmed, his holster hung from his saddle horn on Onyx, across the clearing.

"Now!" Hurd said and aimed the pistol, "now you red-skinned bastard, I'm going to kill you like I should have done in the first place!"

He was going to kill her love. She didn't think—she acted instinctively, raising Hurd's rifle and firing.

"You shot me to save him!" Hurd looked at her in sudden surprise, then down at the blood spreading across his tan shirt. "You—you were such a docile, mind-less girl. . . ."

He took a step toward her, then crumpled and lay still.

Diablo stared at the dead man; then he looked at her and took a deep breath. "Well, it's over."

Her hands felt numb, and she dropped the rifle. "Oh, my God."

"It'll be okay, Princess," Diablo whispered. "Catch the bay, and I'll take you to the train myself."

She nodded dumbly and started through the brush behind the log. That's when she found Joe shot in the back. It was his Colt Hurd had grabbed. "I reckon Hurd killed him," she said. "He really was insane."

The gunfighter strode over and looked down. "It'll be dark soon. I'll bury them both, and you turn their horses loose. We don't need them, but some poor farmer might put them to use."

She nodded and walked out into the brush. Then she cried out with delight. "Hey, the dun's here and her filly!"

She was so glad to see her dad's mare she put her arms around the mare's neck and hugged her while the dun nuzzled her shoulder and the filly ran up to her, nibbling on her pink dress. She turned the sorrel and the white horse loose and led the dun mare back to where Diablo was digging two graves. She and Wolf watched silently as Diablo put both men in the holes. Then she walked over, picked up the running iron, and brought it back.

Diablo took it from her, stared at it a long moment, then tossed it in Hurd's grave. "It's finished, after all these years."

She nodded as he filled in the graves. "Yes," she agreed, "it's finally finished, and now I know the truth."

By the light of the little fire, she looked at Diablo. "Your friends are buried here?"

He pointed. "Right over there. Swen buried them for me, although I tried. I was too hurt to do it."

She walked out through the clearing and came back with an armful of spring wildflowers, and the two of them scattered them under the three cottonwoods.

"Diablo—Jim," she said, "I owe you an apology. Hurd told me he killed my father."

"It doesn't matter. Let's get out of here." He kicked dirt over the campfire. "Let's go back up the trail to where it turns off, and I'll escort you to the train. You can either ship your horses to Boston or sell them in town for a good price."

She didn't say anything as he caught the blood bay and changed the saddle over to the dun mare. It was almost dark when he mounted up and whistled to the dog.

Sunny kept silent as she mounted, and they started back up the trail with him leading the blood bay and the chestnut filly trotting beside its dam. Nothing was said until they reached the place where the trail veered off toward Wildfire. He reined in and looked at her in the moonlight. "All right, Princess, here's where we part. You've got enough money now. By day after tomorrow, you'll be sipping tea in your aunt's parlor."

She sat there a long moment, thinking. This was indeed a crossroads. One direction led to a safe, secure civilized life in Boston. The other trail led south amid much uncertainty and adventure. Had she gained enough grit to make the right choice?

"Well?" the gunfighter said. "Why the hesitation?"

She looked at him, seeing him not with her eyes, but with her heart. She didn't see a scarred monster; she saw a man who would always love and protect her, and she loved him more than life itself. "No," she shook her head. "I've got enough money to start a small ranch and two fine horses to begin a herd. I'm not going to Boston—I'm going to Texas with you."

He looked down at her, shock in his scarred face. "Sunny, no. Don't be a fool. You don't owe me anything, and I don't have much to offer."

She raised her little chin in a stubborn gesture. "Do you love me, Jim Durango?"

"Yes, but—"

"Then don't argue with me," she answered. "I love you, and I'm going back to Texas with you."

He blinked. "Are you sure about this?"

"I've never been so sure of anything in my life. I've been a mouse all these years and now that I've found love, I'm not going to let go of it."

"Oh, Princess!" He reached across and hugged her like he would never let her go.

She kissed him then, kissed him with all the love she had to give while his broad shoulders shook, and he embraced her so tightly, she was breathless. Wolf danced around the horses and barked while the little filly kicked up her heels and neighed.

After a long moment, she whispered, "Let's go to Texas, Jim."

"With you, baby, I'd go anywhere," he agreed.

Then they gave the horses a free rein, and at a gallop, they headed south toward the Lone Star state and the life and love that awaited them there.

Epilogue

The Big Bend area of Texas, Autumn, 1893

Sunny heard the thunder of approaching hooves and Wolf's welcoming bark, and ran out of the stone ranch house. Shielding her eyes with one hand, she waved to the approaching rider on his big black stallion as he chased the band of wild horses into the corral, and she ran across the yard to slam the gate behind them.

He rode toward her, his white Stetson pushed back on his black hair. He wore faded blue denims and a red plaid western shirt, but on his feet, instead of boots, he wore knee-high moccasins. The half-breed grinned broadly and dismounted to take her in his arms and swing her up as he walked, the dog running in circles and wagging his tail. "Well, hello there, Princess. You waitin' for someone, or will I do?"

She kissed his scarred face thoroughly and laid her cheek against his broad shoulder as he strode toward their cabin. "Well, mister, I was waiting for my husband, but I guess you'll do."

He laughed. "I'd better. What you got for supper?" He put her down in the doorway of the cabin.

"Oh, don't you think of anything but food?" she joked.

He winked at her and put his hand on her bottom. "You know what else I think of."

"Later," she promised, whirling away from him. "There's a big pot of hot stew, some biscuits, and an apple pie. "Is that the only reason you married me?"

He grabbed her and kissed her deeply. "Now you know better than that. How's the boy?"

"Come look, Jim." She took his hand and led him to the cradle in the corner where their baby, Swen, slept. "Shh! Don't wake him. I just got him to sleep."

Jim leaned over and touched their baby's cheek with his fingertip. The baby awoke and smiled up at him. He had black hair like his daddy, but the startling pale blue eyes of his mother. Jim turned to look at the petite blonde, his eyes misting. Everything that mattered to him was in this room. "I'd like another just like him next year."

She grinned at him. "I think that can be arranged." She led him away from the cradle. "Looks like you brought in a good string of wild ones this time."

He nodded. "Come out and have a look. I'll get them broke, and then they'll sell for a good price. With the new foals sired by Onyx we're expectin' in the spring, especially from that dun mare, our little ranch is off to a good start."

About that time, the chestnut filly stuck her head in the door, and Sunny laughed and gave her an apple. "I can't keep her in the barn; she keeps getting out."

"Oh, well," Jim shrugged and grinned.

They linked arms and walked out to the corral, Wolf barking and running ahead of them.

"Oh, by the way," she remembered, "while you were gone, we had some more additions to the family."

"What?" He looked baffled.

"You know that stray lady collie that turned up here this summer? We've got pups."

"Why, Wolf, you old rascal," Jim said, and the dog wagged his tail.

Sunny led him to the barn next to the corral, where half a dozen puppies squirmed and whined next to their proud mother. The collie wagged her tail, and Wolf barked again.

"Look like they'll be good stock dogs." Jim grinned.

"Yep," she smiled and took his arm, and they walked to the corral to inspect the new wild horses. Every color—dun, bay, chestnut, pinto—stamped restlessly and watched the humans.

Jim said, "I'll throw them some hay, and they'll settle down."

As he did so, she turned to watch the sun set across the rugged hills. "Brrr! It's getting chilly. Maybe we'll have snow for Thanksgiving."

"I'll shoot us a wild turkey." Jim paused in tossing hay to the wild horses. "Did you go into town?"

She nodded. "It's a long drive by wagon."

"You shouldn't have gone alone. It's too far."

"Wolf went with me, and the baby slept all the way. I can handle a rifle, and there's nobody for miles out here in the Big Bend. People in the general store were talking about whatever happened to that famous Texas gunfighter they'd heard about, Diablo."

He was instantly on his guard. "What did you say?"

She shrugged. "I told them I heard he'd died and was buried up in Wyoming."

"Now that's the truth," he said with conviction.

"Oh, we got a letter. Trace Durango's family want us to come for Christmas."

"It'll be good to see them again," he nodded, "and show off our son. They always have such a big Christmas."

He came over and put his arm around her, watching the sunset for a long minute. In the distance, they could see the bend of the Rio Grande and Mexico beyond. "There's probably not another ranch for almost twenty miles. Don't you get lonely out here?"

She leaned against him, perfectly content. "I've got a wonderful husband and a chubby baby, with more to come. Our ranch is doing well. What more could I want?"

"I feel the same." He kissed the top of her head. "I love you, Princess, more than you know."

"And I love you, Jim Durango. Hey, we'd better go in before my stew burns."

He swung her up in his strong arms and carried her toward the cabin, kissing her all the way. "It's going to be a cold night. Maybe after we eat, we can snuggle down in the feather bed and make that new baby."

She looked up at him, loving him so much she could not speak. "Texan, I think that's a great idea." And she kissed him again as he carried her into their cabin.

Behind the hills, the sun set all gold and scarlet over the Lone Star state. They were home and in love in Texas, the best and biggest state in the Union. What more could anyone want?

To My Readers

The story you have just read is based on the actual Johnson County, Wyoming, range war of April 1892. Powerful big ranchers were upset over homesteaders fencing off the government land where the ranchers had always grazed their huge herds of cattle. The Wyoming Stock Growers Association made up a pot of one hundred thousand dollars and sent an ex-sheriff, Frank M. Canton, to hire some twenty-five Texas gunfighters, and reserved a special train to bring them up to the town of Casper. There they were joined by many of the big ranchers and their cowboys to ride across the county, wiping out or scaring off the homesteaders and small ranchers, whom they accused of rustling cattle. The war got so out of control that Governor Barber finally wired the president to send in troops from nearby Fort McKinney to restore order. By then, the big cattlemen were getting the worst of the fight and had to be rescued by the soldiers.

So what happened in the aftermath? Not much. The big ranchers saw to it that any witnesses disappeared or left the state. The prosecutors had an impossible task in finding an impartial jury, and finally, the whole thing was dropped. In ten years, the ranchers would be in another range war, this time with the sheep men. But that's another story.

Frank M. Canton, the man whom the cattle barons sent to hire and bring in the Texas gunfighters, drifted to Alaska, then down to Oklahoma Territory, where he became a deputy and helped clean up this wild, lawless land. He was later appointed to be adjutant general by the state. Canton died September 27, 1927, and is buried here in my hometown of Edmond, Oklahoma. This information courtesy of a book called *Gunslingers* by Carl W. Breihan, published by Leather Stocking Books, Wauwatosa, WI, 1984.

However, *Frontier Justice*, by Wayne Gard, University of Oklahoma Press, Norman, OK, 1949, says it was Tom Smith who went to enlist the Texas gunfighters.

The Johnson County War has been the basis for many novels and movies such as: Owen Wister's *The Virginian*, *Shane*, *Open Range*, *Heaven's Gate*, and *The Johnson County War*.

In 1894, a brave Wyoming newspaper editor, Asa Mercer, wrote a book condemning the attacks. The book was called *The Banditti of the Plains, or the Cattlemen's Invasion of Wyoming in 1892*. The big ranchers were so enraged over the book they forced Asa to leave Wyoming and drove the print shop that published the book out of business. They hunted down almost every copy available, even in the public libraries, and burned them all, so an original copy is very rare. This book was reprinted by the University of Oklahoma Press in 1954.

If Asa Mercer's name sounds familiar, you may have met him in my earlier romance, *Half-Breed's Bride*. Mercer was a real person who organized a shipload of mail-order brides to take to Washington state after the Civil War. He also founded the University of Washington.

For a readable book about the Johnson County War,

I recommend *The War on Powder River* by Helena Huntington Smith, University of Nebraska Press, 1966.

Another readable book on the subject is *The Great Range Wars, Violence on the Grasslands* by Harry Sinclair Drago, University of Nebraska Press, 1970.

I must tell you about the Cheyenne Social Club. Because of the humorous movie starring Henry Fonda and James Stewart, most people think of it as a bordello, but it was more like a fancy country club where rich ranchers could meet for a good steak, drinks, and cigars. The Social Club may be where the original plan to bring in the Texas gunfighters was hatched.

I like scientific trivia, maybe because I used to be a teacher, so I also want to tell you about the old Indian lore of using willow bark to lower fever. The bark contains salicylic acid and acetylsalicylic acid. From this, a German Bayer Company chemist, Felix Hoffman, created a successful drug, which became commercially available in powder form in 1899. You know it now as common aspirin.

The Texas Big Bend country is a national park of some eight-hundred-thousand acres today and is about as wild and hostile as it was more than a hundred years ago. If you decide to go into that desert and mountain wilderness, take plenty of water and look out for rattlesnakes and scorpions.

You may not know about the tragedy of the Santee Sioux. It is known as the Santee Uprising of 1862, or Little Crow's War. Settled in Minnesota, the tribe was starved and cheated by a crooked Indian agent supplier, Andrew Myrick, who, when told his changes were starving, laughed and said, "let them eat grass." The nation was involved in the Civil War, so little attention was paid to the plight of any Indians.

In the summer of 1862, the Santee revolted and went

on the warpath. One of the first acts they committed was
to kill Andrew Myrick. His body was found with grass
stuffed in his mouth. Before the revolt was over in the
early autumn, hundreds of whites and Santee had been
killed, many whites tortured and women raped. When
troops finally put down the revolt, the army held trials
for the Santee warriors. Three hundred and six were
condemned to hang, but President Lincoln stepped in
and pardoned all but thirty-eight of the Santee.

On the cold morning of December 26, 1862, in
Mankato, Minnesota, at Fort Lincoln, those thirty-eight
Santee warriors were hanged in what remains as the
biggest mass hanging in United States history. Cadavers
for medical research were almost impossible to get, so
later that night, several doctors sneaked out and dug
up some of the hanged warriors for medical research.
One of these doctors was a small-town physician named
William W. Mayo. He dug up Cut Nose, who had admitted to killing twenty-seven white settlers. Mayo's two
sons, William Jr. and Charles, were as fascinated by medical research as their father. When they grew up, the sons
founded the famed Mayo Clinic. This information is
from *The Day They Hanged the Sioux* by C. Fayne Porter,
Scholastic Books, 1964.

While the hanging of the Sioux is the largest mass
hanging in the United States, it is not the biggest mass
hanging that our government has committed in North
America. That dubious title goes to the U.S. army in
Mexico during the Mexican American War of 1846–1848.
However, there will be more about that in my next book:
Rio: The Texans.

If you are one of my steady readers, you know all my stories fit together much as the Cheyenne tell their tales.
Late at night, the Cheyenne gather around a campfire,
and someone tells an ancient tale and ends with, "Can

anyone tie a tale to this one?" Then someone else will pick up the narrative and tell another old legend, each tying to the last one. Sometimes the stories go on all night, but they must stop at dawn because it is forbidden to tell the sacred legends after sunrise.

For more than twenty years now, I, too, have been telling the stories of the old West and tying them together so that it is one long, long saga. It will never end until I die or retire because there are so many tales to tell. There are also two novelettes as part of this panorama that begins in the 1850s and runs through the 1890s. Readers have begged me to explain how the stories fit together because most are written out of sequence. So far, *Warrior's Honor* is the first in the series (the story begins in 1857), although it was the twentieth book published.

My books are listed here in the order they were published, with the date the story begins in parentheses. If two books begin in the same year, look for the month the action begins.

The Panorama of the Old West

1. *Cheyenne Captive* (begins 1858)
   Summer Van Schuyler & Iron Knife

2. *Cheyenne Princess* (begins 1864)
   Cimarron (Iron Knife's sister) & Trace Durango

3. *Comanche Cowboy* (begins 1874)
   Cayenne McBride & Maverick Durango (Trace's adopted brother)

4. *Bandit's Embrace* (begins 1873)
   Amethyst Durango (Mexican cousin of the Texas Durangos) & Bandit

5. *Nevada Nights* (begins 1860)
   Dallas Durango (Trace's sister) & Quint Randolph

6. *Quicksilver Passion* (begins 1860)
    Silver Jones & Cherokee Evans (a friend of Quint
    Randolph's)

7. *Cheyenne Caress* (begins 1869)
    Luci & Johnny Ace (son of Bear's Eyes, Iron Knife's
    Pawnee enemy)

8. *Apache Caress* (begins 1886)
    Sierra Forester (the Foresters are old enemies of the
    Durangos) & Cholla

9. *Christmas Rendezvous* (novelette begins 1889)
    Ginny Malone (Sassy's cousin) & Hawk.

10. *Sioux Slave* (begins 1864)
    Kimi & Rand (Randolph) Erikson (a cousin on his
    mother's side to Quint Randolph)

11. *Half-Breed's Bride* (begins 1865)
    Sassy Malone (Sassy used to work as a maid in
    Summer Van Schuyler's mansion) & Hunter

12. *Nevada Dawn* (begins 1887) (a direct sequel to
    Nevada Nights)
    Cherish Blassingame & Nevada Randolph (Quint
    & Dallas's son)

13. *Cheyenne Splendor* (begins 1864) (a direct sequel to
    Cheyenne Captive)
    The story of Iron Knife, Summer, & their children
    continues

14. *Song Of The Warrior* (begins 1877)
    Willow & Bear (Iron Knife once saved this Nez
    Perce warrior's life)

15. *Timeless Warrior* (begins 1873)
    Blossom Murdock & Terry (brother of Pawnee
    warrior Johnny Ace)

16. *Warrior's Prize* (begins 1879) (a direct sequel to *Quicksilver Passion*)
Wannie & Keso (the children adopted by Cherokee Evans and Silver Jones)

17. *Cheyenne Song* (begins 1878)
Glory Halstead & Two Arrows (Iron Knife's cousin)

18. *Eternal Outlaw* (begins 1892)
Angie Newland & Johnny Logan (Johnny was in prison with Nevada Randolph)

19. *Apache Tears* (begins 1881)
Libbie Winters & Cougar (Cholla's friend and fellow scout)

20. *Warrior's Honor* (begins 1857)
Talako & Lusa (a schoolmate of Summer Van Schuyler)

21. *Warrior's Heart* (begins 1862)
Rider (a gunfighter trained by Trace Durango) & Emma Trent (the girl raped by Angry Wolf in *Cheyenne Splendor*)

22. *To Tame A Savage* (begins 1868)
Austin Shaw (Summer Van Schuyler's former fiance) & Wiwila; also their son, Colt, & Samantha McGregor

23. *To Tame A Texan* (begins 1885)
Ace Durango (son of Cimarron & Trace Durango) & Lynnie McBride (younger sister of Cayenne McBride)

24. *To Tame A Rebel* (begins 1861)
Yellow Jacket & Twilight Dumont; Jim Eagle & April Grant (both men are fellow scouts and friends of Talako)

25. *To Tempt A Texan* (begins 1889)
    Blackie O'Neal & Lacey Van Schuyler (one of
    the twin daughters of Iron Knife & Summer Van
    Schuyler)

26. *To Tease A Texan* (begins 1890)
    Laredo & Lark Van Schuyler (Lacey's twin sister)

27. *My Heroes Have Always Been Cowboys* (novelette
    begins 1893)
    Henrietta Jennings & Comanche Jones (a cowboy
    who once worked for Trace Durango)

28. *To Love A Texan* (begins 1880)
    Brad O'Neal (Blackie's younger brother) & Lillian
    Primm

29. *To Wed A Texan* (begins 1895)
    Bonnie O'Neal Purdy (Brad & Blackie's younger
    sister) & Cash McCalley

30. *To Seduce A Texan* (begins 1864)
    Rosemary Burke & Waco McClain (a cousin on his
    mother's side to the O'Neals)

31. *Diablo: The Texans* (begins 1877)
    Sunny Sorrenson & Diablo (the half-breed rescued
    by Trace Durango)

32. *Rio: The Texans* (begins 1875)
    Rio Kelly & Turquoise (she first appeared as a
    minor character in Cheyenne Princess)

Diablo is still part of the long series, although it is listed
as a new series called "The Texans." In this series, I will
take Texans with different careers and spotlight them.
We've had a gunfighter; next, I'll tell a tale about a half-
Mexican, half-Irish rancher living near Austin. His name is
Rio Kelly. If I were casting his part for a movie, I would

use the smoldering Jimmy Smits, often seen on television, or for my older readers, think a young Anthony Quinn.

Many of you have read *Cheyenne Princess* and written me to ask what happened to the characters and particularly little Turquoise, the half-Mexican beauty who was growing up on the Triple D ranch. Now I'm finally going to tell you that story. The year is 1875, and Turquoise has become a beautiful woman with black hair and pale turquoise eyes. With her father and the old Don both dead, Cimarron and Trace have spoiled their ward, and the headstrong beauty does as she pleases.

Turquoise attracts the eye of two very different men. One is Rio. The other is sophisticated Edwin Forester, older, rich, and powerful, and the bitter enemy of the Durango family. The Durango family is unaware that the beautiful and willful Turquoise is playing these two men against each other while she dallies with their affections. You can expect big trouble and a shocking conclusion.

Stay tuned for this second in this series: *Rio: The Texans*. By the way, Zebra has promised to reprint *Cheyenne Princess,* and later, some of my other early books as this new series unfolds.

If there is a lesson to be learned from *Diablo,* remember, readers, that it is where love is concerned, always look with your heart, not your eyes.

                    Until next time, your faithful writer,
                    Georgina Gentry

Romantic Suspense from
Lisa Jackson

See How She Dies	0-8217-7605-3	$6.99US/$9.99CAN
Final Scream	0-8217-7712-2	$7.99US/$10.99CAN
Wishes	0-8217-6309-1	$5.99US/$7.99CAN
Whispers	0-8217-7603-7	$6.99US/$9.99CAN
Twice Kissed	0-8217-6038-6	$5.99US/$7.99CAN
Unspoken	0-8217-6402-0	$6.50US/$8.50CAN
If She Only Knew	0-8217-6708-9	$6.50US/$8.50CAN
Hot Blooded	0-8217-6841-7	$6.99US/$9.99CAN
Cold Blooded	0-8217-6934-0	$6.99US/$9.99CAN
The Night Before	0-8217-6936-7	$6.99US/$9.99CAN
The Morning After	0-8217-7295-3	$6.99US/$9.99CAN
Deep Freeze	0-8217-7296-1	$7.99US/$10.99CAN
Fatal Burn	0-8217-7577-4	$7.99US/$10.99CAN
Shiver	0-8217-7578-2	$7.99US/$10.99CAN
Most Likely to Die	0-8217-7576-6	$7.99US/$10.99CAN
Absolute Fear	0-8217-7936-2	$7.99US/$9.49CAN
Almost Dead	0-8217-7579-0	$7.99US/$10.99CAN
Lost Souls	0-8217-7938-9	$7.99US/$10.99CAN
Left to Die	1-4201-0276-1	$7.99US/$10.99CAN
Wicked Game	1-4201-0338-5	$7.99US/$9.99CAN
Malice	0-8217-7940-0	$7.99US/$9.49CAN